CITY OF STONE

K.T. HOLDER

For my Wife, and my fluffy little writing companions

AUTHOR'S NOTE

This book is a work of fantasy fiction, and while it contains magical elements and imaginary settings, it also includes themes that may be distressing to some readers.

I believe stories should be immersive, but also that you deserve to make informed choices about the content you engage with. If you'd like to see a list of content warnings for this and my other books, you can find one linked on my website:

www.ktholder.com

Please be aware that some content warnings may be minor spoilers.

Thank you for reading,
KT Holder

THE GREAT CONTINENT OF
VALORIS
AND
SURROUNDING LANDS

CHAPTER ONE

KAS

Rain beat down on the cobblestones. It muffled the footsteps of the guards searching the alleys behind the houses of the Merchants' Quarter. They moved slowly, the frantic pursuit stopped in favour of a systematic search.

Kasperi Ironstone hid in the shadows, listening intently. He gave it another few minutes before they got sick of the rain and gave up their search. After all, it wasn't as if a middling thief like Kas was worth it.

He pulled out the necklace, examining the amulet attached. It was an ugly thing. The costume jewels were too bright to be mistaken for actual gemstones. Kas tossed it in the air, catching it and judging its weight. The metal was real. Probably only gold-plated, but still. Even if it was brass beneath, that was worth something.

A shoe scuffed on stone metres from Kas's hiding spot and he tensed, cursing the lack of cover as freezing rain hit his head and slid down his neck. Sensing the guard move closer, Kas took a deep breath and closed his eyes. For some reason, that helped him bend the light around him. As if the invisibility was powered by the belief that if he couldn't see them, they couldn't see him.

Of course, invisibility wasn't the same as becoming incorporeal, and so the rain continued to tap his head like someone rapping their fingers over his skull. Anyone looking closely would likely notice the sudden disappearance of the falling water, and the lack of dripping into the puddle beneath him. But since when did the guards look that closely?

A shadow fell over him as the guard moved around the corner and stopped right next to Kas. He could smell the city guard's dirty boots. The man was scanning the area, but it was only a matter of time before he looked behind him and noticed the oddity caused by Kas's invisibility. Kas's eyes flitted over the ground looking for something, anything, he could throw to create a distraction.

But before Kas could find anything, or the guard came any closer, a voice sounded loudly, calling from a few streets away, and the mountainous man turned his gaze towards it. A relieved smile broke on his face, and the guard shuffled away. The search had been called off in favour of the pub.

Kas waited until he couldn't hear them anymore before letting go of the light. He slouched back against the wet wall of the building, breathing deeply. Bending light was not a common magic. In fact, Kas had known no one else to be able to do it. Which was why he kept it to himself. He was powerful enough in the normal magics for the rebels to harass him to join every other week. If they knew he could become invisible, they'd never leave him alone.

Standing, Kas exited his hiding spot and walked to the dirty river that paralleled the narrow path. The river ran through the centre of the Merchants' Quarter, but all the buildings faced away as if ashamed of what the river had become. In Hightown the river was a brilliant, sparkling blue, its riverbanks coated with lush grass and trees. But as it split and wound its way through the lower parts of the city, it seemed to become tainted by the less picturesque surrounds.

The Merchants' Quarter was much nicer than the slums where Kas lived, but they used the river for their ovens and forges and to carry their waste products away. The grassy banks had been paved, and the water was murky.

He crouched on the path's edge, as if washing his hands in the brown water. Looking around, Kas saw few people. Those that were out in this weather had their heads down, rushing to get to wherever they needed to go. Some were huddling under cover, hoping the rain might let up. There were two people directly across from him, waiting in the shadows beneath the back stairs of the armourer's store. But they weren't paying him any mind.

Kas stood and shook his hands as if to dry them. No one would notice anything in this blasted rain. He glanced up, as if by looking he might be able to determine when the rain would stop.

And he froze. A figure stood on the roof of Barnes's Hotel. Kas guessed it was a man by the size, and he was leaning against a door that led back down into the accommodation area, sheltering under the measly overhang that wouldn't protect him from the freezing rain.

Glancing back at his previous hiding place against the wall, Kas's heart started to thump. If the figure had been watching, he could have seen him bend the light. But he would have had to be watching in the exact right direction at the exact right time. It was unlikely that—

The figure stepped forward and Kas's heart sank. Jori Devlin. The rebel leader. And the smug look on his face told Kas that he had seen everything.

Jori stalked to the edge of the building and took a deep breath, as if about to call out to Kas, but a sound caught his attention and he whipped around, looking up the street, away from Kas.

Kas lifted on his toes, straining to see what had caught Jori's attention. Feathers were all Kas could make out, but that was all he needed to see. It was a stupid thing to put on top of the guards' helmets. The tall plumes could be spotted in plenty of time to fade into the shadows. Kas didn't understand how the guards ever managed to catch anyone in those outfits.

Glancing up again, Kas met Jori's eyes. The rebel leader hesitated, as if considering whether to still risk calling out, before thinking the better of it. As they both turned to leave, Kas cursed under his breath. He was sure he'd hear from the rebel leader soon.

Kas made his way home, hurrying through the districts of Lorendell, the sprawling capital city of the Empire, famous for its enormous city walls. He entered the filthy slums where he lived, avoiding the corners and alleys where he knew his fellow thieves and beggars would be gathered. Kas didn't want to talk to them. He just wanted to get home.

Finally, he slid around a corner and onto the narrow path next to the city walls. The track was dirt, though the rain had turned it into a mud pit. Kas was careful with his footsteps as he picked his way between the ramshackle shanties that had been pitched against the wall and the sturdier buildings opposite. Peering up, he caught sight of his shanty and smiled. It wasn't much, but it was theirs.

Pushing open a door that wouldn't keep anyone out, Kas was immediately hit by a tackle of a hug.

"You were gone for ages!"

Kas scrubbed his little brother's red hair playfully as the boy tried to push him away. "No, I wasn't. It's not even dark outside."

"It is too."

Kas laughed, leading Sali over to the pile of rags they used as a couch. "Fair enough, but it's only dark because of the storm. I was only gone a couple of hours."

"It felt like forever," Sali complained, drawing out the last word. "It's so boring here."

"Maybe this will help you forgive me?"

Kas drew a cloth-wrapped bundle from his tattered cloak and Sali's eyes grew wide, smelling it before it opened.

"Bread!" Sali exclaimed happily, snatching it from Kas.

"Take it easy." Kas smiled at his little brother's excitement. "And leave me some this time."

"I always leave you some," Sali protested, his mouth full of the stale loaf. "You should let me come. We could have two loaves if you let me help too."

"You can help when you're older," Kas replied as he always did. "It's too dangerous at the moment, and it's easier if I can just fade away on my own."

Sali was the only one who knew about Kas's invisibility. At least before today. Kas frowned, thinking of Jori, and kicked himself for being reckless. That was a problem he would need to fix, but he had no idea how.

"I can fade away," Sali protested, his face reddening as he got mad. "Maybe not like you, but I can hide."

Kas smiled at his brother. It was sweet that Sali wanted to help, but there was no way Kas would be able to concentrate on a job if he was worrying about his little brother the whole time. Though, Sali wasn't the eight-year-old little boy who'd lost his parents anymore. To Kas, even if he was now eleven, Sali was still a kid, and he should be allowed to act like one for as long as possible. Besides, Sali pulled his weight in other ways.

"I need you here," Kas said gently. "You take care of the place. Make sure no one steals anything or moves themselves in. I couldn't do what I do without your help here."

"You want me out of your way, more like," Sali muttered.

"Huh?" Kas missed the comment as he cocked his head. Something had changed outside. The usual noises of the slum had stopped. Someone was here. Someone who shouldn't be.

Knuckles rapped on the door, and it opened before Kas could cross to it. Jori strode in as if he'd been invited and looked around appraisingly.

"This is... nice."

Kas's shoulders went back and his eyes narrowed. He knew their shack was little more than a hovel. But it was theirs. It had taken a couple of years of hard work to get enough to buy the one-room pile of wood and corrugated iron. But it had been worth it. Kas had never felt good about leaving Sali each day in the abandoned building where they had lived with the other homeless folk of Lorendell after their parents died. Even with old Frank keeping an eye on him.

"What do you want?" Kas said in a tone that left no doubt Jori was not welcome.

"Hello, who are you?" Jori ignored Kas, peering around him and smiling at Sali.

"Sali," said the young boy, lowering his voice and trying to sound older. "But my real name is Salomon."

"That's a good, strong name," said Jori, darting around Kas and shaking Sali's hand. Kas tried not to roll his eyes as his little brother puffed out his chest.

"Who are you?" Sali asked, taking control of the conversation, lest Kas kick him out of the shanty.

"I'm the leader of the rebellion."

"Cool!" exclaimed Sali, his eyes going wide. "Did you really steal the emperor's carriage?"

Jori boomed a laugh. "We sure did! But did you hear what we did to his fleet?"

Sali gaped in awe as Jori told him about the rebels and the adventures they went on, omitting anything that wasn't fun or exciting, or that didn't paint them in a noble light. Kas knew the real story. He knew they thought they were doing the right thing, trying to overthrow the Empire. But their methods were reckless and dangerous. And they hurt too many innocent people. Like Kas and Sali's parents.

"I'll bet you get up to some mischief with your brother, huh?" Jori was asking Sali.

"He won't let me go with him." Sali glared at Kas, empowered by his new friend.

"Why not? You're of age, aren't you?"

Sali's face fell. "Yeah, I had my Testing months ago. But I don't have it."

"That's okay," said Jori brightly, and Sali perked up. "I'm sure not everyone can do what your brother can. But we can always use talented men in our organisation."

Kas rolled his eyes at Jori as the rebel leader looked at him hungrily.

"I don't have any of it," said Sali bitterly.

Jori's eyebrow raised and Kas could see the leader's interest in his little brother drain from his eyes. Good. The last thing Kas needed was the rebels trying to recruit his brother.

"Now that's nothing to be worried about," Jori lied. "Some of our best people don't have a skerrick of magic."

"Yeah?" said Sali, looking up at Jori with hope in his eyes.

"Of course. Without them, we'd need to pull our magicals from important missions to take care of the headquarters and get the provisions we need."

Jori tried to sell it with his tone, but Sali saw through it immediately. He had been devastated after the Testing when the Druid declared him a non-magical. And this was only exacerbated the more he saw how valued magic of any kind was. Especially his older brother's.

Kas felt differently, but even he knew it was rich for him to say magic didn't matter. Magic was all the Empire seemed to care about.

Jori stood, turning his attention back to Kas. "Why don't you join us, son? It's not like you'd be giving something up." Jori gestured around at the derelict hut that Kas was fiercely proud of. "We can give you regular work in exchange for food and lodging. You could have a proper bed. Each."

Kas's eyes flitted to the blankets piled in the corner. His cheeks burned. Sali deserved better. He looked at his younger brother, who was still stewing over Jori's dismissal.

Jori followed Kas's gaze. "We'd have work for young Sali here, too. Honest work," Jori cut Kas off. "The movement needs weapons. Maybe he'd make a good blacksmith's apprentice."

Kas's response died in his throat. He couldn't get Sali apprenticeships like that. You needed money or a decent last name, and Kas had neither. But he looked at Sali and all he could see was his little brother heading out on missions with the rebels. Getting hurt. Or worse.

"My answer's still no," he told Jori, ignoring the look Sali shot him.

"Are you sure? With skills like yours, we'd offer you a larger cut than most."

Kas closed his eyes. He wished his parents were here. How was he supposed to make this decision? Did Sali need food and a bed more than safety? And it wasn't like the slums were all that safe, anyway. But people knew them here. Had seen them grow up. Old Frank looked out for them, offering them food when he could, and even giving Kas simple magical items he found that Kas could sell.

Would the rebels look out for them like that? He couldn't imagine any of them seeing Sali as anything other than a resource.

"No." Kas tried to sound confident in his decision. To make his voice sound older than his fourteen years. "Please don't ask again."

Jori exhaled in frustration, but nodded. "Fair enough, kid. You don't have to join, but I do have a job that needs someone with your talents."

"No, Jori," said Kas, frustrated now.

"Hear me out. Just one job. And it'll be worth it. You could probably buy an actual house."

"Woah!" said Sali, interested in the discussion again.

"What's the job?" asked Kas flatly.

"I just need you to steal something for me."

Kas stared at Jori. "What's the catch?"

Jori hesitated. Kas could tell the rebel leader hadn't wanted to pitch the job to him like this. "It's in the palace."

"You've got to be kidding. What, you want me to plunder the emperor's treasury? Take all his coin?"

Jori shifted his weight, rubbing the back of his neck as his face reddened. Eventually he said, "Not all of it. Just one bit of jewellery."

"Oh, and where is it?" Kas saw Jori's face and his stomach dropped. "It's not actually in the treasury, is it?"

"No." Jori exhaled in frustration. "It's... we need his ring."

"Get out," Kas said, shaking his head.

"Kas—"

"Now."

Jori held his hands up in surrender and moved towards the door. "If you change your mind, you know where I am. Do think about it, Kas." He looked around the shack. "One job and you can change your life."

With a pointed look at Sali, the rebel leader left.

CHAPTER TWO

KAS

Kas's shoulders slumped as he made his way back through the slums. Today he had managed to get some work firing the kilns for the potter, and he kept one hand on the coins in his pocket. He was always paid well because he could cast fire for all kilns at once. The only other person around who could do that was Old Joe Hinkley, but when Joe got all the kilns going, the fires were weak. Kas had all of them raging without breaking a sweat.

He fiddled with the coins, running them through his fingers, trying to convince himself that he'd made the right decision. What he'd earned today was nothing compared to what Jori said he'd give Kas for doing the job, but it would still feed them well for two nights. Longer if they weren't fussy about the age of the produce.

And he was far less likely to be executed. That was a big plus.

Still, Kas couldn't help but wonder if he'd let his little brother down. Maybe he should join the rebels. Sali would have a bed, and if anything happened to Kas, there'd be people to take care of him.

But what kind of life would he have?

Kas looked around the slums, smiling at those whose eyes he met. People here would look out for Sali if Kas was gone. Frank would for sure. Kas frowned. The old man seemed to like Kas more than Sali. In fact, sometimes Kas thought he saw Frank looking at Sali with something akin to despair and hopelessness in his eyes, but then, when he looked properly, it seemed more like sympathy. Frank *would* look after Sali. He had to. Even if it was more out of respect for Kas's memory than his love for Sali.

Besides, in a couple of years, Sali could look after himself. Hells, Sali was now the age Kas had been when their parents were killed, and he'd done alright raising them both, hadn't he?

Deciding he had done the right thing in turning Jori down, Kas flung the door to their shack open, fixing a big smile on his face. The smile slipped when he saw that the shack was empty. Dumping the bread and cheese on the small box that was their table, Kas exited the shack, glancing up and down the road, hoping to spot Sali running around with some of the other forgotten urchins living in the slums.

"Lost something?"

Frank looked as old as the worlds, yet somehow he was the only person Kas knew who could sneak up without Kas hearing him. Kas had grown a lot in the last year, and now he could look at the top of the tattered cap Frank always wore. Rough grey hair poked out the sides of the cap and drooped down to entwine with his scruffy beard. Frank's eyebrows were two storm clouds that dominated his face, hiding the tiny black dots of his eyes that sometimes could only be seen when they glinted from happiness or rage.

"Have you seen Sali?" Kas asked, returning his gaze to the street and alleyways.

"Oh yes." Frank nodded. "He left about an hour ago. Went up that-a-way." Frank pointed to where the road bent to the right and wound up the hill to connect to the main street. Kas frowned. They only went that way if they were heading to the Merchants' Quarter, and there was no reason for Sali to be going there.

"I thought he was off to find you," Frank added.

"No," said Kas, distracted. "I was in the Sailors' District today."

Frank shrugged. "Then I don't know where he was going. But he was moving like a man on a mission." Chuckling to himself, Frank wandered off, back towards his own shack, farther down from Kas's.

A man on a mission...

Swearing, Kas took off running. You had to go through the Merchants' Quarter to get to Hightown. And in the middle of Hightown was the palace.

Slowing to a fast walk, Kas felt completely out of place. He knew he was drawing stares. Everything about him, from his scruffy hair to his dirty clothes, screamed that he was a slum rat, and they rarely entered Hightown. Guards stood at the entrance arches specifically to deter the filth of the city from darkening the clean streets of the wealthiest district. There were some from the slums who worked in Hightown, usually cooking or cleaning for the rich people, but their bosses always had strict dress standards.

Kas darted off the main street to get his bearings. He had been to this part of town exactly twice before. Once with his father, and one time after his parents had died. Security was tight, even for someone who could become invisible. He had quickly learned it was better to steal something of lesser value from the Merchants' Quarter than risk being caught thieving in Hightown.

These days, punishments were increasingly harsh, and the rumour was that the prisons were full, so anyone found guilty of even the slightest infraction was instead sent straight to the labour camps.

Kas didn't want to risk being sent to the camps. He needed to look after Sali for a start, but a trip to the camps came with a collar, and Kas couldn't imagine being without his magic. Ignoring the urge to bend light to avoid the glares, Kas darted back out, aiming for the palace walls out of sight of the main entrance.

The palace actually sat on its own island. A huge moat separated it from Hightown, though it had never held water during Kas's short lifetime. Benny, who worked at the market, told him once that they drained it after a would-be thief swam across and climbed over the walls. Kas liked the story, but he knew it wasn't true. The walls were impenetrable, designed to keep everyone out and ensure the palace grounds were for the emperor and his daughter alone.

No, more likely Frank was right. He had told Kas the moat had been drained long ago to prevent water mages from manipulating its contents against the emperor.

Kas found the empty moat and followed it as best he could. The moat wasn't really that wide—maybe two cart lengths across. But it was deep. The palace was the tallest building in the city, but if you sat it at the bottom of the moat, you'd still have to peer over the side to see the flags flying from the tallest spire.

There was no road next to the moat, as if to discourage citizens from walking in the shadow of their sovereign's home. And often the high walls of the nobility's estates backed straight onto the moat itself. After a frustrating period of navigating around sprawling compounds, Kas found what he was looking for.

Separating two walled estates was a small park. It, too,

was walled off, but with a waist-high fence rather than an eight-foot concrete barricade. Kas strolled inside, trying to ignore the screaming from every fibre of his being that he shouldn't be there. He walked slowly to the end of the park that backed onto the moat. A casual observer would think the young boy was simply admiring the park's lush foliage, but Kas was scanning every inch to ensure he was alone.

Perhaps it was because the rich of the great city of Lorendell had their own private gardens that were bigger and more beautiful, or maybe it was just luck, but Kas found himself alone as he reached the fence and looked up at the huge tree that had grown up just inside of it. It was an oak, its trunk thicker than Kas was tall, and its huge branches extended up and out, like an old man stretching.

Kas followed one of those branches with his eyes, examining in particular where it met the branch of a fellow tree that extended from the palace grounds. He frowned. That seemed a particularly large oversight to him, though where the branches met, they were so thin it was unlikely they could support a man.

A boy, however...

Kas drew the light around him. The last thing he needed was someone looking up at the tree at the wrong time. Quick as a flash, he was up the trunk and shimmying along the thick branch. It wasn't until he was out over the moat that he felt the branch sag and questioned whether it could hold his weight.

He'd grown again lately, and sometimes he forgot he wasn't the skinny little rat he'd once been. His shoulders were widening, and if he was able to eat better, he might even be described as broad.

The branch sagged some more and Kas glanced down, immediately regretting doing so. He'd climbed a long way from the park's grounds up to this branch, but now he was over the moat. If he fell now, he'd die on impact. Kas closed his eyes and swallowed, wondering if his body would lie there, invisible, rotting in the sun, or if the invisibility would die with him.

He forced his eyes open and tried to focus on the way forward. The other branch was close now, a few more feet and he'd be on the other tree. But he'd misjudged the amount of crossover. The trees were touching, sure, but where they overlapped, the branches were thin and flimsy. There was no way they'd support him.

Kas estimated he could shuffle another foot on his own branch before he was in trouble. And then there would be about three feet where neither side was safe to hold him. He breathed out in frustration. If he were slipping over rooftops, he'd barely pause at having to leap a three-foot gap. But could he do it from one branch to the other? He couldn't get as good a run up, and he'd have to land on a small, curved surface that he only *thought* could hold him.

Kas looked beyond the branch. The opposite tree sat similarly to the one he was currently on; right up against the palace walls. It looked like part of a park, or garden area, with other trees and bushes. It was a large area. The wall blocked most of Kas's view, but beyond the wall, he could still see grass and bushes.

And there, crouched behind a small hedge, was Sali.

Shit.

Kas had been hoping that perhaps Sali hadn't been going to try to do the mission for the rebels. Or that he might have turned back, unable to get into the palace grounds. But there he was, right in the middle of the palace grounds where, if he were caught, he'd be sent off to the camps, no questions. Let alone if he was caught trying to enter the palace itself.

Kas returned his focus to the gap. He had to try it now.

He couldn't just leave Sali in there. Now that he knew his brother was inside, he noticed small scuff marks on the branch opposite him. Sali might not have a skerrick of magic, but he was agile. Far more agile than Kas was, especially now that he was bigger.

Pushing that unhelpful thought from his mind, Kas told himself that if his little brother could make the leap, then he could too. And before he could think the better of it, he pushed up to his feet and leapt across the gap.

His stomach dropped as he descended, convinced he'd missed the branch entirely and was about to fall the long seconds to the bottom of the dry moat. But then the branch greeted him with a smack.

And broke.

CHAPTER THREE

KAS

THE SMALL TWIGS and leaves of the branch grabbed at him as they fell, determined to pull him down with them. Kas held onto the stump of the branch for dear life. His legs, scratched by the end of the branch on its way down, kicked flimsily at the air.

Kas had managed to grab onto the thicker part of the branch, and now dangled under it. He tried to pull his body up, but his arms were weak with fading adrenaline and he only brushed the bottom with his forehead.

Panic gripped him again. He needed to rest to get the strength back to pull up, but the longer he dangled, the more tired his arms would become.

"Kas?" a frightened voice whispered.

"Sali!" In his panic, he'd let go of his grip on the light, and Kas hadn't even felt the branch move under his little brother's weight.

"I'll pull you up," Sali said, and Kas felt little hands grab his wrist.

"No! No, I need to keep holding on. Shuffle back for me, Sali. I'm going to try to kick up. If I can't get my legs high enough on my own, see if you can grab them. But only if they're in reach, okay? If not, tell me how high I got and I'll try again."

"Okay, Kas." Sali's voice was energised with fear.

"Let me know when you're back far enough, so I don't kick you."

"I'm ready," came Sali's voice from farther down the branch.

Kas took a deep breath. He pushed his legs forward, then swung them back as far as he could before heaving his whole body forward and up with the momentum he'd gathered. He fully expected to hit the tree. Kas felt his body fly up to almost parallel, but the branch was lower where he held it, and he realised too late he'd needed to aim higher.

As his feet started to descend, Kas felt a cold realisation fill his stomach. This had been his one shot. His arms were beginning to shake, and even if he had another try in him, it wouldn't be as good as this one.

A small hand grabbed his shoe, and his leg halted, jerking his body.

"I've got you, Kas," Sali grunted.

Kas's eyes shot wide open. He was going to take Sali down with him! No, his brother would have to let him go. But Sali was lying on the branch, securing himself with one arm, while the other held onto Kas's shoe. Kas was struck with the realisation that his little brother was growing up. He was bigger, stronger than he remained in Kas's mind.

"If you kick your other one up, I can probably grab that and pull your legs up," said Sali, managing to keep his head while Kas lost his mind.

Kas kicked his right leg up, trying to do so without jerking his left down. Without the opposite action, he felt it was a feeble effort, but then his brother's little hand grabbed that shoe too. He felt a tug and, impossibly, his legs were rising and he was guided to wrap them around the branch.

Now hanging underneath like a sloth, Kas felt his breathing relax slightly. Maybe he wasn't going to die right then. But he didn't think he could heave himself back up on top.

"Thanks Sali," Kas said with feeling. "Now, if you head back down, I'll shimmy my way from under here."

Kas worked his way, painstakingly slowly, down the branch. He moved his hands, one at a time, and then legs; lifting one foot and moving it, careful not to let either fall, lest he return to hanging by his arms.

"You can drop onto the wall now," Sali said softly, and Kas glanced down to see that he was over the thick walls of the palace, no longer above the void of the moat. He dropped carefully onto the blessed, firm concrete and Sali dropped down easily beside him. Kas gripped his brother in a bear hug until the little boy squirmed.

"Thanks, Sali. I owe you."

Sali blushed with pride. "I've had a quick look around. I think we could get in through a door over here."

Sali went to lead Kas away, but Kas stopped him, clamping a hand on his shoulder. "Are you mad? We're not doing this, Sali. We'll be killed. Or sent to the camps if we're lucky. And neither option particularly appeals to me. No, we're waiting here while I get my breath back, and then we're heading back across the trees."

"But Kas—"

"No. It's not worth it."

Sali sat on the wall, his legs dangling, his thin arms crossed at his chest and his face in full pout. Kas lowered himself to sit next to him, but Sali refused to acknowledge him at all.

"Sali—" Kas began when the minutes started to run long and loaded.

"I don't want to keep living like this." Sali looked up at

Kas, tears in his eyes. "I know you don't like the rebels, but you can do this job, Kas. I know you can. And then we could have a house. A proper house. With a fireplace. And we could cook proper meals. With potatoes."

The pleading in his little brother's voice was too much, and Kas's heart broke. He wished he could give Sali all of those things. But he wasn't sure this mission was as easy as his little brother thought. And if he were caught, then not only would Sali miss out on the life he dreamed of—he'd also lose his only family and provider.

Kas shook his head. "Sali—"

The garden had muffled the footsteps, and by the time Kas heard them, there were mere seconds for him to grab his brother, jump off the ledge, and dive behind a hedge. Kas clamped a hand over Sali's mouth and lay on top of him, wishing not for the first time that Sali could turn invisible like Kas could.

Kas pulled the light around him and poked his head up. His heart froze and then pounded as if trying to escape its bony cage. The guards were coming straight at them.

"Go!" Kas hissed at Sali, pushing the boy back down as he started to rise. "You'll need to crawl. Go that way."

Sali crawled along the length of the hedge, his butt higher than Kas was comfortable with, but it let the boy move faster, and that was more important right now. Able to stand, Kas kept an eye on the guards. They were relaxed, chatting rather than searching the grounds. Just out for another boring patrol. Kas couldn't remember the last time he'd heard of an intruder in the palace grounds.

"This way." Kas gave Sali's shirt a little tug, leading him away from the guards and towards some leafy bushes near another part of the wall.

Satisfied that Sali was hidden, Kas turned back to the guards. They had stopped right in the middle of the garden.

Even keeping to the bushes at the wall, there was no way to get back to the tree without the guards spotting them. And there was no way out of the palace without getting to the tree.

Sweat pricked Kas's skin. If they were caught, they were done. It had been bad enough thinking of being sent to the camps himself. The idea of Sali suffering the same fate made Kas sick.

They'd have to wait. There was no other way. Surely the guards couldn't stay there too long. But then another pair of guards appeared and sauntered over to where the first pair stood. They were all far too relaxed for Kas's liking. His heart sank as one lit up a cigarette.

"Looks like we'll have to wait them out," Kas hissed, now crouching beside the bush that hid his brother.

"Kas," Sali said quietly. Kas closed his eyes. He heard it in his brother's tone. And the thought was itching the back of his mind already. "Kas. Please."

They were stuck in the palace grounds for an unknown period of time. Those guards might finish their cigarettes and leave before Kas answered his brother. Or they might settle in, preferring to hide out in the garden and chat rather than pointlessly circle the palace for intruders who were stupid enough to try to infiltrate the most heavily guarded building in the Empire.

But if Kas was already in the grounds, already risking the camps if caught... was it really that much more of a risk to try to get into the building itself? Was it that much of a stretch to be able to give Sali the life he dreamed of?

"Okay," said Kas softly. "I'll try."

Kas put out an arm, clasping Sali's shoulder and keeping him in the bush as the little boy's excitement got the better of him and he tried to squiggle out and hug his big brother. His face was visible through the leaves, a big beaming smile lighting it up.

"But you stay right there in the bush. Anyone comes near, you can move that way, back towards the tree. But you do not go anywhere else. Am I clear?"

"Yep." Sali nodded happily. His excitement at being involved and not sent back home to wait was palpable.

Kas fought to keep the corner of his mouth from rising.

"Can you see the guards?"

Sali's face disappeared back into the bush and there was a slight rustling as his brother moved. "Yep."

"Okay, keep an eye on them. If they move, and you're sure they've gone, head to the tree and head home. No arguments," he cut Sali's protest off before it could begin. "If it's safe to get out of here before I'm back, you head back to the shanty and wait there. If it gets dark and I'm not home, find Frank and tell him what happened."

"I'll find Jori—"

"No. You find Frank. Promise." Kas gave Sali the look that said he wasn't messing around and, though he clearly wasn't happy about it, Sali nodded once.

"Okay, this door, you reckon?" Kas nodded to a small wooden door set into the exterior wall of the palace.

"Yeah," Sali whispered enthusiastically, "I've seen some maids and workers go in and out. But no guards or people in fancy clothes."

Kas nodded. It would be easier to get into the servants' quarters than the main palace, but then he'd have to find his way to the emperor's rooms. No doubt they were as far away from the servants as possible.

"Okay. I'll try to come back this way. But get yourself out of here as soon as it's safe, okay? If something goes wrong in there, it'll be harder for both of us to get away."

"Got it."

Kas grabbed Sali's head and gave him a quick kiss on the top of it. "Love you," he said as Sali squirmed and pushed him away. But as he bent the light around him and darted over to the door, opening it as little as he could, he heard a little voice behind him.

"I love you too."

CHAPTER FOUR

KAS

Kas followed the dark corridors, navigating as best he could until he was deposited in a large kitchen. He looked around, eyes wide. The room was bigger than Walton's forge, and that housed four huge fires, cooling troughs, and several anvils, each requiring space enough for the blacksmiths to swing their hammers.

Two thick, long tables dominated the space, and bench seating pushed underneath told Kas that the staff ate here when it wasn't being used to cook enormous feasts for the emperor. The rear wall was dominated with ovens larger than the potter had, and lining the walls were benches for chopping and shelves for holding various pots, pans, trays, and mugs.

Four kitchen staff were busy in a corner, chopping and frying and checking one of the ovens. Whatever they were making smelled amazing, and Kas hurried to the exit before the growling of his stomach could give him away.

Kas followed more winding corridors, turning back when he found himself in dead ends. Most of the doors led to storage rooms or sleeping quarters for the staff, and there were so many different corridors that Kas began to despair he was lost.

Panic threatened to grip him as he realised he wasn't sure of the way back to the exit, and he cursed himself for being overwhelmed by his curiosity at how different the lives of those who lived in the palace were. He knew the staff were hardly living the exuberant life of the emperor or even his nobles, but it was still miles better than his own meagre existence. A thought in the back of his mind formed. Maybe he could get jobs for himself and Sali here. He could get the room and board Jori had offered without the danger.

Pushing open another door, Kas stumbled into the entrance hall of the palace. The official entry was off to his right. Two massive doors, each taller than a house, stood open with guards on either side. The sun poured in, bouncing off marble and quartz, causing the room to glitter as if even the entryway were one of the emperor's treasures.

Kas's mouth gaped open as he stared around, looking up at the impossibly high ceiling. The roof was ringed in skylights, helping to flood the room in warm light. He'd never imagined such a place could exist.

Movement on the far side of the entrance hall caught Kas's eye, and he instinctively moved to the stairwell and positioned himself behind a pillar, though he was still invisible. Guards stood on either side of a smaller set of double doors, nodding at staff as they entered and exited, carrying plates and bundles of cloth and boxes, the contents of which Kas couldn't hope to imagine.

His mind clicked back into mission mode and he started up the steps. That level of activity indicated someone important, likely the emperor, was behind those doors. Or at least, he would be soon. Which meant his rooms should be empty. Kas assumed his bedroom would be upstairs. Rich people always had their bedrooms upstairs so they could look out over a world that, for them, was fun and full of promise.

Following that logic, Kas continued to climb the staircase for another two floors, and then when he glanced around a large, open corridor and spied another, he climbed that too. There were staff and guards on the upper floors of the palace, but they were far fewer than those on the lower level, and they were significantly more relaxed.

Taking care to move slowly and open doors as little as possible, Kas began looking for the emperor's room. One door led to a sprawling office at least fifty times the size of his shanty. It had not only a desk, but a huge lounge setting, complete with a coffee table. An entire wall was glass, with a door leading to a balcony that looked over the city, and had a view where you could see the Frostblood Ranges off in the distance.

Kas would have loved to spend days in the palace exploring and looking at all the wonders it contained. There were bookshelves as tall as the ceiling in many of the rooms, and it was all Kas could do to stop himself from going over and running his hands over the leather bindings of the books they contained.

His parents had owned a few books. He could remember his father reading to him and Sali at nighttime. Kas could even read a few words himself, though books as thick as these were probably beyond him. He frowned, wondering who had time to read all the books the emperor had collected. Or, he supposed, the emperor's father had collected, and his father before him.

Kas turned his mind back to his task, shutting the curiosity off and focussing on the ring. Jori had mentioned it was in the emperor's bedroom, and now that Kas was here, he wondered if that was even right. Why would he keep a valuable ring in his bedroom? A huge palace like this must have a dozen locked rooms full of treasure, guarded day and night. It seemed foolish to think it would be that easy.

The voices came around the corner quickly, and Kas barely had time to flatten himself against the wall as two maids bustled past.

"Got to get his bed done before he retires," one said, stress lacing her tone.

"You have plenty of time for that," the other scoffed. "I've got to get his nightclothes pressed right quick. You know he sometimes likes to put them on and then do some more work."

Kas hurried after the women. They strode down the wide hallway and straight for the doors at the end of the corridor. The guards on either side straightened as the women approached, one opening the door on his side. The women, whose arms were full, thanked the guard, who nodded at them and resumed his watch.

Kas followed the women into the room, so close he almost stood on the shorter lady's heels. But with guards on either side of the doors, there was no chance for him to slip in other than behind someone else. As it happened, he needn't have worried. The guards had no interest in closing the door, and the ladies hurried immediately to work. The taller maid dropped sheets on the bed and began arranging linens from smallest to largest, and the shorter woman headed to the right and around a corner.

Kas stood just inside the doorway, jaw gaping. The room was massive; even bigger than the office he'd found. It similarly had enormous windows leading to a balcony, and a bed that would have taken the entire floor space of Kas's home dominated one end. The other end held a small desk and a vanity table with a large mirror.

Kas walked towards the mirror, wondering where the other maid had gone. As he got closer, he realised there was a room to the right of the vanity that held all the emperor's clothes. The maid was inside, humming to herself as she put things away and retrieved other items, laying them out on a long padded bench.

Kas stayed in the room with her for a few minutes, looking around and peering over her shoulder as she opened various drawers. There were some jewels in one, but they looked to be normal jewellery. Probably the empress's jewels, unnecessary after her death in childbirth. Still, shutting them away in a drawer seemed wrong. Even if the emperor wasn't inclined to gift the wealth to the people, he could at least give them to his daughter. She'd be about sixteen by now, and of age to wear them.

He thought of his dad's cap, permanently shoved under his pillow in the shanty. Kas could neither bear to get rid of it nor wear it. Perhaps he understood why the jewels were dumped in a drawer.

Nonetheless, Kas realised he could grab a handful of the rings and necklaces in that drawer and escape easily. He could probably feed himself and his brother for months. Maybe even get a better place to live. He'd never even have to tell Jori that he'd tried and failed.

But something stopped him. He'd made it this far. The regular jewels would give them a better year. That one ring would give them a better life.

So he left the wardrobe and went back into the main area. The sun was setting, bathing the land in red. Kas thought of Sali. He should be long gone by now, hopefully safely at home in their shanty, waiting for Kas to get back.

Pulling his eyes from the view, Kas walked over towards the bed. Despite her fretting, the maid had worked quickly, and the bed was almost made. Kas wandered to the opposite side of the bed from where she was working and looked at the small table next to it. There was a glass of water and a crystal decanter, should the emperor become parched at nighttime.

A book lay there too, and Kas spent a minute trying to sound out the title. *A History of Valoris* by Archivist Eloi James. Kas raised an eyebrow. An academic text on the history of the continent seemed heavy bedtime reading. He had much preferred when his father read him tales of knights and dragons and mages and epic quests.

In the centre of the table was a strange metal stand. It had a solid base anchoring a thin metal arm that rose up, then bent over, sitting horizontally. Kas had never seen anything like it.

He turned and found himself at the entry to a huge bathroom, dominated by the largest bathtub he'd ever seen. He and Sali could both sit inside it and still have room for friends.

A sigh sounded behind him and Kas jumped, stepping back just in time to avoid being bumped by the maid who had been in the closet. She carried some clothes and went to deposit them on the nightstand with the air of someone wanting a brief rest before getting pulled back into some hard labour.

"No! Not there," called the other maid urgently. "If you hit the stand, you'll set off the alarm."

The maid with the clothes jumped at the warning and moved gingerly away from the nightstand. "Oh gods, I keep forgetting. Thank you," she said gratefully. "If I set that off, I'd lose my job."

"You and me both," said the taller maid, who finished making the bed and ushered the other away. "Let's get out of here before you cause any more trouble."

And they crossed to the door, exiting and closing it behind them.

Kas stared after them. The door was closed, and the

guards were right outside. That meant he was trapped here until someone else came in. Panic threatened, but he took some deep breaths, telling himself Sali would be worried, but he'd be home with his little brother soon enough.

Trying to calm himself, Kas looked again at the stand on the bedside table. The maid had said it had an alarm. That meant it had to be important. Or held something important. *The ring!*

Kas felt sure that was where it was stored. It felt right, and Kas's intuition was usually spot on. An alarm complicated things. He'd either need to find and take the ring before it was on the stand, or grab it and run. Kas wondered what kind of alarm it could raise. He didn't see anything connected to it. Spelled, then? He'd known doors to be spelled to trigger a cacophony if opened. Perhaps this stand did the same thing.

He looked around the now empty bedroom as if the ring might be lying around somewhere within. If it wasn't here, where was it? The ring was the symbol of the emperor's power. It had been handed down from emperor to emperor since the Empire had existed. It was rumoured to be one of the ancient relics, forged by the most powerful Druid of the age, and to have enormous power for one who could wield it.

Kas frowned. The emperor was a magical. Everyone in his line was. But magicals could not perform spells or use enchanted objects. It was unheard of for anyone to have more than one type of magic. In fact, the only person Kas had ever heard of who could do more than one of those things was Kas. And he could do all three. But as a magical, the emperor couldn't *use* the ring. Which was why Kas had thought it would be here, in his room.

But if it was a symbol of his station, then perhaps he wore it all the same. Kas cursed. If it was on the emperor's finger, then Kas would have to wait until he took it off. Which meant hiding in the emperor's bedroom until he went to bed and then stealing the most powerful object in the Empire from right next to the emperor himself, and getting out of the palace, past the guards, all while some kind of alarm sounded.

If there were two guards posted for an empty room, how many would be there to block his exit when the emperor arrived? This was a bad idea. A very bad idea. Kas went to cross back to the wardrobe. He would grab some of the normal jewels and wait for the next servant to enter the room, and then he would flee while the door was open.

But as he crossed the floor, the door opened in front of him. Perfect. He would leave now. Surely there were other valuable things between here and the exit.

Kas took a step back to get out of the way of whoever was entering the room.

And found himself face-to-face with the emperor.

CHAPTER FIVE

KAS

Kas backed away quickly, careful not to make a sound. He wished his invisibility came with a handy soundproof pocket, but it didn't. He'd need to be careful to not draw attention. If the emperor felt something was amiss and had the guards search the room, Kas had no doubt they'd find him.

Several servants followed the emperor inside his room and a tall, thin man with impeccable presentation ordered them about until the emperor was settled at his desk, and then he shooed the other servants away.

As his adrenaline left him and Kas began to think he might not be caught and executed right that minute, he looked more closely at the emperor. He'd never seen him in person. The emperor's face was on their coins and often flew on banners overhead in the streets, but the man in front of Kas looked old and frail—well beyond his forty-two years.

"There now, Emperor," the manservant said gently, fussing about the ruler. "May I get you a glass of water?"

"No thank you Jeremy, I'm fine." The emperor's voice held affection for his servant, but there was an edge to it.

"Perhaps a nice cup of relaxing tea?"

"I'm fine, Jeremy."

Jeremy hesitated. "I'm reluctant to push, my liege, but you are meant to be avoiding stress—"

"Yes, well, a pipe dream, that is. Having to deal with that bunch of self-centred, egotistical vultures... they care nothing for the Empire, only for what they can grab and use to feather their own nests."

"Quite, my liege, but—"

"They have entirely too much power. What my ancestors were thinking, I'll never know."

"We often can't know the circumstances—"

"And to give them the military!" The emperor stood, pacing now as his agitation grew. "Well, basically all of it. Private armies paid more than I can afford. I can't blame the men for leaving, but I can't do anything useful with the troops I have left. Which means I need the nobles. I need their money and I need their soldiers, when all of that should rightly belong to the Empire in the first place!"

Jeremy put a gentle hand on the emperor's shoulder, breaking the man from his rant, and guided the ruler of the Empire back to his seat.

"I'm sorry, Jeremy. I know I'm not supposed to get worked up. But the Controllers *are* coming. And we're just sitting here waiting. I want to take the fight to them rather than wage war in our own lands where our people will suffer."

Jeremy busied himself with brushing the emperor's beard. "Perhaps if the nobles knew of the threat, my liege? Would they then not wish to defend their own lands, if not the Empire?"

The emperor sighed and sat back in his chair. "You might think that would spur them into action. But we let them lead the Great Exploration. They all have lands elsewhere. Lord Flighty and Viscount Cuddy would withdraw from Valoris immediately. They wouldn't hesitate to abandon the continent for their private islands. I suspect they already hoard most of their wealth there anyway. And without their armies, it would be suicide to go on the offensive."

Jeremy snorted his distaste, and Kas was glaring too. He had moved closer to the two men, his footsteps silent in the plush carpet. He'd always hated the nobles. They were obscenely wealthy, and Kas remembered walking through Hightown with his father when he was young and asking why the nobles didn't share with the poor people in the slums the same way their family did.

"If these people had slightly smaller houses, maybe the slum people wouldn't have to live in those shanties," he'd said.

His father had laughed, causing Kas to flush red, thinking he'd said something stupid.

"You would think, my boy, that the people in the Empire who worry about coin the most are those who live in the slums. But it's them." He'd pointed at the concrete walls towering above them. "The more they have, the more they worry. Worry about whether they have the most. Worry about how to get more. You don't need all that money for a good life, Kas. That's why we give our extra to the poor."

From the sounds of it, Kas hadn't understood about the depth of their pockets. He had no interest in politics and hadn't realised the rich owned the armies. That they had more money than the emperor himself. If the Controllers came, it'd be people like Kas fighting and dying to protect the Empire. And if the Empire won, then the nobles would swan back in from their islands and fall right back into running things.

Amid his anger, Kas wondered briefly about those islands. He'd never even left the city, let alone seen any of

Valoris. He thought of the explorers travelling to the four corners of Endarnia. What must it be like to travel the world? What would it be like to visit those faraway places? But travel was not for people like him.

The emperor broke into a bout of coughing. Jeremy fussed over him, patting his back and pouring a steaming, fragrant tea.

Suddenly, Kas worried about his task for a different reason. He'd assumed the emperor ran everything. Ruled with an iron fist. If he was so weak compared to the nobles, what would stealing his ring do? It was the symbol of his position. From the sound of things, the emperor was trying to protect them from an impending invasion. What if stealing the ring sealed the Empire's fate?

Another upsetting thought unfolded in his mind. The whole basis for the rebels was that the emperor was failing his people. Kas had heard Jori telling taverns full of people that the reason they were poor was because the emperor cared only about his own wealth and nothing for them. He frowned at the frail man before him. The emperor did seem to care deeply about his people. And the only concern for his own pockets seemed to be that the nobles wouldn't let him care for his people properly.

If he helped Jori here, was he really helping the nobles? Who, according to what he'd just heard, would hop on their ships at the first sign of this apparently impending war and leave them all to fight it alone.

Kas wandered into the closet and opened the drawer that held the late empress's jewels. He felt guilty stealing from the emperor now, though if the man was that worried about money, he could have sold some of these gems. They would be more used to Kas than they were to the emperor, tucked away in a drawer, and it didn't even seem the emperor would notice they were missing.

He slipped several rings and small bracelets into his pocket. The air changed and Kas turned, alarm coursing through his body as Jeremy strode confidently into the wardrobe. For a second, Kas assumed he'd been caught. He must have let his grasp on the light slip. But then, if he'd been discovered, it was unlikely the manservant would come to deal with him directly. Not with a bunch of burly guards right outside the door.

Kas moved silently as Jeremy aimed for where he'd been standing. His heart thudded against his chest as he was taken with the certainty that Jeremy was about to open the drawer and discover the jewels missing. Maybe he inventoried them each night. Certainly, Kas would check them regularly if he possessed such a fortune.

But Jeremy ignored the drawer, reaching instead for the shirts and robes hanging above. He flicked through them, pulling the occasional one out and considering it with a frown. Kas moved as quickly as he dared, edging back out into the main room and finding a spot to stand where the carpet was less worn.

The emperor sighed, and Kas's eyes jumped to his face. He was pale to the point of being almost ashen, his skin loose and papery, like a man twice his age. Rubbing his eyes, the emperor blinked them back open and looked out the window at the fading day. His eyes were rimmed with red, and there was a strange purple hue to them.

Kas froze, his pounding heart the only part of him still moving.

The emperor was dying.

Worse than that, he had been poisoned. Mottleweed was extremely rare, only growing at the peaks of the highest mountains in the uninhabited Frostblood Ranges. But his father, a talented alchemist, had told Kas it was worth a fortune. Mottleweed in the right hands could make a salve so potent it could cure almost any illness. But in the wrong hands, it could be brewed into a poison so deadly no cure was known for it.

One day a woman had stumbled into his father's apothecary and left soon after, sobbing and wailing. His father had explained to Kas that she had ingested mottleweed. A single drop of mottleweed poison was deadly, he'd explained, but it would take fifteen, maybe twenty years for you to die. The woman had only had a small dose, but there was nothing Kas's father could do. The woman would die a slow and painful death.

And her eyes had looked just like the emperor's.

Panic took Kas. He needed to tell someone. But who would he tell? And what would be the point? It was too late now. The man was going to die. If it was just the one exposure, then the ruler of the Empire had at least a decade left, but his death would be drawn out and painful. If it was more... well. The more mottleweed you ingested, the quicker, but more painful, your death would be. Nausea gripped Kas's stomach, turning it.

The emperor lowered his hands, his fingers toying with his ring.

The ring.

It was a thick and indelicate ring. Clearly made for a man. Red stones sat interspersed with clear gems that sparkled. Such a small thing for all this trouble. Kas had heard all the rumours about what it could do, though he doubted half of them were anywhere near accurate. Depending on who you listened to, the ring imbued the wearer with all the magics available in the world, granted them a longer than usual lifespan, allowed the wearer to kill with a glance, shielded them from any magical attack, or all of the above. Though it would seem it was not able to cure illness. Of course, the emperor was a magical, and so unable to access the true power of the ring.

"Are you alright, my liege?" Jeremy rushed to the emperor, whose head had drooped.

"Fine, I'm fine." The emperor patted Jeremy's hand. "I worry for my daughter. What an awful mess I will hand to her all too soon."

He knew, then.

"The princess will handle everything with the grace she inherited from you, my liege," said Jeremy, doing a fine job of covering the sorrow in his voice.

Kas felt the conflict rise in his chest once more. Surely a ruler who inspired such love in his servant couldn't be as bad as Jori was always saying?

"And I know you will help her as best you can. But what is one to do, charged with the protection of an Empire half the citizens actively resist being a part of? And half the rest don't care about, preferring to build their off-continent refuges? I have no real army with which to defend my people, and almost all of my soldiers are currently busy forcing the tribes to submit to our rule. And I have no money with which to build a bigger army. Curse my ancestors for leaving me with this mess. And curse me for not making it the slightest bit better for Cassandra."

"You are Emperor Ewan Addax, the finest emperor we have seen, and you have raised a formidable daughter. Perhaps you should worry less for her and more for any who make the mistake of standing in her way?" Jeremy smiled at the emperor.

Kas saw the emperor try to smile back, but his worries would not let his smile reach his eyes. He clearly feared for his daughter. Kas felt off balance. His daughter would rule the Empire. She would be one of the most powerful people in the world. That the emperor feared for her struck a panic far deeper in Kas than even the idea of being caught in the palace could achieve.

Come now." Jeremy indicated to the emperor that it was time to get ready for bed. "Perhaps it is not all that bad. Maybe the Controllers won't come after all. They haven't so far."

The emperor sadly shook his head. "They will come, I'm sure of it. The archivists uncovered a pattern. Something has delayed them, but it is a fool's hope to wish the delay is permanent."

The two men moved to the bathroom and Kas remained where he was, adrenaline starting to course through his veins. This was it. Soon the emperor would get into bed and put the ring on the stand. Or would he? Perhaps he wore the ring all the time. It was so small a thing that wasn't out of the realm of possibility.

Kas took some deep breaths, willing himself to calm. He still wasn't sure stealing it was the best idea, but he'd come this far. The fates had been on his side, and so he'd leave the decision to chance. If the emperor removed the ring, he'd steal it and run like mad. If he kept it on, Kas would have no choice but to slip out of the palace, and he could even tell Jori that the problem of getting the ring wasn't going to be solved through mere invisibility.

Disappointment took him at the thought, more so than relief. Something within him was proud of how easily he'd managed to not only get into the palace, but all the way into the emperor's chamber. And with the emperor himself in it. Images flashed through his mind of providing Jori the ring in front of all his rebel cronies. The looks of awe and admiration on their faces. He craved the attention as much as it scared him. He wasn't too keen on everyone knowing what he could do, though he supposed Jori had probably already let his secret out of the bag.

Jeremy settled the emperor into his enormous bed, so big it made the frail man look like a child. As the servant plumped and preened, Kas wandered closer to the desk, peering at the documents the emperor had been reading. Many of the words were not ones he knew, but he could read enough to know it was a brief about the leadership of the Shifters. Kas had heard there were issues in the forest, but he wasn't really interested in the troubles beyond the city. He had enough of his own to deal with right here.

Movement drew Kas's eyes, and he watched, adrenaline spiking again as Jeremy poured the emperor a glass of water then slipped out the door, opening it barely a crack, and shutting it immediately.

Kas remained still, allowing his eyes to adjust to the darkness that had fallen with the extinguishing of the candles, and waited for sleep to take the emperor. He resisted the urge to move closer and see what the fates had decided for him.

He oscillated between hoping it was on the stand and praying it remained on the emperor's finger. A sudden panic grabbed him, trickling over him like a bucket of ice water. He had been preparing himself to grab the ring and run. But how was he supposed to get out of the room? The minute he opened the doors, the guards outside would grab him. Invisible or not, doors opening usually meant a person was there. Perhaps he could push the door open and slip between the guards as they investigated.

Kas shook his head, clearing it. No point in planning his escape until he knew what he was dealing with. Waiting a few minutes more, Kas listened, finally hearing the deep rhythmic breathing that told him the emperor was asleep.

He crept forward, edging towards the bed. It wasn't until he was right at the foot of the bed that he saw it. The ring. Sitting innocently on the stand. Kas's heart began pounding. He almost wished the maid had knocked the stand earlier, just so he'd know what he was dealing with. He tiptoed towards it and reached out, his hand shaking. Assuming it was just an audible alarm, he needed to snatch it and run.

He closed his eyes, took a deep breath, and grabbed the ring.

CHAPTER SIX

KAS

DEAFENING wails and clanging sounded the minute the ring left the stand. Kas jumped at the sound and spurred himself into action. Darting over to the door, he waited, invisible, for the guards. He was barely there when the doors flung open and two guards entered, swords in one hand, balls of fire floating in the palms of their other.

With no hesitation, Kas slipped behind them and out the door, moving as quickly as he dared down the corridor. Footsteps thundered as six more huge guards raced towards the emperor's room. Kas had barely made it to the stairs when he heard the guards from the room calling to the reinforcements that the ring was gone.

Doors opened along corridors as Kas raced down the stairs, bleary-eyed servants poking their heads out at the commotion, some more alert and exiting their rooms to help, pulling on clothing as they went.

Down, down, down Kas went, solely focussed on getting out of the palace. A boom sounded, and he knew before he reached them that the main entry doors had been sealed. He barely glanced to confirm it as he skidded towards the door to the kitchens. The door burst open, almost smacking Kas in the face, and he dove to the left, barely avoiding a collision with a steady stream of kitchen and gardening hands, all moving towards the guards at the doors to get their assignments.

Kas slipped through as the door was closing, his shirt catching in the jamb and jerking him to a stop. He wrenched at it, not caring if it ripped, and it came free, toppling Kas, who had thrown all his weight behind the tug.

More footsteps and a foot caught Kas in the side. He tried to keep his mouth firmly shut, but not before a soft "ooof" had escaped. A tall, thick man fell on the floor between Kas and the door he'd just come through.

"Oooh, Jake, are you alright love?" a matronly woman called to the man.

"Fine," he replied, a twinge of embarrassment in his tone as he squinted at the floor, looking for what had tripped him.

Kas rolled himself to the side, pressing into the wall and willing his body to sink into it. The woman moved forward, stepping where Kas had been a second ago. She offered Jake her hand, but he got up on his own.

"Don't know what I tripped on," he said, his voice both defensive and suspicious.

"Oh, you know what these stones are like," said the woman, eager to get going.

"It wasn't the cobblestones," Jake said. But the woman just gently guided him around, and he moved to the door and through it.

Kas waited, pressed against the door until he was sure they had gone. He moved quickly but cautiously through the corridors, a hint of panic at becoming lost urging his heart to beat faster. There were few people left in the servants' quarters now, and he only saw two more people, but they were clearly late and more focussed on getting to where they were meant to be.

The alarm continued clanging, making it hard to hear any approaching footsteps. Kas registered that the alarm seemed just as loud here as it had been in the emperor's room, but his focus remained on getting out.

He almost cried with relief as he pushed through a door and found himself in the kitchen. He ran the length of the room and hurried back until he found the door through which he had entered the palace.

Kas hesitated. There was no one blocking the door on this side, but that didn't mean there wouldn't be guards outside. Surely they would be stationed at every exit to the palace. His mind raced.

Kas eased the door open, ready to run the minute he heard a cry of surprise, but none came. He slipped out, closing the door behind him, and found himself inches from the backs of two guards. Kas froze. If he'd opened the door a fraction wider, he'd have hit them with it.

"Don't see anything, do you?" one guard asked the other, who grunted in reply. "Best to keep going, then." With another grunt, they turned, Kas moving with them, and they resumed their patrol along the palace wall. Once they were a step past him, Kas rushed over to the hedge, vaulted over it, and crouched down, catching his breath.

A searching hand patted his shoulder, and his blood froze.

"It's me."

"Sali! What in the hells are you still doing here?" Kas whispered, surprised and furious.

"I couldn't leave you," came the quiet reply.

Emotions warred within Kas. He was so angry his brother had kept himself in danger and was now at risk of being caught alongside him. Escaping had seemed much easier when he thought his little brother was safely at home.

But he could understand Sali staying. Kas was all he had. The idea of waiting at home, not knowing what had happened to his older brother, would have seemed like torture. At least here he could listen out. Hear it if the guards were gossiping about a boy who had been caught stealing and was now in the dungeons or dead.

"It's okay," said Kas, giving Sali a quick hug and keeping hold of his hand so his little brother would know where he was. "But we need to move. You go first, head to the tree, and we'll go back along the branch. Focus on keeping low and I'll keep an eye out for anyone coming."

Sali moved quickly, darting through the gardens, using the bushes well. Kas was impressed; Sali was almost as invisible as he was. Kas followed closely behind, his head on a swivel, checking for guards that might see them moving through the garden.

In no time, he was up the tree, crouched behind Sali, who had paused on the branch.

"You go. I'll wait here until you're across. Don't wait for me though; once you're on the other side, head down and hide in the park, okay?"

"Okay," Sali whispered back. He crept along the branch, but when he reached the gap, he hesitated.

"What's wrong?" Kas hissed.

"It's... it's a long way," Sali whispered back. "It didn't seem this far before."

Kas cursed. Realistically, it was the same distance, but since he'd broken the branch, the gap looked much bigger.

"You've got this Sali," he said, trying to sound reassuring rather than impatient. "You jumped farther than that gap when you came across."

Sali nodded, staring at the chasm. Kas saw his brother take a deep breath and leap.

"Hey!"

The voice came from the direction the two guards had walked off in.

"Run," Kas called to Sali as the footsteps of the guards crashed into the garden.

Kas willed Sali to move faster as his little brother crept along the branch on the other side.

"There he is," called one guard as the other said, "I see him."

Watching his brother's form disappear down into the park on the other side, Kas let his hold on the light go as he hurried along the branch. Let the guards focus on him, not Sali.

With no time to think, Kas leapt across the branches, imagining his weight breaking the other branch. There was no way he'd be able to get up on his own. Would the guards come after him, or just watch as he grew tired and eventually fell to his death?

His feet hit the wood and Kas ran down the branch before dropping into the park and hurrying to Sali, who was perched near a tree, not hidden at all.

"Let's go," Kas said, turning his brother around and pushing him along in front of him.

"Why are you visible?" Sali asked, alarmed.

"Better they come after me," said Kas. "Come on, this way."

Kas pulled Sali through the streets of Hightown. It was late, but the rich were still out, off to the theatre or on their way to the taverns, though some were already stumbling home.

The boys drew stares, and Kas cursed. Of course they would stand out, grubby little slum urchins that they were.

All the guards needed to do was ask, and the nobility would point them straight to the thieves.

He tried to move off the busy main streets, but Kas didn't know this area. Hitting another dead end, Kas swore, tears of frustration threatening to fall.

He pulled Sali back towards the opening of the road and saw a familiar figure flit by.

"Adeline," Kas called as loud as he dared. As he pulled Sali out onto the main street, his best friend looked his way. Her face creased, looking for who had hailed her.

"Oh! Kas, hi." Her face broke into a smile. "And how are you, Sali?"

"Hi Adeline." Sali beamed, seeming to forget their predicament.

"Adeline, I need you to take Sali. If the guards ask, say he's your brother, and you took him to work with you to train him up."

"What in the world—"

"There's no time! Adeline, please. I wouldn't ask if it wasn't important."

Voices sounded back up the road, and Adeline's eyes locked on something over Kas's shoulder. She seemed to want to ask more, but she simply nodded, grabbing Sali's hand and hurrying away.

"Gods bless you," Kas whispered after her. Adeline was risking everything by taking Sali. If the guards had seen his little brother clearly and found Adeline with him, they would take her in for aiding his escape. Or worse, think she was the other figure. But Kas was almost certain the guards thought they were looking for two boys. Adeline should be fine, and he wouldn't trust his brother to anyone else.

He heard the commotion moving towards him, and with one final look at his brother disappearing around the corner, Kas took a deep breath and headed back towards the guards.

"Hey!"

It took longer than he'd expected for them to see him, but once he was sure they had, Kas ran. They might not have gotten a good look at him, but a slum kid running would be enough to grab their attention. He led them away from Adeline and Sali, thinking only to buy them enough time to leave Hightown. After that, he could pull the light around him and disappear.

Kas sprinted down the main road, bumping into people and knocking some of the more inebriated ones to the ground. Ensuring the guards kept him in sight, he darted off to the right, praying that the road led somewhere.

The gods answered him, but only to the letter. The road led to a bridge. With a cart blocking its other end.

"Move!" Kas cried. The owner of the cart was an old man, and he peered around his cart at Kas. The donkey, who was refusing to move, similarly glanced back, but was unimpressed by Kas's terror.

"He's here," called a guard to his fellows.

Kas panicked. There was nowhere else to go. Rows of tall concrete walls paralleled the road, and Kas could only jump off the bridge or try to climb over the cart. He peered over the edge of the bridge. It was a shorter drop than the moat, but it would still kill him. Or he'd just be seriously maimed, and Kas wasn't going to risk that.

He grabbed hold of the cart and something immediately snapped at his fingers. Kas caught a glance at what the man was transporting. *Crocodiles. Great.*

Recently, the wealthier of the Empire's citizens had been taken by a fad that involved eating small crocodiles. The animals were brought to the table and snapped around, exciting the rich folk, before being taken back to the kitchen and cooked. Poachers looked for the smallest they could find, and some industrious people had begun breeding miniature crocodiles for this very purpose. As a result, lots of guys in the slums had lost fingers hunting or breeding them to sell to street vendors and restaurants in Hightown.

Kas felt the bridge shudder. The guards were at the other end. Climbing over the cart was out. It'd have to be under. Kas glanced over the side of the bridge again. At the bottom of the drop was the trickle of a small section of the river that had been diverted to carry the waste of Hightown away from the rich and into the rest of the city.

Reluctantly, he dropped the ring over the side, aiming for a clump of brambles. It would be a nightmare to retrieve, but likely no one else would be poking around in the prickles and find it. Kas hated to part with it, but to get caught with it on him would be a death sentence. The rest would just earn him a ticket to the labour camps. But then, he wasn't planning on being caught.

With the footsteps of the guards unnervingly close, Kas dove under the cart, pulling himself along and kicking out at the hands grabbing at him.

"Move this cart!" the guards bellowed at the old man.

"Jinky moves when Jinky wants to move," he whined back at them. "I can't make him go if he doesn't want to."

Kas blocked out the ensuing argument as he got to the front of the cart and Jinky kicked down, almost stomping his hand. Kas tried to move around the donkey, but the crea-ture, unnerved at so many people behind him, kicked and stomped and generally made it impossible for Kas to get past.

A sudden heat blew over Kas, and he heard the croco-diles screech while Jinky brayed. With a clatter, Jinky decided that the bridge wasn't the place to be, and lurched forward. The blast of fire from the guards had burned away the catch on the cart, and as Jinky moved forward, revealing Kas sprawled on the ground, the crocodiles made their escape, dropping from the back of the cart onto Kas and the ground surrounding him.

Kas heard screams, though they might have been his.

The old man was bellowing, "That's my livelihood! Don't crush them!"

Kas was pushing and sweeping them off him, trying to crawl away from the tiny snapping mouths. He wanted to give them a blast of fire, but he was so panicked he might burn the bridge. Plus, if he got any of the guards, it would be over. One crocodile snapped at his shirt, nipping his chest underneath, and Kas twisted and shoved, forcing the crocodile and several of its friends off him.

He barely had a moment of relief before a thick hand grabbed him by the collar, yanking him to his feet. Unfortunately, clearing the crocodiles had given the guards a path to him, too.

Kas's mind ran through impossible options. He could turn invisible, though that wouldn't help him slip the guard's grip, and would likely just make things worse. He could fight, but he was fourteen, and these guards looked like they'd give the Trolls a run for their money. They wouldn't be expecting his magic to be as powerful as it was, but if he used magic on the guards, even if he got away, he'd be dooming himself to a life on the run. And they'd go after his family, too.

A rough hand patted his pockets, locating the one with the jewels and pulling some out.

"You're coming with us, thief."

Kas's heart sank. He prayed Adeline would look after Sali.

CHAPTER SEVEN

CASSANDRA

EIGHT YEARS LATER

THE VIEW from her room normally worked as a salve, a meditation, distracting her mind from all her worries. But today, not even the beautiful view could stop the anxiety. She was due in the council chamber in less than an hour. These monthly meetings with the nobles had always been terrible, and they were only getting worse.

At first, she was able to convince herself it was because she was new. It seemed understandable, even fair, that the nobles, who had been attending the meetings far longer than she, and had all the knowledge and background, would be frustrated at needing the approval of someone new.

She had asked all sorts of questions, trying to get across all the issues being discussed, but each question was met with sighs and subtle shakes of heads. Understandable, she told herself. It would get better when she was up to date on everything.

But she had now been empress for three years. And so she had to admit to herself it was not because she was new. The old men just had no respect for her at all. Maybe it was because she was young and female. But the nobles had not even a skerrick of the deference they had shown her father for her. And even that hadn't been the respect an emperor deserved.

She had tried being nice and understanding. Even apologising that she was new and had to be read in on so many issues. That had been a mistake. She had lost ground that had so far proved impossible to make up.

And so now she dreaded the monthly meetings. Sitting in a room with all those pompous, arrogant assholes. The derision that sounded at any suggestion she gave. The patronising tones that gilded their responses. Responses that were always saying she was wrong.

She hated the meetings. She hated the nobles. Most of all, she hated that she needed them. She played with the ring on her finger. It was lighter than the real one and had not a scrap of magic in it. Not that she could have used the magic. She had power over water, but she couldn't command powerful objects. That was for others to do. Yet her father had insisted the ring always kept the emperor or empress safe.

"Is everything okay, ma'am?"

The empress jumped, jerking her hand away from playing with the false ring. She pulled her gaze from the view out her window and turned to her mirror. The worried eyes of her lady's maid stared at her as the woman fixed her hair into a knot. She didn't seem interested in the ring, and shouldn't be.

Only a select few knew it wasn't the real ring. That the real one had been stolen from her father's nightstand eight years ago and was never recovered. Someone had been sent to the labour camps for the crime, but the ring had not been found on him. She stopped the frown that usually came whenever she thought of the camps. If there were a way, she would shut them down today. But, of course, the nobles would never allow that. How had they managed to get into such a mess that the ruler of the Empire could do nothing without the acquiescence of the nobles?

The empress plastered a smile on her face and assured the maid that she was perfectly fine.

Sadness settled in her chest. She wished she could confide in someone. She wished she could confide in her maid as her father had his manservant. But the woman was a plant, she was sure of it. Sent to the palace by Lord Emery Flighty, no doubt. Or Baron Derron Shamble. Both would love to have something over her.

The empress closed her eyes, willing the loneliness away. Her father was dead, and she had no friends. No allies. She couldn't even trust her lady's maid.

The meeting began poorly and was now going worse than she had feared. The nobles used to jump to their feet as soon as the doors opened for her father, but they barely rose an inch for her until the doorman bellowed her name.

"The empress, her magnificent defender of the Empire, Cassandra Addax."

She was relieved her father forewent middle names for her. He'd had several and told her the best gift he could bestow on her on the day of her birth was not to take up half her life listening to people announce her.

Initially, Cassandra had hoped to forgo being announced at all for regular meetings such as this one. Everyone knew who she was, and she'd thought they would develop a strong working relationship that wouldn't need a reminder of her authority. How wrong she'd been.

"And so surely now you can see, Princ—forgive me. Empress..."

Lord Flighty. Such a jerk. It had been three years, and he still expected her to think his slip—almost referring to her as the princess—was accidental. Perhaps the only thing that stung worse than the disrespect was the constant insinuation that she was stupid.

But Cassandra was not stupid.

"Lord Flighty," she interrupted, "I think we can all see why raising the price of grain across the Empire is a good idea from your side of things, but I'm afraid increasing your wealth just isn't a compelling argument from the Empire's point of view."

Baron Zachariah Page sniggered before he could catch himself. He was perhaps the only one of them on Cassandra's side, but as a baron he was a minor noble, and offered very little power to their meagre team.

"We are in a famine." Lord Flighty was angry now, and he dropped the simpering, patronising tone and glared at her. It didn't escape Cassandra's attention that he failed to use her title. "If we do not raise the prices, those who can afford to buy in bulk will stockpile and nothing will be left for those who cannot afford to do so. Do you wish to see your people starve?"

Blood boiled in Cassandra's veins. The bastard was really going to insinuate that he wished to raise the grain prices on humanitarian grounds at the same time as accusing her of not caring for her people?

Cassandra slowly leaned forward and dropped the temperature in the room with a clench of her fist. Fear graced the eyes of some of the nobles, and Baron Shamble, a small and stout man, flinched as the water in his glass froze. Lord Flighty had gone too far. For his part, Lord Flighty tried to hold her gaze, but she saw fear there too. Good.

"You will keep your prices low. The Empire will buy bulk stocks and we will ensure enough is kept for rationing in the event our people are going without."

Lord Flighty nodded and relaxed in his high-backed chair, trying to suppress the smile that threatened to break out. The Empire buying bulk stocks would net him almost as much as raising the prices. She'd put him in his place, but he'd still gotten what he wanted. As she intended.

She hated these men. She hated so much more that she needed them. And she hated that she couldn't tell them the truth. That she couldn't lay it all out for them as her dying father had for her and explain to them why they all needed to work together. Why they needed to pull their heads out of their asses and focus on something other than lining their own pockets.

How was it that the men with the power and resources to defend the Empire were the ones who would leave at the first hint of danger? She'd learned about the Great Exploration in her lessons as a child. It must have seemed a great idea at the time. The first annexation had failed and with nothing to do, the Empire's military had been sent on what appeared to Cassandra to be little more than state-sanctioned raids on other nations.

Her great-great-grandmother had rebranded the raids into the Great Exploration, ordering an end to the violence and thieving, but in return, granting the nobles more ownership of their troops, and allowing them to keep the spoils of their adventures.

The woman had fixed her own problem, oblivious to the yoke she was building for her ancestors. It was the power these men now had that caused her father to insist they couldn't be told of the threat of invasion. Once the archivists had uncovered the pattern of the Controller invasions and realised the next war could be predicted, he had ordered those who knew to silence. He had been so sure the nobles would take their soldiers and hide on their islands until the war was over.

But Cassandra wasn't so sure. Oh, she didn't doubt for a second that the nobles would hop on the first ship out of the harbour the minute they learned of the inevitable invasion. But would they take their forces with them? Could they?

The logistics involved were one thing, but Cassandra couldn't for the life of her see the nobles expending the resources required to transport and feed their entire armies. And surely some of their troops had families. The nobles wouldn't take them, so logically some of their soldiers would desert.

But as sure as she felt about that, Cassandra still couldn't bring herself to disregard her father's warning and come clean.

"Perhaps we should discuss the unrest in the outer reaches of the Empire?" Viscount Pol Cuddy simpered. Though as a viscount he had more power than a baron, Cuddy held himself as if he were a lord, and therefore the pinnacle of Empire nobility. His face was long and his right eyebrow seemed permanently raised. His voice reminded Cassandra of the one her father would use for the villains in the stories he used to read her when she was little.

Lord Flighty nodded at Baron Page, who, as the least powerful noble in the room, was treated almost as an assistant. Baron Page hopped up from the table and peered out of the door, ushering in a general in full dress uniform with medals sparkling in the light.

As the general outlined the unrest within the minor tribes, Cassandra frowned. The Empire had annexed all the tribes in the southern reaches just before she was born, twenty-four years ago. It was the second time the Empire had annexed the tribes, but unlike the first, on this second attempt, the Empire had tried to assert control. Had insisted on bringing them into line by forcing the ways of the Empire upon them. And the tribes had fought against it.

Thankfully, tensions had not risen to outright conflict, but the presence of the Empire's soldiers was resented, and the imposition of the Testing was hated. The collars were perhaps the cruellest twist of all.

One of Cassandra's favourite things as princess had been to travel the Empire and visit the tribes. She had wondered at their differences, enjoying the easy, laid-back nature of the Trolls, the fluidity and openness of the Shifters, and the mystique of the Druids.

She had seen firsthand the impact of the collars, and that had been the focus of the biggest arguments she'd had with her father. He used to smile sadly when she'd declare the collars to be the first thing she'd get rid of when she was empress.

"When you are empress," he'd say gently, "you'll understand why that cannot be."

And he was right, of course.

I still don't think they help, she argued with her dead father in her head. But she had yet to think of a viable alternative. And so the collars remained.

"Yes, thank you, General," said Lord Flighty, dismissing the man. The general left, pausing to salute Cassandra at the door. At least the military respected her. Those *she* owned, anyway.

"It seems that the unrest has significantly increased over the last three years," said Viscount Cuddy.

It was all Cassandra could do not to roll her eyes. The man must be given a commission from Flighty every time he pointed out that the unrest had increased after Cassandra became empress. There was no other reason she could think of for him to raise it at every meeting.

The worst was she couldn't argue the point. It *had* increased since she took the throne. And she knew why.

She had made promises to the tribes. Stupid, naïve promises that she would restore their sovereignty when she took over. But she hadn't known then. Her father hadn't told her.

"... only thing to do is increase the number of soldiers. And I can assure you all that the Thackray's agree with me on that point." Baron Shamble nodded eagerly at the table, his jowls jiggling.

"Perhaps it would be better to hear their views directly? I would prefer the Viscountess Thackray attend this meeting and speak for herself." Cassandra's voice held no passion. She had raised and lost this argument too many times.

The men chuckled.

"Empress." Lord Flighty smiled at her as if she were a precocious child. "I'm sure the viscountess has better things to do with her time than attend boring meetings such as this one."

Like needlepoint or planning garden parties. Like a good woman should.

"You may find this meeting dull, my lord, but the matters discussed here are important, and a large house such as the Thackrays should have a voice at the table."

"And they do, Empress," insisted Baron Shamble. "I make sure to speak with the viscountess before every meeting."

I'm sure you do.

Cassandra gave the baron a look that told him she knew exactly what was going on and had no time for his lies. Baron Shamble flushed a mottled red and stared at the table.

"It would be good to have a full crew again," said Lord

Flighty. "Has anyone heard from Lord Sandison? I miss his wise counsel, as I'm sure do we all."

Cassandra froze, willing her body to stillness. Lord Flighty looked at her, daring her to respond. She had allowed Lord Sandison to provide his opinions on relevant matters remotely for the last three years. If she were to push for the viscountess to be allowed to attend the meeting, Lord Flighty would insist on Lord Sandison being present in person too. And Cassandra had her own reasons for seeking to avoid that.

A thin smile spread across Lord Flighty's face as he sensed victory, and he turned the discussion back to the 'war effort'. Cassandra only half listened. It wasn't a war. Not yet. And to call the enforcement of their border with the Controllers a war displayed a pitiful lack of understanding of the gravity of the threat on the nobles' part.

When the Controllers came for them, the entire Empire would know what war really was. And it couldn't be far away now, though according to her father's calculations, they should have invaded years ago. It was the delay that was causing such dangerous apathy.

The expected invasion was why everything was bad in the Empire. The annexation had been intended to bring all the tribes in the southern parts of Valoris together to fight an enemy that threatened them all. The collars were intended to prevent a civil war that would hand the Controllers the entire continent on a platter. And yet, they did not come. Had her father been wrong?

Talk turned to the cost of the border enforcement, and predictably Baron Shamble suggested again that he might reduce his house's troop contributions.

Cassandra had had enough. She slammed her hands on the oak table as she rose, causing all the men to jump.

"Contributions remain as they are." She stared at each man in turn, her eyes letting them know she was not joking.

"But Empress—"

"Any alteration of troop numbers at the border must be approved by me personally. Any house who unilaterally reduces their contributions will face consequences." She stared around again, keeping her expression stern but desperately willing that no one ask what those consequences would be. "This meeting is over."

No one stood as she stormed out, though her guards' armour clanged as they came to attention. Immediately, the anxiety hit her. The nobles would all remain behind and talk about her, and gods knew what else. She should have stayed. If not to hear the discussions, to prevent whatever ones would be taking place now.

What if she really upset them? What if they withdrew their funds? Their troops? She cursed her ancestors, who had allowed the nobles to grow this powerful. Without their money and soldiers, the Empire was nothing. It would fall in a day. And never mind the minor tribes; Lorendell itself would dissolve once again into different factions aligned per allegiance to the noble houses, type of elemental magic, or both.

She shook her head, willing away the rising panic. If the nobles withdrew their support, she wouldn't have to worry about the fallout of the Empire fracturing. The Controllers would kill them all before any civil war truly took hold.

Cassandra took a deep breath, calming herself. Let them come. She'd rather die with dignity than grovel to those men.

CHAPTER EIGHT

KAS

THE SUN BURNED down on Kas's broad shoulders. Of all the camps he'd spent time in over these past eight years, he hated the southern quarry the most. The guards were crueller, the food was worse than at the other camps and in short supply, and even though it was cooler down in the south, there was no way to avoid the sun.

The skin on his shoulders burned even as the old burns peeled, and his chapped lips cracked. Kas was sure his lips would bleed if the water rations weren't so limited. But the guards treated water like a luxury they were keeping from naughty children, rather than a necessity.

Sweat dripped into Kas's eyes and he didn't bother to wipe at the stinging, instead blinking it away as he continued to swing his pick into the stone wall in front of him. He'd only been at the camp a month, but already Kas was itching to leave.

The guards rotated the prisoners between the camps. They said it was to avoid the prisoners forming ties and banding together. But there was no apparent logic behind who was selected to move and when. Almost as if some higher up had had the idea of rotating them, but the subordinates who were carrying it out didn't understand the purpose. Or didn't care.

Either way, Kas hoped that his stay in the south would be brief this time. He'd been stuck for over a year once and that had almost been the end of him. Kas scratched at an insect bite on his neck but found his fingers swiping the cool metal of his collar instead. The collar somehow always felt cool, even out here in the blistering heat. It was a thin band of smooth metal, as wide as his thumb was, and so light that sometimes Kas even forgot it was there. Probably designed to not get in the way of the prisoners working. After all, its point was to block their magic. Heavens forbid it get in the way of production.

He swung his pick again, trying to focus his mind on the monotonous labour. But he couldn't help it from drifting to Sali. Lorendell wasn't far from the southern quarry. Maybe a day by cart, two at the most. Thinking of his little brother so close, but being unable to see him, talk to him, was torture.

Kas had spent the first few years going over his capture in his mind. Surely there was something he'd done wrong. Something he could have done instead to evade capture. Maybe he should have turned invisible. Maybe he should have climbed up onto the roofs. Maybe he should have turned left instead of right.

It ate at him constantly until Ossi had told him to let it go. It had happened. He was here. Fighting against it wouldn't change anything. It'd only drive him mad. Ossi had been right, of course, but it had taken Kas a while after that to eventually make peace with his capture.

Kas had seen the Trolls who occasionally visited the Lorendell markets when he was younger. He'd even spoken to one once, but he'd never really gotten to know a Troll until he came to the camps. Or a Shifter, for that matter.

But here, they were everywhere. Ossi was a smaller Troll than most, but he still towered over Kas, and Kas had grown strong and tall. And even with the collar preventing him from accessing his magical strength, Kas was sure Ossi could take out half the guards on his own. Well, maybe, if the guards didn't also have access to their own magic. Hard to punch someone when they were burning you to death, or drowning you, or stealing your breath.

Kas was one of the strongest fire magicals around. If he didn't have this collar, *he* could probably take out half the guards himself. His pick slammed into the wall with more force than the last swing. He missed his magic. He missed how it made him feel. But he would happily give it away to be back with Sali.

Quiet voices murmured to his right. Ossi and Tia arguing again. Their main topic of conversation was what they would do if they weren't here. And still, the Troll and the Shifter found something to argue about. Tia, like all Shifters, was passionate and spoke her mind, letting everyone know her opinion on everything. Like a typical Troll, Ossi rarely had an opinion about anything that he didn't feel was his place to judge. It had almost become a mission for Tia to get him to take a side on something.

Honestly, if they weren't from entirely different tribes, Kas would have thought they were brother and sister. He'd never met two people who could argue so passionately with each other, and then simply move on to something else, the apparent conflict forgotten.

"Keep it down," Kas hissed as the guard paced back towards them. Kas glanced up to make sure they'd heard him.

"Eyes on your work," the guard's voice boomed as a rough hand grabbed the back of Kas's neck, pushing him roughly towards the wall. His hands were holding his pick and so his head cracked against the stone. Thankfully, he'd been glancing at his friends, or his nose would have broken. Again.

Kas swiped futilely at the trickle of blood and slammed his pick into the wall. If you stopped work for any reason, even injury, the punishment was harsh, and Kas knew the guard would be watching, hoping for an excuse to hurt him more.

It was a while before the guard's footsteps faded. Shortly after they did, Kas felt gentle hands on his shoulders, turning him.

"Thanks for the warning," said Tia, apology in her voice. She pulled a tin from somewhere in the rags she wore and quickly dabbed some salve on Kas's cut.

"Of course," Kas replied, his mood immediately lifting. Tia was beautiful. Tall and lithe, with skin darker than Kas's, she was exotic to him. A mysterious beauty from a tribe so completely different from his own. The Shifters lived in Ravenswood Forest, a far cry from Kas's home, Lorendell, which was often called the City of Stone due to its huge stone walls and multitude of stone buildings.

Something in the effortless grace of her movements put Kas in mind of the elves in the stories his father used to read to him. There were no pointy ears, or anything like that, but the Shifters were all strong and slim, and seemed to have the haughty confidence that made you think they knew more than you did.

Empire folk were much broader than the Shifters. If the Shifters were made in the image of elves, the people of the Empire were cast from dwarves. They weren't short, though Kas felt it standing next to Ossi, but they were stocky. Even the Trolls, huge as they were, looked like warriors who had been stretched, but proportionately so.

"He is returning." Ossi's voice was a deep baritone, even when he whispered.

"Thanks," Kas whispered to his friends as they returned to their positions and began working as if there'd been no pause.

They fell into the silence of their work, the guards pacing more frequently than before, preventing any communication at all. Kas's mind drifted back to Sali. What had happened to him these last eight years?

He was sure that Adeline and Frank would have taken care of him. Still, he couldn't help but ask every new prisoner if they had any word of his little brother. None did, but that didn't mean anything. Sali was fine.

He would be nineteen by now, fully grown. He'd have a job and maybe even a place of his own. Kas wondered what his job would be. He tried to picture Sali in a forge, slamming a hammer and making weapons. But the image just wouldn't come. Kas slammed his pick into the rock over and over. No, his little brother was smart. He'd have a job as a shop assistant, work his way up, and take over the shop someday. Or maybe a scribe. Wouldn't that be something? He could scribe for one of the nobles, attending meetings in the palace or trade deals in the market.

Kas's pick bounced off the wall of the quarry, distraction sapping his strength. What might he have become, had he not been caught that day? Would he have continued with the only thing he'd known and spent the rest of his days thieving to survive? Or once Sali was old enough to work too, would Kas have tried to find himself a trade? His mind began to drift, but Kas blinked, refocusing on the task at hand.

Kas didn't like to let himself dream like the other prisoners. Some of them had big dreams. If they ever got out of the camps, they would travel the world, or have the most successful chain of forges, or marry the empress and live as a king for the rest of their days.

When he was younger, Kas used to dream of travelling the world. Of the different things he might have been, or adventures he would have had. Now, all he wanted was to be back with his little brother. They would have a house together and Kas would get a job and they'd meet in the tavern at night and discuss their days over an ale.

He knew they wouldn't live together forever. Hopefully, they'd find wives and start families. But they'd live close by—maybe even next door—and their kids would be more like siblings than cousins.

"He is fine." Ossi's voice startled Kas out of his reverie, and he realised the guard's footsteps were no longer pacing behind them.

"Who's fine?" asked Tia before Kas could reply.

"His brother," said Ossi simply, still working, lest a guard be looking from afar. "When Kas gets that look on his face, he's wondering about him."

Tia frowned at Kas, examining his face. "What look?"

"The faraway dreamer's eyes."

Tia scrutinised Kas again, causing him to blush. Any attention from Tia had the butterflies in Kas's stomach going into hyper gear.

"His eyes are normal. Pretty and green. Like the trees." Tia smiled at Kas and he beamed back, but he saw the sadness creep into Tia's own blue eyes. She'd been taken from her home at just five years old. The only trees she saw these days were the ones they were forced to cut down in the lumber camps.

"I think they are the colour of the weeds that coat the bottom of the Suncrest River on a sunny day," mused Ossi.

And they were off, both Tia and Ossi verbally sparring in voices even Kas could barely make out, though he was right beside them. Kas smiled to himself. Ossi had a way of pulling people from their melancholy without them even realising it.

"Hey, Ironstone," a harsh whisper came from his left, away from his friends. Kas inwardly groaned as he glanced and saw who it was.

"Hey Crispin," Kas hissed back, keeping his eyes on his work, his body angled to the wall.

"You sure you're out? There's still time."

Kas felt his entire body tense. When he'd first arrived in the camps, he'd been scared, but also full of the bluster of youth. He'd had hope. Kas had been sure there was a way out. This could not be the rest of his life. And so, when he was approached by some of the rebels in the camp to join their escape, Kas'd jumped at the chance.

They'd given him the role of lookout. He was to watch for guards while the team ran to the fence and cut a hole in the wire. On reflection, Kas knew he'd been used. He had been young and naïve, and the rebels had no intention of taking him with them. There'd never been enough time for Kas to remain at the wall as a lookout, then run to the hole they'd created and escape with them.

His warning hadn't helped. When the guards saw them, the men had been so close they could almost taste freedom, and began jostling to squeeze out of the hole they hadn't had time to make large enough. All of them had died at the fence.

Kas was grateful in retrospect not to have been a part of their team and died with them. But he'd been whipped so hard he almost followed. Some of the Shifters had nursed him back to health, and Ossi had helped him work during the day, covering for his injuries.

But Kas had been young, and the only lesson he'd learned was that next time, he wouldn't miss out on the escape. Ossi had urged him to give up his dream of freedom, but he hadn't listened. He'd really thought the next plan would work. Kas had just been moved to one of the lumber camps and had sought out the rebels being held there. He pitched his idea. Make a diversion by loosing some logs down the hill and slip out of the gate during the chaos.

The rebels had liked his idea. Just not him, as it turned out. Kas had been on the other side of the camp when they enacted his plan. And it had worked, too. Well, to some extent. Three of them got out. But at the eastern lumber camp, there just wasn't anything around, the area having been cleared out over the years. With nowhere to hide, the men hadn't lasted long.

Kas spent the next few years observing and noticed that the only ones trying, and failing, to escape were Empire folk. He'd asked Ossi about this, and his friend had merely shrugged, suggesting those of the Empire found it harder to accept their reality if it wasn't to their satisfaction.

The hope of escape had never left Kas, but it had become abundantly clear that it was an impossible dream. Everyone who'd tried in his eight years had died. He'd also never let go of his resentment for the rebels.

"I'm out, Crispin. And you'd be better off leaving it alone, too."

There was an angry pause, but Kas knew Crispin had only asked because their fourth had broken his leg. Kas was just a number, and he was done being used. Still, it stung when Crispin hissed at him, "I'd heard the stories, but I hadn't realised how much of a coward you truly are."

Kas saw red.

He didn't remember dropping his pick, but when Ossi grabbed his shoulders, stopping him from moving towards Crispin, Kas's hands were empty. Ossi thrust the pick at him.

"Good luck to you Crispin," Ossi said, his voice firm. "I will take care of your young friends when you are gone."

Both Kas and Crispin's eyes snapped to Ossi. It sounded like the Troll was wishing him well. But 'gone' could relate to either outcome of the escape attempt.

Crispin's attention, however, had been snagged by another implication. "I'm coming back for them." Defensiveness dripped from his words.

"And I will care for them until you do."

They all heard the footsteps at the same time and, without another word, each man slipped back to his position on the wall.

"That was the right decision," Ossi hissed at him.

"Keep it down," a guard snarled at Ossi.

"And you are not a coward, Kasperi Ironstone."

"What did I just say?" The guard strode up to Ossi, moving so he was an inch away from the Troll. It was meant to be intimidating, but the guard's face was in the middle of Ossi's chest, and the sight of Ossi looking down at the guard with a pleasant smile almost made Kas laugh.

"You asked me to keep it down," said Ossi in the reasonable tone he reserved for the guards. It reinforced their assumption that Trolls were slow minded. "So I whispered."

The guard pulled his arm back, preparing to strike, but was distracted by Kas, who hadn't been able to stop the snort of laughter that time.

"Something funny?" the guard asked Kas, stalking towards him. The guards would always take the chance to beat on someone who wasn't a Troll.

"Sound the alarm!"

At the cry, the guard's attention snapped away from Kas and all the prisoners froze, instinctively hunching in on themselves, trying to become smaller targets. As the guard rushed off, Kas chanced a look.

He saw two men sprinting for the fence. A third was behind them, picking himself up after falling over on the uneven terrain. He barely took a step before he screamed and appeared to shrink before their eyes. Kas glanced back towards the wall and saw the guard who'd nabbed him. A water mage, and his concentration was intense as he dehydrated the prisoner.

Fireballs flew at the other men; one now trying to scale the fence as the other, Crispin, turned and sprinted its length. Kas wondered where Crispin was running to. There was only one way in and out of the camp, and it was permanently guarded. Perhaps he hoped his friend would keep the guards' attention long enough for him to find another place to scale the fence.

But a gale-force wind blew Crispin's legs from under him, and he fell to the ground with a thud and didn't rise. Kas heard the screams from the man on the fence as a fireball hit true.

Kas turned his eyes from the carnage and joined back in with the monotonous clinking of metal hitting stone.

CHAPTER NINE

KAS

Kas sat with his back to the wall, the cool ground pleasant now, even if he knew it would be biting in the freezing night. Everyone was on edge after the failed escape. Some had lost friends, and Crispin's nephews mourned their uncle. But the main source of the tension was the anticipation of the guards' response. They were always hyped up after an escape attempt.

The guards were under strict orders not to kill the prisoners unless absolutely necessary. After all, fewer labourers meant less production. The nobles owned the mines and the logging camps and the farms of the plains. This was all business to them, and nothing upset a noble more than losing money. Three dead meant the guards would be eager to ensure a drop in production was not felt, and that meant harsher working conditions and more punishments. They weren't supposed to kill the prisoners, but they could maim them all they liked. So long as the prisoners could still hold a pick.

As Kas sat in the rough, man-made cave that was used as a dining hall for the prisoners, he saw the resentful looks. Heard the harsh whispers. The people were angry. Nothing made them feel more impotent than a failed escape. It reminded them of how powerless they all were with these collars on. Without them, the prisoners would have risen up years ago.

Kas absentmindedly fiddled with his collar. He remembered when it was lashed around his neck. He'd been dumped into a cell under one of the guard towers for a few days, and then suddenly the guards had come and shoved him into a line with a dozen other prisoners.

They'd filed through into a large room and Kas had been watching the front, his eyes darting frantically, wondering what was happening and expecting someone important to appear. Suddenly the thin metal band was slipped around his neck, and a warmth pulsed at the back.

And that was it. He had felt the absence of his magic like a physical blow. Kas didn't even remember how he got back to his cell, but he did remember spending the night scratching at the collar, trying desperately to get it off. But he felt no latch, no join. It was as if the metal band had been slipped over his head and shrunk.

It was later they told them that the collars could not be removed. That regardless of the futility of trying, there was a harsh punishment for tampering with them. Even now, if a prisoner's hand strayed to their collar, the guards watched eagerly, hopeful for a chance to punish.

A shadow passed over Kas and a thud sounded beside him as Ossi lowered himself heavily to the ground. Wordlessly, Kas passed Ossi his mouldy bread roll. He'd picked as much of the mould off as he could, and the stale bread looked like a dried up ocean sponge.

"What's this for?" asked Ossi, one eyebrow raised.

"I know you gave your ration to the kids. Again."

The corner of Ossi's mouth twitched. "It was a mix-up with the kitchens," he said drily.

"Uh huh," said Kas, pressing the roll into his friend's hand.

"I promised to look after them," Ossi said quietly before crunching on the roll.

"You were slipping your food to Crispin's nephews long before you made that promise."

Ossi finished the roll quietly. "This is not a place for children."

On that, they agreed.

"You're a good man, Ossi Planchard," said Kas, "but if you keep giving your food away, you'll die."

"I will be okay," said Ossi, grinning. "Because you are a good man too, Kasperi Ironstone."

Kas bumped Ossi with his shoulder, trying not to smile. "Maybe we can work something out as a group. If we all gave a little of our food so the kids could have extra, you wouldn't need to starve yourself."

"He's too huge to starve," came Tia's voice from above them. "Think quick."

Ossi snatched the package Tia tossed to him, opening it as she sat, squeezing between them, to reveal some kitchen scraps.

Kas tried not to be overly aware of her arm pressed against his own as he felt warmth spread in his chest. Clearly, he was not the only one aware of Ossi's sacrifice. That Tia had noticed only made him like her more.

"But you're not." Tia looked at Kas, making him blush. She pressed a small lump into his hand, and he looked down to see a small bread roll, only slightly mouldier than the one he'd given Ossi.

"You boys need to eat up. Otherwise, you won't grow up big and strong."

There was sporadic chatter as Ossi and Kas focussed on

wolfing down their food, and the tension Kas had felt began to fade.

"Blessed Harvest, Tia Siren." A group of Shifters paused as they passed, bracing one arm across their chests and bowing at Tia.

"Goddess's Blessings to you too," Tia said, returning the bow.

"Is it the Harvest already?" asked Ossi.

"Harvest Moon is next Thursday," Tia said, "but our festival lasts the full week."

"Tell me about it," prompted Kas. He loved hearing all about the other tribes. "You have different celebrations for the different villages, right?"

"Sort of," said Tia. "The smaller villages are really just different collections of magicals. Those who can shift into water creatures often prefer to live by the river, whereas the winged ones like the treetops. But most of us live in the capital. For the Harvest, all the smaller tribes come to the capital and everyone cooks their favourite meal and shares it. And we eat and dance and then collapse and sleep until midday." Sadness tinged Tia's voice as it always did when she spoke of home. Kas knew she was vigilant, recalling the few memories she had, desperate to hold on to them. Tia had been taken from her tribe when she was just a child, collared, and sent to the labour camps. Kas hadn't met anyone else who had been in the camps as long as her.

"And then what would you do?" asked Ossi.

"Those who could, would shift and join their animal tribes." Tia paused her work, smiling at the memory. "It's quite a thing, watching so many people shift all at once."

Kas cast a glance at her, smiling himself at the look of joy on her face, but it faded before he looked away. They fell into silence again, and Kas struggled to think of something to say to cheer Tia up.

But there really wasn't anything to say. He missed his magic like a lost limb. He couldn't imagine what it must be like for her to not even know if she had magic. And if she was a magical, what kind of animal she could shift into.

"The only other time we have such a big shifting is when a child turns eleven. There's a huge celebration when they find out whether or not they have magic. If they're a full magical, they shift for the first time, and those who can become the same type of animal shift with them. Well..." Her face fell again. "That was what used to happen, anyway."

Kas's face fell too. The imposition of the Empire's Testing had put a stop to the Shifter's rituals.

The Testing was a day of joy in Lorendell, and since Kas had arrived at the camps and learned more about the rest of the Empire, he'd realised that the city of Lorendell was really all the Empire was. The other tribes did not think of themselves as part of the Empire at all. But the Testing was done at ten. It gave families a year to prepare and decide what path their children would take when their magic—if they had any—came through.

Kas remembered his Testing. He had been so nervous, but his parents kept saying there was no bad outcome, it was just that afterwards he would know more about what his life would bring. He had been ushered into the room. It was dark and ominous, a light falling on the mysterious orb in the centre.

The Druids had created the artefact, imbuing it with the ability to read a person's magical potential. Putting a hand on the orb would reveal if you were a magical, a spell caster, or an object wielder. It could also tell how powerful you were. The Empire adopted the artefact's classification system and applied it to everything. There were certain jobs or opportunities that were only open to people who were a certain tier. His father had only been allowed to own his apothecary because he was a tier three spell caster, the most powerful tier available.

Kas had cautiously approached the orb, jumping when a voice came from the shadows.

"Place one hand on the artefact, boy, and hold it there until I tell you to remove it." The voice was old, but not unkind. It sounded almost bored, as if it gave that instruction regularly, which Kas realised it probably did.

He squinted into the shadows, trying to see who was there.

"Come on boy, it won't bite you." The voice sounded amused now.

Blushing, Kas reached for the orb, reminding himself of his parents' words. There was no bad outcome.

Immediately the orb glowed a bright blue, and he heard a creaking to his right, like someone standing.

"A magical. Well done, boy!"

As if it were something Kas could control, or study for.

"And a tier three! You can expect a letter from the Academy, I'd say."

It wasn't until later that Kas had unexpectedly uncovered the limitations of the artefact. He was indeed a very powerful magical, but it hadn't glowed the green for spells or yellow for objects, and Kas could do all three forms of magic. He had wondered if the orb's identification of the tiers was limited too, and suspected it was when he found he could bend light.

Of course, now that he was collared, he couldn't do any of that. He was as good as a non-magical. Worse, since the collar identified him as a criminal.

"In my village, we celebrate the Harvest with a big fight," said Ossi, breaking the sombre mood.

"In your village, you celebrate everything with a big fight," said Tia.

"This is true. There is no better celebration than a big fight."

"I don't understand that," said Kas, smiling at his friend's bizarre enthusiasm for violence. "Aren't you Trolls just in pain all the time?"

"There is some pain," Ossi allowed. "But there is an art to fighting. To defeating your opponent with as little pain as possible."

"You're telling me you try to punch people in the head in a way that doesn't hurt them?" asked Tia, incredulous.

"There should be some pain in defeat. This is how you learn. But there is no victory in trying to cause as much pain as possible. An opponent should be defeated efficiently."

"When we break out of here, I'm going to cause these soldiers as much pain as I possibly can," said Tia, a blood-thirsty look falling over her features.

"Hurting them is a waste of time. They are ordered to be here. They have not chosen to personally detain us all and make us work. You spend too much time causing them pain, you'll waste the life you may have outside of here."

"Fine," said Tia, crossing her arms. "I'll save the hurting for the empress. She's the one behind it all."

"She inherited all the issues of our land," said Ossi reasonably.

"She said she would lift the annexation and close the camps. And then she turned out to be just like the rest of them."

"There must be a reason she changed her mind," mused Kas.

Tia looked at him, her jaw dropping. "Not you too."

"I just mean..." Kas searched for the words that didn't involve revealing his trip to the emperor's bedroom. "I saw the emperor once. He seemed to really care about the people."

Tia snorted. "Maybe *your* people."

"I think it's more complicated than that," Kas pressed. "I don't think the empress has as much power as we think she does."

Tia opened and closed her mouth, as if thinking better of what she'd been about to say. Eventually she said, "Fine. But when we get out of here, *someone* is going to pay."

"I can get behind a celebratory fight." Ossi smiled.

CHAPTER TEN

KAS

"Siren! Blanchard! Ironstone!"

Kas and his friends turned in surprise as they heard their names. A soldier was standing on the porch of the guardhouse reading names from a scroll.

"Return your picks and form up here in five minutes."

With a quick glance at each other, Kas, Tia, and Ossi broke into a jog towards the shed up near the top of the quarry. The prisoners rarely got exercise other than the monotonous labour and took every opportunity they could for something different. Kas was quickly puffing, reminding him of how little running he'd done in the last few years.

"What do you think? Time off for good behaviour?" Ossi joked.

"You know we're being moved, dumbass," Tia said good-humouredly. "Do you think we'll stay together?"

Tia kept the same joking tone, but she couldn't hide the hopefulness in her voice. Kas could understand. He and Ossi had started at the same camp when they were first sentenced and had somehow been located together in several camps since. Still, every time they were moved, anxiousness settled in his gut, worried they would be separated.

"It's possible they don't think we need separating, being from different tribes and all," Kas said. "But more likely, they'll drop us at different camps along the way."

They returned their picks and hurried back down the quarry, seeing people already lining up by the guardhouse.

"Don't worry, Tia, if we're separated now, we'll be reunited again soon." Ossi grinned down at her.

Kas inwardly cringed. Ossi meant to be reassuring, but somehow the reminder that they were doomed to spend their days travelling from one hard labour camp to the next just didn't pep him up.

The three arrived at the guardhouse just in time and were ushered into the second caged cart. Three other prisoners were locked in with them, but thankfully none were Trolls like Ossi, who dominated the small space. Tia sat next to Ossi, since she was smaller than Kas, and Kas sat down across from Tia.

Two men were sitting on Kas's bench. He recognised them as rebels, but hadn't spoken to them before. They cast assessing eyes over their cagemates, each giving Kas a serious, manly nod when they saw him watching.

Squeezed into the far corner next to Ossi was a small woman. She looked younger and more petite than Tia, and by the size of her arms, she hadn't been at the camps long. Kas saw Ossi shift a little closer to Tia as he glanced at the woman, obviously worried he was squashing her.

"Oh, you're fine," she said to Ossi, briefly touching his arm to let him know he didn't have to move.

"Let me know if I crowd you." Ossi smiled at her. "It's a little cramped with how much room Tia here takes up."

Tia swatted Ossi, rolling her eyes, and the woman laughed, some of her nerves evaporating.

The soldiers yelled, reins cracking, and the carts creaked into motion, bumping over the uneven path out of the quarry. Kas looked out through the rear bars, wondering how long it would be until he saw this quarry again.

Normally prisoners used the transport time as a chance for extra sleep. It was rare that they got a few hours where they could do nothing but sit. And if you went from the southern camps to the northern ones, you might catch up on a full day's rest.

Kas positioned himself in the cage's corner, shifting this way and that, trying to find a relatively comfortable position where he was unlikely to fall off the bench when the prison wagon hit rocks or potholes.

He cast one more look around before closing his eyes. Ossi was already asleep. The man could fall asleep before you clicked your fingers, no matter the conditions. Tia was leaned against him, already nodding off too. He smiled at them and then his eyes met the small woman's. She was watching him watch his friends and smiling at the expression on Kas's face. When she met his eyes, her smile turned nervous, and she quickly looked away, staring out the front of the cage.

Kas glanced at the Empire men again. They were wide awake, which immediately put Kas on edge. Their heads were together, conversation whispered. Furtive glances were aimed at the guards up front, driving the cart, and Kas prayed they weren't planning something.

If any prisoner attempted to escape, the entire cage was punished on the basis that they had all been in on the plan, or failed to turn their fellow prisoners in. And Kas was likely to be thrown in with the men since he was also Empire-born, which meant suffering whatever fate they did.

Maybe they were just nervous. Kas forced his eyes

closed. Even if he couldn't sleep, he needed to rest. The bumping and jiggling of the cart soon lulled Kas into a relaxed state, but his mind remained with the men. He told himself they were just giving each other information. As they were unlikely to be sent to the same camp, they could be passing messages to old friends that the other might see. Besides, even if they were planning something, what could they achieve from inside a cage?

The explosion came out of nowhere. No shouts or warnings preceded it, and before Kas realised the convoy was under attack, he felt the cage slowly tilt before it crashed to the ground and began to roll downhill.

"Brace!" bellowed Ossi, grabbing the women to him and trying to shield them with his body. Kas reached out his arms, hoping to grab onto something to stop himself from tumbling with the cage.

"No!" Ossi called to him before he was cut off by a scream from one of the other Empire men. Kas balled himself up, trying to protect his head. Finally, the cage came to a jarring stop before rocking back onto what used to be its top.

Kas unfurled himself cautiously, checking for injuries. He could feel blood on his skin, and his body was going to be sore soon from being tossed around. Flexing his hands, he saw the skin on his knuckles was scraped and torn as if he'd been in a fight, but everything worked. Most concerning was an ache in his ankle. Hopefully it was just bruised, but when the adrenaline wore off, it might be an issue.

Looking at his friends, he could see Ossi had some gashes that would need attention, but he was moving fine, and Tia was bleeding from a bump to the head and holding her arm as if it pained her. The other woman, having been protected by Ossi, seemed to have made it out without much damage at all.

One of the Empire men was groaning and swearing, pulling at his arm that had become wedged under the bars of the cage.

The man was pale, and Kas felt his own blood leave his face as he saw the man's pinned hand with mangled and missing fingers. The man was, however, doing better than his friend, who lay unmoving, his body twisted in a way that told Kas he was dead.

"That is why you shouldn't grab the cage," Ossi said softly to Kas, checking him over quickly to make sure he was okay.

"I wasn't thinking," said Kas, shock still making him numb. "Thank you. If you hadn't called out..."

Ossi waved his gratitude away, already moving over to the pinned man, looking for a way to free him.

"Help me," the man begged Ossi. Ossi ignored him, focussed on his arm and how the cage lay. Apparently satisfied with his assessment, Ossi grunted and turned to move to the cage's crumpled door. "Wait!" Panic entered the trapped man's voice as he grabbed at Ossi.

"There is no way to help you from in here," Ossi said gently. "I must open the door."

The man let him go, nodding. Kas looked at Ossi's face. Trolls wouldn't lie, but they also wouldn't necessarily tell you everything, unless you asked specifically. And then they would, without hesitation. But most people weren't used to having to ask for details. They were used to people offering everything relevant. Kas, able to read Ossi easily by now, noted the man who was stuck had not asked if there would be a way to help him from outside of the cage.

Kas and Tia had been trying to open the door while Ossi assessed the trapped man. Both had tried pushing, individually and together, as well as kicking it and shaking it and swearing at it. But somehow, it had survived the journey down the hill with the lock intact.

"No good," Kas told Ossi as the Troll peered out of the bars, trying to see the lock. "We've tried—"

Metal clanged and screeched as Ossi burst the door open with a well-placed kick. He grunted, pleased with his effort, and jumped out of the cage, turning to help the others down.

"Lucky we loosened things," Tia commented as she accepted Ossi's hand and hopped gracefully onto the ground, immediately looking back up the hill, still cradling her arm.

Kas jumped out too, forgoing Ossi's hand and landing awkwardly on his injured ankle. Swearing, he fell onto his rump. The small woman also took Ossi's hand and exited the cage with significantly more grace than Kas.

Ossi helped Kas to his feet, and they joined Tia, scanning the road above them. The other cart was on its side on the road, and though there was still smoke, nothing appeared to be burning, and the black clouds from the explosion were dissipating.

Fire and lightning and sparks flared in the distance. His heart leapt at seeing magic again. The only magic seen in the camps was when someone tried to escape, but that usually only produced a fireball or two, and then it was all over. The fighting up the hill was intense, neither side holding back. The hair on Kas's arms rose with the crackling power in the air.

He watched a water mage raise what must have been a small lake or river nearby, and fling the torrent at her enemies. Kas's fingers twitched, longing to feel that power again.

"Hey!" called the man from inside the cage. "You've got to help me."

Ossi moved around to where the man's arm was pinned and then back to the now open entrance.

"There are only two ways to free you, and both will result in your death."

"Goddess above, Ossi," said Tia, looking at Ossi in shock. "Break it to the man gently, why don't you?"

Ossi glanced around at her. "What is a better way to convey that information?"

Tia hesitated, then frowned, thinking.

"You can't leave me here," called the man, returning everyone's attention to him. "You've got to help me."

"I can lift the cage," said Ossi gently, "but I have seen injuries like this before. You will not survive long after the limb is freed. We can find something sharp and remove the trapped portion. But with what little is available to us here, I don't think you'll last long following that procedure either."

"They're down here!" a voice called, and everyone who was out of the cage braced, scanning for its origin.

"We should have run," Tia cursed quietly, dropping into a crouch as if ready to pounce on whoever came down the hill.

All of them tensed up, preparing to fight if required. Kas looked to see who was coming and spotted three large men hurrying down the hill. He frowned. They might be soldiers, but he didn't recognise their clothing. Maybe they were reinforcements from a different unit attracted by the battle.

Kas also felt they should have run as they exited the cage, but he also felt a guilty wash of relief that they'd stayed. If they now could not escape, appearing as if the thought hadn't crossed their minds would serve them well. Maybe the soldiers wouldn't kill them immediately.

But as the men got closer, it became obvious that they were not soldiers. Kas saw they were not wearing the uniform of the Empire, nor any colours of the noble houses. And they had beards. Soldiers were not allowed beards unless stationed in particularly cold climates.

But then, who were they?

The men positioned themselves so that the cage was between them and the strange group of ragged prisoners staring suspiciously at them. They shot particularly wary looks at Ossi, and Kas couldn't blame them. He knew Ossi, and even he would be scared if the Troll looked at him as he was the three strangers.

The men were armed with crossbows and swords. One carried an axe. But they all held their weapons at their sides, raising their free hands to show they were not a threat. Two of the men kept eye contact with the prisoners as one peered into the cage.

"Bluey's dead. Looks like Randy's trapped," he reported.

Almost immediately, Randy started up. "Help me," he bellowed before taking on a more pleading tone. "Please, please, please." He began to sob.

The man in the middle, apparently the leader, raised an eyebrow at the man who'd reported. That man shook his head, and the leader sighed before nodding his head at the cage.

"Yes! Please, thank you," Randy blubbered as one of the men approached the cage door. "No!" His face turned to horror as the man raised his crossbow and fired one bolt, catching him between the eyes. Randy slumped down, silent.

Kas jumped at the noise. At the swift and efficient ending of Randy's life. He stared at the crossbow, still in the man's hand, and trembled as the man squared up to the group, looking to his boss with one eyebrow raised, asking a silent question.

Kas's eyes jumped to Randy's ruined head before locking on the boss, waiting to learn his fate. Freedom had been so close.

CHAPTER ELEVEN

EMILIA

Emilia Skrok walked slowly through the enemy's campsite. Scouts. All men. And *what* were they cooking on that fire? Whatever it was, it smelled horrible, and Emilia's nose scrunched up as if even her nostrils were trying to avoid the foul odour as she repositioned herself upwind.

She listened to the blokey banter as she scanned her surroundings, picking out all three of her compatriots in the surrounding brush. The area was sparse and so hiding places, especially close enough to gather intel, were few. However, that didn't mean you tried to hide your body behind a tiny patch of grassy reeds, as Reiko was doing now.

But then, Reiko had never worried about the ire of his superiors. His father was an archpriest, and so Reiko got away with murder. Literally.

Emilia scowled at Reiko, whose eyes were locked on the largest of the enemy soldiers. It wasn't beyond the realm of possibility that his terrible attempt at stealth was deliberate. Reiko had been known to allow himself to be found just so he could kill the enemy. Why he was a spy rather than infantry, Emilia could not comprehend.

She moved away from Reiko, her colleague none the

wiser, as ignorant of her presence as the soldiers she now turned her attention to. She could kill them all right now, if she wanted. If she were a psychopath like Reiko. And none of them would know what hit them.

But Emilia was not a psychopath. She was one of the top spies in the Divvinium. *The* top spy, but for the fact that women could not be the top of anything. Emilia was skilled at infiltrating an area and leaving without anyone even knowing she'd been there. She could blend into the shadows better than any of her peers, and she was the only known Imperius so stealthy she could even slip past the Empire's wards without setting them off.

It was that talent that really pissed off her male counterparts. Her success on missions was readily handed over to her commanders (always male) and even the praise for her solo infiltration of the blasphemous cult who'd sought to overthrow the Divine Prophet had been laid at Gavin's feet. Gavin hadn't gotten within twenty feet of the door to their headquarters before their sentries had become suspicious.

And so it drove them crazy that she wouldn't tell them how she did it. And she never would. Because then she wouldn't get high-profile assignments. And also because it would get her killed.

Emilia had never told anyone about her special gifts. In the Divvinium, any magic that was not the ability to control another's mind was blasphemous. And she remembered what happened to her mother.

"I hear you're leaving us, Lukey," one of the soldiers said as Emilia returned her attention to her task.

"What? Are you missing me already?" the largest of the soldiers joked back. She could see their rank insignias. This 'Lukey' was not the leader, yet they all angled their bodies towards him and sought his attention and approval.

"Nah, can't wait for you to go."

Emilia moved so she stood in front of the large man. His hands were huge, making the tin cup he gripped look like a plaything. She was taking a risk standing so close, boredom making her cocky. She liked to look into their eyes and know that she could take control. Just like that.

And if anyone bumped into her out here in the dark, they'd probably just think it was a vengeful spirit. That was how she thought of herself when she bent the light around herself and disappeared. A ghost. Nonexistent. Dead. She wondered if the One True God would forgive her the blasphemy of using a magic other than mind control. But then, it could just as easily be insulting to Him for her to be given a gift and not to use it.

"So how'd you get out of border patrol?" someone was asking Lukey. Emilia moved away from the fire and stood behind the soldiers, forcing herself to pay attention. From the positions of her compatriots, she was the only one who would hear anything they said.

"Boss gave me leave to head home for a couple of weeks. We haven't heard from my father for a while and my mother is getting worried. She wants me to look into it. See what I can find."

"I thought he was travelling?" one of the soldiers piped up. "It can be tricky to get letters back from the Faraway Isles."

Lukey nodded. "And hopefully it's just that and I'll be back up here bothering you all in no time. But he's been travelling for three years now. Every time he's about to come home, something comes up and he remains away. And now, with his letters stopped..."

The mood around the fire darkened, everyone processing Lukey's predicament. Emilia frowned at Lukey's hope. Clearly, his father was dead. Probably at the hand of some entrepreneurial pirate who was now fleecing the family for all they were worth. Yet he seemed to hope all was fine. Such naivety in a grown man.

"Well, enjoy your leave," said one of the soldiers, trying to restore some levity to the group.

"Oh, it's not leave," Lukey corrected him. "I'm being sent to the palace for duty."

Whistles and teasing ensued, with a good deal of banter about Lukey's childhood friend. The empress.

Interesting.

The men settled to chatting and playing cards, and Emilia silently withdrew, circling around until she was hunched right behind Reiko.

"This has to be the worst attempt at hiding I've ever seen," she said, happiness flooding her as he jumped. At least he didn't squeal as he had previously when she'd appeared behind him.

"I've told you not to do that," Reiko snarled, glancing around as if he might be able to see where she came from.

"Come on, we'll get nothing more from these ones." Emilia left before Reiko could ask any questions because she knew that irritated him more than her scaring him. He waited while she retrieved their fellows and then the team began their trip home, blending into the shadows like wraiths on the land.

The two junior spies reported what they'd observed, which was nothing useful. They directed their comments to Reiko. Because, of course, Reiko was in charge. Reiko just grunted at the juniors and turned to Emilia expectantly.

"I'm sure I got nothing better than you did, Reiko," said Emilia. He frowned at the use of his name, instead of the title 'dominus', which the position he hadn't earned demanded. But he didn't pull her up on it. Reiko was too smart to upset Emilia before he got her information.

"Well, why don't you tell me anyway and I can compare

it." Reiko's voice was firm, the restraint of not simply ordering her to tell him clearly grating at him. She smiled. Good.

"Soldier's banter," she said dismissively. "Leave plans and such." Not a lie.

Reiko glanced at her, trying to figure out what she was holding back. She was always holding something back. Because she was better than they were. And she never got the credit for it.

Emilia would have preferred to be upfront. To operate as a team. But if she'd done that her entire career, she'd probably still be a junior spy who was responsible for the promotions of all her classmates. Things weren't too far off from that. But at least she got to operate relatively independently. Reiko was in charge here, but both would report to Patron Smolka.

Because Patron Smolka was smart enough to get the information from Emilia directly. That way he could use it to further his own career rather than Reiko benefitting.

It wasn't her preferred outcome, but her choices were limited. She'd much rather almost anyone but Reiko benefitting if she couldn't get the kudos herself.

Reiko kept quiet for the rest of their journey, and when he tried to pin her against the wall just around the corner from Patron Smolka's office, she was ready for it. Reiko grabbed her left shoulder with his left hand, ready to push her so his forearm pinned her. Emilia took a step back, grabbing his wrist and pushing the rear of his shoulder with her other hand, slamming him into the wall instead.

She immediately pulled him back off the wall.

"Reiko!" she feigned concern. "Watch your step!"

Reiko wheeled on her, snarling, and began to advance. Emilia took a step back, assessing her options. Much as she'd like to punch Reiko in the face—repeatedly—that would earn her a punishment. Likely being assigned under his command. She could run, but then who knew what he'd tell Patron Smolka.

"Ah, there you are." Patron Smolka himself appeared around the corner, saving Emilia from choosing. He smiled blandly at them, as if nothing were out of the ordinary about a large man advancing on a small woman as if he might kill her. "Reiko, I'll hear your report first."

Normally Patron Smolka had them brief together before dismissing Reiko and hearing what Emilia had found. But not today, apparently. Maybe he just thought they needed separating to allow them to cool off.

The two men left without another word, and Emilia leaned casually against the wall outside Patron Smolka's office. Where she could hear every word Reiko said.

Of all the masters she'd had so far, Patron Smolka was the best. He still stole all her intel for his own benefit. And he'd never so much as scolded Reiko for attacking her—not with his father so powerful. But he did his best to keep her safe. And even if that was mainly for his own benefit, at least he made it seem as if he cared about her.

She listened as Reiko ranted and raged about how insubordinate she was. What a terrible team player. An awful spy. She could hear Patron Smolka's reasonable tones trying to steer Reiko back to his own information. A good tactic to calm the large man, but it would be difficult to make it work when Reiko had no information to give.

The voices lowered and, even straining as she was, Emilia couldn't make out what the men were saying. Then the door slammed open and Reiko stormed off without so much as a glance in her direction. Emilia counted that as a win for her. Patron Smolka popped out into the corridor and told Emilia to make herself comfortable in his office while he made himself another cup of tea. He liked to be comfortable for Emilia's debriefings so he could concentrate and pull the best intel that suited his needs. He never offered Emilia a refreshment, but he did allow her to sit.

She wandered into the small office and glanced around. The room was sparse, his desk impeccably neat. But for the absence of dust, it could be a spare, unoccupied office. Emilia wandered over to the sole painting on the wall. A small, framed canvas illustrating the Divvinium prevailing over their enemies, the One True God behind them, controlling their victory.

It troubled her for reasons she couldn't articulate. Most things she had been taught since birth she followed without question. Like it or not, that was the way it was, and the Divine Prophet brokered no deviation. But the idea that the One True God would smite all who had been gifted magic other than the gift of controlling minds...

"Ah, that is one of my favourites," said Patron Smolka as he shut the door and seated himself behind his desk. His tea steaming before him, he gazed over at the painting as Emilia took the seat opposite. "I look at that painting and I feel rejuvenated in our mission."

"Victory as He wills it," said Emilia, as was expected of her, and she inclined her head.

"Indeed." Patron Smolka beamed at her. "Now, I expect you overheard Reiko's report."

There was no judgment in Patron Smolka's voice. The opposite, in fact, since it was expected of Emilia to gather information. To fail to do so would be frowned upon. If Patron Smolka had not wished her to hear, he would have ordered her to wait elsewhere.

"Yes, Patron Smolka."

"Good. Now. Tell me something useful." He lifted his quill as he said it, his conviction that she would have something for him absolute.

It was this trust that gave Emilia pause, and at her hesitation, Patron Smolka lowered his quill, his indulgent smile slipping slightly.

"Of course, Patron," said Emilia respectfully. "Only, I wonder if I could make a request first?" It was a ploy Emilia used sparingly. Once her masters understood her value to their own career, she found she could ask for favours, but she was rarely successful if she had already provided what they needed.

"Of course," Patron Smolka said, as if such a question was silly. As if anything she needed would be granted as a matter of course. "What do you need, child?"

"I wonder if it might be possible for me to serve... individually. Or at least in another section."

Patron Smolka nodded. "I thought you might ask. Reiko is... difficult, for most people. And he seems to have a special interest in you. But my child, the One True God has already provided for you!"

Emilia's head snapped up. This was unexpected. "Blessed is His benevolence," she said as she looked curiously at her master.

"Indeed it is. The grand cleric has seen fit to send you on a most blessed mission. You are to go to the very heart of the Empire and set the conditions for the Cleansing."

Emilia blinked. The heart of the Empire? That could only mean the enemy's main city.

"I'm to join our brothers in the City of the Damned?"

"Yes, my child, but *you* will be the gem set in our ring of control. You are to infiltrate the palace."

Emilia met this news with stunned silence. The palace? It wasn't entirely unexpected. After all, she was the only one who could slip through the wards unnoticed. When they'd sent the other spies south, it took a great deal of planning to arrange several attacks along the border so that the wards might be sounding for any one of the known incursions, and not wherever the spy crossed.

The palace was similarly warded, and clearly their strategy wouldn't work there. By the time they had forces enough to attack the palace, spying would be the least of their concerns.

But they were trusting her with what had to be the pinnacle of positions. Though women were, in theory, allowed to have any job and try for any role, they were never actually granted anything in a leadership position. Or anything a man wanted instead. In the palace, she would be getting information right from the empress herself. Control someone who might influence the empress's decisions. And no one could get in to monitor what she did.

Again, Patron Smolka's smile slipped at her pause and she hurried to reassure him, bowing her head, wondering if she might need to slip from the chair and prostrate herself on the floor.

"I am humbled and honoured by the trust of the grand cleric, and the One True God who guides his hand."

"Of course you are." Patron Smolka resumed his indulgent smile. "And of course, *I* did what I could to ensure *you* were the one chosen."

As if there was someone else. As if she only received this mission due to his great advocacy on her behalf.

"I am eternally grateful to you, Patron Smolka."

"I'm sure you are," said Patron Smolka in a voice that told Emilia he would be calling in a favour from her in the future. "All that we need to do is identify an appropriate proxy for you to target, and once that proxy is approved, you will be on your way. In the meantime, however..."

"But I have a target," said Emilia excitedly. "That was to be my report to you. The soldiers we observed this evening. Among them was one about to be sent to the palace—"

"Yes, but a mere soldier," Patron Smolka interrupted, waving her away.

"He was said to be a childhood friend of the empress."

That got the patron's attention. "Really?" His right eyebrow raised, calculations occurring behind his eyes.

"Yes, Patron. He was chosen for the palace specifically for this connection. I would imagine he will speak to the empress in private and be most influential in his advice. Additionally, as he leaves from here, I can use the journey to study him and connect to him. With the opportunity to subtly establish control, by the time we reach the palace, he will barely notice my guidance."

That did it. Patron Smolka's eyes were alight with the promotion he was surely due for finding their spy such a promising proxy.

"Of course, this man does seem someone we should consider," Patron Smolka said. "And of course, if he proves inappropriate once you are there, Handler Dunat will advise of a new proxy."

Emilia's stomach dropped. Sigmund Dunat was known to throw anyone under the cart at the hint of an advancement for himself. Even if that advancement was only in the queue for a cup of tea. The man was a poor Imperius, but his ability to weave information and influence emotions was legendary. Some whispered that the man was the only one who could come close to controlling the Divine Prophet himself.

Still... she would be on her own in the palace. Would only have to deal with Sigmund whenever she was required to check in. And she wouldn't have to work with Reiko anymore.

"The only issue, Patron Smolka, is that the man leaves for the palace tomorrow." It wasn't a total lie. The men had not mentioned when the soldier would leave. It could well be tomorrow. But if she was ordered to shadow him, she wouldn't have to see Reiko again.

Patron Smolka smiled broadly at Emilia. "Then, my child, we will need to ensure you are ready to leave tomorrow as well."

CHAPTER TWELVE

KAS

"Sorry about that," the rebel boss said to the group of prisoners, who were now more alert and tensed for action. But the leader barely noticed, shaking his head. "This whole thing was to get Bluey and Randy out. Ah, well." He blew out a breath. "Good luck to you all." And he turned to leave, his associates falling in behind him.

"Wait," called Kas, causing the men to stop and Tia to glare at him.

"What are you *doing?*" she hissed.

"Who are you?" Kas asked.

The leader took a few steps back towards the group, eyes narrowing on Kas. "We're the people who got you out of a cage, boy. That's all you need to know."

Kas looked the man up and down. The weapons were concerning, but after years of hard manual labour, Kas felt confident he could handle himself if the men turned violent. Plus, he had Ossi with him.

But he wasn't worried about danger. There was something familiar about the men. About how they were all dressed.

"You're rebels, aren't you?"

"What does it matter?" Tia hissed. "We need to go."

The men smirked. "You should listen to the lass, boy. I'd say the city guard will be here soon, and the soldiers will be reinforced soon after. I'd have thought you wouldn't want to be here when they arrive."

"Is Jori still in charge?" Kas's mind was barely catching up with the idea that he was free. It had happened so fast, so unexpectedly. But his heart was ten steps ahead of him, trying to find a way back to Sali.

Sure, he could just head to Lorendell himself, but how was he supposed to get in the gates with a collar around his neck? And even if he snuck in, he couldn't exactly wander the streets asking questions. The collar branded him as a criminal. And an escaped one at that. Anyone who didn't scream for the guards at the sight of him would likely hand him over in anticipation of a reward.

Jori owed him. Big time. If he could make contact with him, the very least Jori could do would be to find a way for Kas to get into the city and return to his little brother.

"What's it to you?" the leader asked, glancing over his shoulder, eager to leave the scene.

"He looks familiar," one of the other men muttered, and all three suddenly looked at Kas with furrowed brows.

Realisation hit the leader, his eyes growing wide. "Gods above... you're not Salomon's brother, are you?"

Salomon?

No one ever used Sali's full name, and Kas had never been referred to as Sali's brother, for that matter. It was usually the other way around. But it wasn't beyond the realm of possibility that in finding a way for himself without Kas—without the last member of his family—Sali had finally shed the nickname he'd always disliked.

"Sure," said Kas. "How is Salomon? He alright?"

"Oh, he's grand, he is," said the leader jovially. Apparently, they could be friends now. "I'm Derrek. I'll let him know I've seen you and you're out. Good luck, mate."

"I need a way into the city," Kas called before the men could get too far away.

They turned once more, shooting looks at each other.

"You don't want to go to the city, mate," said Derrek. "Not with that around your neck."

"Please. I need to see Sali—er, Salomon."

Derrek looked at the man on his left, who shrugged, and then the man to his right, who nodded. Derrek sighed. "There's a big drain east of the main gate. It's patrolled, but not regularly. If you're smart, and keep an eye out, you might be able to get in there. But if you're in the tunnels and you hear the soldiers coming, scram back out the way you came. There's only one way in and out. And there's nowhere to hide once you're inside."

With that, Derrek nodded at them and hurried with his men back up the hill.

"Come on," Tia said urgently, grabbing Kas's arm and pulling him away from the cage.

———

They walked for about an hour, aiming for the dead ground between the southern quarry and Lorendell in the hopes that anyone tracking them would first search the roads leading as far away from the labour camp as possible. They were tired, the adrenaline having long gone and the aches and pains from the crash now making themselves known. Kas was limping heavily and Tia had fashioned herself a sling for her arm from a strip of fabric from the bottom of her shirt.

Spotting a cluster of trees close to a small lake, Ossi led the group over, and after drinking from its slightly dirty water, they collapsed about in the shade. It wouldn't take long for the shade to become cold, but having walked for so long in the sun, it was a welcome relief. Kas was pulling a makeshift bandage tight around his ankle when Mira, the small woman who'd been with them in the cage, asked the question on all of their minds.

"What now?"

"We won't last too long out here by ourselves," said Ossi. "But we could camp outside my settlement. That place I've been telling you about." He nodded at Kas.

On so many nights, Ossi had painted Kas the picture of his favourite place to camp. In Kas's mind, it was a lush field with a crystal blue river winding its way lazily through it and a giant tree with fresh green leaves spilling down like a waterfall, brushing the water. Ossi loved to fish there, and had even once confided to Kas that if he had to put down roots like an Empire man, he would build his house there.

"My people will bring us food and bedrolls," Ossi continued, "and the soldiers don't often patrol the marshes nearby."

At the beginning of the annexation, the Empire had insisted the nomadic Trolls live in a fixed settlement. The Empire even went so far as to construct the settlement for the Trolls, but they'd built it in the marshes. Ossi had told Kas that the marshes were where the Trolls traditionally spent the least amount of time each year. Of course, Kas realised building a settlement on the plains where the Trolls used to spend most of their time took up valuable farming land. Land that had quickly been acquired by the Empire's nobles. Ossi's fishing spot was at the edge of the marsh and the plains. Close enough to the settlement that the nobles didn't farm it, and far enough that the soldiers didn't bother with it.

"I need to see my family," said Tia. "From everything

I've heard over the years, our tribe isn't doing well. I might be able to help..." She trailed off, and they all unconsciously touched their collars. None of them would be much help to anyone while they were shackled with them.

"I need to find my brother," Kas said quickly. They all wanted to see their families, but his brother had been left to fend for himself for eight years. At least everyone else's families had had their tribes to help them.

"I'm not sure we should split up," said Mira, looking slightly alarmed at the idea. "We're stronger together."

"We're more of a target together," countered Kas, thinking back to his days of thieving. But even as he said it, he felt a pang of anxiety at the idea of leaving his friends. How would they ever find each other again if they needed to?

"We should keep moving," said Mira, trying another approach. "Perhaps we could visit each of your homes, but the group could remain outside the settlements? That way, if the person visiting their family gets in trouble, we could all help."

"Don't you want to see your family?" asked Tia, frowning at Mira. "Where are they, anyway?"

Mira's face burned. "We used to travel. Last I heard, they were in Lorendell, but that was years ago..."

"So we should start there, then," said Kas happily.

"I am going to see my family," said Ossi with a note of finality. "You are all, of course, welcome to join me. You may accompany me now or seek me out after you have found your own families. But I will not wait."

Kas looked at his friend curiously. Normally, Ossi was the first to bend to the desires of others, and Kas couldn't think of a time Ossi had been as firm as he was now. But it was understandable. Kas had no intention of waiting to find Sali, either. Still, the anxiety at splitting up was palpable.

None of them wanted to leave, but the desire to find home was stronger.

"Fair enough. I'm going to find my brother. But if that doesn't go well, or it gets too dangerous to stay in the city, then I just might come and look you up." Kas smiled at Ossi and Ossi nodded at Kas, their eyes meeting in understanding.

"I hope you will, little Empire man." Ossi's eyes twinkled as he teased Kas. "I will look forward to seeing you again."

The two men clasped wrists in such a manly farewell that Tia groaned and both women rolled their eyes.

"Well, I guess that's that then," said Tia. Though she was clearly as eager as the others to get to her family, there was an anxiety there about the group separating. "Mira, are you going with Kas? You're also welcome to come with me if you want."

It hit Kas that Tia had probably never been alone in her life. She had been so young, her tribe would have cared for her, and then the camps told her what to do and when. Freedom and the idea of being left to her own devices must be overwhelming.

Kas suddenly felt an intense desire to put off heading to the city to be with Tia. Travelling together on the roads and in the forest could be a lot of fun. Not to mention bringing them closer. The nights were chilly. They'd probably need to snuggle together for warmth—

"I've always wanted to see the Shifter's villages," said Mira, breaking Kas out of his fantasy. "I think I'll come with you, if that's okay."

Tia nodded it was and Kas felt guilty. Guilty for so quickly jumping on a fantasy that would lead him away from his brother, and guilty for not ensuring Mira knew she was welcome to accompany him.

She seemed a lovely girl, but selfishly, Kas didn't want any responsibilities that might keep him from finding Sali. Whether or not Mira expected his help, he could hardly travel with her to the city and then wish her luck evading the guards as he left to find his brother. Especially when she had no idea where her family might be. He could travel faster on his own. Fade into the shadows.

Thinking about Sali made Kas want to be in the city now. His desire to go was only increased by the awkwardness that now permeated their group. The decision to split up loomed above them, highlighting the differences that hadn't seemed to matter in the camps. Unspoken was that in a blink they had gone from expecting to see each other regularly for the rest of their lives to likely never seeing each other again.

"Well," Ossi finally said, rising to his feet. "It looks clear. I think I will get going."

The rest stood too, and Kas offered his hand again. Ossi grabbed it, smiling as they shook once, before Ossi pulled Kas into a crushing bear hug.

"Do not forget me, little Empire man."

"That seems unlikely," Kas wheezed, extracting himself and giving Ossi a friendly slap on his shoulder.

"Keep safe," said Tia, giving Ossi a brief squeeze. She then turned to Kas. "I think we'll head off too."

Her arms went around his waist and Kas's heart thumped as if he'd run from the city to the border. He squeezed her back, wanting to hug her longer, but not wanting to make it weird. The smile she gave him as they pulled apart filled his chest, but it ached as he realised they were separating. Possibly forever.

They all said their farewells in a moving feast of murmured good wishes and hugs.

And then they were gone.

Kas watched his friends as they moved over the land and out of view. He felt a strange sadness. Not only that his friends were gone, especially Ossi, who had been an almost constant in his life for the last eight years, but that *something* was ended.

Kas turned and looked towards the northeast. The day was still clear and he could just make out Lorendell.

The City of Stone.

Lorendell was ringed by a huge stone wall, thick enough for the guards to patrol the top of it. It was this wall that the Empire claimed saved the city from the last Controller invasion over two hundred years ago.

Inside the city, stone walls also separated the various districts. These were far smaller than the main one, but still taller than a man. As he walked, Kas thought about how he used to be so proud of the city. That was what he had been told he should be, after all. He'd been taught by listening to the city dwellers that they were superior to the minor tribes. They had constructed and lived in a modern city made of stone. The Shifters lived in the woods like animals, and the Trolls wouldn't even have a settlement if it wasn't for the Empire's benevolence.

Kas frowned, suddenly realising that the Druids seemed to escape the condescension. From what he'd learned in the camps, the Druids lived in a simple village in the north. Some people said they lived in straw huts, others said they were simple wooden houses. Either way, it didn't sound like they were much different from the other minor tribes. Yet the Empire folk didn't ridicule them. They didn't speak of the Druids much at all from Kas's memory.

Having walked for long enough that the sun was a mere cart length above the horizon, Kas took a short break, crouching in the cool shade of a barrier wall. He couldn't halt for long, or his ankle would start throbbing again.

The crumbling stone structure he crouched by used to form part of the Great Barricade. Sometime after the Empire had defeated the Controllers and forced them to withdraw, the enemy had returned, this time to attack the Trolls. The emperor at the time had ordered the erection of a huge barricade outside the city to slow the Controllers if they defeated the Trolls and once again came south. But the Trolls had defeated the Controllers and the Great Barricade fell into disrepair, never having been needed.

The stone was cool on his sweaty back and Kas relaxed as he looked up at the city that was his home.

The City of Magic.

Ossi had used the name once, and Kas had liked it, repeating it himself until Ossi had explained that the minor tribes used it to describe the Empire city in a derogatory way.

"But magic is a good thing," Kas had said, confused.

"But it is not the only thing," Ossi had replied. "The Empire places too much stock in magic, and not enough in the person."

Kas thought of the Empire's citizens, wandering the streets in clothing specially dyed to reflect the colour the Testing Orb had shone for them. He thought of the badges that tier threes had sewn onto the arms of their tunics. He remembered the look on Sali's face when he'd learned he was non-magical, and how Jori had lost interest in him when that had been revealed.

Even as a prisoner, Kas had left his city proud to be a citizen of the Empire. Sure, not everything was great. The wealth distribution could have been better. But it was a great city. He had been told as much. Returning, however, Kas's eyes had been opened. The Empire wasn't so advanced. The minor tribes weren't so primitive. The

Empire didn't necessarily treat the minor tribes well, just as it didn't care for its most vulnerable citizens.

City of Slaves.

Kas hadn't needed to ask Tia about that title, nor had he repeated it. The Empire was founded on slavery, when the Fire Tribe had conquered the other elemental tribes and forced them to build Lorendell. Now it seemed the minor tribes were to be conquered as well.

Reluctantly, Kas left the cool wall and pushed to the right, heading away from the road that led to the main gates. The sun was setting now and soon he would miss the heat that had bothered him most of the day. But he picked up his pace, ignoring the twinge from his ankle. He wanted to reach the drain before it was too dark to see. He'd need to get a good look at it while there was still light.

Derrek had said there was only one tunnel, but he hadn't said how wide it was. Sure, with only one passage, anyone trying to sneak in would be seen by the guards patrolling its length. But if it was wide enough, it might be possible for someone invisible to sneak by.

Kas got all the way to the entrance of the drain before he remembered, automatically touching his collar. He could no longer become invisible. Somehow, being free of the camp and returning to familiar ground had chased his restrictions from his mind. He would have to do this the hard way.

Calling the tunnel a drain seemed to completely miss the epic nature of the construction. It was higher than Kas was tall, and even Ossi could have entered it without stooping. There was a thin stream of water and waste travelling along the bottom, but it looked similar to the volume Kas used to see in the gutters throughout the city. He looked at the huge width of the drain and couldn't imagine what would need to happen for water to fill it.

Kas picked up a small stone and threw it as far as he could into the darkness, ready to run if he somehow managed to hit a guard skulking in the tunnel. The silence stretched before Kas heard the faint clicking of the stone bouncing along the tunnel's floor.

Satisfied with his reconnaissance, Kas hesitated. Perhaps he should risk it and just head into the tunnel now? But he didn't know how long it was. What if he made it all the way to the other end and then the guards appeared? He was already tired from the walk and his ankle wouldn't last a lengthy pursuit.

Kas retreated to the bushes that had sprouted at the base of a tree, several cart lengths away from the drain's entrance. As he saw it, he had two options. The first was to do as Derrek had suggested and try his luck, observing the patrols and then timing his run to avoid the guards.

There was a lot of risk involved in that option, and Kas had no idea what the other end of the tunnel was like, or where in the city it emerged. For all Kas knew, it could open up into the guard barracks on the other side of the wall from the slums.

The second option was to fashion himself a weapon and deal with the guards as it suited him. Once they were unconscious, Kas could relax. At least until they awoke and raised the alarm. He could kill them, though the thought turned his stomach. But then it would be a matter of someone finding the bodies and raising the alarm. That might take longer, but the search for the culprit would be significantly more intense.

Kas didn't like the idea of hurting anyone. Though his time in the labour camps had made him physically stronger, it hadn't hardened him the way it had some of the others. If push came to shove, Kas knew he could defend himself, but the idea of setting out to hurt someone just to get what he wanted made him sick. Sneaking it was, then.

Kas sat there for an hour, and nothing happened. The dull ache in his ankle was making itself known, and the cold was a few degrees away from making him shiver.

He knew the smart thing to do would be to spend the night and next day in hiding, learning the patrol timings and selecting the perfect time to try his run. After all, it wasn't like he was on a schedule or anything. But he could sit here all week and still be wrong-footed by a change in the patrol schedule. Plus, he really wanted to see his brother.

So, more confident than when he'd thrown the pebble, Kas decided there was no time like the present, and snuck over to the mouth of the tunnel.

And right into the path of two city guards.

CHAPTER THIRTEEN

TIA

As Tia crested a hill and set eyes on Ravenswood Forest for the first time in eighteen years, she realised she had forgotten what home felt like. She hadn't been ready for the physical pull of her heart. And until Mira gently wiped Tia's cheeks, Tia hadn't noticed she was crying.

Suddenly, she couldn't wait a moment longer. She wanted to set off at a sprint, never mind the day of travel she knew they still had until they even reached the forest's edges. She was going *home*.

Tia had spent the journey so far feeling a chaotic swirl of contradictions. The buzz she'd felt at escaping the camps had worn off with the adrenaline, and as she and Mira had set out, leaving the others, the enormity of her freedom had truly hit her.

She'd never had true freedom before. When she was with her family, she'd been too young to feel the burden of choice. But it struck her now that she could literally go anywhere, and that terrified her. The world suddenly felt overwhelmingly vast, and she had a strong urge to find a safe cave or abandoned hut and hide.

But then she'd feel the breeze, or see some of the

animals her people could take the form of, or take in the beauty of a world she'd never had a chance to know, and all she wanted was to be able to shift into something that could fly so she could soar above and explore everything.

Though she was an emotional whirlwind, until Tia had seen the forest, she and Mira had passed the time with idle chatter. Wondering about what had changed in the world, beyond the snippets of information they'd gleaned from new arrivals to the camps. But now, as Tia's mind turned to her family and she opened her mouth to talk about them, she wondered about Mira's.

What must it be like to suddenly be free, but to have no idea where her family was? And Mira had chosen to accompany Tia, rather than going to the City of Slaves with Kas. She couldn't imagine wanting to go anywhere but the forest, even if her entire family had been wiped out—which it almost had been.

She glanced at Mira, the smaller woman seemingly unbothered to not be off questing to find her kin. It was odd to Tia, though she recalled speaking with Kas about this. Her people, the Kikachi, were a true tribe. It sounded like Ossi's people were too. But the Empire folk... they lived together in that stone cage, but it sounded as if they bore no ties to one another. Only to their birth family. Perhaps that was why Mira felt no pull to go to the city.

"You must be getting excited," Mira said, breaking into Tia's thoughts.

"I am. I'm just sorry you're not getting to see your family. You really have no idea where they might have gone?"

The flash of pain was so quick, if Tia hadn't been looking at Mira, she would have missed it. She *was* aching to see her family then. So why was Mira here?

"No," said Mira quietly. "They were travelling merchants, so we never really stayed in one place long."

She never really had a home.

Sadness spiked Tia's chest at that, trying to comprehend what it must be like to have nowhere you inherently belonged. But looking over at Mira, something felt off. She was clearly sad about not seeing her family, but she seemed to have a complete absence of desire to find them. To look anywhere. Indeed, they'd seen some taverns as they paralleled the main road, but Mira hadn't given them a second glance. She hadn't even asked if Tia would be okay if Mira risked going inside to ask after her family. If their situations were reversed, Tia probably wouldn't even have asked Mira. She'd have just gone.

Biting down on her curiosity, Tia turned her mind back to her own family.

"My family has lived in the forest for generations," she said. "The farthest anyone ever moved was to one of the minor Kikachi tribes within the woods."

"Who are you most excited to see?" Mira asked with genuine curiosity.

Tia tried to keep her face from falling. "There aren't many left," she said quietly. "My mother was the Matriarch. The leader of our tribe. When we didn't fall in line after the annexation, the soldiers came with orders to force it. My mother thought we could settle the matter civilly. But the soldiers had other plans."

"They killed her?" Mira asked quietly.

Tia nodded. "And most of my siblings. For my people, the Kikachi, families are more fluid. The person you mate with for offspring is not necessarily the person you choose for your life partner. The soldiers killed my mother and her Chosen, and they took those of us born of my mother, but they did not take her Chosen's children, nor the children of my father. Some were killed in the fighting, though I am told my brother Fabian and sister Aurora still live."

Tia felt Mira reach out and give her arm a quick, sympathetic squeeze.

"Did they take you all to the camps? The children they took?"

Tia shook her head. "First, they took us to the City of Slaves. The Druids there had asked for us. To study."

"What?" Mira looked horrified.

"Apparently, some of them were hoping to replicate the relics. They thought by studying us they could imbue our magic into objects and allow others to shift."

Mira gaped at her, stunned. Tia's mouth was a thin, angry line as she remembered. The blasted Empire and their relics. None were so taken by the ancient objects as those from the City of Slaves. In fact, beyond the Empire and the Druids, many people thought they were a myth.

"The relics?" Mira asked, her brow furrowed in confusion. "Aren't they just some objects the Druids made ages ago? How would they replicate them with people?"

"The rumour my people heard was that the relics could grant the user all the magics of the tribes. The City Druids wanted to study our magics so they could try and imbue an object with shapeshifting."

"But..." Mira struggled for the words. "You were all children. You said you were five. You wouldn't have had magic to study."

Tia's mind took her back to the large cage they had been placed in. Her anger boiled, remembering how it had felt as the hooded people had stared at them, talking about them as if they couldn't understand. Like they weren't even people.

"Apparently, they thought the magic was already there. That before eleven it's present but not accessible. Either way, it didn't work."

Images flashed through her mind. Her siblings being taken, one at a time. No one returning to the main cage. She thought she had heard screams, but she wasn't sure if that was her imagination. After three of them died, some of the Druids weren't as keen on their experiment. She and her brother were taken to the camps, but her brother had been injured when they'd been wrenched from the forest, and the City Druids saw no use in healing him. He'd died the day after they arrived at the logging camp.

"I'm so sorry, Tia," said Mira.

Tia shrugged, not wanting to deal with the memories. "There's something wrong with those City Druids. Like their connection to the world has been severed. We should camp here for the night. If we leave at first light, we can make it to my home before midday."

The two women busied themselves making camp, and while Tia hunted, Mira made a small fire. They were close enough to the forest that it shouldn't draw attention. Few but the Kikachi ever came near the forest.

Full bellies relaxed them, and Tia felt the pull of sleep. One more night sleeping on the ground wasn't so bad. Not when she would see her people tomorrow. She was about to open her mouth to bid Mira goodnight when the shorter woman spoke.

"I think my family is dead."

Tia froze, staring at Mira, who in turn seemed hypnotised by the flames.

"That is why I don't seek them out. They were with me when I was caught by the soldiers. They tried to run, but... I think the soldiers killed them."

Tia got up and moved around to Mira's side of the fire, putting an arm around her shoulders. "Why would they attack you all like that?" she asked gently.

Mira shook her head, wiping at her tears and her nose.

"I don't know. I don't know why they stopped us. I just remember my father talking to them and then yelling for us to run."

Silence settled over them, save the crackle of the fire and Mira's sniffing. "I asked about them in the camps, but no one had heard of them," Mira said after a while, her voice flat. "I can't imagine any of them escaped, and there's no way the soldiers let them go."

"Mira, I'm so sorry," said Tia, embracing Mira. Tia's heart hurt for her friend. Both had lost so much, but Tia was about to be reunited with her siblings and her tribe. Mira had neither.

"It's okay," said Mira, waving Tia's sympathy away and wiping at her face. "I've made my peace with it. I don't tell people because I don't want the sympathetic looks. The pity. But I wanted you to know. To understand. Why... why I'm not off looking for them."

Tia nodded and poked at the dying fire, separating the embers and causing sparks to chase the stars.

***

The women were up and moving before the first curve of the sun kissed the horizon. Mira's story weighed heavily on Tia's heart, as did her own. But she focussed on her excitement at seeing her siblings and her tribe, and Mira appeared almost as excited to join her.

She babbled at Mira as they passed through the first sparse trees, telling her all about everything she remembered. About the village that was almost as big as the City of Slaves, but completely open and made of the materials of the forest. About the huts built up in the canopies that the shifters who could fly preferred. And the houses that jutted out into the water, a corner of their floor missing so that water shifters could dive right in.

And about the capital, her home, where shifters of all kinds lived together with the spell casters, object wielders, and non-magicals. She remembered playing and laughing and the festivals they used to have, and as they drew closer, she wondered if they had them any more.

A shadow loomed, quelling her joy.

"Are you okay?" Mira asked, noticing the change in mood.

"The Kikachi I met in the camps told me that after my mother was killed, the soldiers declared the witch doctor the new Matriarch."

"Is that bad?"

Tia frowned. "The witch doctor is usually someone with a talent for spells. Sometimes even a non-magical. But the Matriarch is always a shifter. And a woman."

"And this witch doctor is a man?" Mira asked.

Tia nodded. "I remember him as a good man, but I was so little. And power changes some people. The stories I've heard... they say he's turned families against one another. That with the Empire abolishing our education, he's taken us back to the darker days. Insisting that the Goddess requires sacrifices. Retribution. Retaliation."

She had heard such horrible stories. The witch doctor telling the family of a sick boy that one of the witch doctor's own rivals had cursed the boy, causing his illness. That the only way to end the curse and save the boy was to kill the man. The family refused, and the witch doctor declared their inaction was akin to telling the Goddess to take the child, and they should prepare for his death.

As the boy worsened, his father felt he had no choice, and killed the man. The witch doctor had then prayed for the child, who immediately recovered. No doubt from some potion the witch doctor slipped him.

The worst was that when the family of the slain man demanded justice, the witch doctor made a big show of considering it, before declaring that the man was killed in service to the Goddess, and as such, no justice was owed.

However, the man's son had been injured attempting to protect his father, and that injury was beyond what the Goddess demanded. And the witch doctor declared that they should take their justice against the first family's newly recovered son.

The dead man's family withdrew, claiming they had no quarrel with the child and the witch doctor declared to the tribe that the Goddess demands balance and if they insisted on displeasing the Goddess, her wrath would be felt. The family left, not wishing to maim a child in cold blood. And perhaps not believing in this vengeful Goddess the witch doctor seemed intent on creating.

The next day, the soldiers came and took their daughter, collaring her and sending her to the camps for some imaginary infraction. The witch doctor told the family he had warned them—the Goddess would not be ignored.

Tia's stomach had turned as her fellow prisoners had ended their tale reporting that the family had been so scared that the Goddess would take their other children, they had attacked the boy, but became so frenzied he had died too.

Tia had left her tribesmen before she could hear any more. So much pain with seemingly no end. She wondered if anyone still trusted anybody else anymore. Perhaps they were now more like the Empire. Guarded and individualistic.

"Do you think we'll be safe?" Mira asked, hesitation slowing her steps as the trees thickened around them.

"We should be wary," said Tia, checking her surroundings and realising they were close to the village now. "The good thing is, they've collared so many of my people, they had to leave some in the tribe, so we shouldn't stand out too much. But we'll approach carefully, hiding on the outskirts, and when I see someone I trust, I'll ask them to fetch my siblings. They'll know what to do."

Mira nodded and then jumped, hearing the snapping of twigs to her left too late.

"Hello Tia," drawled a voice that made Tia's skin crawl. She looked over to see Valto Hipolit, the witch doctor and Matriarch of the Kikachi, leering at her. From the trees and bushes around them, several tribesmen, apparently loyal to Valto, appeared, surrounding the women.

"Welcome home," Valto said, his smile at odds with the cunning gleam in his eyes. "Take them both."

CHAPTER FOURTEEN

KAS

THE THREE MEN stood outside the tunnel under the wall and stared at each other for a split second, each too surprised to immediately comprehend what was happening. One of the guard's eyes fell on Kas's collar, narrowing slightly as his brain struggled to make sense of what he was seeing.

Kas reacted first. Years of being on high alert for the next beating from the soldiers in the camps had honed his reflexes beyond what the training of the city guard could provide.

He moved purely on instinct, grabbing the men and smashing them together before throwing one to the ground and the other into the wall beside the tunnel entrance.

As the guard bounced off the wall, Kas caught him and slammed his head into the concrete and stomped down at the guard trying to get up, his foot finding the guard's head and bouncing it off the hard ground.

It felt like mere seconds had passed, but both guards lay silent and unmoving at his feet. Kas began to come back to himself, the horror of what he'd done dawning on him. Kas wasn't used to his strength. He felt numb. He checked the guards and, finding no pulse, swallowed, trying to keep down his nausea.

He couldn't leave them lying there, so Kas grabbed one of the guards, throwing the body easily over his shoulder. There was no cover in sight other than the bushes Kas had been hiding in minutes ago, and so he dumped the corpses there, moving back to the entrance of the tunnel and checking that they weren't visible.

They wouldn't stay hidden for long. Anyone sent to search for the missing guards would surely check the bushes first. And animals would come to feed. The smell would attract them soon.

Kas shook his head, then forced himself to turn and start walking. If he waited for the next patrol to come, this would all be for nothing. And if he had to fight them too...

The dank dark of the tunnel did nothing to stop Kas's mind obsessing over the fact that he had just killed two people. He tried to tell himself he'd had to. It was them or him. And he was not going back to the camps.

But years of hanging around with Ossi had inconveniently blurred the lines of good and bad. It had been easier hating the soldiers, but as Ossi often told him, they were just doing their jobs. Kas had watched Ossi talk quietly to soldiers who had been ordered to punish him. Sometimes, by the end of the beating, the soldier was crying more than Ossi.

To be fair, he'd seen Ossi talk to the bad soldiers too. The ones who enjoyed the beatings. Who looked for any excuse to hand one out. But that was to mess with them. Ossi knew the soldiers were ordered not to kill the prisoners, and so he liked to push the bad ones as far as possible.

Maybe these guards were bad. But Kas thought about all the city guards he'd dealt with over the years he'd lived in the city. Some didn't like the scum of the slums, as they called those who lived there, but he'd never known them to be heavy-handed. There had been a crackdown on the use of force by the guards after the food riots. After his parents had been killed.

Did those men have families? Children whose fathers Kas had just taken from them? Kas forced his mind back to the present. To listening for anyone approaching. He had to focus. He could worry about the men he'd killed later.

The tunnel twisted and turned and felt like it went on forever. Why couldn't the bloody thing simply go straight through the wall? Thick as the walls were, he'd probably have been able to see out the other end. The longer he was in the musty, dark tube, the more convinced he was that at any moment, more guards were going to appear in front of him.

When, finally, faint light glowed from the dark ahead of him, Kas sped up, breaking into a jog, ignoring his ankle. He turned another corner and squinted, the light bright, as if someone had lit fifty candles all at once.

Kas approached the thick metal bars and peered through. He could see the slums. The familiar shanties and dust and smoke. Kas pulled at the bars, wondering why the hells there weren't bars at the other end. He was grateful there weren't, but it seemed if the point of the wall was to keep intruders out, there should be bars on the other side of the wall. Not here inside the city.

Unwilling to give up but unsure of how to proceed, Kas stood there staring at the bars as if waiting for someone to solve the problem for him. But he couldn't stand around all day. He needed to get out of there before the next set of guards came. Maybe he could find another way into the city, or even find someone on their way in who could get a message to the rebels.

Kas turned, but froze.

The next set of guards.

If this end was barred off, how did the city guards enter the tunnel to patrol it?

The spark of hope died as Kas realised it was far more likely the soldiers who patrolled the outside of the city walls simply deviated up the tunnel, turned, and continued on their way. But maybe, just maybe, that wasn't the case.

Kas moved back to the bars and tugged on them harder now. None moved, and in frustration, Kas jerked his hand away from the last bar at the right of the tunnel. And it twisted in his hands.

Excited, Kas twisted the bar as quickly as he could, thinking his current luck would have the next patrol arrive just as he'd almost escaped. But it seemed his luck had changed, and Kas exited the tunnel and replaced the bar without a soul coming near.

Of course, aside from the patrolling guards, no one came down to this end of the slums. The slaughterhouse was right next to the drain, and the smell was atrocious.

Kas walked quickly away from the drain and into the slums. Immediately, he panicked. This was a terrible idea. He had nothing to cover his collar and if that wasn't enough to attract attention, the people here knew him. They knew he had been sent to the camps. And no one came back from the camps. The soldiers must have discovered them missing by now and there'd be a price on their heads. And if anyone could use money, it was these people.

"Come on boy, in here."

An old but strong hand clasped Kas on the shoulder and steered him inside a wooden shanty that was so run-down it didn't even look like the folk of the slums wanted to live there.

"Frank!" Kas gave the old man a hug, dismayed to feel

his ribs. He seemed to have shrunk in Kas's absence, even beyond what could be explained by Kas's growing.

"It's good to see you, boy," said Frank warmly. "Here, cover that thing up."

Frank tossed Kas an old and smelly scarf and Kas wrapped it as best he could around his neck. Frank frowned at him and Kas looked down, trying to take in his appearance. He was in tattered and faded labour camp shorts and shirt. His old leather shoes were little more than rags at this point. The cloth around his neck did little to help disguise him.

"Let's see," Frank muttered to himself as he dug through a small wooden chest in the corner. "Nope. Not that one either. Definitely not—ah."

Frank turned to face Kas, holding up some old brown trousers and a tattered coat. The coat was so dusty, Kas couldn't even tell its colour.

"They might be a bit tight, but give them a go, boy," Frank said, tossing them to Kas and shuffling through a small doorway.

Kas pulled the trousers on. They actually fit relatively well, as did the coat, though it sent Kas into a bout of sneezing.

"You can take it outside and beat it against the wall," Frank said, coming back into the room with a cap that he handed to Kas.

"Nah, it might give me a head start if the guards try to nab me and the dust gets them sneezing. Hey! My dad's old cap." Hesitantly, Kas put it on. He never used to wear it, but doing so now gave him a sense that his dad was with him, helping him.

"Kept it for you," Frank grunted. "Figured you might want it some day."

Kas was hit with affection for the old man. He'd known he'd never see Kas again, but he'd kept his cap anyway.

"How have you been, Frank?" Kas asked. "How's Sali?"

"Oh, I'm fine." Frank waved him away. "But that brother of yours." Frank shook his head, the smile he'd worn for Kas falling as he thought of Sali.

"What's wrong? Is he in trouble?" Kas braced as if to run from the shanty to take on anyone who might be troubling his brother.

"He *is* the trouble," said Frank. "I tried to keep him here with me. And even that Adeline of yours offered to take him in. Though I think her family might have said no. But it doesn't matter. He turned her down. Stayed here only long enough for him to find Jori, and then he went and took up with those rebels." Frank shook his head again. "Goes by Salomon now. Won't answer to anything but," the old man added, as if that were another strike against Sali.

Kas felt a sinking feeling in his stomach, battling with the relief that washed over him. Sali was fine. He was alive and, from the sounds of things, unharmed. Frank would know if something bad had happened to him. But he was with the rebels. Kas tried to tell himself that Frank's disdain was for the rebels in general, and not anything specific that Sali was doing for them. After all, Sali was a non-magical. Most he would be doing was forging weapons or getting supplies, right?

"But you'll be wanting to see him," Frank said, bringing himself back on track. "Maybe you can talk some sense into him. They've set up over in the Merchants' Quarter. Jori somehow got Victor's old shop and they've set up in there."

"Victor's? He retired?" Kas was surprised. Victor was the best smith in the Empire. He couldn't see the man putting down his hammer easily.

"Died," said Frank bluntly. "Apparent robbery as he left the shop one evening."

"Apparent?"

Frank looked at Kas, his eyes dark. "Just seems convenient that Jori's looking for a new place and then Victor dies and suddenly Jori has a location with everything he needs. Well, not convenient for Victor..."

Victor's shop was a huge building. The shop was all most people saw, but behind a door at the back was a forge in an area that was easily twice the size of the shop, and the shop was one of the largest in the quarter. Behind the forge was a warehouse that was twice as big again. Kas had only seen it from the outside, but it was one of the largest buildings in the Merchants' Quarter.

"Victor's was next to the barracks, though. Seems a risky location for the rebels to set up right next to the city guard."

Frank grunted. "These days it's hard to tell the two groups apart."

"What does that mean?"

"Ask that brother of yours," said Frank, not unkindly. "You'd better get on if you're going to blend in. Folks'll be heading home soon."

Thanking Frank, Kas exited his shanty, pulling his cap low to hide his face as best he could. He popped the collar on the coat up, tucking the fabric that hid his collar inside as if it were a scarf.

Not much within Lorendell had changed, but what had felt jarring. Some buildings were gone, others stood where before there'd been nothing. The tavern near the slums had changed its name.

But people were the same. Those heading to the slums were dirty and thin, older than their years, and as he moved farther into the Merchants' Quarter, he saw the wealthier folk who spent enough money for a month of bread on a single hat that they barely wore twice.

Kas wandered through the streets, heading to Victor's. He kept to alleys where he could and the edges of the roads when he had to move in the crowds. It felt strange to be among them again and Kas allowed his eyes to brush over the people of the City of Stone as he tried to figure out why.

At first he just assumed it was because he was a fugitive. He felt apart because he was hiding. But then it struck him. It had been so long since he'd been in a place with *only* people who were Empire-born. Kas felt an odd pang of longing for the peoples of the other tribes. There was something energising about being around so many different people. Suddenly his home streets felt lifeless and monotone.

Kas looked around, hoping to see one of the rare Trolls visiting the market. But a Troll would have been obvious and a quick scan of the crowds told Kas none were nearby. But a smaller figure caught his eye. There was something familiar about the woman, though Kas knew he'd not seen her before. He followed her for a little while, keeping to the shadows as he tried to get a look at her face.

She turned, and Kas felt like he'd been punched in the gut but was oddly happy about it.

Adeline!

She was older now, and looked more like an adult which was why he hadn't immediately recognised her. He supposed he must have changed too. Adeline hadn't seen him, but picked up speed, a destination clearly in mind now. Kas pushed past people, trying not to draw too much attention, but trying to get ahead of his friend.

A lucky break with a slow cart had Kas slipping into an alley a little ahead of Adeline. Just as he'd realised his mistake at letting her out if his sight—what if she'd turned down a different street?—he saw her bustle into view and very nearly missed his chance.

"Addy," he hissed. When she didn't turn, he tried a little louder. "Adeline!"

He could feel her hesitation. Someone calling her name from a back alley probably wasn't enticing, but he willed her to turn, and finally she did. At first she stared blankly at him, her face stern, ready to rebuff any unwanted advances.

But then, just as he'd found her in her older skin, he saw it click behind her eyes and they grew wide. She started to say his name and then clapped her hands over her mouth. With a furtive glance each way up the street, she hurried into the alley and stopped in front of him, running her eyes over Kas in disbelief.

"Kas!" Adeline whispered. "It can't be you."

"I, er, managed to get away." Kas smiled, suddenly feeling awkward. "How have you been?"

Adeline let out a little squeak of happiness and threw her arms around him. Kas returned her hug, smiling. Adeline and Kas had grown up together while Kas's parents were alive. They'd all lived in the Servants' Quarter, an area that once had been little better than the slums, but was being reclaimed, and life had been good. They hadn't seen much of each other after his parents died, and he and Sali moved to the slums. There just hadn't been time. He was trying to provide for him and his brother and he'd heard Adeline had found work in a noble's house. But he'd still thought of her as his best friend. And he couldn't think of anyone else who would have taken Sali as she did, without asking questions.

"How are you here?" Adeline asked, her face falling as she touched the fabric around his neck, feeling the cold steel beneath it.

"It's a long story, but I have to keep a low profile."

Adeline nodded, glancing back at the entrance to the alley to ensure they were still alone. "How are you, Kas? I've missed you."

"I've missed you too." Kas smiled.

Adeline's face lit up. Kas's smile widened, looking at his old friend. Aside from Sali, Adeline was the only person who could make him feel at home. Like everything was back to normal and was going to be okay. "All I dreamed about in that place was being back here with you and Sali."

"Really?"

"Oh yeah," said Kas, his eyes unfocussed as he thought about the fantasies he'd indulged in to be anywhere but the camps, if only in his head. "Sometimes I'd imagine we were all nobles, living in some big house with servants bringing us anything we might even think we wanted. But most of the time, it was simpler. Just a small house. Maybe in the Servants' Quarter. Or maybe even in the Sailors' District. And we wouldn't have much, but enough to be comfortable, you know?"

"I've thought about us together too," said Adeline, her voice slightly breathy. "I mean, I've dreamed of it for years."

"In my mind, Sali's still a kid, but I suppose he's older now." Kas was still lost in his imaginings. "He'd have a job, but stay with us until he could go out on his own. Or he'd be married, I suppose," said Kas with a small laugh. The idea of Sali being old enough to marry seemed odd. It was going to take some getting used to, but seeing him would help. Maybe Tia would join them. Suddenly, Kas's imagination was full of images of Sali and his imaginary wife living next door to him and Tia. But that was silly. She'd never leave the forest, would she?

"That sounds wonderful," said Adeline, bringing Kas back to the present. "Is that something you really think about? Us together?"

"Of course," said Kas, looking at Adeline in surprise. "You and Sali are the people I love most in the world. And we're such a good team." He caught Adeline looking at him. There was something in her expression that he couldn't quite read. As if she couldn't believe what she was hearing. Like she doubted how much Kas cared about her. Perhaps she'd thought he'd forget about her in the camps, but that was ridiculous. She was his best friend. As much his family as Sali.

Kas grabbed Adeline, pulling her into a hug. "I really missed you, Addy," he said into her hair. "You're like home to me."

Adeline squeezed him back, and for a moment they stood there. Two old friends, as if no time had passed.

Eventually she let go, pushing him back to look at his face but still holding onto him, like he might disappear again. "I've got to get back to work and, um, sort out a couple of things. And you'll be wanting to find Sali, but I'll meet you later?"

"Definitely." Kas smiled, nodding, but his face fell slightly. "Frank said Sali was running with the rebels now."

Adeline's face fell too, and she rolled her eyes. "We tried to stop him. To keep him with us, but he's as stubborn as you are and he had his mind set on joining them. I know a couple of guys there and they let me know how he's doing and try to keep him out of the more dangerous stuff."

Kas smiled appreciatively at her. "Thanks for that. And I mean, at least he's not a magical. No risk of them sending him on missions."

Adeline didn't return his smile. "Sure, but... the rebels have changed, Kas. They're more like they were when... well, when your parents were alive. Jori wants to keep them peaceful, but there's a group of younger folk that think there should be more action. They're not just about trying to keep the empress honest; they seem to want full-on revolution."

"Sali wouldn't want any part of that," Kas said confidently. "Not after our parents."

Adeline's expression turned sympathetic. "I'm not sure he remembers it like we do. He was so young."

Kas's stomach dropped. He hadn't wanted Sali anywhere near the rebels, but the memory of Jori's reaction to his non-magical status had given him comfort during his time away. He'd been confident that even if Sali joined them, he'd be doing something ancillary. Something out of the line of fire.

But if there was a push to violence... you didn't need magic to wield a weapon.

"Sounds like I'd better go find him," he said to Adeline.

She nodded. "I'll find you later. The rebels have turned the warehouse at the back of Victor's into their own tavern. I'm allowed in because of Amos and Patty. I'll head there once I'm done with... everything." Her face lit up, and she gave Kas a little kiss on his cheek. Surprised and blushing, Kas watched as Adeline hurried to the end of the alley. Before she entered the main street, she turned and gave Kas a little wave, and then she was swept away with the crowd.

CHAPTER FIFTEEN

CASSANDRA

"Please, all I ask is just a little news of my son. Is he alright?"

Cassandra closed her eyes briefly, fashioning her features into a look of bored frustration. She didn't like it when he asked about his son. She didn't like anything that reminded her of who he was. That he was a real person. That reminded her of what her father had done. And what she was failing to put right.

Opening her eyes, she exhaled loudly, waving away the man's question. "There is no change, for good or bad. And there won't be. Not unless you can help me sort the Empire out."

The man deflated in front of her, his shoulders slumping, and the bones poked through his threadbare shirt. He shuffled away from the bars and sank down onto a small straw pallet, rubbing his face in his hands. Cassandra reminded herself to have them increase his rations and give him new clothes. And much as she hated it, she was going to need to visit more. It had been too long since she'd seen him.

"You speak as if we are a team," the prisoner said, lifting his head from his hands and looking at her.

"We are a team."

"Are we now?" He looked pointedly at Cassandra, standing on the right side of the bars in one of her fine dresses, and then around his small cell. It stank down here. She knew they cleaned his bucket before she arrived, but the palace dungeons had no air flow and everything smelled stale.

Unable to help himself, starved for information as he was, the prisoner moved on without forcing a reply. "Tell me what's happening."

"The northern border is stable, as I said. No indication that the Controllers will advance soon. Or at all," she muttered, but the prisoner heard her comment.

"They will come. Something must have happened. They've been operating like clockwork until now. Something's thrown them off, but they will come."

"Well, regardless of how much extra time we have to prepare, we won't be ready." Cassandra couldn't hide her frustration.

The prisoner looked up, his eyes shrewd. "Ah. This is why you've come to see me."

Cassandra hated that he read her so well. He read everyone well. That was why he was her best advisor. That and the fact he was locked away with no possibility of contact with anyone outside. His enforced solitude made him the most trustworthy person Cassandra had to talk to.

"I'm having no luck uniting the nobles," she admitted. "They won't play ball. They're all so obsessed with their own fortunes. None of them care for the Empire. They don't respect me."

"Give them a reason to."

"I am the empress," Cassandra snapped. "That is reason enough."

She felt like a spoilt child as the words came out, and

the look the prisoner gave her made her feel about five years old. She knew the title shouldn't be relied on alone for the respect of her subjects. Her father taught her that. But it still grated that it didn't inspire at least a modicum of respect. Even if the nobles hated her, they should have a love for their Empire. But worse than hating her, they were indifferent. And no one seemed to care for the Empire anymore.

"Whether or not the nobles should respect you, they don't. So let's address the reality of the situation rather than wishing for a dream." The prisoner was firm, but gentle. It was the same voice he'd used when she was a child and had snuck into the kitchens and gotten caught snacking on the desserts intended for her father's royal feast. He had always been kind to her, even when disciplining was needed. Cassandra felt sick. As he had been back when she was a child, he was right. Of course he was right.

"I know, chasing dreams rarely helps. And I'm dreaming of things being easy, and they are far from it. The nobles are doing what they always do. They are using their wealth and power to secure more wealth and power. And the only place they can take it from is the Crown. Unless they were to turn on each other, and amusing as that might be to watch, the last thing we need in the face of an impending Controller invasion is a civil war."

"And you're still unwilling to tell them of said invasion?"

Cassandra sighed. "My father urged me not to."

The silence that fell was charged. The deceased emperor was a topic the two usually avoided. Adding to Cassandra's discomfort was her increasing feeling that not telling the nobles was the wrong thing to do. But aside from the fact that her father had ruled the empire for much longer than she had, it felt somehow disrespectful to his memory to go against his wishes.

Are you really going to damn the Empire out of misplaced loyalty to a dead man?

Cassandra shook the thought away. Besides, the risk of the nobles taking their resources when they inevitably left was real. And that was a mistake there was no coming back from.

"I see the wisdom in that advice," said the prisoner, careful not to mention the emperor. "But I know the nobles. They will leave, on that we all agree. But they will not think to take their armies."

"They may order their forces to secure their lands," Cassandra argued. She didn't know why she parroted her father's thoughts. She was personally more of the mind that the prisoner was right.

"Perhaps," he said reasonably. "But it would not take much, particularly once it becomes apparent that the invasion is close, to *encourage* those men to join the defence of the Empire. One might even argue that doing so is essential in completing their task of securing their masters' lands."

Cassandra was again struck by how different things would be if the man before her hadn't been made a prisoner. If she hadn't continued his detention. Maybe he would have been able to help her avoid all the other bad decisions she'd made by act or omission.

The two fell silent once more. The only sound was the dripping of water from the stone walls into a puddle somewhere off in the dark of the dungeon.

"As if the nobles aren't enough to deal with," Cassandra continued, wanting to change the subject, "the rebels are acting out again. I haven't seen them this bad since... well, since the food riots."

The prisoner sat up straight. "There's your answer."

Cassandra looked at him as if he were mad. "Dozens of innocent civilians died in the food riots. I can't see how—"

"No, no," the prisoner interrupted her, shaking his head in frustration. "Quell the rebellion and you show the nobles your power. What you are capable of."

"Even if I could," Cassandra sighed, "how would that help? The nobles aren't the ones having issues with the rebels. If I get rid of them, the nobles are hardly going to care. Other than not being able to snigger at me about not being able to deal with the 'disorganised rabble' anymore."

The prisoner closed his eyes, steeling himself, as if dealing with an obtuse person. "You said the rebels are acting out. What is it they are doing, exactly?"

"Stealing," said Cassandra, then catching the frustration on the prisoner's face and expanding her answer. "Stealing supplies. Food, weapons, even building materials."

"Stealing how?"

"They're attacking the convoys. Some of them fight with the soldiers while the rest steal the goods. A lot of soldiers have died. They even attacked a prisoner convoy the other day. Blew it up while it was transporting them between the camps."

The prisoner gave Cassandra a meaningful look. "Are all of these targets Empire convoys?"

"No, but—"

"Then they *are* hurting the nobles. The prisoner convoy alone will cost them in mineral profits. Less workers means less product which means less money. The rebels *are* an issue for the nobles. They're just not worried about it because they see the rebels as being worse for you."

Cassandra stared at the prisoner, stunned. She hadn't looked at it that way. Hadn't realised. Of course, they were suffering the losses too. Their goods. Their soldiers. Their profits. But they had more riches than they knew what to do with and they could ride it out, when the upshot was the empress looking like she couldn't handle a small rebellion.

"You're right," she said, the prisoner nodding with her. "But then, how do I defeat them? I don't have the soldiers to go after them. Not with the border and the camps and the minor tribes. And they're mainly operating out of the city. The city guard is stretched to breaking with general security and I don't want to risk fighting in the streets. I won't show power by endangering civilians."

"There are two ways to make an enemy disappear," said the prisoner. His face twitched briefly with the irony, before the expression fled, his face neutral as ever. "Defeat them— either wipe them out or force a withdrawal. Or you can subsume them. If your enemy joins your side, then they are no longer your enemy, no?"

Cassandra's eyes grew wide as she stared at the thin, ragged man on the other side of the bars. The man was a genius.

"You said it yourself. The guard are few in number and you don't have a strong military at your back. Bring the rebels onside and you've increased your forces as well as demonstrated your power. And your cunning."

"But how do I do that? How do I bring them over to my side? They hate me."

"They hate the idea of the *Crown*. They'll work with you." He waved her concerns away. "You will need to give concessions, of course. Now, what is it they want?"

CHAPTER SIXTEEN

KAS

THE WAREHOUSE SEEMED LARGER than Kas remembered, though he'd only ever seen it from the outside. Being inside, seeing exactly how much *stuff* it could hold, somehow made it seem so much bigger.

He had thought to just enter through what had been Victor's shop, but something stopped him. He hadn't ever trusted Jori, but even if he had, a long time had passed. Who knew what the rebels were like now, and from the sounds of things, they were moving in the wrong direction. Maybe they'd grab him as soon as he entered. Hand him to the guards for whatever reward was no doubt on offer for the escaped prisoners.

Sure, Sali might see and try to stop them, but he was nineteen, only just a man. What could he possibly do to stop the rebels from handing him over, or whatever else they might want to do with him?

So Kas remained in the shadows, circling the building before he spotted an open vent above the forge. They built forges with holes in the roof so the smoke could escape. There were flaps that covered the holes, designed to be larger, so they provided protection in the rain. All were propped open, thin metal rods holding the flaps ajar. One was open wider, the rod used to prop it open broken and jammed.

Climbing to the roof was neither more difficult, nor easier than it had been when he'd been young. It was just different. He hadn't needed to climb in the camps and his muscles were slow to remember. But he was stronger now, and pulling himself up onto ledges felt so easy it was as if he'd been doing it his whole life.

Getting through the hole was more difficult. Kas knew intellectually that he was bigger than he had been eight years ago, but he'd not had much opportunity to realise it. Now back in the city, it was as if he'd slipped back into his fourteen-year-old mind. He dove at the opening just as he would have before, and promptly wedged his shoulders in the hole, snapping him to a halt. After some squeezing and twisting, Kas plopped onto one of the high walkways that ringed the upper reaches of the warehouse far less gracefully than he had intended.

Kas lay there for a beat, listening to the voices below, ensuring no one had heard his entrance. The conversations continued in the same rhythm and Kas flipped onto his stomach, peering over the side of the thin walkway to see workers busily forging weapons for the rebellion.

The familiar heat of the forge blasted him, and there was something soothing to him about the clanging of hammers on metal. Kas pushed up to his feet and made his way to the end of the walkway. He slid down the ladder and, pulling his cap a little lower, slipped into the warehouse and faded into a dark corner.

The warehouse, as Adeline had told him, had been partially converted into a tavern. In fact, the back half of the enormous space had been given over to what looked almost like a rebel village. In the opposite corner to where Kas skulked was a bar heavily stocked with liquor bottles, and behind that was a door. If the smells were anything to go by, there must be a kitchen back there. The bar was ringed with wooden stools, and smaller tables were scattered about the floor nearby.

In the middle of the rear half of the warehouse were two long tables, each with benches on either side. They were probably full at mealtimes, but at the moment no one was sitting there, most of the patrons gathered at the bar or sat at the smaller tables. To the right of the long tables were row upon row of bunk beds.

Kas frowned. There were so many of them. The rebels must have grown their numbers significantly since he went away. And still, he couldn't imagine Jori sleeping in a bunk near the foot soldiers. That meant there was likely another sleeping quarter for the leadership.

The scale of the operation hit him, and an ominous feeling engulfed Kas. It was like they were preparing for a war.

Voices to his left made Kas jump, and he quickly tried to cover his movement, turning it into a stretch that culminated in his rubbing his face to hide it from view. But the men who'd entered the warehouse paid him no mind.

"I'm telling you," a broad man, taller than Kas, was saying, "it's time for Jori to move on."

"Come off it Rubén," said a shorter man. "Jori's the boss. Always has been."

"That's my point," replied Rubén as they moved towards the bar, their voices fading.

Kas glanced around and, satisfied that no one was paying him any mind, followed the men, listening to them debate Jori's leadership. Two of the men excused themselves, ostensibly to sneak in a quick nap, though possibly they were sick of the debate.

Rubén and the shorter man sat down at a table near the bar, and Kas slipped behind some boxes in the part of the warehouse that was still being used for its intended purpose. Here he was hidden from view, but could see the two men and hear their conversation.

"I'm just saying." Rubén held his hands up in mock surrender. "Jori's been in charge for what? Ten years? More? And what have we achieved? We're still running the same missions we were when I started here. And nothing's changed."

"Plenty's changed," said the shorter man, gesturing around the warehouse. "Weren't like this when I joined up."

"Aw, come on Jimmie," Rubén said, frustrated. "You know I don't mean that. I mean, the empress is still in charge. Still sitting in her fancy palace with her rich friends and the poor are getting poorer. We were meant to change all that. Balance things. Jori's not willing to do what needs to be done to force *real* change. He doesn't have the stomach for it. We need someone like Salomon in charge—"

"Salomon!" Jimmie laughed in surprise. "The boy's nineteen. He can barely grow a beard, let alone run the rebellion."

"He might be young, but he's got some good ideas. It were him that organised the raid on the supply convoy last week. And he blocked the west gate. Tied the guards up for hours, letting us raid their armoury. Not only do we have swords for everyone now, but it's a pretty bad look for the guards."

Jimmie wasn't convinced. "That raid killed some of our blokes. Good blokes—Harry, Alfie? And for what? We didn't need the supplies, just like we didn't need those weapons. It seems to me that embarrassing the guard isn't that much more than Jori's doing."

Rubén smiled, taking a swig from his wooden tankard, his beard coming away covered in foam. "Ah, you just don't like Salomon."

"That's not it," said Jimmie quickly. Was that fear Kas heard in his voice? In the way he glanced around as if scared someone heard what Rubén had accused him of? "I just think he's too young. It's good the way it is now. Jori in charge and Salomon his deputy. The boy can learn from Jori and take over in a few years."

Rubén scoffed. "I don't want to wait around a few years to make changes. Salomon's action-oriented. That's what we need right now. You want another?"

Jimmie nodded, and Rubén grabbed their tankards and headed to the bar. "Action-oriented," Jimmie muttered to himself. "Preference for violence, more like."

Kas withdrew into the boxes and crates of supplies and weapons stacked on top of each other, thinking about what he'd just overheard. It sounded like the rebels were at a crossroad—some comfortable with the way things were, others wanting more significant change, no matter the cost.

But what really hit him was how they spoke about Sali. Or Salomon, he supposed. He felt both proud of his brother, and scared. Sali had always had a way about him. People flocked to him, wanted to be around him. Kas smiled as he thought about how worried Sali had been after the Testing. How he had thought he'd never make anything of himself. Kas had never really been able to explain to Sali how magnetic he was. People wanted to be around him and to do what he suggested. And it seemed the rebels were the same.

Deputy at nineteen! Kas's chest swelled. He'd been accepted by some adults when he was young, but that had been because of his magic. Sali had done this all on his own.

But Kas's smile fell as he thought about the rest of it. It

sounded like Sali was pushing for more action. More violence. Sali hadn't been affected in the same way as Kas by their parents' deaths. He'd been too young to remember the surge in operations by the rebels and the subsequent crackdown by the emperor. Too young to really understand that their parents were killed because the rebels were pushing things for the sake of pushing.

They hadn't needed to protest at the ration point. The emperor was trying to show the people he understood their plight. That the food shortage was hurting. He had his guards set up carts to hand out food to the poor. Kas and Sali's parents had gone to get rations for the family. All their money was being put into savings for Kas to go to the Academy. They'd heard there would be a protest, but had been told it would be a peaceful one. Chanting and speeches and the like. Kas's father had told him to stay in and take care of Sali.

But it hadn't been peaceful. The rebels had never intended it to be peaceful. They wanted the violence. They wanted the message it sent if the guards who were there to hand out food to the poor wound up killing them instead.

And that was exactly what had happened. Their parents had been at the front of the crowd waiting for food. When the rebels began to push people forward, they'd been trapped, unable to get away when things went bad.

They were among the first to die when the guards panicked and began swinging their swords. Kas had been told exactly what happened. But he hadn't seen the need to give Sali all the details. He'd been so young, and Kas hadn't really wanted to talk about it. Maybe that had been a mistake.

Instead, Kas forgot about the Academy and where such training might have taken him—what he might have become

—and instead took the money his parents had saved and tried to take care of his brother.

Wandering through the crates and boxes, Kas's mind wandered where it hadn't dared travel in years. Where might he have been now if his parents hadn't been killed in the food riots? Would he have found work in one of the emperor's forges? For fire mages like Kas, they were coveted positions, and they only took the best. He'd have earned a decent wage, maybe enough to open his own forge one day.

Or perhaps he might have been selected for a security position in a merchants' caravan. Or even found a spot on a ship marked for an exploration mission. They were rare these days, but he could have been sailing around Endarnia and seeing lands he couldn't even imagine.

Shaking the thoughts away, Kas turned his mind back to the task at hand, circling around the stacks of crates stretching to the high roof of the massive warehouse. Finally, Kas found what he was looking for. The stack was slightly offset, creating a ladder of sorts, and Kas pulled himself up onto some of the higher boxes, keeping himself as flush to the stacks as he could so as to remain out of sight.

From this angle, Kas saw a door just beyond the rows of cots. It was possible it was a bathroom, but from the steady stream of people heading for a door that was back towards the forge, Kas had a feeling it wasn't. He remained up high, watching for a time. After a while, someone approached the door and knocked.

When it opened, Kas saw Jori's head poke out. The man had aged since Kas last saw him. His head of black hair was more sparse and riddled with grey, and he seemed thinner, smaller. Jori followed the man who'd knocked, and they hurried out the main exit near the tavern.

Kas slid down quickly. If the door led to rooms for the leadership, it was possible Sali was in there. And if not, he could get in and hide and wait for Jori to return. The man owed him, after all. His eyes constantly scanning, Kas approached the door and listened as best he could. Nothing sounded from the other side, so at least it was unlikely there was more than one person in there.

Now or never.

Before he could think better of it, Kas opened the door and slipped inside.

CHAPTER SEVENTEEN

KAS

Kas entered what looked like a small sitting room, or a study. right across from the door was a roaring fire, two easy chairs facing the flames.

To his right were tables piled with equipment. Back packs and tools and clothing and weapons, strewn around in the type of disarray that made no sense to him, but still seemed as if formed a system for someone.

He felt a presence to his left, but before he could turn his head, a voice that was deep, yet still familiar cried out.

"What are you doing here?" a gruff voice asked. Kas looked over and locked eyes with the man. Recognition slowly registered in the other man's face. "Kas? Kas!"

Kas was knocked backwards as a body, only slightly shorter than his own, slammed into him, gripping him in a bear hug. His brother was almost as strong as he was. Sali released Kas and held him at arm's length, looking at his face to confirm it really was his older brother, before squeezing him tight again.

Kas smiled wider than he had in years, hugging his brother back.

"Gods, Sali, what have they been feeding you? You're huge!"

"So are you!" Sali finally released Kas and added, bashful but firm, "And it's Salomon now."

"So I hear," said Kas with a smile, and he reached over, giving Sali's red hair a quick tousle as he used to do. "But you'll always be Sali to me."

Sali's face fell slightly as he led Kas over to the chairs by the fire. They weren't much, but looked more comfortable than what was available to the masses outside. The brothers sat down, each still staring at the other, taking in the changes.

Sali was maybe an inch shorter than Kas, but broad. He'd kept his hair short compared to the rebels Kas had seen wandering around with ponytails, and it was scruffy, as if Sali spent half his life running his hands through it. There was the ghost of scruff on his chin, and Kas suspected Sali could only grow a patchy beard at the moment and was keeping it short until he could manage something more impressive.

"I feel like I'm dreaming," Sali broke into Kas's thoughts. "I can't believe you're really here!"

"I've missed you," said Kas, struggling to keep his voice steady.

"Me too." Sali smiled. His face fell, his eyes cast down to the ground. "I'm really sorry, Kas."

"Hey," Kas leaned forwards, reaching for Sali's hand and squeezing it. "It's not your fault."

"If I hadn't—"

"I mean it Sali. It's not your fault. It was a good idea, and we almost had it. But you know what they say." Kas smiled at Sali, who looked confused. "Nothing screws a good plan like a wayward donkey."

The two fell into laughter, the tension broken.

"From the sounds of things, you've done well for your-self, little brother," said Kas.

Sali puffed up at the compliment from his older sibling. "It's alright," he said modestly.

"Deputy leader?" Kas raised an eyebrow. "Seems more than alright."

Sali laughed. "Yeah, I think I really fit in here. People listen to me. They value what I can do, and it doesn't even matter that I'm non-magical. I can still help, you know?"

Kas's heart broke a little as he heard pain in Sali's voice. He still felt less than because he had no magic. But Kas was happy his little brother had found a place that recognised his talents, magical or not. He just wished it wasn't with the rebels.

"Yeah, that's great." Kas did his best to sound enthu-siastic.

"They even let me go on missions sometimes," said Sali, completely missing Kas's mood drop. "I mean, sometimes I can't. If it really needs magic, or sometimes it's just too dangerous and neither Jori nor I can go."

"How'd you get to be deputy?" Kas asked, again straining to sound like he thought this was a positive thing.

"At first they just had me running errands. Simple stuff. But then Patty let me help him at the forge, and I was really good at it. They still ask me to make things sometimes. Because I'm better at it than some of the other guys. Anyway, they wanted me to deliver some swords to some of our guys who were preparing for a raid outside the city, but when I got there, they'd been discovered and were fighting with the soldiers. I got them their weapons and picked up a sword I'd made and joined in. Got a couple of soldiers myself," Sali said with a pride that turned Kas's stomach. "Then they let me go on raids, and I had some ideas and, well, now I work with Jori."

Kas tried to smile. To show he was happy for his brother. But he'd wanted such a different life for Sali. He'd wanted so much more. His face crumbled. It felt like he'd failed his parents. Failed Sali.

"Hey," said Sali, grabbing Kas's hand again. "I know how you feel about violence—"

"I don't think you do," said Kas gently. "It's more than worry that you might get hurt. Mom and Dad... they wouldn't have wanted this for you."

Sali dropped Kas's hand, his face hardening. "I never really knew them, Kas," he said quietly. "I can't live my life for ghosts."

Kas closed his eyes. Sali had a point. Kas knew their parents better, and even though they were gone, he felt a certain pressure to live up to their ideals and make them proud. But if he did think differently to them, would he hold himself to what they might have wanted? And even if he did, would that be the right thing to do?

His mother had always ended their talks by telling Kas that she and his father wanted to guide him. To show him what they thought was right, but that ultimately it was for Kas to decide his path. Still, the few times he'd gotten in trouble, both his parents had seemed pretty disappointed. Maybe he was wrong to cling to the memories of their parents, and Sali was right.

Opening his eyes, Kas took a deep breath. This wasn't about their parents. Kas didn't think a violent rebellion was going to help anyone. The slums weren't great, but people weren't dropping from hunger and disease. Well, at least they hadn't been when he lived there. So many would die or be maimed if they went to war with the empress. Maybe Sali among them.

"You're right," Kas said to Sali's obvious surprise. "We can't live for them. But—well, you know better than I do. Is there really a need for a violent uprising? Isn't there another way?"

Sali opened his mouth to fire back a response, but stopped himself, taking time to consider the question. "I don't think there's ever a good time for a violent uprising, as you call it. But if it comes to a fight, is it better to attack first, while the people are in relatively good health and can add to your numbers, or wait until they're dropping and can be wiped out by the guard?"

Kas considered Sali's response. It was difficult to argue with.

"But I think we both agree that violence for the sake of violence isn't the way," Sali added.

Kas nodded. "You make a good point, little brother. I came in here ready to argue that it's not the time for aggression, and now that you mention it, I wouldn't be able to tell you when the right time is. I'm not so naïve as to think there's never a time for fighting. Sometimes your hand is pushed, whether you believe in violence or not. But these raids... tell me, brother, is there a plan behind them? Are they part of a larger strategy?"

This gave Sali pause. He considered Kas's question and then laughed. "It seems we both make good points, big brother. The aim of the raids is to cause disruption, but disruption for what? To what ultimate end? How does that serve our cause, other than sticking it to the Empire? I can't say we'll stop the raids, but I will speak with Jori. See if I can make him see my vision."

Kas relaxed in his chair. Somehow, in the space of a few hours, he'd turned his little brother into a monster in his mind. A madman obsessed with violence for violence's sake. Shame bit at the relief he felt. Did he think so little of his brother that he'd conjured such evil from a couple of comments from strangers?

No, it was just that he didn't know his brother anymore. He'd not seen Sali turn into the man before him. That had been robbed from him by his time in the camps.

But the boy he'd raised for a time would still be there. Kas just needed a chance to get to know him again.

"I really missed you, Sali," said Kas quietly.

"It's Salomon," said Sali, more firmly this time.

Kas blinked. His little brother had remade himself in Kas's absence. He'd been left alone so young and had to forge his own path. Perhaps he *had* left 'Sali' behind and become 'Salomon'. But he was still Kas's brother. Kas needed to get to know him again. And if that meant using the name he preferred, that was a small concession. He nodded and continued.

"All I dreamed about in those camps was coming back here and being with you like old times. We'd have a house, and I'd get a job and everything would be fine. Now that I'm here, we could make it happen. We could both work a forge. You wouldn't have to fight anymore."

"That is a nice dream, big brother," said Salomon sadly. "But how can that happen with a collar around your neck?"

"I'll get it off."

"How?"

"I don't know. I'll find a way." Kas was disheartened to the point of panic by Salomon's resignation to Kas's situation. As if it were set in stone. Sure, Kas had never heard of someone getting their collar off, but he'd never heard about them trying, either. But Salomon didn't even seem interested in giving it a go.

"Don't you see?" Salomon said, smiling gently at Kas. "*That's* why we need to fight. What right does the Empire have to put collars around people's necks with no chance of redemption? They just want to fill their pockets with gold, and if people could leave the camps, the production rate would fall."

Kas rubbed his face. This was not the homecoming he'd imagined. He felt his brother's hand on his shoulder.

"There's got to be a way," Kas said weakly.

"Sorry brother," Salomon said. "I'll get off my soapbox. I'm just so passionate because of what happened to you. To us. Because they won't let us have your dream."

"What about your contacts?" Kas asked, unwilling to let it go despite Salomon clearly not wishing to discuss it further. "Surely you must know *someone* we can ask?"

Salomon frowned at Kas thoughtfully. He opened his mouth, but closed it, thinking some more. "Perhaps there is, brother. Let me ask around and see what I can uncover."

"Thank you," said Kas meaningfully.

Salomon stood. "Come, let's get a drink. There is no need to hide here. No rebel will defy me and turn you in. And if they did, we would all fight so you never have to return to those camps."

Kas stood and gave his brother another hug. "I appreciate that, brother. But I don't want anyone to die for me. If the guards come, I will run. You will deny ever knowing I was here."

Salomon led him out to the tavern, greeting almost everyone they passed on the way to their table. Kas was struck by the respect the rebels all seemed to have for Salomon. It was jarring, in a good way, to see men older than he was being deferential to his little brother.

"They really love you," he said to Salomon after they were seated with their drinks.

"Ah." Salomon waved him away. "They like my ideas. For now, anyway. Come back in another eight years and see what it's like."

He knew Salomon was making light of his success, and

clearly the praise from Kas meant a lot to him. But the reminder of how quickly Salomon had risen to second-in-command made Kas pause. There was something going on here, but he couldn't quite put his finger on it.

"Hey Salomon," two burly men wandered over. "The patrol went well. We—Kas? Is that you?"

Amos and Patty were older than Kas, but growing up in the same neighbourhood as Kas and Adeline, the four had become good friends.

Kas stood and embraced the two men, all three of them broader and stronger than the last time they'd met.

"Little Kas, all grown up," teased Patty, who, as a blacksmith, had arms like tree branches.

"Yeah, shame you've let yourself go." Kas smiled.

"How are you, man?" asked Amos. "When'd you get back? And how'd you get back, for that matter?"

"What did you need to tell me about the patrol?" Salomon asked before Kas could answer. Salomon hadn't stood with the rest of them and still sat, legs crossed, coolly sipping his beer.

"Oh yeah," said Patty, then launched into his report, apparently oblivious to what was blatantly obvious to Kas. Salomon had always been sensitive to the attention Kas got growing up. First, it was just that he was the older brother. Kas was given more tasks, more responsibility by their parents, and it always made Salomon feel left out, no matter how many times Kas let Salomon go with him.

Things had gotten much worse after Kas's Testing. Salomon had somehow taken any praise for Kas's result as a pointed comment on his own lack of magic, and this was before he knew that would never change. Any positivity thrown Kas's way Salomon saw as negativity directed towards him, though Kas couldn't think of one instance where anyone told him he was less than.

It hadn't bothered Kas growing up. He'd only been worried that Salomon seemed to have such low self-esteem that he took everything as criticism. But it needled Kas now that Salomon couldn't let Kas catch up with his old friends without needing the attention back.

Intellectually, he knew that Salomon's position in the rebels was a huge deal for him. Something he had achieved that Kas had not, and really could not. But hadn't Kas just spent eight years in the labour camps? And while he didn't feel blame for his younger brother, it was a direct result of Salomon pushing the matter and forcing the mission on Kas.

Kas shook the thought away, sitting back down. It wasn't Salomon's fault, he reminded himself. Sure, Salomon had pushed the issue going to the palace, but Kas had made choices too. It had been his choice to go looking for Salomon. Had he not, it was likely Salomon would have given up and come home. Having found his brother, Kas chose to enter the palace, and once inside, he'd made several decisions, not the least of which was to actually steal the emperor's ring. So why was he suddenly feeling resentful?

Amos and Patty left, promising to have a drink with the brothers later, and the tension left with them. Alone, it was easy with Salomon, and he seemed pleased to have Kas back. They caught each other up on things, telling stories and laughing, the years falling away.

And then Jori came.

CHAPTER EIGHTEEN

KAS

"There's a face I never thought I'd see again." Jori's gruff voice preceded the heavy hand that clapped Kas's shoulder.

"Good to see you too," said Kas. "You look old."

Jori laughed, then nodded at Salomon. "Patty tell you about the patrol?"

"Yep," said Salomon. "I've handled it."

"Good," said Jori, returning his attention to Kas, his expression one of consideration. Apparently making a decision, Jori grabbed a nearby chair and dropped it by the brothers' table, sitting on it backwards and leaning his arms on the backrest. "Something urgent's come up."

"What is it?" asked Salomon, dropping his voice and leaning in.

"A mission. An important mission."

"Shall we—" Salomon pushed back his chair, standing, but Jori cut him off with a slice of his hand.

"I need Kas for this one."

A charged silence fell over the table. Kas saw Salomon struggling to maintain control, swallowing whatever outburst he'd been on the edge of making. Kas admired his maturity. If it wasn't for the soldiers and their truncheons in the camps teaching him restraint all those years, Kas wasn't sure he would have had the control over his emotions that Salomon seemed to hold.

"Kas? What could you possibly need Kas for? He doesn't even have his magic anymore!"

Kas knew Salomon's anger was directed at Jori, but the reminder of his lost magic still stung. As did the implication that he had no other skills. Salomon, of all people, should know better.

"And besides," Salomon continued, oblivious to his brother's reaction, "he's only just arrived."

"And it's lucky he has. Besides, it's his strength we need, not his magic." Jori stared into Salomon's eyes. A challenge. Salomon didn't look away. Refocussing on Kas, Jori said, "Come see me in the back room. As soon as you can."

Salomon seethed at Jori's back as the old rebel leader headed back to his room.

"You two not getting along?" Kas asked. He was interested in the dynamic, but also wanted to put a little distance to the request.

"You could say that." Salomon sat and drained his tankard. "He resents that the men follow me. That they like my ideas better. I think he hates that he's grown too old for this, and that I'm the one they've chosen to follow is like salt in the wound since I'm so young."

"But you're leading the rebels together?" Kas didn't see the two of them agreeing on much.

"Kind of," Salomon said, his temper fading now that Jori was gone. "He's still in charge, but the guys mainly come to me. And I'm the one coming up with the missions."

Something flared in Salomon's eyes and Kas finished his drink, putting the tankard on the table just loud enough to break into Salomon's thought process.

"I don't have to meet with him," Kas told Salomon. "I

have no interest in doing another mission for the rebels. Especially after how the last one worked out. Besides, our focus should be on getting this thing off." Kas tapped his neck.

Salomon smiled sadly, but his eyes were still angry. "No, it's fine. Actually, I'd like to know what he's planning, so if you wouldn't mind..."

"Consider it done," said Kas, standing. "Just have a beer ready for me when I come back."

<hr>

Jori was sitting in the chair Salomon had occupied earlier. He had pulled it close to the fire and was warming his hands, looking as if he was a million miles away. But Kas could read people well now. He'd always been intuitive, but eight years of needing to read body language and micro expressions in order to avoid beatings had honed his skills considerably. Jori knew he was there. Was monitoring his approach.

Kas sat next to Jori and waited for the older man to speak. He wasn't interested in playing games.

"Guards have picked up Derrek," Jori said eventually, dropping his pretences. "You remember him."

"His mission allowed our escape," said Kas. "Though it seemed to kill everyone he was trying to rescue."

"I told them not to use the explosives." Jori shook his head. "But that brother of yours—"

Kas looked at Jori as he stopped himself with an effort. The rebel leader used to look vibrant and energetic. Ready to take on the world. Now he just looked old.

"Anyway." Jori glanced over at Kas for the first time since the younger man had entered. "Since he helped you out, intentionally or otherwise, I thought maybe you'd like to return the favour."

Kas stared at Jori, his eyes squinting as he assessed what he was up to. His reason made sense, sure. It was easy to assume that Kas of all people would be up for rescuing the man who'd enabled his escape. But that wasn't it. And Kas wasn't buying his strength as an asset, either.

Kas exhaled loudly, shifting his posture, continuing to look at Jori, who was becoming increasingly unnerved by Kas. Jori wasn't stupid. He'd have to know the likelihood of Kas ever agreeing to undertake a rebel mission again was zero. But he'd still asked. No, he hadn't asked, Kas reminded himself. He'd walked right up and pointedly suggested Kas was the only one. Ah.

"You don't actually need me for the mission," Kas said. "You just wanted to stick it to Sali."

Jori looked at Kas, his eyes narrowing. "You're half right," he conceded. "I did want to stick it to Salomon."

"What is going on with you two?"

Jori stood, leaning on the mantel above the fire and staring at the flames. "Some of it is me resenting getting old. Well, resenting the constant reminder from everyone that I'm getting old. But mainly it's that he doesn't listen. He's so desperate to prove himself, and he takes any adjustment to his plans as an indictment on the whole idea."

Kas could see that, but he remained silent, letting Jori talk. Jori had been holding a lot in, and now he seemed desperate to get it all out.

"His ideas... there's a bunch of guys who think we should be doing more. They want more action. And Salomon gives them that, and they support him. Look, I know I'm resistant to violence. I was there. When your parents..." Jori shot Kas a sympathetic look that Kas chose to ignore. "I know it can go wrong. There's a time and a place for it, you know? But Salomon just won't listen to me. If he'd just learn from my experience rather than ignoring everything that I say..."

Jori sat again, shaking his head. "Maybe it is time for me to quit."

That got Kas's attention. The Jori he remembered was a rebel for life. He lived this cause, had given his whole life to it. Things must be bad if he was considering leaving it. Kas sighed.

"Look, we both know Sali's got a chip on his shoulder about the magic stuff. He's been trying to prove himself since he was born."

"Well, having an older brother like you can't have been easy."

Kas frowned, bristling at the implication that he was somehow to blame, and confused about the assertion that Salomon was trying to live up to him, when he hadn't even known about his magic until he was ten.

"Anyway, maybe try praising him. When you're in public, throw the kudos his way and when you're in private, try to steer him right. I'm sure if you got him to temper his missions and then told everyone what a great success they were, he'd come 'round."

Jori leaned forward, rubbing his face in his hands. "There's a reason I didn't have kids," he muttered before looking at Kas again. "I did try that at the beginning. He found it patronising, and frankly, I don't have the time to coddle his emotions. I'm running a rebellion here."

"Are you?" asked Kas, and Jori flinched. "Look, I'm just saying they seem to be listening to him, so if you want to keep the rebellion on track, you're going to have to work with him. At least for a while."

Jori raised an eyebrow. "What does that mean?"

"Well, it's just that I'm back now. I can take care of him

again, or," Kas mentally corrected himself. It was hard to remember his brother was grown now. Could take care of himself. "We'll take care of each other. With both of us working, we can get a place of our own. He doesn't need to stay here anymore."

Jori stared at Kas like the younger man was a dreamer. "You think he *wants* to leave? And just what job are you going to get with that around your neck?" He nodded at the collar.

"We'll figure it out. Sali says he might know someone who can help."

Jori grunted in a way that told Kas he didn't believe him. "Does he now?"

They lapsed into their own thoughts, and Kas felt Jori would probably leave the movement before he tried to manage Salomon. It was sad. They'd probably actually make a good team if they could work together.

"You said you needed me for this mission. Why? And don't give me that line about my strength."

"Your strength is a factor," said Jori. "But yeah, it's not the only reason I want you. You've been to the camps. You know what it's like. Some of these guys," he said, waving at the door, "they don't get it. They think it's a game. They don't understand the consequences."

Something clicked in Kas's head. "You want me because I'm expendable."

Jori had the grace to look embarrassed. "I want you because you'll fight to avoid going back to the camps. And because you can climb—the best way in is the roof. But yeah. There's not a great chance of success and I can't risk my men on it."

Kas exhaled angrily. "Why does this sound familiar?" he muttered.

"Derrek's in the tower at the south gate."

Kas sat back in his chair, wrong-footed by the information. He'd thought Derrek would be in one of the holding cells at the north gate. That was where they normally put people awaiting trial because anyone breaking out, or looking to break someone out, would need to pass through Hightown, and the type of people involved in jailbreaks tended to stand out in the upper class district.

South gate was where they held the prisoners sentenced to the camps. It was more solid and tightly guarded, since once you were headed for the camps, you were revenue for the nobles. If Derrek was there, then they'd already decided his fate, and it was unlikely the rebels would be able to free him.

"You'd probably have better luck attacking his convoy," said Kas.

"There's not going to be a convoy," Jori said darkly. "They've seen him at raids before. Derrek's going to swing."

CHAPTER NINETEEN

TIA

Tɪᴀ ɢʟᴀʀᴇᴅ ᴀᴛ ᴛʜᴇ ᴅᴏᴏʀ. One way in and one way out. It looked feeble. Old planks cobbled together to make a covering to protect the witch doctor's supplies. Supplies she had already smashed in anger. She knew he'd taken anything of value from his underground storage before it became her prison. And she'd been careful to hide anything that might come in handy later. But, unable to smash the door open despite its appearance, she'd laid waste to the dark, dirty hole she was trapped in.

Now it smelled funky, and Tia hoped she hadn't unleashed anything that would harm her. She moved closer to the door. It didn't meet properly in the middle. Likely because the craftsmen hadn't wanted to help Valto Hipolit and he'd been forced to make his own door.

No one liked Valto. She could tell from the looks the tribe's people had cast his way as his lackeys hurried her through the village to his personal storage area. Though he must have some support, or he'd have had to imprison her himself. And Tia knew that altercation would have gone very differently.

The only upshot was that Mira had escaped in the ruckus. Obviously Valto and his men were focussed on her, but Tia had seen at least one swipe at Mira, trying to prevent her from leaving. But Mira had moved swiftly and been gone in a flash.

Tia slammed her hand futilely against the door. For something so shoddily made, it was remarkably resilient. Spelled, most likely. She returned to pacing the small, dank space. It almost made her miss the camps. At least there she'd been out in the air and had something to do, even if the manual labour had been rough. She kicked out at the remnant of a chair she'd smashed earlier.

How had she managed to be caught again? And so soon after her escape? It felt so unfair that her brush with freedom had been so brief. Tia blinked angrily at the tears that threatened. There'd been a sense of overwhelm at the enormity of her freedom, but she certainly wouldn't have sought to deal with that by finding herself another cage.

Tia's chest ached and she returned to her pacing, hoping the movement would sooth or at least distract. It hurt that it was her own people who'd done this to her. It was one thing for the Empire to enslave her for all those years, but for her own family to lock her up, knowing what she'd been through...

Not family, she corrected herself. She used to think of the tribe as her family, but that felt like a child's fantasy now. Her family was her brother and sister, and maybe the people loyal to the old ways. Certainly not anyone who followed the witch doctor. And certainly not anyone who would imprison her on his orders.

Valto used to have a level of respect. Tia could remember the deferential tones used to speak about and to the witch doctor when she was little. But now that she was older, she recognised the respect had been for the position, not the man himself.

Tia's head shot up. Noises from outside. She crossed the space in a couple of strides and pressed her face to the door, straining with her right eye to try to make out something. Anything. But she couldn't. She rested her forehead against the wood, taking the opportunity to breathe in the fresh outside air. And then she hit the door again with both hands in frustration.

"Now, now," came Valto's patronising voice from outside. Tia felt her stomach turn just hearing it. "I'm told you've been making quite a racket. Which seems strange to me. I would imagine that someone in your... predicament, wouldn't so readily try to attract the attention of the Empire soldiers."

Tia flinched and closed her eyes. She'd largely forgotten about the soldiers in her desire to cause as much damage to anything Valto might want or need. How could she have been so foolish? If they came to investigate the noises, she was as good as dead.

"I'd like to see you while we chat," Valto's drawl slid through the gap in the wood. "So be a dear and back up. If I feel I'm in the slightest bit of danger when I open the door, I might scream, and then the soldiers will come."

Tia had no desire to be anywhere near Valto and so moved to the back wall. The door creaked open, blinding her with the sudden light. Then it was gone, but a softer light remained. Valto set a lamp in an alcove dug into the wall and looked around at the damage.

Tia watched him and could see that the damage she'd caused bothered him. Good. But the witch doctor kept his face passive and merely tutted.

"So much damage. So much rage. And even after I fixed that arm for you."

Tia rubbed her arm at the reference, suddenly feeling as if her limb was tainted and needed to be cut off.

"I could give you a potion for anger. Something to calm you down."

"I don't want anything from you," Tia spat.

Valto smiled. "I can only imagine the lies your fellow Kikachi prisoners told you in those camps."

Tia glared at the older man, her face caught between a sneer and a snarl. His voice managed to both patronise and sound sleazy. One of the other female prisoners had told her stories that made Tia uncomfortable about being shut in such a small space with the man, but she'd refused to go into much detail. Tia's mind had filled in the blanks, and her skin crawled.

"But I was not involved in the massacre. That was the Empire. Our common enemy. I did not ask for them to place the burden of leadership on my shoulders after your mother died. But I did not want another to have to suffer in my place, and so I did not fight them."

Tia dug her fingernails into her palms, trying to create enough pain to distract herself. She hadn't even been born the last time the Empire tried to annex the other civilisations in the southern lands. And at first, the Kikachi thought it would be like last time—largely impotent.

But this time, the Empire forced the satellite villagers to move to the capitol. They wanted everyone in one location so they could use fewer soldiers to guard them. When the Kikachi fought back, the Empire imposed their Testing upon them, collaring anyone deemed to be a 'tier three magical' which the Kikachi quickly discovered were the powerful shapeshifters. Those who usually shifted into a powerful animal form, such as lions or stags.

Though the Empire felt they were offering an olive branch by allowing collared Kikachi who toed the line to remain in the tribe, taking away their magic was too painful to be tolerated. And besides, the Kikachi might have been secluded in their forest, but even they knew the main reason all collared Kikachi weren't sent to the camps was because of the risk of overpopulating them, not out of a misplaced sense of kindness for their people.

The tribe had tried to hide their children, sending anyone they could to a secret village, hoping to save as many warrior magicals as possible. But Valto had given them up. He'd told the Empire soldiers who was running the rebellion, and the soldiers found them. And slaughtered them.

Tia's mother, the Matriarch, and her warriors had attacked the soldiers in response, but had quickly been killed. The soldiers had carried off her children and told the tribe they were dead. Valto was then put in charge, and everything had festered.

"You're a coward," Tia spat.

"I'm a leader and a realist. What good would it have done anyone for me to die too? For more of the tribe to die? I had overheard some of the soldiers talking. There was a push to collar us all and force us into the camps. We would have died out."

"You sought to save yourself and improve your position. You're a coward and a fraud."

Tia saw a glint in Valto's eyes, her words striking a nerve, but he waved her away as if they meant nothing to him.

"Your anger is understandable. But I'm not here to talk about that. What I want to know is what happened to you and your siblings after the Matriarch's murder. They told us you were all dead." His snake eyes slid over Tia's body, meeting her glare with mere curiosity. "Imagine my surprise when the Empire soldiers who assist the village told me of a recent escape. And one prisoner sounded an awful lot like Angelique's littlest pet."

"Don't you *dare* say her name," Tia spat.

The satisfied smile on Valto's lips aggravated Tia to the point she felt her feet shift in the dirt, ready to pounce on him. But he wasn't worth being sent back to the camps. Or getting killed. She forced herself to look closer. To see beyond the sleaze that oozed from his every pore.

Behind the smug smile and curiosity were fear and anger. A satisfied smile curved her lips. That was what he was worried about. A challenge to his authority. Her half-siblings were one thing, but a full-blooded descendant of the last Matriarch? That was a symbol for people to rally behind.

"So defensive of her, even now," said Valto, a cruel smile playing on his lips. "Despite the lies."

Lies?

Tia tried not to bite. Clearly Valto was trying to get her off balance. Likely trying to pique her curiosity so that she would tell him whatever he wanted in exchange. But still... she couldn't help but wonder what he meant.

"I'm not telling you anything," Tia said, trying not to sound petulant.

"Pencurcero," Valto muttered.

Pain, a kind Tia had never experienced, lanced through her body. All she could do was gasp as she collapsed, her mind going blank but for the white-hot agony. And then, just as suddenly, it was gone.

Tia's muscles ached as she pushed herself to her feet, clocking Valto wiping the potion that powered his spell from his hands. It was forbidden to use the dark magics on members of the tribe. Kikachi knew of spells that could harm people, even kill them. But they were reserved for battle.

Or at least, that was the old way. It seemed Valto was comfortable using any power he could find to retain what little the soldiers had given him.

"Let's try again, shall we?"

Tia did a quick calculation. He couldn't have much of the potion required. They never kept much in stock, as it was so difficult to make. Though again, she hadn't been here in years. Maybe Valto had shelves of the stuff. But he clearly didn't have a lot with him now, so there was a limit to the torture he could inflict. At least on this occasion.

But was it worth the pain to keep the information from him? What could he really do with it?

"I want to see my siblings," she said. Tia doubted Valto would entertain such a thing. But he might accidentally confirm they were alive. That they were safe.

"Oh yes, your *siblings*," Valto sneered, his eyes narrowing. "You don't really think that's going to happen, do you? That I would allow you to conspire with Aurora and Fabian? Allow them to recruit you to their little rebellion?"

Tia's heart swelled with relief at hearing her siblings were alive, but she carefully kept her expression neutral. And they were fighting back!

Something clicked in her mind. Valto wasn't worried about her assisting the rebellion. Aurora and Fabian, as her mother's Chosen's children, were as much the children of the Matriarch as she was. At least, that had been the way when she was young. But the people should follow them as much as they would follow Tia.

No, Valto wasn't worried about the Kikachi threatening his power. He was worried about the Empire. It was the Empire who would look upon her as the heir to her mother's position. Perhaps, if there was unrest in the village, he worried that the Empire would hand her the leadership, thinking it might settle everyone.

She subconsciously touched her collar. Surely Valto must know the soldiers would likely kill her before they even realised who she was to the Kikachi? That they'd never let an escaped prisoner rule. Unless... a ray of hope flared in her gut. Unless they were willing to forgive her escape in exchange for her fealty.

The hope fizzled out. She couldn't become a traitor to her people. Even if it meant forgiveness from the Empire and getting rid of Valto. Her people would expect her to fight the annexation. And the minute she looked like she was doing that, she'd be back at the camps or dead.

Tia's attention was caught by Valto pulling a small vial out of his robes. He swirled it at her. Whatever potion he'd used to cause her so much pain.

"You were about to tell me what became of Angelique's children?"

Tia didn't want to tell Valto that she was the last of the line. He would relax, knowing that the only threat to his rule was currently detained in his cellar. But was there harm in telling him the rest? That they'd been taken to the City Druids and used for cruel experiments? What would he do with such information?

And what would she say about what happened next? Lying that they'd all been sent to the camps was akin to admitting they were dead. And if she claimed they'd escaped, the question became why they'd failed to return. Either way, Valto would be happy knowing no other threats were likely to show up out of the blue.

Tia had all but decided to tell Valto when she closed her mouth again.

What worth did she have beyond that information? Once he'd confirmed that Tia was, in fact, the biggest threat to his position, the smartest thing for him to do would be to have her killed. In handing her over to the soldiers, he would manage to expunge a challenger and ingratiate himself with the Empire.

Her eyes hardened and Valto's thin lips spread into a leer. And Tia knew he had been hoping she would refuse to answer. She opened her mouth to tell the witch doctor exactly what she thought of him, but before a sound could be made, she was again on the floor, writhing in pain.

CHAPTER TWENTY

KAS

Kas tried to celebrate with Sali and his rebel friends, but the conversation with Jori had left a sour taste in his mouth. He stood by his decision. And he believed what he had told Jori—that there were plenty of rebels who could break Derrek out just as well as Kas could. He appreciated what Derrek had done in enabling his escape, but it hadn't been for him. And it might be harsh, but Derrek just wasn't worth risking everything for. Not when Kas had just been reunited with Sali.

Sali was in great spirits. Kas turning Jori down, coupled with the fact that Kas hadn't been selected for his talents after all had buoyed Sali significantly, and he was holding court at the head of one of the long tables. Kas had sat by his side most of the night, but having secured his latest drink, he now took a seat farther down the table.

He was trying desperately to hold on to that feeling he'd had when he first saw Sali again. When they'd hugged and looked at each other with unadulterated joy. But if that feeling was a beautiful pond, resentment was slowly polluting the waters.

Kas could feel it happening, but his attempts to stop it

were futile. He'd had enough of Sali's antics. His brother was showing off, and the couple of mugs of ale he'd had weren't helping. Maybe it was just that Kas's tolerance for what he felt was juvenile behaviour had been frayed by his time in the camps, where he'd had to grow up so fast.

He felt his dream slipping through his fingers. All he'd wanted in the camps was to be home with his brother. But the rebel warehouse wasn't the home he'd wanted. And it was like he didn't even know his brother at all.

He had to do something about his collar. He was free of the camps, but in just a few short hours, it had become glaringly obvious that he could have no life while it was clamped around his neck. He would get the collar off and then things would be better. He would show Sali that they could have a normal life, away from the rebels and conflict. And when Sali could relax, when he didn't feel like he had to do everything by himself, then he'd return to the brother Kas knew.

He glanced over, attention grabbed by a particularly loud bout of laughter. Sali was imitating someone Kas didn't know as part of a joke he didn't get. Sali got louder and Kas tried to stem the feeling of dislike growing inside.

It was insecurity causing Sali to act this way. He was insecure with his big brother back, and it hadn't helped that Jori had played into that. It also didn't help that there were a constant stream of people genuinely happy to see Kas. It had made things worse when each person approached the table, greeting Sali in a friendly manner, then becoming animated at seeing Kas. Couldn't Sali understand that they seemed happier to see Kas because they hadn't seen him in so long?

For Kas's part, he'd focussed on keeping a smile plastered on his face. It was a lot to see so many people after so long. And he'd be lying if he said he was happy to see that so many people he'd known as a child had joined the rebels.

Still, the legions of people coming to see Kas and being openly thrilled to have him back had only increased Sali's jibes. Subtle at first, his jokes and comments were progressively derogatory to Kas. They all stung, but the pointed remarks about getting caught were really pissing Kas off. Still, he knew it was unintentional. Right?

"Hey," Adeline said breathily as she sat on his right.

"Hey," Kas smiled, happy for the distraction. Sali was still talking loudly to his left, and he blocked his little brother out as he focussed on his friend. "How's it going?"

"Good. Well," she hesitated, looking serious for a moment. "I spoke to Micah."

"Micah?"

"My fiancé." Adeline looked at Kas with a frown.

"Oh! Congratulations." He took a swig from his mug, trying not to be distracted by another obnoxiously loud bout of laughter from the other end of the table.

"No, I—" Adeline's frown increased as she stared at Kas. "I guess I didn't tell you before."

"No, though we didn't really get to talk much then. But tell me now. What's he like?"

Try as he might, Kas's irritation was like an itch, and his focus kept slipping back to Sali's voice, telling yet another rendition of the same story he loved from their childhood where Kas had messed up and been embarrassed. By this stage, the story bore little resemblance to what actually happened, and Kas was being portrayed as a hapless oaf with barely a brain cell between his ears. So focussed was Kas on ignoring the story and listening to Adeline that he completely missed the look of hurt and confusion on her face.

"He's a jackass, to be honest," Adeline said distractedly.

"But look, when we met before, you were saying about dreaming we were together..."

"Yeah." Kas brightened, really looking at Adeline now. She lit up in response. "Thinking of everything and everyone back here was really what kept me going, you know?"

Adeline nodded, but her smile dimmed.

"I missed hanging out with you, and Patty and Amos. And the whole crew. Who now all seem to be here." Kas's smile slipped, but not as far as Adeline's.

"Of course," she said, staring at the table. "But you mentioned us living together..."

"Yeah!" Kas's smile lit up again, but this time Adeline's didn't match his. "I used to think about that when we were little. You know, before I knew what marriage really meant. I figured our parents were friends like we were." He laughed, and Adeline managed a strained smile. "I used to think about that old dream a lot in the camps. Especially when things were rough. All I wanted was my best friend. I had Tia, of course, and Ossi. You'll like Tia, she's... well. She's amazing, really."

Kas smiled dopily at Adeline and she downed her tankard, replacing it heavily on the table and muttering, "Shit."

"Are you okay?" asked Kas.

"No. Yes. No. It's just—are you going to finish that?" Adeline pointed to Kas's mug. He shook his head, and she grabbed it, drinking half and sighing heavily.

"Addy—"

"It's fine," she lied. "It's nothing."

"Is it this Micah?" Kas asked, becoming concerned.

Adeline gave a rueful laugh. "Oh yes. More than you know." She closed her eyes as if fighting back tears.

"Addy, if he's hurting you..." Kas put a hand on her arm.

"No, no, nothing like that. Let's not ruin the night talking about him. You're back! We should be celebrating."

"Yeah." Kas smiled at her before cringing as Sali's voice rose and he was reminded of his little brother's antics. "Though maybe we've had enough celebrating for one night."

"What's up?" Adeline asked, brow furrowed.

"Oh, it's just Sali. He's insecure about me being back."

Adeline smiled supportively. "He's always been insecure about you, you know that."

"I do. It's me, I know it is. I'm tired and I probably have a shorter fuse now than I used to."

"Understandably," said Adeline.

"I just don't know how much more I can take. I was so looking forward to being home and back with Sali. And I know he's happy to see me, but it's like there's a part of him that liked me being away."

Adeline took a swig from the mug and swallowed. "I mean, I think there's probably some truth to that. Not in a bad way," she added quickly at the scowl on Kas's face. "I mean, he absolutely hated that you were in the camps. For years he was bothering Jori about trying to break you out. And I know for a fact he missed you terribly. But he also feels like he's in your shadow when you're together."

"I don't—"

"It's not anything you're doing," Adeline stopped Kas, her hands raised as if in surrender. "It's all on him. And I think he knows it's all him. That's why he's getting like... that. He's insecure about you being back, and he's frustrated with himself for feeling like that and not just being happy about it."

Kas grabbed his mug back from Adeline and took a swig before giving it back to her. She was right. He knew she was right. But he couldn't shake his irritation and resentment. It was probably best he went to bed before he said something he regretted. But he wanted to spend a little more time with Adeline. Besides Sali, she was who he'd missed the most.

"It's good to be back," he said with the air of changing the subject.

"What do you think you'll do?" she asked.

"I don't know. It's going to be hard doing anything with this around my neck." He tapped the collar in frustration. "I'm not sure how to get it off, but I'll find a way somehow. I'd love to settle down. This kind of life is not for me." He gestured around the warehouse.

"No, you were never keen on the rebels."

"I just want something simple. Maybe a house and a family. If I can find the right woman." He thought again of Tia.

Adeline downed the rest of the ale. "I need another," she announced, standing suddenly. "I'll be back."

Kas watched in confusion as Adeline abruptly left, winding her way to the bar. She seemed in an odd mood. Though, Kas reminded himself, so much time had passed. Did he really know her anymore? He certainly didn't seem to know his little brother.

Kas's mood soured further, caught in the unfairness of it all. His dream had fuelled him in the camps, letting him put one foot in front of the other and endure. The idea of coming home had helped him survive. But in his dream, everyone was beside themselves with happiness to see him, weeping and hugging him. And, he realised guiltily, in his dream they were all also as enamoured with his idea of a simple life as he was.

Had he not expected them to move on? Did he really think they wouldn't make lives for themselves in his absence? Or had he been expecting them to drop everything they'd built—all that they'd worked for—the minute he strode back into their lives?

Kas pulled at his collar in irritation. Even if his unrealistic expectations were not so, he couldn't very well expect them to gamble their lives on a man with a collar. What if he was caught?

Kas pushed up from the table, thinking to get another drink, but instead wandered over towards the cots. More ale was not going to help him, but sleep might.

Finding an empty cot, Kas fell heavily into it, tossing and turning and trying to get comfortable. He was exhausted, and it was hard to believe that when he had woken up that day, he'd been in the camps. So much had happened since then.

The cot wasn't much, but for Kas it was luxuriously soft. He'd spent so long dreaming of a proper bed, but now that he was in one, sleep proved elusive. His mind kept returning to his broken dream.

But maybe it wasn't broken. At least, not beyond repair. He had been unreasonable, expecting his brother to abandon everything he'd built for himself. Kas would meet him halfway. Perhaps if Sali could see that Kas saw him as an equal—not simply his little brother—then he might realise he didn't need the rebels anymore.

And that meant finding a way to get the collar off. If Sali could ask around like he'd said, find someone who could help them... but Jori's dismissive grunt kept echoing in Kas's mind. Kas shook the doubt away. Sali wouldn't have said there might be a way if there wasn't.

Kas turned over, feeling more relaxed now. He'd talk to Sali tomorrow. Ask what he might be able to do to help around the warehouse. Show he was willing to pull his weight, and that he didn't completely hate the rebels. Or at least, didn't hate what his brother had made for himself. And then they'd look into getting rid of the collar.

Together.

CHAPTER TWENTY-ONE

KAS

THE NEXT FEW days were some of the most frustrating of Kas's life—notwithstanding the eight years he'd spent in the labour camps. His offers of assistance were met with placating smiles from his younger brother, and when he insisted he could be useful, Sali had patted his arm and asked him to inventory the supplies.

Kas had jumped into the task, desperate to show Sali that he was willing to work. Willing to meet him where he was at. That they could be a team again. But he received enough comments from rebels passing by with curious looks that he knew Sali had just given him busywork to keep him out of the way.

Sali himself wasn't around much. In fact, it had been a couple of days since Kas had seen him. The last time he spoke to his little brother, he'd pressed him again about the collar, and Sali had again responded that they'd get to it. That he had a couple of things to sort out first, and then he'd make some enquiries.

Sali had actually laughed when Kas offered to make the enquiries himself. Pointing to his collar, Sali had suggested that Kas spend his time in the warehouse relaxing. Kas could tell Sali was passing off his reaction as thinking Kas should recover from his incarceration rather than a reminder that with that thin band of metal, Kas was basically useless.

Adeline hadn't been back either, and Kas was feeling cooped up and lonely. He missed his friends, and his mind drifted to them often, wondering what they were doing and jealously imagining them enjoying their freedom when he'd seemingly swapped one cage for another. At least in the camps he'd been out in the fresh air. And doing something.

The fact that he was ostensibly free made his restrictions worse. No one was keeping Kas in the warehouse but him. Several times he thought to leave. To go and find Ossi, or Tia and Mira. But each time, he let the idea go. Sali would have to return soon. And then Kas would make him focus on getting the collar off.

But Sali didn't come back. Worried that Sali had been hurt, Kas even went to ask Jori where he was. Jori hadn't spoken to Kas since Kas turned him down. But the older man did glare at him whenever their eyes met. Jori didn't know where Sali was, but he would know if something had gone wrong, and so Kas stopped worrying and went back to being frustrated. He almost considered telling Jori he'd do the mission. Partially to see if that loosened the man's lips about where his brother was, but mainly for something to do.

But it would be just his luck that his brother would return while Kas was out on the mission, and feel betrayed. A break in the monotony wasn't worth the risk of capture, and it certainly wasn't worth rupturing his relationship with his brother.

Kas was grumpily washing the dishes in the small kitchen, running through all the arguments and pleas he'd use to get his brother to spend some time on the issue of his collar, when he heard a commotion.

He stuck his head out the door, and a grin broke out across his face. Sali was back. The rebels were gathered around him and his team, peppering them with questions about how whatever mission they'd been on had gone.

Kas wiped his hands on his apron, but before he could join them, Sali raised his hands and told the crowd that he and his men needed to clean up and eat something. Everyone rushed to get out of their way, several people hurrying off to prepare the baths, several others pushing past him into the kitchen to make some food.

Several hours later, Kas was drumming his fingers on his own tankard of ale. A dark mood had settled over him. He'd tried to get a minute to talk to his brother, but it had proved impossible. So he'd taken a seat, sure Sali would come out of his room soon, but minutes turned to hours, and Kas stewed in his irritation.

Finally Sali exited the room he shared with Jori and headed for the bar. Kas jumped up as if spring-loaded. He'd barely taken two steps toward Sali when his little brother raised his hands as if warding off an attack.

"Tomorrow brother, please?" Sali said, a gentle smile on his face. "I'm too tired to think clearly."

It seemed reasonable, as Sali was no doubt tired from his mission, and though Kas agreed, his disappointment was palpable. Sali threw an arm around Kas's shoulders.

"Ah, forgive me, brother. I know how important it is. But that's why we need to do it right. I can't risk asking the wrong person, you know? What if someone were to tell the guards that I was asking around for a way to get a collar off? It can't have escaped their attention that you've escaped and we're brothers."

Kas nodded. It made sense. Though, another thought

popped into his head. "Why don't the guards raid this place?" he asked. "I mean, I've been gone eight years and found out where you were based within an hour of my return."

Sali laughed. "You'd think they'd be all over us! But I have a few well-placed friends, big brother. They make sure we're not inconvenienced."

"They never come here?" Kas didn't doubt his brother had useful contacts, but unless he had the entire leadership of the guard in his pocket, someone must be asking questions.

"Oh, they do," said Sali, leaving Kas at a seat along the side of the table as he headed for his seat at the head. "But we get fair warning, and there's nothing suspicious here when they turn up."

Kas sat heavily, feeling dismissed. He knew it was his own frustrations making him feel that way. Even so, as those dark clouds descended again, Kas felt very much as if the world had moved on without him, and now he had no place in it.

It didn't help that Sali launched immediately into regaling everyone with tales from the mission he'd just returned from. As his little brother gleefully detailed killing Empire soldiers, even those they probably could have snuck past, Kas's mood darkened further, and now, as he returned to drumming his fingers, Kas wondered if the boy he'd known eight years ago was gone for good.

And if this was the man Sali had become, well... Kas wasn't sure he even liked him at all.

Sali began regaling his men with how he'd managed to extract information from a guard they'd captured, and Kas decided he'd had enough. He stood and walked towards the bar, looking around hopefully for Adeline, but she wasn't there. He scanned the rebels, looking for Patty or Amos, thinking maybe they could get word to her and ask her to swing by.

He couldn't see them, and his feelings of impotence increased. He couldn't even send a message to ask a friend to hang out with him. Kas placed his tankard on the bar and tried to catch the bartender's eye, but he was busy. Irrationally, this just made Kas feel even worse. Now he was invisible, too. A bitter laugh escaped his lips. Several times a day, he made bargains in his head with the gods, offering anything to be able to become invisible again. Perhaps the gods had a cruel sense of humour.

What is wrong with me?

Kas left his tankard and wandered into the warehouse area, finding a cool and deserted spot and sitting on a crate of crowbars. Three hundred and sixty-four crowbars, to be exact. Who even needed that many crowbars? Was there a large market for them?

Kas exhaled loudly, trying to rid himself of his frustration. He felt lost, and he felt trapped. And worst of all, he felt alone. It wasn't Sali's fault. Not really. His brother had made a life for himself, and Kas couldn't begrudge him for it. He was annoyed that Sali wasn't putting in more effort to help him with his collar, but really, that was Kas's problem.

And all Kas had done to rid himself of it was to sit here for almost a week. Kas closed his eyes, realisation dawning. He couldn't stay here. Not anymore. If Sali really had someone who could help him, surely he would have done something by now. Or at least made some progress towards making contact with them.

Irritation flared within him. Why would Sali lie to him? He knew how important it was to get Kas's collar off. He'd said it himself. Kas tried to tell himself that Sali had lied to him to keep him there. To keep him close so they could rebuild their relationship.

But it felt hollow. You didn't make someone a virtual prisoner and then leave for days on end if you wanted to spend time with them.

Kas stood and began walking back towards the rebels. He'd done enough work in the kitchen over the last few days that he'd surely earned some provisions. And his brother wouldn't begrudge him a weapon. He'd speak with them tomorrow, gather his supplies, and set out for the Troll settlement when evening fell. Despite his mood, Kas's heart felt lighter at the thought of seeing Ossi again soon.

"There you are."

Kas turned at hearing his brother's voice, hope immediately flaring in his chest. Sali had left his audience to find him. Maybe he realised how Kas felt. Maybe he'd made contact with someone about the collar.

"Here I am," said Kas, plastering a smile on his face. "Did you need something, brother?"

Sali looked around. "I noticed you slipped away. I thought maybe you were with Adeline."

"She's not here," said Kas, his mood plummeting. Sali sounded annoyed.

"You left before I got to the good bit," Sali said, looking around as if he'd bumped into Kas on his way to finding someone else, and hadn't sought him out. "But then I realised it might be hard for you to hear about the missions. Since you can't do any and all."

Kas bit back his reply. He'd noticed his brother was meaner when he drank. Kas had just decided to deflect and extract himself when Sali barrelled on.

"So I thought maybe you'd gone to console yourself with Addy. She still likes you."

Four little words, and somehow Sali had made the sentence sound insulting to both Kas and Adeline. Why would anyone want Kas as he was now, and Adeline must be less than for wanting him all the same.

"We're friends, little brother. We've always been friends." Kas's anger bubbled, and though he knew he should just walk away, he'd had it with Sali's needling. Especially when he'd abandoned Kas. Especially when he seemed to have time to insult him, but no time to help him free himself of his collar.

Tired as he was, Kas cast around for a barb to hit back with and settled on the one thing that had bothered him since he'd arrived.

Besides Adeline, he'd only seen a handful of women in the rebel headquarters, and they'd only turned up in the evening, arriving for drinks and socialising. When Kas had been growing up, there'd been lots of women in the rebellion. Now it appeared there were none. Had they all just gotten tired of it? Or had they been kicked out for some reason?

"Why don't you come back over?" Sali said, his tone as if he were the most benevolent man in the room. "I was just about to tell the boys about—"

"Why is it 'the boys'?" Kas asked, his voice angrier than he'd intended.

"What do you mean?" Sali frowned.

"I mean this literal boys' club." He gestured wildly, as if he were the patron saint of gender equality. "Can women not join the rebellion anymore?"

Sali frowned as if it hadn't even occurred to him that there were no women in his movement. "I dunno. I can ask Jori..." he trailed off. "And if it's bothering you, I'll make sure we do something about it."

Kas immediately felt bad, despite Sali's behaviour. He was the older brother. His father had always told him to rise above. Getting down in the dirt with Sali trapped them both there, but if Kas took the high road, it gave Sali a chance to join him.

The guilt immediately disappeared when Sali muttered, "Heavens forbid *our* organisation somehow offends the great Kas—"

"That's enough," Kas snapped. "Give it a break, alright? I know you feel like everyone's comparing you to me, but they're not, and you need to get over it."

Sali looked like Kas had slapped him across the face. A little voice in the back of Kas's head told him to stop. He ignored it.

"And even if they are, that's not my fault. Don't take it out on me, okay? If you think people think I'm better than you, do something about it. Don't just try to bring me down to your level."

Kas knew that he'd gone too far, even as it left his mouth. But Sali would yell back and the fight would carry them away from that comment. Except Sali didn't. He just stood there, staring at his older brother.

Conflicted, and unsure that any apology he attempted wouldn't just make things worse, Kas turned and walked away to find his bunk. He felt bad about what he'd said. Or at least the way he'd said it. But he still felt justified in being upset about how Sali had treated him. Hadn't he been in the labour camps for eight years for these people? And he hadn't even been home a week.

Kas threw himself onto his cot, expecting Sali to have followed him, and feeling worse and worse when his brother failed to appear.

He kept running over the argument with Sali. He came up with several different ways he could have handled that situation. In some of his scenarios, imaginary Sali realised what he'd been doing, apologised, and everything was fine.

In others, Sali denied it, and Kas articulately laid out

what Sali had been doing, arguing with him when he denied it, and providing more and more examples. Kas dwelled the longest on these imaginings, even though all they did was drive him further from sleep.

<hr>

When Kas jolted awake the next morning, he couldn't remember falling asleep the previous evening. He remembered the fight, and obsessing about it. But he'd never actively thought to put that aside and get some sleep, which meant he probably fell asleep mid-internal rant.

He didn't feel rested and cursed himself for getting so worked up over something so minor. Especially when the true source of his anger was at Sali for abandoning him.

Either way, he shouldn't have had it out with Sali when they were both tired and under the influence. He should have left it for this morning, but he knew deep down that if he'd left it, he wouldn't have had the heart to raise it in the cool light of day. He didn't trust himself to explain how he felt without Sali taking it as an accusation, and so he probably would have just left it and instead asked for his supplies.

Kas wasn't sure that would necessarily have been a bad thing.

Now, as it was, he'd need to go find his brother and apologise. The resentment festering inside woke up at that. Why was he always the one to apologise? Especially with how Sali had been treating him. His parents had told him it was 'because he was older' but such reasoning would condemn him to always apologise, no matter which brother was in the wrong.

Still. He loved Sali. He'd missed him terribly when he was away. And, he reminded himself, it couldn't be easy to always come second. It had been rare, growing up, for there to be something for Sali to try that didn't already come with a standard set by Kas having tried it first.

Kas paused as he washed his face. He'd never really thought about it like that. When he'd had a go at different things, there was little pressure. His parents encouraged him to try, but there was no pressure to achieve anything. But Sali would never have had that. Even with his parents delivering the same message, Sali had been aware that Kas had been good at this or that, or scored this or achieved that. That couldn't have been easy.

Kas finished washing and resolved to find his brother and apologise. He'd ask once more about the collar, and then, if Sali again put it off, he'd let his brother know he was leaving for a while.

The antics of last night seemed petty now. He'd been separated from his little brother for eight years, had thought he'd never see him again, and having been given the unexpected gift of reunion, the first thing he'd done was fight with him. Kas felt deeply ashamed.

"Hey, Kas."

Sali's voice turned him and Kas saw that his brother looked as if he'd slept as well as Kas had.

"Hi Sali," said Kas.

"Salomon," his brother automatically corrected him.

"Sorry—Salomon."

"I wanted to apologise, Kas. I was a jerk last night. I was proud of the mission and I was hurt that you left when I was telling everyone about it."

"I didn't—"

"Please," Salomon interrupted, "let me finish. I was a jerk—expecting you to sit there and listen to my adventures when you've been cooped up in here. And you've barely returned and I've been gone for most of the time you've been back. You must think I'm not happy to see you, but I am. It's a gift you've come back to us. I was a jerk. A total jerk. I missed you, big brother. And I'm so glad you're back. I'm really sorry."

Kas swept Salomon up in a bear hug, and the younger man gripped him back.

"I'm sorry too," Kas said, releasing his brother with a smile.

"I do want to ask you something," said Salomon as he led Kas to the tavern where breakfast was being served.

"Okay," said Kas, trying not to sound hesitant.

Salomon grabbed plates and heaped them with eggs and bacon and big hunks of bread that he covered in butter and honey. He waited until they were seated before continuing.

"Will you help me get Derrek back?"

Kas raised an eyebrow. He had not been expecting that. His heart had leapt, thinking Sali was going to ask Kas to go with him to talk to whoever it was that knew about the collars.

"We really do need Derrek," Salomon continued. "He's an earth mover, but he can grab the ores rather than the dirt. Makes him really good with explosives some- how." Salomon shrugged, biting off a chunk of bread and chewing it. "Plus, I feel I owe him since it was his mission that broke you out. Anyway, I'm heading out soon. Guards change in an hour. I think I can do it alone, but— don't tell Jori I said this—he was right. You'd be the best to help with the mission. I can climb, but nothing like you."

Kas shovelled eggs into his mouth, both because they were delicious and he hadn't eaten a proper breakfast in forever, and also to give himself time to think. He had not been expecting this at all. From how Salomon reacted when Kas told him what Jori had asked him to do, Kas had thought Derrek was disposable. There had certainly been no hint of it being worth risking lives to get him out.

But then Kas wondered if this wasn't Salomon's way of showing him he was sorry, rather than just telling him. Showing him that he was grateful for Kas being back, and maybe even wanting to spend some time with him. Kas could think of better bonding trips that wouldn't have them captured or killed, but maybe this was Salomon trying. Wanting to do something together.

"I..." Kas cleared his throat. "I thought maybe you were going to ask for something to do with getting my collar off."

Salomon hesitated for a beat and then closed his eyes, shaking his head. "I'm a goose. Sorry brother, I'm so tired, I forgot I hadn't told you. I've a meeting with my contact this afternoon. In fact, if you can help me with Derrek, you could bring him back and I can head straight to the meeting."

Kas blinked. He'd resigned himself to leaving. Convinced himself that Salomon had been lying and there was no contact. But now... excited as he'd felt at the idea of seeing Ossi again, his heart soared to think the simple life he'd dreamed of might be back within his grasp. And if he got his collar off, he could find his friends and help them be free too.

Sali mistook Kas's hesitation. "I completely understand if you don't want to risk it. I mean, you've only just gotten out. So if you want to stay here, that's fine. I need to go though. Derrek was on one of my missions when he was nabbed, and it's really important to me to try to get my guys back. And I want them to know I will try. I think it'd be hard to send them out on missions if I didn't try to get them back if something goes wrong."

Right then it hit Kas like a punch to the heart. It was the old Sali in front of him. His little brother who'd spent days tiptoeing around because he was terrified he was going to step on the ants and bugs on the ground. When his mother had asked Salomon what he was doing, the little boy had explained, adding, "Why should they die just because I want to go somewhere?"

In his heart, Salomon was a good person. Probably a better person than Kas.

"Alright. Let's do it. Together."

Salomon beamed. "Really? Amazing."

Kas smiled, but an ominous feeling settled over him. He dismissed it as nerves.

Salomon swallowed his last bite of breakfast. "It'll be just like old times."

CHAPTER TWENTY-TWO

KAS

"Oh, excuse me!"

"No, it was my fault. Are you—"

Kas's eyes met Adeline's, and the surprise on their faces melted into amusement.

"Kas! I didn't think you'd be out and about." Adeline cast a nervous glance around as if several city guards might spring out of nowhere and grab Kas.

"A guy can't stay cooped up all day." Kas smiled. "I haven't seen you in a while. Are you alright?"

"I am." A blush kissed her cheeks. "Just a little embarrassed. About the other day? The misunderstanding?"

The blush vanished, replaced with irritation as Kas's expression remained blank.

"Misunderstanding?" he said, mind racing, trying to pinpoint what Adeline was talking about. He had no idea, but it seemed important. "You mean…" he reached, "when you went to get a drink and didn't come back?"

Adeline stared at Kas for a beat, seemingly torn between being annoyed or relieved that he had no idea what she was referring to.

"It doesn't matter," she told him, then muttered, "just my entire life down the drain is all."

"What?" Kas asked, not hearing that last bit.

"Nothing."

Kas couldn't stand the sadness in her eyes, much less that he seemed to be the cause. "You look really pretty today," he said, pleased when her eyes twinkled again. "Hot date?"

The light dulled and the smile on Adeline's face now seemed forced, but all she said was, "Job interview."

"I thought you liked working for the Maxwells?"

"I did. I do," Adeline corrected herself quickly. "But it's for a job in the palace, so..."

"Oooh! That sounds good," said Kas.

"Yeah." Adeline perked up a little. "I mean, the pay is a little less, at least at first, but it comes with room and board."

"Time to move out of your parents' place?"

Adeline hesitated, as if wanting to say something else, but then she just said, "Yeah, I think it's time."

Kas couldn't stand that there was something wrong that Adeline wasn't telling him. When they were five, if she hurt herself or was crying, Kas would dance or tell jokes, anything to cheer her up, and he never stopped until she was laughing.

"Where are you off to in such a distracted hurry?" Adeline asked.

"Mission," Kas said. "For the rebels."

"Is that such a good idea?"

"It's to rescue the guy who ran the mission that let me escape," Kas said.

"Fair enough. Just... be careful, won't you, Kas? The rebels, it's like they've gone off course. I feel like they're more of a gang than a cause these days. Half their missions seem to be about increasing their own power rather than forcing change for the betterment of everyone."

"I know. But Salomon's doing the mission, with or without me. And he thinks it'll go better with my help, since I've climbed the south tower before, so..." He shrugged.

The uneasiness from earlier lingered. If he was honest, he really didn't want to do this mission. But he could hardly let Salomon try to carry it off on his own. He'd never live with himself if Salomon wound up in the camps, or worse, and there might have been a way for him to stop it.

Adeline frowned. "South tower? I've seen Salomon there before. He was chatting with the guards, having a right old time."

The uneasiness increased. "Probably trying to butter them up to get intel," Kas said reasonably.

"Yeah, probably," Adeline said, her tone indicating she didn't think so.

A bell sounded in the distance.

"Shit, I've got to go," said Adeline. "Look, be careful, okay?"

"Of course. Good luck with the interview. Even though you won't need it. Buy you a drink later?"

"Thanks, and yes. Though I'll buy you a drink, since you don't have any money." Adeline smiled as she set off.

"I'd better have some after this," he called after her, smiling as she waved back at him. Having plans to see Adeline later dispelled some of his uneasiness, and Kas set off in slightly better spirits. The mission would be fine. Everything was going to be okay.

Everything was not going to be okay.

Kas felt it as soon as he approached the tower. There

was nobody outside. Literally no one. No guards, but also no citizens milling around, trying to sell the guards their goods. No passersby heading from one part of the city to another.

It was too quiet.

Kas paused in the shadows and considered leaving. But he couldn't go without seeing Salomon and making sure he was safe. They had agreed to meet behind the abandoned stable, a ramshackle building barely more than a skeleton of a structure that had fallen into disuse after the south gate was blocked off.

Nothing stirred in the shadows of the stables, and Kas couldn't tell if Salomon had been and gone, or if he was running late. Kas felt paralysed. It was possible Salomon had arrived earlier, observed the odd silence and, realising something was off, left.

It was equally possible that Salomon had charged in, desperate to do the mission himself and show that he didn't need his older brother. In fact, if he had done that, it might explain the lack of life surrounding the tower.

Kas could go ahead with breaking into the tower with a view to completing the original mission, if not also rescuing Salomon as required. Or he could leave and head back to the rebels. He could get more people, perhaps have them create a distraction.

But if they did have Salomon, returning to the rebel headquarters might take too long. Kas ran a hand through his hair, cursing his collar. Without it, he could easily approach the tower and find out what was going on and what he'd be facing.

In the end, concern for Salomon won out and Kas, keeping to the shadows, approached the tower. The first window was overhead and Kas shimmied up the tower to peer in. The ground level was the guards' day room. There were tables and chairs and a large fire set into the wall, with a huge pot sitting over the flames. Several guards were sitting about, casually talking and laughing. Certainly not on edge and ready for a fight.

In the corner were two small cells where short-term prisoners were kept, but the cells were empty. Either Derrek was a concern enough to keep in the dungeon cells, or he'd already been moved.

Kas scanned the room again, preparing to jump down, when his eyes fell on Salomon. Fear stabbed his stomach seeing his little brother surrounded by all those guards. Salomon was laughing nervously, his eyes darting around. Perhaps looking for an escape.

Kas scanned the room too, but there wasn't much that looked useful for rescuing his brother. Kas could climb to the top of the tower and come in from above, as had been the plan for Derrek, but unless some of those guards left the common area, he didn't have much hope of freeing Salomon.

Kas looked at his brother again and their eyes met, Salomon's going wide. Kas gave him a nod, trying to communicate that he would get Salomon out, and he saw Salomon relax a little, his smile becoming less nervous. That little smile, so confident in his older brother, was all Kas needed to spur him into action.

Forcing himself away from the window, Kas began to climb, but he'd barely reached the top of the frame before noises sounded from below and a gruff voice called, "Better for you if you drop down now, lad."

Kas glanced down to see all the guards who had been in the common room staring up at him. They still seemed relaxed, and Kas tensed his muscles, preparing to climb the tower as fast as he could. Maybe they'd follow him and he could still drop into the tower and free his brother.

Glancing over his shoulder to see if they were likely to follow, Kas froze.

There, in the middle of the guards, completely unrestrained, was Salomon.

Kas's heart thumped even as the rest of his body refused to move. His arms began to shake and his stomach turned. He might vomit.

"Come on down, Kas. It's okay."

Salomon's voice was calm, but there was an edge there. A confidence. Whatever was going on wasn't a surprise to Salomon. Whatever was happening had been planned.

Kas pushed off the wall, landing comfortably, but allowing himself to run a few paces as if thrown by the momentum. He positioned himself as best he could with as few guards between him and the exit as possible.

"What's going on, brother?" Kas asked, willing more confidence into his voice than he felt.

"You were right." Salomon strode towards him. "All that talk about our missions. Too much conflict. And then, as if to prove your point, Derrek is captured, and I thought to myself, 'Kas is right'. We need a better solution where our people aren't in so much danger."

Kas's eyes danced over the guards, but they remained as relaxed as if Kas was already in a cell. He shifted his weight, shuffling as he did, trying to plan the best route to the exit.

"I made a deal," Salomon continued, now in front of Kas. He moved to his older brother, fussing with his collar and patting it as if dressing a child. "The empress needs more forces under her command. We need better conditions. It's a win-win."

"Better conditions for who? Everyone? Or just you?"

Salomon smiled. "Baby steps, brother. At first, it will just be the rebels. We'll have conditions similar to the city guards, and we'll work together. Once that's bedded in, we can look at the bigger issues."

He's sold out.

Alarm bells were screaming in Kas's head now. If the rebels and the guard were working together, it explained why Salomon was safe among them. But Kas wasn't a rebel. He was an escaped prisoner.

"So they let Derrek out?" Kas said as he shifted again, closer to the exit.

Salomon moved with him, alive to what Kas was doing. "Well, no," he said, affecting sorrow. "Moving forward, as a legitimate security force, we need to be seen as doing the right thing. And Derrek broke the law. So he will remain a prisoner of the Crown, as will anyone else currently in custody. But otherwise, the rebels' past misdeeds will be forgiven. Of course, it would undermine my bargaining position to allow a collared criminal to roam freely about the city. Even if he is my brother."

Kas shifted again, but this time Salomon stepped between him and the gate. Kas looked into his little brother's eyes and saw something he'd never noticed before. Resentment, bordering on hate.

"You don't have to do this," Kas said quietly, talking so only Salomon could hear him. "I'll find a way to get this collar off. You can leave the rebels. Leave this life, the dream—"

"*Your* dream," Salomon hissed, before shaking his head. "It's never going to happen, don't you get that? You have a collar that *doesn't come off*."

Kas blinked. "I'll find a way."

"There is no way! Have you ever heard of someone getting their collar off?"

"That doesn't mean it can't be done. Listen to me—"

"You *left*, brother," Salomon was angry now. "You left,

and with that thing around your neck, you may as well still be gone. I've had to find a way for myself. I can't keep waiting for you. I have to live."

"It doesn't have to be—" Kas said, but Salomon turned, signalling to the guards and walking back towards the tower.

The guards lost their relaxed posture instantly and began converging on Kas. But they were too confident. It was understandable; seven armed guards against one collared criminal. But the years of hard labour had made Kas stronger than they realised, and the fury of betrayal turned Kas into a machine.

He barrelled through the first guard, knocking the man clean off his feet. Another guard dove at Kas, but Kas stopped dead and when the guard flew in front of him, Kas punched hard, slamming him into the cobblestones. He didn't get up.

"Earth movers!" called the guard leader. "Blocks in place!"

Kas didn't wait to hear the rest of the orders. He ran, sprinting at the gate that would lead him back to the Merchants' Quarter, but as he approached, the very ground erupted, forming a solid wall in front of him. Kas turned to aim for the road leading to the slums. It was still open, but it was also behind all the guards. A ring of fire engulfed them and began pushing out, inching closer to Kas. Kas had seen this before. It was a basic guard tactic. The fire mage would protect the other guards, but if their target tried to breach it, they would burn.

Kas glanced to the steps of the tower, expecting to see Salomon watching him with that sick grin. But Salomon was yelling at the guards. The next stage of detainment was to engage the water mages. They would gain control of the very water in Kas's body, making it impossible for him to move. Killing him if deemed necessary.

Salomon was arguing with the lead guard. Apparently killing Kas wasn't the agreement. Just a return ticket to the camps.

He supposed he should be grateful for the distinction, but since the lead guard was arguing back, Kas took his opportunity. Sprinting straight at the tall, smooth wall separating the courtyard of the south tower from the slums, he kicked off it, one step, then two, as if he were running up the wall. He heard the surprise behind him, but didn't lose focus.

Reaching for the top of the wall, Kas's fingers found it, and he used his momentum and all the strength he had left to heave himself up and over. He stumbled on the other side, but didn't try to halt his momentum, instead going with it and falling into a controlled roll before leaping up and running as if his life depended on it. Which apparently it did.

Kas's mind whirled through the possibilities, and as he got deeper into the slums, his pace slowed as he tried to figure out where to go. He could head straight for the main gate. They might not have closed it yet, and if the guards there weren't expecting him, he might have a chance if he sprinted right through.

Or he could head for the east gate. The main gate was closer, and so that would be where they'd expect him to go. If he went for the east gate, he might even be able to blend in with the crowd and sneak through.

"In here, boy."

Rough but surprisingly strong hands grabbed him, pulling him into a run-down building.

"Frank—"

The rough hands clapped down on his mouth, and Kas saw Frank standing ramrod straight, listening intently. He heard the guards running through the slums, their armour and weapons clanking with each step. Then voices.

"Spread out. He can't have gone far. Ask around. They will know which way he went."

"Stay here," Frank hissed at Kas, tossing a dusty, mouldy blanket over him. Kas immediately threw the blanket off him. It was gross, and if the guards entered the building, it would hardly hide him. But even in the split second it took for Kas to do that, Frank had crossed to the door and gone outside. Kas crept to the wall, peering through a crack in the old wood.

"Old man, did you see someone running through here not too long ago?" A guard approached Frank, his eyes scanning the area.

"Oh yes." Frank nodded eagerly. The guard's eyes snapped to Frank's face. "He headed towards the gate. Running like the clappers, he was. You'll have to hurry to find him, that's for sure."

The guard made to move away, but something stopped him. He peered at Frank, his eyes narrowing. "You wouldn't be lying to me, old man?"

"No, sir," said Frank, sounding astounded at the accusation. "He went barrelling past. Almost knocked me over."

"Sir." Another guard approached the one talking to Frank. "Some people are saying he headed for the main gate, others that no one's come through here at all."

"Bloody slum scum," the guard leader muttered.

"No need for that kind of language, young man," said Frank, affecting deep offence.

The guards ignored his comment, but the one who'd questioned Frank peered at him again, thinking.

"Call in reinforcements," he ordered the other guard. "We'll search the area. Send word to the main gate to monitor who exits."

"Now just a minute—" Frank started, but the guards ignored him, the one in charge walking straight for Frank's shanty. Straight for Kas.

Frank lunged, grabbing the guard by the shoulder. "That's my house!"

The guard leader pushed Frank off him, sending him to the ground. "Do not touch me!"

The guard was taken by a fury that surprised Kas, and before he could move, the guard pulled his truncheon and began beating Frank.

The beating didn't last long. It didn't take much to subdue an old, frail man. The guard didn't check to see if Frank was alive or dead. He simply walked away, leaving him in the dust, the search seemingly forgotten.

As the guards ordered his men to hurry for the gate, Kas exited the building and hurried to Frank's side.

"Frank?"

The old man's eyes were swollen shut, blood coating his face and staining his clothes. He coughed, which Kas took as a good sign, until he saw the pink bubbles around Frank's lips.

"I'll get you help, Frank. It's going to be okay."

Kas looked around, trying to decide if it was best not to move Frank, or to risk it and carry him to the doctor. Frank coughed again, raising a battered hand to pat Kas on the chest.

"I don't need a doctor, boy," Frank wheezed. "The undertaker will do."

"Frank—"

"I'm going to die, and it's okay. I've lived long enough."

Frank made it sound like he was tucked in a comfortable bed surrounded by grandchildren, rather than bloody and beaten in the dirt of the slums. Kas choked back a sob.

"Listen to me, boy, and listen well. My name is Francisco and I am a Druid."

An old memory stirred. Kas as a boy asking Frank's name. Kas had both butchered Frank's name, resulting in the shortened version, and refused to believe that the man didn't have a last name.

"Everyone has a last name," little Kas had said obstinately.

"Do you have one?" Frank asked suspiciously.

"Of course. It's Ironstone."

"Well then." Frank had considered. "You may call me Frank Ironwood."

Kas hadn't thought about that moment since it happened. Of course, now older, he knew that Druids did not use last names. He vaguely wondered why Frank had made up a last name rather than just tell him he was a Druid.

"I didn't tell anyone I was a Druid," Frank wheezed as if reading Kas's mind. "Druids in the City of Magic are permitted to work magic for the empress and nothing else. But I am a Druid of the Veil. I needed to remain free of the palace. I had to keep close to you."

Kas blinked. Frank had been a constant in his life, especially after the death of his parents. But he hadn't really stepped into any key role. Sure, he had been there and helped Kas and Salomon where he could, but they certainly didn't have any kind of deep relationship.

"There was a vision," Frank said urgently as his voice grew weaker, his strength failing. "It told of things to come. You will play a role, but we need to get that thing off your neck. Here." His spindly fingers pressed a ring into Kas's hand. It was metal, but looked like twigs that had been woven together. "Take this to the Druids in the north. Tell them to help you. Tell them I said they should."

"I will. Thank you, Frank," Kas said, looking around for anyone to help them.

"Go—" Frank's words dissolved into wet coughing. "Use the tunnel you came into the city through. Don't worry about me. They'll catch you if you don't leave now."

The old man began coughing again, and Kas went to lift him up. He would get him to a doctor, or at least somewhere safe before he left, but Francisco pushed him off with hands surprisingly strong for an old man dying on the street.

Kas felt awful. He'd never leave anyone hurt, let alone someone who'd given him and his brother food whenever he could as they grew up. But Francisco had been clear, and he was right. Kas stood, telling himself that being sent back to the labour camps would help neither him nor Francisco, but it felt hollow. He really should get the old man to a doctor.

Voices began to fill the silence. People were starting to poke their heads back out now with the guards gone.

"Something wrong with your feet, boy?" Francisco spat, blood peppering the dirt. "Go!"

Kas left.

He left Francisco dying in the street. He left the city that had been home for so long, but now felt like an enemy. He left his little brother, who had betrayed him.

CHAPTER TWENTY-THREE

CASSANDRA

Cassandra crept towards the kitchens, hoping to find them deserted so that she could comfort eat about the day she'd had. What she mentally termed her 'dirty secret' had recently become alarmingly routine. Pausing as the hallway came to a crossroads so she could listen for any movement, she wondered that she'd never met another soul during her nighttime trysts with the cooks' amazing desserts.

Was it just that by this time everyone was in bed as normal people should be? Or had she been spotted without realising, and the staff ordered to remain hidden? The idea irked her, but she knew she was projecting the frustrations of her day.

Lords Flighty and Cuddy had been particularly patronising earlier, and worse, it was as if now her outbursts didn't even phase them. They had become so routine the nobles simply averted their eyes as if the sovereign was having an embarrassing tantrum and simply waited until she calmed down.

She half wished the staff *were* here, milling about. Cassandra fantasised about chatting with them, befriending them, and finally having normal people to talk to. People who didn't have scheme upon scheme to advance, and who weren't looking for every opportunity to seize upon her mistakes for their own gain.

But it wouldn't be like that, and she knew it deep down. The staff couldn't be themselves with her. She would bring the royal pallor to their refuge and taint it with her station. Depressed as she was by this thought, Cassandra nearly didn't hear the voices in the kitchen in time to stop herself barrelling in. She caught the door, holding it ajar, and listened.

"I mean, it really is all in a name, innit?" came a voice Cassandra recognised as Mrs Pipe, who was in charge of the palace maids.

"Don't be daft. Royalty is all about the blood." That tired voice was Mrs Cameron. She was in charge of all the palace staff, though really only got involved in hiring, firing, and wages.

"Sure, but I mean, take this one. 'Tracey' is hardly a name for a queen. Can you imagine? 'Oi, Trace! Spare us some rations.' Ridiculous."

"Actually, Tracy is my middle name—" a woman's voice Cassandra hadn't heard before piped up and was cut off.

"I don't think they actually call out the queen's *name*—" Mrs Cameron said, sounding thoughtful. "I do quite like Trish, though."

"Well, that's not her name. It's Tracey," said Mrs Pipe, drawing out the name as she wrote it down.

"Oh, actually there's no 'e' before the 'y'," said the unfamiliar voice. There was an awkward silence before the unknown woman added, "But I suppose it doesn't matter…"

"Right, now you sign here. Good. And now you can move into your room. Sheets are in the main hallway, and if there's no pillow on your bed I can find you one, but it won't be until morning, okay?"

Cassandra listened as the new woman futilely tried to ask questions while the older women extracted themselves, insisting they would explain everything in the morning. The door at the other end of the kitchen shut and Cassandra heard a sigh and the scrape of a chair being pulled out.

She peered inside and saw a pretty woman, about Cassandra's own age, sat at the table that ran the length of the kitchen, her head in her hands. Sympathy stabbed at Cassandra's heart, and upon seeing someone who appeared to feel as defeated as she did, Cassandra decided to join her.

"You look as if your day was as bad as mine," said Cassandra, slipping into the seat beside the girl and sliding her a slice of chocolate cake that Cassandra had liberated from the ice chest on the way past.

The woman looked blankly at Cassandra for a beat before horror slid over her features and she scurried to stand.

"Your Majesty," she said, trying to get up and curtsey at the same time. "I mean Grace. Your Grace? No, Majesty—"

"It's fine, please sit." Cassandra smiled, indicating to the girl to take her seat. "I didn't mean to interrupt, but I was going to eat this cake to feel better about my day, and it looked like you might need something to make up for yours." She nodded at the cake in front of the woman and took a bite of her own, closing her eyes at the hit of sweet, baked, chocolatey goodness.

The woman hesitated and then took a very small bite. The cake seemed to melt her inhibitions and terror at being found in the kitchens by the empress and she visibly relaxed.

"I didn't think empresses would have bad days," she commented quietly. The horror quickly returned to her face. "Oh my gods I'm so sorry," she said so fast it sounded like one word.

Cassandra waved her away. "That's fair. I live in a massive palace and have emotional cake on hand. I certainly have little to complain about."

The woman shoved a large bite of cake in her mouth as if as a precaution.

"Being empress does have its perks," Cassandra continued, feeling oddly at ease with this stranger, "but my father left me to continue carrying out an absolutely terrible plan. And none of the nobles listen to me. Bunch of old, crusty men," she muttered, taking another bite of cake. "Sorry, I don't even know your name," she said thickly, covering her mouth with her hand.

The woman swallowed and said, "It's Adeline, Your Majesty."

"Cassandra," said the empress. "Pleased to meet you."

Adeline's handshake was tentative but firm, and Cassandra knew she would never use her first name, but dearly wished that wasn't the case.

"So, Adeline, I've told you why *I'm* eating cake." She looked at Adeline expectantly.

Adeline sighed. "I thought the boy I'd been in love with for years had finally seen me. Really seen me. But I was wrong. Of course, I only realised he still saw me as his childhood friend *after* I dumped my fiancé and my parents had already planned on me being gone. So now I need to work here so that I have somewhere to live. But the wage is less than I was getting at the Maxwell's and half of that is taken for room and board."

Silence followed Adeline's tale of woe as Cassandra took the woman's situation in. Adeline misinterpreted the silence and hurriedly added, "For which I am eternally grateful and am incredibly lucky to have this job at all."

Cassandra stared at Adeline. "You win." She pushed her plate closer to Adeline, who had already finished her own slice. Somehow the act of sharing her dessert broke the tension and the two women began chatting as they ate, almost like old friends.

But once the cake was done, Adeline seemed to remember that she was the newest member of the household staff, and Cassandra ruled the entire Empire. Cassandra's heart fell. She so desperately wanted a friend. Needed one. And were the circumstances different, she honestly felt she and Adeline could be the best of friends.

"So what job did they give you?" Cassandra asked.

"They said the only opening they have is a scullery maid. Cleaning the kitchen." Adeline glanced around her new domain. "They said if there's an opening, and I'm doing a good job, then I can look at maybe being a household maid. I get the feeling they like to start people here to get a feel for them."

Cassandra nodded. That did sound like something Mrs Cameron would do. But Cassandra felt she had the measure of Adeline, and she admired her tenacity.

When a rock causes your cart to lose a wheel, her father used to tell her, *you can fix the problem and keep going, or sit in the dirt and hope someone fixes it for you.*

She'd used to tease him that he forced her to travel with so many guards, she'd never even know the wheel had broken. He'd smile at her and say that he knew if the guards weren't there, she'd hop down, hike up her sleeves, and get mending.

Cassandra smiled sadly. She missed her father. What would he do here, in her place? Her smile faded. Given the plans he had left for her to continue implementing, she wasn't sure he was who she should emulate anymore.

"Is your heart set on the kitchens?" Cassandra asked

Adeline. Adeline looked caught. Clearly, being a scullery maid wasn't the job of her dreams, but Cassandra could tell she didn't want to be ungrateful. "It's just that I've been thinking of looking for a new lady's maid. The current woman has... untenable allegiances, and I'd really feel more comfortable with someone who might join me for cake from time to time."

Adeline's face broke into a huge smile. "I'd love to, Your Majesty, but—"

"Don't worry about Mrs Cameron or Mrs Pipe. I'll take care of them." Cassandra frowned. "Though it's too late to do anything about it tonight, I'm sorry. I think it best you sleep in the room they allocated to you. I'll leave word with my guards, and they'll tell Mrs Cameron as soon as she wakes. Would you prefer to be in the rooms down here?"

"Um..." Adeline looked confused.

"It's just that there's a maid's room up near mine. My current maid doesn't use it, at my request. But you'd be welcome to it. Of course, you may prefer to stay down here and get to know the other staff. Think about it," Cassandra said quickly, realising it was a lot for Adeline to take in. "Spend the night here and see how it is, and tomorrow we can look at the other room. There's no pressure to decide, and of course, you can always change your mind."

Cassandra stood, and Adeline hurried to follow.

"Thank you, Your Majesty," Adeline gushed, looking on the verge of tears.

Cassandra smiled and waved her away. "Thank *you*, Adeline. I enjoyed our chat. See you in the morning."

CHAPTER TWENTY-FOUR

MIRA

MIRA LEANED against a tree and tried not to cry. She would not cry. She was strong. Strong like Tia, who had fought despite the overwhelming number of people trying to take her. Tia, who had stood her ground while Mira had run.

She bit back the shame she felt at running. There was no honour in both of them being caught. And this way, with one of them free, there was a chance to find help.

It was just that the wrong person had escaped. Had it been Tia, they would likely both be free by now. But Mira was horribly lost. She pushed off the tree and looked around. The southern realms of Valoris had mountains and plains and a forest and swamps, so how come everywhere she'd gone in the last few days all looked so damn similar?

Pushing down the wave of hopelessness, Mira turned, found the highest point, and started walking. She would have thought the hardest thing would have been getting out of the forest. All those trees, so close together, it would not have been hard to get turned around. But somehow she had managed to keep her line and in what felt like no time, she'd pushed through the last of the tight woods and emerged into the sunlight.

The bright calm had been jarring. Tia was in danger, maybe hurt, or worse, and the sun was shining, with a lazy breeze blowing the scents of spring flowers. It should have been overcast with people screaming and running from bands of pillaging bandits.

Her first thought had been to find the road. If she found the road, she could find Lorendell, and then she could search for Kas. As she started walking, despair crept in. Lorendell was so large, and Kas would be hiding, not wandering around, waiting for Mira to find him.

But the road would also lead her to Ossi. While the idea of going anywhere near the Troll settlement filled her with dread, Mira figured Ossi would be easier to locate. She'd just have to find the settlement and then wander around the outside until she found his camp.

Why hadn't they made sure there was a way to find each other in an emergency? Maybe they should have all stayed together. Mira had wanted that. Sure, she didn't have a family to hurry off and look for as the others had, but there was still safety in numbers. Mira's mind slid over the thought that somehow this group of strangers felt as close to having a family as she had since her own was killed, and therefore she had felt the same urgency they had, but to stay together rather than separate.

Mira wondered at the strength of her feelings for these people who had been strangers mere days before. They'd bonded during the escape for sure, but there was something more than that. Mira hadn't made many friends during her three years in the camps. She was quiet and small, and didn't have the natural tribal bond of the Kikachi or Trolls.

And Mira had only recently arrived at the southern quarry. Not enough time to really get to know anyone, but she had noticed Kas and Ossi and Tia. She'd envied their natural friendship and wished she could have somewhere to belong again.

But she wasn't the type to simply insert herself into groups, and so she'd continued on, never dreaming that fate would bring them all together. Nor that they'd so easily accept her into their little tribe. She felt completely comfortable with all of them. And with Tia especially.

Mira had never clicked with someone the way she had with Tia. Their conversation just flowed, and she felt they'd been friends for years, not days. And then her new best friend had found herself in trouble, and Mira had just run away.

She hurried up the hill, shaking the unhelpful thoughts away. It didn't matter now. All that did matter was getting help for Tia.

How she missed the road, Mira did not know. But she'd managed it. The first hour, she told herself that the road must wind at this point and that was why it was farther north than it should have been. But by the second hour, she had to admit she'd gone past it.

She must have exited closer to the entry to the forest that the Empire had built than to Lorendell. Closer to Lorendell, the road was wide, but she supposed near the Kikachi settlement it was probably only ever used by Empire soldiers. It must have been one of the tracks she'd barely looked at on her way to find help.

But Mira had kept going. Turning around felt too much like failure, and besides, if she'd missed the road once, she didn't trust she'd find it the second time. The Troll settlement was roughly north of Ravenswood Forest. Maybe a bit to the east. Mira adjusted her path and kept going.

She would succeed this time. If she didn't find the Troll settlement, or Ossi's camp, she would definitely find a road. The road to the Troll settlement was an already existing one that went from Lorendell to the Crossroads, and from there to the north or other areas of the south. Either way, she'd be fine. And soon, she'd have help, and she'd rescue Tia.

But Mira wasn't fine. She eventually found the road, but was so sure she was close to the Troll settlement, she pushed ahead, crossing it and continuing north. When she'd not seen any sign of the massive people or their Empire-built town, Mira backtracked to the road.

She felt safer on the road. Despite the threat it posed given she was collared, at least she couldn't get lost. And this time, Mira was sure she knew where she was. She shouldn't have far to go on the road before she found the Troll settlement.

Mira had made good time, despite having to duck off the road and hide when she ran into travellers. But she'd walked on the road for a day, and as the sun began to set, the settlement had still not appeared.

She'd stemmed the panic, telling herself it was fine. She'd find somewhere to shelter for the night and get moving first thing in the morning. The road would take her to the city. She could look for Kas, or, worst case, turn around and follow the road back to find Ossi.

During the night, as Mira shivered in the icy breeze that blew down from the mountains, she found herself at her lowest and was ashamed that she entertained the possibility of giving up. She had never been to this part of Valoris before and the overwhelming feeling of being lost made the idea of just giving up and heading north suddenly appealing.

But there was nothing left up north for Mira. Her family had been killed and her home was gone. They had been heading south when they were stopped. When the guards had taken her and killed her family.

Sitting in the cold and dark in an unfamiliar land, Mira

suddenly felt completely and utterly alone. She had nothing and no one.

No one, except the eclectic group of people who had taken her in, no questions asked, and accepted her as a friend immediately. And Tia, who'd offered to take Mira to her home without hesitation. And was now trapped, so soon after escaping a life of captivity.

Mira almost set off again right then, determined to see Tia free as soon as she could find help. The only thing that stopped her was the realisation that her navigation had proved abysmal during the day, and the darkness of the night was unlikely to improve her efforts. And if Mira failed, then no one would know that Tia was in danger.

But midafternoon the next day, just as she began to believe that everything might be okay, she spotted a large contingent of Empire soldiers marching right towards her.

Mira had been taking a break. The hill she was climbing was steeper than it had looked. That was good—steeper meant a better viewpoint. But seeing the soldiers increased her heart rate, and her heart was already pounding from the climb.

How could she be so unlucky? She darted off the road, as she had for dozens of passing carts and wagons. But when the soldiers in their neat lines pulled level with the bushes she was hidden within, they halted.

Had they seen her? She couldn't think how. She'd left the road the minute she saw them. And then the order sounded that turned her veins to ice.

"Set up camp!"

They were going to camp right here, where she was hiding! How long would they be there? Was it a short stop on their way to wherever they were going? Or would she be stuck, cramped in the bushes all night?

Were it only her own safety on the line, Mira likely

would have stayed. But an image of Tia bravely fighting off those men who had pounced on them in the woods flitted through her mind, and Mira ran.

The irony that the image of Tia fighting inspired her to run, as she had done when the fighting had broken out, did not enter Mira's mind. There was no time. As soon as she darted from her hiding place, she heard the cry of being spotted. She didn't dare turn to see who had called out, or who might be following. She kept a point on the horizon in her sights and ran with everything she had.

Luckily, a small girl in rags didn't pique the interest of the soldiers. No footsteps came thundering after her. No arrows whizzed past her head. No magicals froze her blood or blew her over. She'd had a go at hiding her collar, but it wouldn't have held up to any scrutiny. Perhaps she'd been far enough away from them they hadn't seen?

As she slowed, trying to suck air into her aching lungs, Mira wondered if the soldiers even knew a group of prisoners from the camps had escaped. Surely she looked like one such prisoner, dressed in her rags and running from the soldiers. But she didn't think too long on it, as if doing so might alert whatever gods or goddesses or powers were in charge of the world to their oversight.

And though she'd escaped the soldiers, Mira was, once again, horribly lost.

Mira crested the hill she was climbing and looked around. The God of Light must have been shining on her. For though she'd wished fervently that she'd look down the other side of the hill and conveniently see Ossi's camp and the Troll settlement a little way off, she could at least see Lorendell, standing tall, and not too far away.

Mira frowned. She must have run farther than she'd realised in trying to escape the soldiers. She avoided looking down, but suddenly her feet hurt and she wasn't sure that what she thought was just sweat wasn't in fact blood.

Before all her aches and pains and hunger and thirst could catch her, Mira pushed off and started down the hill. She could see a stream in her path. She would allow herself to stop for water. It wouldn't help Tia if she dropped from dehydration before she found anyone. But after that, she would not stop until she found someone to help her rescue her friend.

CHAPTER TWENTY-FIVE

KAS

Kᴀꜱ ʙᴀʀᴇʟʏ ʀᴇᴍᴇᴍʙᴇʀᴇᴅ his trip through the tunnels. Thankfully, this time it was uneventful. Kas was in such a daze after leaving Francisco to die in the streets that he probably wouldn't have registered any guards until they had him detained.

He'd paralleled the main road in the same fugue state, trying to process how everything had managed to go so spectacularly wrong in the course of less than an hour.

Salomon had betrayed him.

Kas had always known his little brother held resentment. But he'd thought it was at the constant comparison to his older brother. About the things that Kas did well that Salomon was not as proficient at. Not for a minute had he considered the resentment might be aimed at Kas himself. Nor that it might be so strong.

But to turn him over to the guards... to have struck a deal that would see Kas returned to the camps... Kas's mind struggled to make sense of it. No one who hadn't been there really knew how bad the camps were, but everyone knew they were bad. You'd rarely find someone willing to send their worst enemy to the camps. And Salomon had willingly negotiated to send his own brother.

Kas's mind was frantic, searching for some excuse, some logical reason why Salomon would do that. Why Salomon would hate him that much. But he was at a loss. Perhaps the part of his brain that might have found an excuse for his little brother was busily in denial about leaving an old man to die. From a beating he'd received for saving Kas.

Frank—Francisco—had never been what might be described as paternal. Had never sought to replace the parents Kas and Salomon had lost. But he'd looked out for the boys. Shared food and resources whenever he could. Helped them whenever they needed it.

And in those final minutes, after Francisco had sacrificed himself to steer the guards away from Kas so he might escape, Kas had just left him in the dirt. Dying.

What kind of man was he? Part of him felt he was little better than Salomon.

But I didn't arrange for the guards to beat Francisco...

Taking a deep breath, Kas shook the thoughts away. He didn't have time to dwell on all this. He needed to escape—to get as far away from Lorendell as possible before the guards expanded their search. If he was caught now, Francisco's sacrifice would be for nothing.

Kas looked around. He'd been standing in a field near a crossroads. The grass was up to his waist and so dry it scratched against him in the breeze. The main road in southern Valoris ran from the border with the north, all the way down to Lorendell. As if in a long-forgotten time, the tribes of the north and south of the continent had happily traded with one another, rather than waging war every few years.

Kas wondered at its purpose. There were several smaller

Empire cities dotted around southern Valoris, so perhaps the main road connected Lorendell with the other main centres. Indeed, there were a number of inns located along the road to accommodate travellers undertaking the several-day journey to the border towns, or just travelling between the smaller cities of the Empire. But it was more likely the Empire had built it to hasten troop movements to the north to prevent the Controllers from marching too far south.

Another road, similarly well made, stretched west to Ravenswood Forest, which lay a couple of days walk away. Kas supposed it had been established after the recent annexation. Which would also explain the third road leading from the city that headed northwest and lay between the other two, that likely headed for the Troll settlement.

A steady stream of travellers plodded along the road heading north, going both into and out of the city. Less followed the Troll road, and in the time Kas had been standing there, only a couple appeared on the road to the forest.

He needed to go north. That's where the Druids were. But his heart, stinging from his brother's betrayal, was pulling him towards his friends. Francisco had told him the Druids would help him. Maybe even get the collar off. But if that was possible, why should he be freed, and not Ossi and Tia?

Kas had all but decided to set off to find his friends when a rustle nearby had his heart racing. He'd just been standing there. Not even squatting down, avoiding being seen. Had the guards spotted him? Were they now sneaking towards him, about to bring him down?

He would not be taken easily. Kas planted his feet, ready to fight. He'd not go back to the camps. Not again.

The rustling stopped, and Kas looked about, becoming frantic as the fear and adrenaline built.

"Kas!"

The soft voice came from behind him. Kas squealed and jumped, trying to turn towards the voice as he did, but twisting his feet in the process and winding up landing hard on his backside.

"Oh! Sorry, are you alright?"

Kas blinked as his body screamed at him to run, but his mind processed who was there.

"Mira, hi, I wasn't expecting..." Kas's embarrassed explanation trailed off as he stood, dusting off his clothes. "How are you?"

What he really wanted to know was why Mira was here, but that seemed impolite as a first question.

Mira's eyes filled with tears. "Oh Kas, I've been looking for you. Well, you and Ossi—either of you. But I got lost, and then there were soldiers—"

"Woah, Mira, slow down." Kas put his hands comfortingly on Mira's shoulders. He looked at her properly now, noticing her exhaustion and dishevelled state. She really did look like she'd run the length of Valoris and back.

Mira merely shook her head at him. "No, Kas, we have to hurry. They took her." Mira grabbed one of Kas's hands and started pulling him back towards the forest.

"Wait." Kas gently pulled Mira back around to face him. "Took who? Tell me what happened."

Mira looked like she was going to argue, but with a furtive glance back towards the forest, she told Kas what happened.

"They took her, Kas. Took Tia. We were headed to her village. We weren't going to go right in. Tia said we should hide just outside it and wait until we saw someone she knew and trusted. But then they just appeared."

"Who appeared?" Kas's own instincts were now pulling him towards the forest, and it was all he could do to stop himself mimicking Mira and pulling her along as he raced to help Tia.

Mira shook her head, the tears on her cheeks flying off. "I don't know. One man seemed to know Tia. But they tried to take us. Well, they really wanted her. Only one was coming for me and I ducked and then... I ran," Mira whispered the last words, her shame painted over her face. "I left her there."

"You did the right thing," Kas said earnestly, despite his own guilt at leaving Francisco. "If you'd both been caught, no one would know. But now you've found me and we can help Tia."

Mira nodded, though Kas could see she would not be forgiving herself for abandoning her friend anytime soon.

Kas looked towards the forest, the deep green visible even from here. He desperately wanted to head there immediately and free Tia. But he hesitated. He had no idea who had taken her or where she was now. Kas had never really left the city before the camps. He'd not stepped foot in Ravenswood Forest, let alone had any idea where the Shifters lived, or anywhere a prisoner might be taken.

As if reading his mind, Mira said, "I think I can find my way to their village. I know where we entered and the bearing we took. I'm terrible at navigating, but once I've been somewhere, I can always find my way back along the same path."

"Even in a forest?" Kas felt like that had to be next to impossible. There would be no landmarks other than trees, and they all looked the same.

"I used to spend a lot of time in the woods as a kid," said Mira, almost defensively.

"Okay, but then we'd need to find her. Presumably she's

in the village. Unless she's already back at the camps," Kas said, voicing the concern neither wanted to consider. *Or dead.*

"I don't think she would be," Mira said. "It wasn't soldiers who took her. They were other Kikachi."

Kikachi. That was the name Tia had used for her tribe. Their real name. Kas flushed red, thinking he'd known Tia longer but hadn't adopted the correct name for her tribe. It was habit to call them Shifters. Would they really have kidnapped one of their own?

"And they took her to some storage bunker or something. It certainly wasn't the cells."

"How do you know where they took her?" Kas raised an eyebrow.

Mira flushed. "When I realised they weren't following me, I circled back around. I caught up to them, but kept my distance. They went to the village, but they were avoiding being seen by the soldiers. Like they didn't want the soldiers to know they had her. They took her to this ramshackle place and threw her inside, and then two of them stood guard outside. I waited to see if there was a chance to sneak up and speak with her, but they didn't budge. So I thought it'd be better to find help."

Kas nodded, looking at Mira. Neither of them looked like Kikachi. Kas was too broad and Mira too short. It wasn't like they could simply head into the village and wander around. Before the annexation, the Kikachi had been notoriously private, and afterwards, it was probably the one thing the Empire had respected of their culture. Likely because it was easier to control the tribe without visitors.

Kas took a deep breath. They were going to need help. "Before she was taken, did Tia mention anyone in the village that might be able to help us?"

"Her siblings!" Mira's eyes lit up. "She has a brother

and a sister... Fabian and Aurora. I'm sure they'll help us. If they're not already trying to get her out." Her face fell. "I should have tried to find them myself."

"You did the right thing," Kas said. "If you'd asked the wrong person, you probably would be locked up too. This way, we have some redundancy."

Kas looked back at the forest and then over to the road leading to the Trolls. And then his eyes drew north.

"We need magic."

"What?" Mira asked.

"Listen, before I left the city, a Druid told me if I went to their village, they could remove my collar."

Mira looked at Kas as if he'd suffered a head injury.

"It's a long story," he said, waving her off, "but listen, if I had my magic, I could probably get Tia out myself. And it'll be a cinch with your spells."

He'd meant it to be complimentary, but Mira looked distinctly uncomfortable as he mentioned her spells. Maybe she didn't know any beyond simple housework spells. He knew some people limited what girls were taught.

"Before you popped up—"

"Sorry again about that."

"—I'd decided to come and get you all before I went to the Druids. I figured if it were true, we could all get our collars off. Have a chance at a new life. I hate the idea of leaving her there as much as you do, but I really think finding Ossi and getting our collars off will give us the best chance at savin Tia."

Mira opened and closed her mouth, turning towards the forest as if she might be able to see Tia there. Kas felt the same pull. The desire to run in and save her. The guilty shame of even considering going somewhere else. Especially when that somewhere else was to remove their collars, while Tia remained collared and locked up once more. But they were no help to their friend sitting beside her in a cage.

"You're right," Mira said eventually. "But I feel awful."

"You and me both," said Kas. "But I'm happy to feel like an ass if it means we manage to get her out."

Mira nodded.

"And it'll be good to see Ossi again," said Kas, trying to lift the mood. "Maybe he'll have a better idea of what we should do."

Mira gave him a small strained smile, and they started walking towards the Troll settlement. Part of Kas wondered if they shouldn't split their efforts. Maybe someone should head straight for the Kikachi village and try to make contact with Tia's siblings. And remain close by in case anything changed.

But he didn't want to send Mira back there. Not only would he feel like an ass sending the small woman back into danger, but she seemed so quiet and nervous. He worried she might not be up to the task. And guiltily, he didn't want to miss the chance to get his collar off. Kas told himself that he was the one with the ring. The only one Francisco had said the Druids would help. He needed to go. What if Ossi and Mira got there only to learn the Druids wouldn't help them?

And besides, it was his magic they needed. He missed it terribly, but it was also the most useful. Aside from the obvious benefit of invisibility, with his elemental magic, Kas could create a pretty impressive distraction. He imagined forest dwellers would be quite alarmed by fire.

Kas picked up his pace, almost convinced he was doing this because it was the best way to save Tia and not because he was being selfish.

CHAPTER TWENTY-SIX

KAS

Ossi had been easy to find. He'd told Kas so many times about his favourite camping spot by the river that Kas felt he'd already been there before. They found him right where he'd described, by a large willow tree a few miles from the Troll settlement. Though he'd been happy to see Kas and Mira, he was angered when they told him about Tia, and it had been difficult to stop him from immediately marching down to the forest to rescue her. Despite that, he readily agreed that the removal of their collars would help with Tia's liberation and he had instead immediately started walking north, Kas and Mira running to catch up with him.

"Don't you want your stuff?" Kas had asked, looking back at Ossi's campsite.

Ossi shrugged. "It is just stuff, as you say. It will be there when I get back."

"Someone might take it." Mira frowned.

Ossi shrugged again. "Then it will be gone."

It was very difficult to get a Troll to worry about anything, and they certainly had a different attitude to possessions than anyone else in the Empire. Kas had seen someone steal from a Troll selling wares in the market once.

The Troll watched the small boy run away, then simply turned back to his stall. Kas, feeling bad, had approached the huge man and offered to get his goods back, but the Troll had just smiled at him.

"To take it and run like that, the boy must need it much more than I." His deep voice had boomed down at little Kas.

"But," Kas had said, frowning, "if you have a stall, then you need the money from your sales."

"That does make sense, little man." The Troll had kept smiling at him. "But I just enjoy being here in the markets of your beautiful city. It makes your soldiers nervous if I enter with no purpose, and so I have a stall. It makes them feel better." He'd whispered the last comment as if imparting a big secret.

It had made no sense to Kas, but he'd found the relaxed nature of the Troll very comforting. As if nothing could ever go wrong.

Kas glanced back at Ossi's camp again. It made him nervous to leave it all there.

"You are projecting your own sense of loss," Ossi said, seeing Kas's worry.

Kas blinked. Perhaps his friend was right. He had needed to leave everything he'd ever owned in the city. Twice. Unconsciously, Kas's hand reached for his father's cap. The only thing he still owned. The only reminder of his parents. Kas tried to pull his thoughts from what he'd lost and focus on the mission at hand. Tia was far more important than some trinkets and keepsakes.

"There is nothing wrong with it," said Ossi. "Any loss can be painful."

"But not to you," said Kas. Ossi raised an eyebrow and Kas rephrased, "Sorry, I mean, you aren't worried about your stuff back there. Not that you wouldn't be upset at a loss. A bigger one, I mean."

"I think it's normal to be upset about losing your things," said Mira thoughtfully. "Not to say it's not normal to not be worried about it," she amended with a quick glance at Ossi, who smiled, unconcerned. "Just that it's okay to be upset about it."

"We Trolls don't worry about possessions as some other tribes do because we are nomadic by nature," Ossi said. "Often we craft items that will only last the duration of our stay. Anything more durable is usually stored somewhere for when we return to the area. Sometimes it is there when we do. Sometimes it is not. We are not taught to form attachments to things, and so we do not. It is not right or wrong, it is simply our way."

The trio walked in silence for a while, both Mira and Kas thinking about what Ossi had said. Kas found it difficult to imagine such a life. He thought about how hard he'd worked to get the shanty that had been his and Salomon's home. It had been hard enough being torn away from it—he couldn't fathom simply leaving it and setting up somewhere else. Though to be fair to him, the Trolls didn't have to buy a new house wherever they went.

"Do you call yourselves 'Trolls'?" Mira asked, breaking the silence.

"Sometimes," Ossi replied.

"But surely you have another name for yourselves," Mira pushed gently. "Like how we all call the Kikachi 'Shifters'. What is your tribe's real name? If you want to tell me, of course." Mira suddenly looked worried that she'd caused offence, seeming to realise that their true name might not be something they shared with outsiders.

"We call ourselves Jatte," said Ossi. "But we are not bothered if people wish to use another term for us."

Kas frowned. "Yeah, but 'Trolls' is a bit derogatory, isn't it?" He'd never given it much thought. Everyone had always just called them Trolls. He'd never considered what the term meant. Why people might have called them that.

Ossi just shrugged. "We tend to see it more as a simplification. Outsiders all have names for other tribes, and often they are descriptive. The Shifters shapeshift; the Controllers control minds. We are big and strong like trolls."

Kas glanced at his friend, trying to see past the relaxed smile on his face. Ossi was far too intelligent to not know that another aspect of the description was that trolls in fairytales were seen as big dumb oafs. He couldn't imagine that this didn't form a part of the reason that name had been given to them.

For anyone who hadn't spent any real time with a Troll, their laid-back, easy-going nature could lead a stranger to believe they were unthinking. But Ossi knew more about how the world worked than Kas did. Knew about the politics within and between all the tribes. Knew about what was going on in the north.

"I like Jatte," said Mira. She frowned again. "Do you think the Druids call themselves 'the Druids'?"

Both Ossi and Kas frowned, too. "My people say they do," said Ossi.

Kas shivered as a particularly cool breeze brushed by them. The Druids always seemed like the exception to the rule. Always standing slightly apart from all the other peoples of Valoris.

He was nervous about going to their village. Nervous about being so close to the border—especially if an invasion was imminent. But hopefully they wouldn't need to be there long. The collars had taken mere seconds to lock onto their necks. Surely it would be a similar process to remove them.

They made good time travelling north. Their collars meant they had to travel off-road, and that would usually be an issue for food and water, especially since none of them had any supplies. But Ossi knew how to live off the land, and showed them bushes and plants that they could snack on during their journey, and at night he would make a fire and hunt or fish.

Kas asked if Ossi would teach him, and Ossi reassured Kas that he didn't mind doing these things. Kas told Ossi he appreciated that, but really, he'd like to learn. Mira did too, and soon they were all hunting and fishing and cleaning and cooking.

If the spectre of Tia's incarceration wasn't looming over them, the trip would actually have been quite enjoyable. As it was, Kas felt a level of relief at having distractions from thinking about Salomon's betrayal, though even with everything going on, his mind drifted back from time to time.

"You are troubled," said Ossi as they sat fishing one evening. It was just the two of them, Mira having gone in search of berries or roots to go with the catch.

Kas went to reply that he was worried about Tia, but Ossi had a way of looking at people that made them think he already knew the answer, and Kas was sure he'd at least know Kas wasn't being entirely truthful. And so he told his friend of his brother's betrayal.

"The man you met does not sound like the boy you spoke of in the camps," Ossi said simply when Kas was finished.

"That's what's so hard, Ossi. I'm so angry at him for what he did. But at the same time, it's like I can't let go of my memories of him. I still love him."

"And you will always love him," said Ossi. "He is your brother."

"But he betrayed me!"

"And you are allowed to be upset about that." Ossi pulled in a fish and set it in the hastily woven basket beside him. "But you can't expect to replace a lifetime of loving someone with the pain of one betrayal. Even a betrayal as significant as this."

Kas thought on Ossi's words. His friend had a habit of being wise, and while Kas had hated every moment he was in the labour camps, the idea that if he hadn't been caught that day he might never have met Ossi made him incredibly sad.

"I'm so angry at him, Ossi. For the betrayal, of course, but also... all I've dreamed of for these last eight years is getting back to him and living a simple life. And now, it's all ruined."

Ossi paused as he did when he had a response, but wanted to ensure the person he was speaking with felt heard. "Your dream doesn't have to be ruined," he said gently. "You can still have the simple life you've dreamed of for so long. It's just that Salomon's part in your dream might be different."

They packed up their makeshift rods and headed back to camp. The idea that Salomon might not play a prominent role in his life made Kas's heart ache, but Ossi's words had lifted a weight from his chest.

Travelling overland cut a couple of days off the journey and after only three nights, they were in the northern reaches of the southern lands. And what they saw shocked them. Villages and towns were abandoned, some of them completely burned out. And the northern labour camps had been shut down.

"I thought we were just enforcing the border," Kas said

as they wandered through another burned-out town, black charred wood broken and bent. They looked for supplies but found nothing that had survived the blaze. "This looks like a full-on war."

"It's possible this was deliberate," said Ossi, examining a gutted building. "The Empire may have evacuated the people and burned the village to create a buffer in case the Controllers do come south. This way they have no access to resources and it stresses their supply line. Makes it more vulnerable."

Kas and Mira stared at him. Ossi shrugged. "My people know conflict."

"But you're all so laid-back," said Mira, picking up and dusting off a charred lump of what might have once been a toy.

"Sometimes it's good to be prepared. Much as we like to fight, we don't like war. But we make sure we know it, so if it is brought upon us, we can end it quickly."

"Wait." Kas held up a hand to silence his friends and stop their progression through the ruins. "Quick, hide."

He'd heard someone picking their way through the ruins on the other side of what would have been the main road. The three friends hid behind a wall that was barely standing. Kas and Mira ducked below the hole that was once a window, and Ossi stood behind the bulk of the wall. All three risked glances when they could.

Kas spotted them first. Two people, a few metres apart, moving south. He chanced another look. The first one was definitely a man. The Empire armour left little doubt, moulded to the wearer's chest as it was. This guy was a human version of Ossi. Big and broad, but not massive like the Troll. *Jatte*, Kas quietly corrected himself.

The one trailing the first was more curious. At a second glance, Kas wondered if it might be a woman. The figure was smaller and dressed in black robes, a hood concealing their face. The person looked... wrong. Faded somehow.

"Should we do anything?" Kas hissed to the others.

"Like what?" asked Ossi.

"I don't know." Something about them felt off. And being so close to the border... but it was hardly an invasion. Something about that second figure, though. Could it be a Controller?

Kas had never seen a Controller, but he'd imagined them to be large and ominous and intimidating. Perhaps in real life they were small. All the better to infiltrate. But they'd still set off the wards. Wouldn't they?

"Should we stop them?" Kas whispered.

"He's an Empire soldier," whispered Mira. "Why would we stop him?"

"And he might have something to say about our collars if we did," added Ossi.

"Yeah, but the other one bothers me," said Kas.

"What other one?" Ossi frowned, peering out again.

"The little one in the cloak."

"I just see the soldier," said Mira, poking her head up too.

Kas popped up as the others pulled back into cover. The figure was right there in front of them. How could the others not see it?

As if alerted by his thoughts, the figure turned towards Kas and froze, seeing Kas looking right at them. Kas ducked back down and told the others the figure was directly across from them, but when they looked out again, they said nothing was there. This time, when Kas popped up, he saw nothing but the soldier walking away in the distance.

———

They spent the rest of their trip discussing the state of things in the north, debating whether the Controllers were going to push into the south, or whether the desolation was a rather extreme preparation tactic by the Empire.

Kas tried to bring up the cloaked figure again, but as neither Ossi nor Mira had seen the figure, both would only go so far as to agree that seeing a lone soldier travelling through the ruins was odd before they'd turn the conversation back to the devastation around them.

Kas fell into silence, thinking about the cloaked figure, almost convinced now it had been a Controller. Was it controlling that soldier? Had the Controllers now infiltrated the Empire military, so conveniently stationed at the border? And if they were freely travelling within the Empire, how many other people were under their control?

More importantly, did that mean the wards weren't working anymore? The Druids had placed wards along the border that would alert if a Controller passed into the southern lands. He'd heard there were wards at the palace, too.

The Controllers had always been something of a fairy-tale to Kas. A cautionary tale told to children to help illustrate right from wrong. In his mind, he had built them up as a race of unstoppable demons intent on the destruction of the world. And looking around at the burned, barren, and abandoned landscape, it was hard not to fall back into that way of thinking.

But the cloaked figure hadn't been some huge, red-eyed beast. It was small and had seemed almost scared to be seen. Still, Kas felt it was healthy to have a base level of fear for anyone with the power to control another's mind.

The Controllers did actually have red eyes, which probably didn't help their image. They were striking, but that was part of the trick. Once they had eye contact with you, they struck, penetrating your mind and taking over.

Kas had overheard some old guys in the tavern once who claimed to have been controlled. One had said he felt the Controller push into his mind, like a splinter of wood. Something foreign that wasn't meant to be there. The other said he had no idea he'd been taken. He was aware of some odd ideas, some thoughts that didn't feel like his usual thoughts. And his friends and family had said he was saying weird things. But it wasn't until he managed to break the connection that he realised what had happened. And that was only because he travelled far enough south that the connection was broken.

Kas had felt at the time that the two men were probably making it all up. Convenient excuses for behaviour they now regretted. Hadn't Ricardo also tried to claim he was controlled when he'd gotten drunk and slept with that barmaid? His wife didn't buy it for a second, yelling at him that the Controllers had better things to do than make him cheat.

Kas shuddered. He felt wary being so close to the border. To the Controllers. He looked along the horizon for the wards, as if he might see huge pillars with glowing runes carved into their faces and crackling electricity passing between them. But now that he thought about it, he realised he had no idea what a ward even was, let alone what one looked like. Just that they sounded an alarm if a Controller crossed them.

"What even is a ward?" he asked Ossi and Mira.

"I saw them once," said Mira hesitantly. "My family travelled up here when I was young. The border wards are big stone plinths, taller even than Ossi, and they have intricate carvings. I don't know if the carvings were the wards, or if they're something imbued into the stone, but the alarm they're supposed to sound if someone from the Divvinium crosses is meant to be deafening."

"Divvinium?" Kas asked.

A slight blush graced Mira's cheeks. "I think it's what the Controllers call themselves. Or, so I heard."

"I heard the soldiers talking about the wards when we were in the camps," said Ossi. "All soldiers at the border must pass through on their way back from patrols, and again before returning south. Apparently, the wards alert if a Controller passes through, and also if a person is under control."

Kas felt a little better hearing that, but his mind immediately returned to the soldier and the hooded figure following him. Did the Empire or the Druids ever check the wards? It wasn't like they could just ask the Controllers to send someone over every so often to make sure they were working.

The memory of his Testing popped into his head. Everyone just assumed anything the Druids made worked perfectly. But Kas knew all too well the limitations of the Druids' devices. What if the wards were the same?

"I think we're here," said Ossi, pausing at the top of a hill.

CHAPTER TWENTY-SEVEN

KAS

Mira and Kas joined Ossi at the top of the hill and took in the view in front of them. They were at the foothills of the Frostblood Ranges, but the foothills looked like gigantic mountains in their own right up this close. Trees nestled at the base of the range, and among the trees were several thatched huts, smoke curling gently from some chimneys.

The village was larger than Kas had imagined. Somehow he'd pictured a handful of houses, all set in a circle around a large communal firepit. But as he looked at the medium-sized village, with bisecting main roads and several smaller alleys cutting between huts, he realised how silly he'd been.

The Druid village looked to be a peaceful settlement. He could see people going about their day. There was an efficiency to their movements, but no rush. Something about the relaxed nature of the place felt calm, like the exact opposite of Lorendell.

A small field sat to the southwest of the village. Or maybe it was a community garden. Certainly, Kas saw no farming equipment. Just some cloaked figures kneeling in the dirt. Their cloaks put him in mind of the strange figure again, but the Druids' cloaks were the grey of the mountains in the background, and seemed designed for warmth, not concealment.

North of the village, the trees got thicker, though Kas could see a small clearing. There was some kind of rock formation there. He could barely see it for the trees, but the stone in the centre was almost white.

Kas looked nervously for soldiers. After all, the Empire had annexed all the minor tribes, including the Druids. But he saw none in the village. Frowning, he scanned the outskirts of the settlement, and eventually spotted some tents set up to the east, where the woods began to thin. Apparently, the soldiers would rather camp in tents than live in houses near the Druids. Curious.

The three set out once more and soon entered the village. Kas was tense, expecting to be stopped on the outskirts, but no one even challenged them. They walked farther into the village with still no issue. Druids who passed them nodded and smiled, as if three strangers were nothing out of the ordinary.

"Should we ask someone?" Mira whispered, clearly also unnerved.

Kas shrugged, continuing towards the town centre. What would he ask? He had Francisco's ring, but now that he was here, he realised the old man had not told him who to approach for help. He'd simply said 'the Druids'.

The centre of the village was a large dirt square set where the two main roads intersected. At first glance, Kas thought it was a market, but then he realised there was no actual trade taking place. People were taking what they needed, and only what they needed, and dropping off other supplies that presumably they did not need. Some of the stalls weren't even monitored by anyone.

"Greetings, friends," said a friendly voice. Kas turned

and saw a Druid of about forty years of age bowing at them. "Is there anything I can do to assist you? You are, of course, welcome to simply visit with us."

Kas felt incredibly wrong-footed by such an open greeting. He was used to guards and questions and suspicion. Mira shuffled, seemingly from Kas's school of thought, but Ossi simply smiled, returning the bow.

"Thank you, master Druid—"

"Oh please, brother is fine. Or, if it makes you feel more at ease, Davide."

"David?" asked Kas, reminded of how Frank was actually Francisco.

"It's Da*vide*," the Druid explained, still smiling. "Though David works too, if it pleases you." He bowed again.

Kas felt his discomfort grow. There was something different about the Druids' easy-going attitude to that of the Jatte. He couldn't put his finger on it. Both seemed to go with the flow, to bend where possible to accommodate others. But somehow the Jatte felt genuine, and the Druids seemed... calculating. But maybe he was just more used to the Jatte.

"Brother," Ossi continued, "we are looking for some help. My friend here met one of your kin in the City of Magic, and he sent us here, suggesting that we might find assistance with... our little problems." Ossi touched his collar.

Kas knew his friend was telling the Druid of their reason for being there, but he also wanted to make sure the man knew who was in their midst, in case he was uncomfortable and wanted them to leave. Davide didn't flinch and barely looked at Ossi's collar, clearly having clocked it immediately.

"But of course," he said, smiling, before turning to Kas and looking at him expectantly.

"Uh." Kas rummaged around in his pocket, finding the ring and pulling it out. "My friend Frank—uh, Francisco. He gave me this and said if I brought it to you, you could help with the collars. Not *you* specifically," Kas babbled uncomfortably. "He said the Druids…"

Davide blinked at the ring and whispered, "Francisco." Shaking himself, Davide sprang into action. "But of course, please, come with me."

Kas shoved the ring back in his pocket and they hurried after Davide, who was now walking at a swift pace. He led them through the village, past buildings of various sizes that seemed to be houses and taverns and meeting halls. Kas wondered about the tavern. He couldn't picture Druids having a few pints and letting loose.

Eventually, Davide stopped at a small, nondescript house and knocked on the door. A young girl who couldn't be more than ten answered.

"Blessings, Davide."

"Blessings, Sofia." Davide bowed deeply. "Some friends have come to visit us. Francisco sent them."

Sofia peered around Davide, looking curiously at the group. "Did he really?"

"He gave them his ring."

Sofia's eyes snapped back to Davide's, and they looked at each other for a beat longer than Kas would have been comfortable with before Sofia nodded and turned back to the group, a big smile on her face. "Would you like to come in?"

Kas, Ossi, and Mira entered Sofia's house and looked around. They were in a large room that took up most of the building and served as kitchen, dining room, and sitting room all in one. There was a door to their right that Kas assumed led to the bedroom.

Sitting in a comfortable chair by a cosy fireplace was an old man with a long white beard. He reminded Kas instantly of Frank. Kas couldn't put his finger on it, but despite their similarities, Frank felt older.

"Father, we have visitors," Sofia said to the old man gently. He looked over at them, an eyebrow raised in curiosity, but otherwise seemed unperturbed that a bunch of strangers with collars marking them as criminals had appeared in his living room.

"Greetings," he said, getting to his feet with an ease that was incongruent with his age and beaming at them as if he knew them well. "Please come in and have a seat. Davide, would you mind popping to the tavern and fetching them some afternoon tea?"

Davide gave something that was either a nod or a bow and left.

"They have Francisco's ring, Father. He's asked us to help them."

The old man stared at the young girl, again for longer than seemed usual. He turned back to the group and blinked, shaking his head slightly.

"Forgive me. Where are my manners? I am Tacito, and you've met Sofia, I presume?" Everyone nodded, and Tacito turned his gaze to Kas. "May I see Francisco's ring?"

Kas stood, plunging his hand into his pocket and pulling it out. He handed it to Tacito. The old man turned it slowly in his long fingers, staring at it as if it might deliver a message.

Kas had just sat again when the old man said, "He is dead then."

It didn't seem a question, but Kas answered anyway. "Yes... I think so."

Tacito and Sofia exchanged a look, and Tacito placed the ring on the table in front of him. "Francisco was once our leader. This is the ring of his office. It should only be passed on once he has left us." Tacito gazed at the ring for a beat longer before looking up and directly into Kas's eyes. "He must have thought highly of you to give you his ring."

Kas felt uneasy again. Sure, Frank had been a staple in their lives, but he searched his memory once more for any sign that he had felt particularly strongly for Kas. Nothing came to mind. Other than, of course, that the old man had given his life to let Kas escape the city.

"Are you able to help us with our collars?" Mira asked. "I don't mean to be so forward, but one of our friends is in trouble, and we need to get them off so we can help her."

"Yes, of course," Sofia said, but didn't move. "We can release you from your collars. I understand the urgency of the situation regarding Tia."

The three friends froze. Davide chose that moment to return and he and Sofia busied themselves laying out plain but appetising dishes of sandwiches, baked goods, and meats. Davide collected the trays he'd used to transport the food and left. Kas and Mira stared at Sofia, waiting for some explanation as to how she knew Tia's name, or anything else about her. Ossi tucked into the food, seemingly oblivious to the tension.

"Please, help yourselves." Tacito smiled at Kas and Mira and gestured to the food.

"I think they're worried about how you know Tia's name," said Ossi thickly around his sandwich.

"Ah, of course. That is understandable." He smiled at the pair. "We Druids are creators, of sorts. We imbue objects with powers and magics. Some that require object wielders to operate, and others that just are. Some of our kind created those collars you wear."

Kas had expected at least a slight change of tone as Tacito mentioned the City Druids. Their allegiance to the Empire was said to be seen by the Druids of the Veil, the true Druids, as a betrayal of everything they believed and held sacred. But there was no inflection, no pause, nothing to indicate any feeling at all for those who the Empire used to create their collars and subjugate the land.

"Sometimes powerful Druids may see possible futures. One such foretelling was that three travellers would return something precious to us." He nodded at the ring. "And we would help them free their friend and—"

"More tea?" Sofia leaned forward, proffering the teapot. "Forgive me, Father, I shouldn't interrupt." She smiled as if embarrassed. "I worry our friends are parched from their journey."

"Right you are." Tacito chuckled. "They should be eating and drinking, not listening to the ramblings of an old man. Please, rest a while here and replenish yourselves. Sofia and I will prepare what is needed to remove the collars and return when everything is ready."

The two Druids smiled at the group before leaving, the door shutting quietly behind them.

"Should we be worried that they're going to get the soldiers?" Kas asked.

"No, they wouldn't do that," Ossi said, grabbing another sandwich. "The Druids dislike the annexation as much as anyone. If they didn't want us here, they'd just tell us to leave. They wouldn't turn us over to the Empire."

"They're nice enough," said Mira, trying a pastry. "But somehow, still pretty creepy."

"Right?" Kas said earnestly. "I can't put my finger on it."

"Like they're happy for us to be here, but really don't want us to be here."

"Exactly."

"You two are allowing childhood myths and legends to colour your minds." Ossi smiled, finishing his tea. "The Empire has always thought the Druids are secretive and devious. As if they are keeping something from all of us."

"If you Jatte think they're normal and not hiding anything, why aren't any of you here?" Kas asked. "We'd see at least one Jatte visiting the markets in Lorendell every month or so. They used to bring their own goods and goods they traded off the Shift—Kikachi. But never the Druids, and there's not a non-Druid in sight. Even the soldiers are camped as far away as possible."

Ossi frowned at that, opening his mouth to respond before closing it again and continuing to think.

"So long as we get these collars off, they can have all the secrets they want," said Mira, standing and wandering around the room.

"This is true," said Ossi, but Kas could see his friend was still bothered by what he had pointed out.

A bell rang out, causing Kas to jump. He joined his friends at the window, watching as all the Druids they could see seemed to abandon whatever they were doing and head off somewhere else. But they didn't move in the same direction. It clearly wasn't a bell telling them to assemble together, unless they all needed to go and get something before meeting. Instead, the Druids immediately moved with purpose in all manner of directions, some entering buildings, others heading for the main square, others walking straight into the woods.

No one heard Sofia re-enter the room, and they all jumped when she spoke.

"Quickly now, we're ready for you."

CHAPTER TWENTY-EIGHT

CASSANDRA

"Lord Flighty, I must insist—"

"We simply can't do it, Your Majesty." Lord Flighty shook his head sadly, as if tired from explaining something simple to someone too thick to grasp it. Not shamed as he should be for interrupting his empress. "It is a fine idea, truly. But to provide that much food to the citizens all at once would simply cause unnecessarily high tensions in the street. Tensions the city guard are ill-equipped to deal with."

"Yes, Lord Flighty." Cassandra gritted her teeth, trying to keep her temper in check. "But the rebels are now on side, and they have assured me they can work with the city guard to ensure appropriate and civilised distribution of the rations."

"Ah yes." Lord Flighty smiled, as if slightly embarrassed for her. "Your deal with the rebels."

He didn't use air quotes, but his tone implied them. Viscount Cuddy chuckled, and Baron Shamble shifted uncomfortably. "Forgive me, Empress, but perhaps the rebels are not the right group to assist with rations. It might conjure up unwelcome memories of the food riots. You were just a girl, but—"

"I'm well aware of the food riots, Lord Flighty."

"Yes, well, still. Even if your new... allies were appropriate for the task, I'm just not convinced the task itself is without issue." Lord Flighty shot a barely perceptible look at Viscount Cuddy, who sprang into action.

"I quite agree," he simpered.

Of course you bloody do.

"Providing rations to our less fortunate citizens is admirable, Empress," Cuddy began.

"The gods would surely smile upon you," added Shamble, perhaps seeking favour with Flighty for joining in, though clearly out of the loop about what he was joining in on. Cuddy shot him a look and Shamble sat back in his chair, flushing a light red.

"But I worry we might create a dependency."

"What?" Cassandra was furious. She knew where this was going. She just couldn't believe they were really going to run this argument.

"You see, my liege, if the citizens think you'll step in whenever things are hard, as noble as that sentiment might be, they may come to rely on your assistance. Some even to the detriment of their own attempts to better themselves."

"They'll stop looking to support themselves due to an assumption that the Crown will feed them?" Baron Page asked, frowning at the idea.

"I'm not saying they all will, but certainly a significant portion of the population—"

"A significant portion of the population will starve if we do nothing. Are we not in agreement on that?" Cassandra's tone belied her anger. Flighty smiled as if he could tell how angry she really was and how difficult it was to hold it back.

Baron Page nodded, and after a beat, Flighty allowed a slight nod of his head. Cuddy nodded after waiting for the signal from Flighty, and Shamble agreed only after seeing the two of them nod. Cassandra closed her eyes, taking a deep breath. How were these the most powerful men in the Empire?

"I am not willing to allow my people to starve to death, and certainly not when there are stores enough in our warehouses to prevent their deaths."

"But of course, Your Majesty. I don't think any of us are suggesting we should simply let the people starve," said Lord Flighty, as if that was not exactly what had just been suggested. He gave a little laugh, causing a tittering to break out from Cuddy and Shamble. "We simply query the proposed method of distribution."

"So long as the people get what they need, what does the method matter to you?" Cassandra's voice was low and dangerous as she leaned across the table, staring into Lord Flighty's eyes. The other nobles sat back, as if not wanting to be in the way.

Lord Flighty opened his mouth, but was interrupted.

"An excellent point, Your Majesty. I'm sure everyone here trusts whatever methodology you wish to utilise." The door slammed shut behind the newcomer and everyone jumped to their feet, smiles on their faces.

"Lukas!" Lord Flighty moved quickly to hug the young man. "Welcome home. I thought you were to remain at the border?"

"I will return, my lord, but I have been permitted a brief respite."

"And you've come to stand in for your father at the council meeting? Surely there are better ways to spend your leave?" Lord Flighty smiled at Lukas as if he were a naughty child, or something of a rogue. It turned Cassandra's stomach.

"Not at all," said Lukas easily, smiling around the room. "My family and I have always found these meetings of the utmost importance. Feeding the poor, for example, is something we would always support."

He said it with a smile, but the message was delivered firmly, and the smiles on the nobles' faces faded slightly.

"But of course, as do we all," said Lord Flighty with a deep nod. "I'd say that settles it then. Your Majesty, we'll leave you to implement your plan. Gentlemen, shall we?"

The nobles left before Cassandra could fully process what had just happened and realise exactly how mad she needed to be. Had she just been dismissed? As if it were Flighty's meeting!

She looked over at Lukas, who was frowning after the older men. She'd missed him since he went to the border. He'd joined the military so quickly and headed north almost immediately after bootcamp. Cassandra had barely seen him since she'd become empress.

He was her closest childhood friend. His father, Lord Sandison, was one of her own father's closest advisors and the two children had grown up together, running through the palace creating their own adventures. He'd accompanied her to events and balls and parties, protecting her from awkward pairings with suitable bachelors as she got older.

As they'd grown, she'd become increasingly aware of how tall he'd become and how his shoulders had broadened. But then his father had begun looking for a suitable match. And Cassandra hadn't been in the running. She'd pushed her feelings aside, telling herself she'd settle for friendship.

And then he had left. And she had missed her best friend.

She didn't know the full story of why he'd gone. She assumed some falling out with his father, but he'd sent her a letter apologising for his abrupt departure and promising to explain one day, and so she hadn't pushed. No matter how curious she was.

The military seemed to have suited Lukas. He was a man now, tall and broad. He filled his uniform well with both his bulk and his confidence. Lukas saw her looking and smiled at her. That smile could melt snow, it was so warm. Cassandra blushed.

"Thank you," she said, though she couldn't keep all the bitterness out of her voice.

"I'm sorry they only came around after I supported your idea. What was it, anyway?"

Her bitterness melted. She did resent that the nobles only agreed after Lukas sided with her, but how could she remain angry when her best friend was still happy to support her, no questions asked? Even now that her decisions weren't about which of their toys should be soldiers and which should be the enemy.

"It doesn't matter." She smiled, grabbing his arm and pulling him to her side. "Can you stay and visit? I'll have lunch sent to my room."

"I have all day." Lukas smiled down at Cassandra. "I'm not due home until dinner. I told my mother I had duties until then. But surely the empress doesn't have all day to sit around with a simple soldier."

She playfully bumped him. "I absolutely do not. But I do have all the time in the world for an old friend."

He squeezed her arm, and her heart jumped. What was wrong with her? She'd thought these feelings had gone, that she'd extinguished the flame years ago. But it was as if she'd simply locked them in a box in her heart. A box to which Lukas seemed to hold the key.

Cassandra mentally shook herself. Lukas was her oldest friend. *Oldest friend who's somehow even more handsome than he was before.* Cassandra expelled the thought from her mind and concentrated on the fact that she had her friend back.

She opened the door to her room and a little cry of surprise sounded.

"Sorry, Empress," Adeline said, falling into a deep curtsey.

"It's fine Adeline, I didn't mean to startle you. This is Lukas Sandison, an old friend."

"My lord," said Adeline, curtseying at Lukas.

Lukas laughed easily, crossing to Adeline and shaking her hand. "I'm no lord." He smiled. "Just a simple soldier. You can call me Lukas. Pleased to meet you, Adeline."

Adeline looked at Cassandra, her eyes huge, begging for guidance.

"You can call him Lukas here, Adeline. But out in the palace, it'd be safer to stick to 'Master Sandison' as the son of a lord." Cassandra gave Lukas a look. "You might not like it, but I'd rather my maid and only friend in the palace is kept out of trouble."

Adeline's face burned at the compliment, and Lukas sighed but didn't argue.

"Adeline, will you ask the kitchen to make lunch for two today and have it sent up here? Lukas and I are going to catch up."

"Yes, Empress." Adeline curtsied and headed for the door before curtseying again. "Your Majesty. My—Lukas." Flustered, Adeline left quickly.

"She's a gift from the gods," Cassandra said to Lukas's inquisitive smile. "But the other staff are not necessarily happy about my selecting someone so new for my maid. I think they're giving her a hard time, and Mrs Cameron caught her failing to curtsey on her way out yesterday. Gave her a bollocking in the kitchens. I want to just decree that she can call me Cassandra and not curtsey when we're in my rooms, but I know that would only make it worse."

"Much worse." Lukas laughed. "I can imagine Mrs Cameron's face if you even suggested that! She'd probably have you on extra chores again."

Cassandra laughed with him. The two had often been given extra chores as a punishment for getting up to mischief when they were young. Her father had thought it was a good idea for her to have some chores anyway, so as to better understand what went into running the palace and what the staff really did.

Mrs Cameron had taken to the extra chores punishment with vigour and always found the most difficult or disgusting tasks she could. Cassandra had often wondered if they were real tasks that someone had to carry out, or if Mrs Cameron had made them up.

"Tell me about you," said Cassandra, beaming at Lukas as she led the way over to the love seat by the window. "How have you been? How's the border?"

Lukas sat on the seat with her. There was room for another person to sit between them, but Cassandra suddenly felt flustered. As if they were engaging in some tryst. Lukas seemed oblivious to any such feelings, resting his right ankle on his left knee and sitting back, his arm casually resting on the back of the seat. Cassandra tried not to be obviously aware of his hand so close.

"I'm good." He smiled. "The border is..." He cast her a look. "Well, I don't need to stick to the cover story here, I guess. It's pretty terrible up there. The Controllers probe our defences regularly. It's taking a lot of patrols to catch them all and keep the border enforced, but I get the feeling that they're toying with us. Probing because we're there, rather than actually intending to do anything. If they invade, I'm not sure we can stop them. *When* they do."

The light fled his eyes, and he looked almost haunted.

"We'll be ready," Cassandra said with a conviction she did not feel.

Lukas looked at her as if sensing the lie. He nodded though, before forcing his smile back on his face. "The army suits me. Though I think I'm at ceiling rank."

"Impossible." Cassandra frowned. "You've always excelled at anything you've tried. Next time you visit it will probably be as commanding general."

Lukas barked out a surprised laugh. "Hardly. But even were that true, I don't think I'd want the job. Where I am now, we're all about the mission. Getting the job done. From what I can tell, any higher and it all becomes politics."

Cassandra's expression darkened. "Would that we all had such a choice."

"I know." Lukas smiled apologetically. "I'm sorry you're stuck with it. But being empress must have some perks, right?"

"I'm sure there must be," Cassandra muttered before catching herself. "No, you're right. I live a very privileged life, particularly in times where people are starving. Thank you, by the way, for backing me up."

"Of course. I'm sorry you needed it. I've never liked Flighty. Dad never liked him either."

"If he didn't have the largest private army of anyone, I'd seriously consider banning him from the council."

"Now *that* is a meeting I'd be happy to attend." Lukas laughed.

"I just don't understand how we got to a place where the Crown has no allies at all on the council." Cassandra shook her head. "I don't know if it's my father's doing, or his father before him."

"Or just an unfortunate changing of the guard on the

nobles' side?" Lukas suggested. "It doesn't have to be your family's fault."

Cassandra nodded, her eyebrow raised. "True. But there's so much mess my father left for me, it's easy to assume this was his mistake too."

Lukas dropped his hand onto Cassandra's shoulder, giving it a gentle squeeze and causing an eruption of butterflies in her stomach. "I hear you. That's the whole reason I'm back, actually. My dad," he explained at Cassandra's confused expression. "No one's heard from him in some time and my mother is worried. She fears for his safety, and so I was able to negotiate a couple of weeks' leave to look into it."

"We only have you for a short time then," said Cassandra, her mood falling.

"Not necessarily." Lukas smiled. "My boss said if I need a bit longer, he can swing me a position here at the palace."

"What? As my personal guard?" Cassandra was teasing, but her heart skipped a beat. Suddenly she felt fifteen again, when she'd thought she loved him. But they never seemed to be in the same place for long after she turned fifteen. She'd heard the palace gossip that it was her father's doing. That he knew they were close, but had another suitor in mind for her. A more powerful house than the Sandisons. And that he kept them apart to avoid unnecessary complications.

And then Lukas started courting Delilah Armengou. Or at least, that was the rumour. She saw Lukas's father at some party bragging that they would be married within the year. Cassandra had been crushed. She was yet to meet anyone she loved as she did Lukas. More terrifying, she hadn't met anyone who respected her as he did. Her stomach flipped as she remembered being worried that any husband her father selected for her would try to gain power.

To rule by proxy. She imagined the nobles siding with her imaginary husband over her.

But then, no wedding had eventuated. Not even an engagement. Without any warning, Lukas had up and joined the military, heading for bootcamp without even saying goodbye. And Cassandra had told herself it had been just a teenage crush and the pain in her heart was just her missing her friend.

"Cassandra?" Lukas's hand was on her shoulder again. "Are you alright? Are your imaginings of me as your personal guard so awful?" He smiled.

"No, of course not." Cassandra smiled too, shaking her head. "Sorry, for some reason Delilah Armengou popped into my head. Whatever happened to her?"

"No idea," said Lukas, sitting back, his hand withdrawn, the topic cooling his warmth.

"I heard you were to marry at one point," Cassandra said quietly, deciding to push the subject.

Lukas looked at her, fire in his eyes. "My *father* wished to join our houses. I'm sure she's a lovely woman, but I did not wish to marry for power."

"Is that why you left?"

Lukas nodded. "My father and I fought about it. I had always liked the idea of the military, but I'll admit my joining was more about escape than service. And then, once I was at the border, service was all it was about. I was needed. I was doing something *real*. So I made career choices that kept me there, but my father thought they were about avoiding him. I never really got to explain it to him, and now..."

Cassandra's heart contracted at the pain on Lukas's face. He and his father had always been close. He was the eldest of Lord Sandison's children, and as he'd gotten older, the two had almost seemed more like brothers than father and son. That they fought and now his father was missing must be killing him. Cassandra felt the familiar twinge of being trapped.

"I thought he was writing to your family?" Cassandra asked.

"Yes, he was, but it's been a while since we've received a letter. And he really should have been back by now. At least to check in and see the family. It's been almost three years since anyone's seen him."

"Three years?" Cassandra felt sick. "Surely not. He's been abroad, dealing with your island holdings, I thought. Someone must have seen him."

"We thought that too. His letters were coming from our outposts. But then mother went to our closest island, Boomver, and they said they'd not seen him at all."

"That's terrible," said Cassandra. She had no idea Lady Sandison had gone abroad. How had she become so out of touch?

"When she arrived home, there was a letter from Dad. It said he was at one of our other islands, having deviated from his planned trip to Boomver. The letter said he'd not been there in years and intended to go soon, on his way home."

"That seems a little too convenient," said Cassandra, frowning.

"That's what I thought too."

"Clumsy, though. If something untoward has befallen him, you'd think whoever had him would be smarter than that."

Lukas considered this. "True, but everyone makes mistakes. Mother's trip may have caught them off guard. Or if he's only recently been captured, they might not know we have reason to worry."

"That's true," Cassandra said quickly. "We really don't even know how long he's been actually missing."

"Which leads back to my being here." He smiled at her, and her chest filled with warmth and light. "Though I'd prefer better circumstances, it is good to see you again, Your Majesty."

"Nope." Cassandra immediately shook her head. "Do not ever call me that again unless completely necessary. It's weird, coming from you."

"Whatever pleases you, Your Grace."

CHAPTER TWENTY-NINE

EMILIA

A DONKEY BRAYED, and Emilia wrinkled her nose. She'd been watching for over an hour now, and it was clear the animals did not like traversing the drawbridge.

'Drawbridge' seemed the wrong term for what was little more than thick wooden planks lying across the hideously deep and empty moat. The bridge was as wide as the main road running the length of southern Valoris. The rusted chains attaching the bridge to the palace walls were rusted and set, giving no indication that the bridge was ever raised.

Perhaps they maintained the title merely to avoid installing any kind of safety barrier. The bridge was simply the wooden planks with no railing on either side. Emilia shuddered to think how many unfortunate souls had been lost over the edge. The people seemed less bothered by it than the animals did. The donkeys and mules all pressed as much as they could into the centre, creating an unnecessary crush of people trying to get to the palace.

Poor things. Emilia wished the people would leave the animals on this side of the drawbridge and carry their wares themselves. But the people of the Empire were lazy. And godless, by the looks of things.

She hadn't had a chance to explore the City of the Damned as she followed the soldier through the maze of streets, but everything here seemed so... commercial. Back in the Divvinium, almost everything was done in the service of the Divine Prophet. Food was grown to feed the One True God's people. Not to sell. Not to use to make a profit while others begged in the streets.

Everything about the city had been jarring from the moment Emilia had followed the soldier through the gates. So much colour. So much noise. And so little cohesion. It did not seem the Empire folk cared for one another at all.

Emilia had her own issues with the Divvinium, but at least she knew she would be cared for. She would be fed and clothed and healed if she fell ill. Here they walked past the sick in the streets, the pain of their brothers and sisters none of their concern.

For the first time, Emilia could find little fault with the idea that the One True God had ordered the obliteration of an entire people. She'd had her doubts as they destroyed the Communicators. She'd kept them to herself, of course, but she'd had a hard time understanding what was so offensive about a magic that allowed communication with animals.

She looked around as another donkey brayed, having been prodded forward onto the drawbridge by its owner. Her eyes narrowed. Perhaps the Communicators had been like this too. She'd never seen their villages before the masses of Divvinium troops had engulfed their lands. Maybe they'd been disconnected from His light, as the Empire clearly was.

The man prodded the donkey again, the beast turning and snapping its teeth at him. Emilia fought the urge to prod the man off the drawbridge.

The Divvinium didn't care for animals, though cruelty was outlawed. Emilia, however, had always held a soft place for them in her heart. She'd used her invisibility to free a number of mistreated animals back home. If she didn't need to get a move on and find the soldier, she'd be tempted to follow the man home and address the situation.

Emilia pushed off the wall she'd been leaning against and started forward. She kept closer to the edge of the drawbridge than she was comfortable with, but everyone avoided it, so it was the safest way to cross without bumping anyone and alerting them to her presence. Though there were so many people here, all pushing against each other, she doubted anyone would notice a bump from a ghost.

Telling herself to not look down, Emilia fixed her eyes on the palace gates. She failed to notice she'd moved too close to a couple who were moving slowly across the drawbridge with their donkey and cart. Before she could move away, the man shifted, bumping into her.

"Sorry," the man called without looking as he jostled Emilia.

"For what?" his female companion asked.

"Bumping you."

"You didn't bump me, you silly sod."

They continued bickering as Emilia froze, allowing them to get farther away. Taking a deep breath, Emilia shook her head, then her body. She was better than this. She needed to concentrate. How awful to come this far only to fail because of a fear of heights? She'd never live it down.

Getting her mind back in the game, Emilia set off again, this time fully aware of her surroundings and focussing her mind on the task at hand. It had been a gamble, letting the soldier go, but necessary. It was well known the palace was warded to alert if someone under the power of an Imperius passed through the gates. It was also warded to sound an alarm if an Imperius themselves entered the palace walls.

But then, the wards at the border were also supposed to alert for an Imperius, and they'd given her no issues.

The trick, she'd learned, was to pass through when she was invisible. Apparently, the wards didn't pick up on her when she bent the light. But they would still notice the connection if the soldier entered under her control, and so she'd had to release him.

Which meant entering the palace, somehow locating him again, and then bringing him back under control. Establishing the connection was the hardest part, even for a magical as powerful as Emilia, who could take someone's mind with a mere glance. But the other peoples of Valoris tended to freak out at the Imperius's red eyes, and some people with a strong will could break the connection at that point.

The soldier's will was strong. But Emilia had been stronger.

She looked up at the palace. She'd never seen anything so huge, and that included the Divine Prophet's Grand Temple. So gaudy, so unnecessary. The building loomed above her, the perfect effigy to what stood out so glaringly.

The Empire worshipped money and things. If you had them, you were powerful. If you didn't, you were worthless. They spoke of gods, but from her brief glances, they had largely forgotten their false deities. There was no faith. There was no soul. There was no heart.

She frowned, again taking in the colourful outfits, the strange hairstyles. All things offensive to the One True God. These people were lost. Emilia wondered that the One True God didn't tell the Divine Prophet to bring them back to the fold. To help them find the righteous path. Sinners though they all were, obliteration as a first step still struck Emilia as extreme.

Spotting a gap, Emilia darted forward, slipping between bodies like the very wind itself. And then she was through the gates before she'd even had a chance to wonder if these wards were different to the northern ones that had offered her no issues.

Nothing. Silence.

Emilia allowed herself a beat to breathe a sigh of relief before she again took in the monstrosity of the palace, wondering how in Hades she was going to find the soldier again. Frowning as she scanned for entry points, it occurred to her she didn't necessarily need to find the soldier again.

Who knew how long he'd be staying at the palace? Perhaps he'd simply check in with his old friend the empress and then leave in search of his missing father.

Emilia walked to the main entrance. All she really needed was someone close to the empress. The empress herself couldn't be taken. Not with the relic on her finger that repelled all magics. And so Emilia needed the next best thing, which at this point was the soldier. She could find someone else once she was inside, but... she'd liked the soldier. He'd seemed... noble. Good in a way she hadn't expected. Not in a man, and certainly not in a blasphemer.

Plus, her handler would be pissed if she switched her target without seeking permission. They always were when she changed things up while the mission was in progress. And Sigmund was particularly sensitive to anyone going rogue. He fancied himself quite the puppet master, and if yours were strings he couldn't pull, they'd be cut.

She'd have a certain amount of leeway, given how much praise her success garnered for her superiors, but Sigmund was certainly no Patron Smolka.

The main entrance was busy, but it was open. Several other, more private entrances were all closed. The last thing she needed was someone on the other side to be startled by a self-opening door. But the main entrance was also heavily guarded. The guards were alert, scanning people as they entered and left, and occasionally taking people to the side and searching them.

Peering beyond the entrance, she saw more guards scattered around what looked like an enormous entry hall. She looked back at one of the doors along the wall of the palace. No doubt an entry for servants. Preferable, but it hadn't been used in the short time she'd been here. No way to know how often it was used or where it likely led.

Emilia would prefer to wait out here for at least an hour. Longer, if possible. Get the feel of things. Who went in and out. How often and from where. Make an appropriate plan to infiltrate while simultaneously plotting several exfiltration avenues for emergencies and enter only when the time was right.

But the longer she took tracking down the soldier, the more information she missed. The empress might be giving the soldier orders. He might be laying out their upcoming plans. She was missing opportunities to prod and nudge and alter the course of the impending war.

Main entrance it is.

The couple she'd bumped into were there already, now arguing with a guard who seemed unwilling to let them in.

"Never had produce this good, I'm telling yer right now," the woman was saying to the guard, who looked like his patience was running out.

"Freshest in the land, true enough." The man nodded.

"I don't care about the produce," said the guard, restraint close to breaking. "Do you have an appointment with the chief cook?" He looked from the woman to the man, both hesitating. "The chief maid, perhaps? Or even the head of housekeeping? No?"

"I'm sure that—"

"No appointment, no entry," said the guard with a note of finality.

"Well, how do we make an appointment?" asked the man, and they stepped back from where they'd been blocking the entrance as the guard began pointing and explaining where they needed to go.

A gap opened and Emilia slipped inside, no one any the wiser.

She looked around the expansive entryway, noting doors leading away in all directions, and a staircase heading up into the higher floors. She strode confidently towards the stairs.

Now, to find my soldier.

Emilia walked swiftly and silently past all the watchful guards, careful not to pass too close and create curiosity with a breeze or her scent. She hurried up the stairs, certain that whoever owned this monument to hedonism would be located as high as possible, taking advantage of what must admittedly be a spectacular view.

Heavy footsteps sounded above her, voices low, but not whispered, and Emilia hurried up farther, pressing herself into an alcove as four men, draped in clothing and jewels that would feed a small village for a year, descended slowly.

"Of course, he'll come round to our way of thinking," said the one the others looked to. He was in charge then. Two of the other men looked up at him as if he were responsible for hanging the stars. The other didn't appear to be sycophantic, but his presence told Emilia that he wasn't as powerful as the one who'd spoken.

"You don't think he'll side with her?" asked a small, stout man, wringing his hands.

"Not at all." The main man's jowls shook with his head. "I know Lukas's father would have ensured he knows what needs to happen. And I myself instructed the boy in business and finance when he was younger."

"But they are very good friends," suggested the one man not hanging off the main man's every word. "It's possible she will find Lukas an ally. And if his father is not found—"

"Charles Sandison is not missing," the main man snapped at the other, who shrugged as if used to his temper and unconcerned with his disapproval. "And I will bring Lukas around. He's nothing to worry about."

The men's voices grew quiet as they descended, and Emilia continued her climb through the palace. It seemed there was plenty of discord already. Exploiting it to weaken the Empire before the invasion should be simple.

They'd been talking about the soldier. His friends at the border had called him 'Lukey'. It had been a boon to find someone with a personal connection to the empress, but a noble with a seat on the empress's council was a bonus. And a missing father could be useful, too. So much easier to manipulate powerful emotions that were already there. And for spies, the key was a soft touch.

Her compatriots at the border were looking for blunt weapons. Soldiers to control who could be walked back into camp and turned on their units, for example. But when an Imperius took full control, the host was immediately aware of the incursion.

For spies behind enemy lines, you might need to take control for a moment and then release it. Just as she'd had to release the soldier in order to pass through the wards. Spies had to gently caress the target's mind. Linger without disturbing them and lightly nudge them where you wanted them to go.

Making someone yell at a friend would leave them wondering why they'd become so angry, whereas picking at the scab of an irritation already present left fewer questions.

On the top floor now, there were more servants, but they were quieter. She was in the right place. Two guards stood alert outside double doors and Emilia stood silently nearby, waiting for another servant to enter, or for her target to exit. A smile tugged at her lips. This was going to be an interesting mission.

CHAPTER THIRTY

KAS

Sofia led the group out of the hut and in the opposite direction of the town square.

"Where are we going?" asked Kas, trying to sound curious rather than worried.

"It's best if we keep as quiet as we can," was Sofia's reply. It did not help Kas's anxiety.

They passed a few Druids heading towards the square. Each nodded at the group but no one seemed at all surprised to see little Sofia leading a group of non-Druids through their town. Sofia's pace didn't change. Not even when they left the huts and walked into the woods.

Though he'd been unsettled, until now Kas hadn't been worried that anything untoward might befall them. But why else did you ever lead people into the woods but to kill them? He'd heard the stories. He knew people who had never left the city for fear of coming upon such psychopaths.

But their direction was not towards the soldiers' camp, so at least it didn't seem she was turning them in. Unless there was another camp.

"Hold."

The voice was calm, deep, and entirely unexpected. The three outsiders all jumped and swore. A large man in a grey Druid robe holding a staff appeared just off the path they were following through the trees. Kas was immediately embarrassed by his reaction, especially since Sofia didn't even flinch, but felt better that Ossi had also jumped.

"Hail, Defender," said Sofia politely, bowing at him. "They are permitted."

The large man stared at each of the companions in turn before apparently deciding they were okay. He nodded and faded back into the trees. Sofia started off again and Kas followed, looking to see where the man had gone, but there was no trace of him.

The unsettled feeling that had started when Kas entered the Druid village grew. His instincts were beginning to scream at him to leave.

Suddenly, the trees parted, and Kas found himself at the foot of a mountain. There was no sloping start to this mountain. It simply seemed to have exploded out of the ground, reaching for the sky. The resulting cliff extended so high, Kas had to look straight up to find where it started tapering into any kind of peak. The true peak must have been permanently in the clouds.

"In here," said Sofia.

She was standing near the mountain face, where the stone was jutting out. Looking along the cliff wall, Kas could see several such divots, as if the mountain were somehow made of frozen waves. Kas's first thought was that the divots were large enough to hide a small band of mercenaries, and his heart pounded in preparation for an attack.

But Sofia just stood there, patiently waiting. There were either no mercenaries, or those who were hiding had been hired by the Druids. Though if they wished to harm the interlopers, surely they could have had that huge guy in the woods do it.

Kas moved closer to Sofia, trying to dispel the unsettled feeling and trust the little girl. There was no reason for the Druids to want to harm them. And Sofia was what? Ten? That seemed a little young to be plotting the murder of three strangers.

As he got closer, he realised the gap where she stood hid a cave. And standing in the mouth, smiling, was Tacito.

"Apologies for the cloak and dagger," he said, ushering them inside. "It's important we keep this cave secret."

Kas was about to ask why when the reason appeared before his eyes. The cave opened into what could only be described as an underground village. It was rudimentary, seemingly just caverns and tunnels without anything much carved into the walls. But it was clearly lived in by the dozens of Druids who were now staring at him.

There were Druids of all ages, and at least half of them were collared.

"The Testing," Tacito said, gesturing at the group. "Terrible thing. Though we are grateful that a collar doesn't come with an automatic ticket to the labour camps."

"Didn't you create the Testing?" Kas frowned. The Druids made all magical objects. Including the Testing Orb.

"Oh yes." Tacito nodded. "But only because the Empire requested it. We told them it was rudimentary. Unable to cope with nuances, as you'd well know." He inclined his head at Kas, who flushed immediately. "But they insisted. We, of course, don't need the Testing. But with the annexation..."

Tacito shrugged, and the smile left his face. It was enough of a shift for Kas to realise the Druids were actually quite angry about the whole thing, understandably so. But they seemed incapable of anger like Kas knew it. He'd be yelling and swearing and rebelling.

And that would probably have resulted in his friends being killed or sent to the camps. Still, Kas felt there was an honour in that. In fighting back, no matter the cost. And yet, looking around, it seemed however the Druids were approaching things was working for them.

"Of course," Tacito continued, "we need our powerful Druids to create objects and maintain the wards, and so the collaring of our tier threes is somewhat inconvenient. But the Collaborators—the Druids who left us—were not the most powerful of our kind, so we have been able to develop a way to remove their collars."

Kas looked about the cave, this time examining the Druids with free necks. Now that he looked closer, he could see several thin bands of metal lying within arms' reach of a number of Druids, all of whom were sitting at woven mats, working magic into various objects.

"So why are you hiding in here?" asked Mira. "Why wear the collars at all?"

"We can't very well rip the collars off and wander around the town," Tacito said, as if correcting a child's misconception. "That would make the soldiers angry, and we might then find our collared brothers and sisters sent to the labour camps, where we wouldn't be able to free them. I'd also expect the soldiers may not feel as comfortable camping outside of our settlement, and may decide they need to relocate and set up their camp within to keep a closer watch on us."

Kas looked around again, his brow furrowing. The Druids had suffered a minor inconvenience to their daily lives. Not only had they invented the collars—they'd also found a solution to them, but they'd kept that solution to themselves. He thought of Tia, imprisoned before she even knew she had magic, and the rest of her people who were collared if they tested as powerfully magical, and were never been permitted to use their magic. To feel it. Anger welled up inside him.

"It is very important at this stage that it not become widely known that we are able to remove the collars." Tacito's voice became firm, and Kas could feel the old man's eyes on him.

"Why?" Kas asked, fighting to keep his voice even. "Why not just release everyone? If we all had our magic back, the Empire would be hard-pressed to collar us again."

"If the Empire believed their collars could be defeated, they would have the Collaborators create another way to stifle magic," Tacito said simply. "But the likelihood of us being able to release everyone swiftly enough that the Empire couldn't simply round us up and prevent us from removing the collars in the first place is low. You will understand soon."

"But," Kas said, gesturing around, "how is it fair that your people get to be free when others aren't?"

Tacito looked Kas dead in the eye. Gone was the impression of a pleasant old man. Kas felt the power of generations bearing into him, the force of the stare making Kas want to get on his knees.

"It isn't," Tacito said simply.

Kas blinked and Tacito's smile returned, the power within him hidden once more.

"Are those wards?" Mira asked, and Kas followed her gaze to the faint etchings on the walls. He had seen similar patterns near the palace gates.

"We must teach our young," Tacito said. "So, they hide here and remove their collars while they work. Then the collars are reattached and they return to the village. It's not ideal..."

Kas recognised the anger in the Druid's voice this time.

"We've almost perfected a way to nullify the effects of the collar while it is still being worn." Tacito perked up. "That will allow us to work more easily and with less hiding. Of course, that's not what you're after."

Tacito turned and nodded at Sofia, who crossed to a crude wooden bench and retrieved a long, thin metal rod. It looked like a larger version of a lock pick. Sofia returned, and Tacito held up a hand.

"There is one... small task we'd ask in return."

Kas's heart sank. *Of course there is.* His mind ran through fantastical possibilities of what the Druids might ask in exchange for the removal of the collars, and he was halfway to panicking about the impossibility of what he was imagining before he got a hold of himself.

They're going to remove the collar. I'll be able to use magic again. I can free Tia. And then Salomon...

A slightly nauseous feeling settled in his stomach as he remembered his brother's betrayal. But despite what Salomon had done, he couldn't simply give in to the anger and hurt he felt. He couldn't shake the care he felt for his brother, the worry at what had made him change so completely. As much as he dearly wanted to give Salomon the punch in the face he'd truly earned, he paradoxically still wanted to fix whatever had gone wrong with him.

Either way, he needed the collar off. Resolve settled over Kas. He would do whatever was asked. Anything to get this thing off his neck.

"What is it you ask of us, Druid of the Veil?" asked Ossi, formal as ever.

Tacito hesitated and then gestured to the firepit, inviting the friends to sit on the logs placed around it.

"What do you know of the Controllers?" Tacito asked, and Kas's stomach turned. It was going to be worse than he expected. Tacito was going to ask them to steal something from the Controllers. Or sabotage them somehow. Kas, despite his wish to travel and see the world beyond the Empire, had no desire whatsoever to enter Controller territory.

"We defeated them the last time they came," said Ossi confidently.

"As did we," Kas added. "Though I always felt from the stories that it was more the Controllers just left, rather than we defeated them."

Tacito beamed and nodded at Kas's answer.

"They've changed," said Mira quietly.

Kas felt the attention of the Druids home in on Mira. "Changed, how?" Tacito asked.

"They used to attack and withdraw, like Kas said. But now they seem to want to obliterate the other tribes, rather than just take slaves."

Kas watched Tacito study Mira, then share a look with Sofia. The little girl smiled at the old man, as if she'd won a bet.

"Very observant. Especially from an... Empiran," said Tacito. There was something in his tone that Kas couldn't place. And he didn't like the way Tacito was looking at Mira.

"The Controllers have always been cyclical." Tacito returned his gaze to the group. "They descend on a tribe and begin the Reaping, taking as many citizens that can be placed under the mind controller's power as possible so that they can perform the menial tasks no Controller wants to perform. But they have always been careful not to take too many. To leave the tribe able to recover, so that they may become ready to Harvest in later years."

Kas's mind reeled. The concept of taking slaves to live out their days under mind control was awful, but the clinical nature of what the Controllers had been doing was sickening.

"Until now," said Ossi, his face showing he was as appalled as Kas.

"Until now," Tacito agreed. "The Controllers descended on the Communicators in line with their schedule—"

"And you didn't think to warn anyone?" Mira asked, her voice hard. "Having figured out their routine and patterns, you didn't think to pass that along?"

"It is not our place to interfere with the way of things." It was Sofia who answered.

"What's that supposed to mean?" Mira sounded angry now.

"We are the Keepers. Our role is to protect the sacred relics until the world is ready for Unification." Tacito spread his hands as if to say everything was beyond his control.

"How can the world be unified if the Controllers destroy everything?" Mira asked, seemingly appalled by the abject lack of responsibility of the Druids. "If you'd told the tribes, they would have unified against the threat."

"That is not what history tells us would happen." Tacito sounded apologetic. "And some have argued in the past that were the Controllers to rise, defeating all the other tribes, that could be seen as another form of Unification."

The three friends' jaws dropped.

"You can't believe that?" Kas stared at the man, aghast.

Tacito shrugged. "It is not for me to say how the Unification will occur. What I prefer matters not in such things."

Kas wasn't too sure what this 'Unification' was, but it was frustrating that the Druids seemed to desire it, yet were completely against doing anything to make it happen.

"But our leader," Tacito continued, regaining Kas's

attention in an instant, "wished to gather more information."

"Wait, I thought you were the leader?" Kas asked, confused.

Tacito laughed. "Oh powers, no. I am a steward. Outsiders often wish to speak with the person in charge, and so, particularly with Francisco... away, I have become that person. If Francisco has truly returned to the energy, we will have a new leader."

"But not you," confirmed Kas. This all struck him as weird.

"Not me." Tacito smiled. "Our proposal, such that it is, is that you will remain here tonight as our guests. We shall remove your collars, and tomorrow you will escort our new leader to the City of Magic. With a short detour, of course, to free your friend Tia and remove her collar also," he added, sensing Mira ready herself to interrupt.

"That's it?" asked Kas. That seemed far too easy.

"Yes." Tacito shrugged. There was hesitation in his voice.

"Speak freely, Druid," said Ossi in his deep tones. "Let us discuss the bargain openly."

"We would ask that you help our emissary gain an audience with the empress. We would also hope that you might remain open to helping further, depending on the outcome of that audience."

"Is that all?" said Kas sarcastically.

"Of course, your collars will be long gone by then," said Tacito, unperturbed by Kas's tone. "And we have no bargaining chip as such with which to entice you to help."

"So why would we stay?" asked Kas, earning a glare from Ossi. He didn't mean to be rude, but once his collar was off, Tia freed, and the debt paid, he was going to resolve things with Salomon one way or another, and start his life.

The life that had been taken when he was caught and sent to the camps.

Tacito gave Kas a sad smile. "I believe you will stay because Francisco saw it."

Kas blinked. What did that mean?

"Often, our leaders are blessed with visions of what the future may hold. Before he left us, Francisco received such a vision. He did not divulge all of what he saw, but his vision was powerful enough that he left the next day, explaining only that he was to go to the city to guide and protect a boy who would be instrumental in the events that will herald the Unification."

It took Kas a beat to realise they were all now staring at him. It took him a beat longer to realise why.

"What? Me?"

"He told me the one he was to protect would return bearing his ring."

Kas felt incredibly uncomfortable with the implications and accompanying weight of expectation and responsibility. "He gave me his ring because I was the only one around after... when he got hurt."

"And how was he hurt?" Tacito asked with a smile that said he knew how, even though he couldn't possibly. "You are the one he left to protect. You are the one he has sent to us."

"We accept your terms," said Ossi decisively.

"Ossi!" Kas looked at his friend in disbelief.

Ossi held up a hand to Kas. "We will escort your emissary to the city after we free Tia, and we will consider what comes of the meeting with the empress."

"And how are we supposed to make that happen? Knock on the palace door and ask to see her?" complained Kas, annoyed at Ossi, even though he realised his friend was right to agree.

"I believe she will meet with the travellers seeking to return this." Tacito opened his hand, revealing the empress's ring. The ring Kas had stolen the night he was caught and sent to the camps. The ring that he'd thrown over the bridge.

"How did you... ?"

"The relics often find their way back to us," Tacito said, evading the question. "The empress will agree to an audience with the one who found and seeks to return her relic. And then our emissary will speak with the empress and determine the way forward."

Kas looked at Tacito. He just looked like a kindly old man. His pleasant smile was fixed to his face, but his eyes... if you ignored everything else and just looked in his eyes, there was something shrewd there. Something with a singular focus.

Druids had a mixed reputation. While some merely saw them as kindly people who made useful magical objects, others resented their aloofness. The way they seemed to see themselves as apart from the goings on in the world. They also somehow seemed to avoid ever getting caught up in conflict. Indeed, now that Kas thought about it, the Controllers had reaped from all the peoples of Valoris, except the Druids.

But while those who complained about them felt they didn't care, looking at Tacito, Kas could see he did care. He cared deeply. It mattered very much to the Druids what happened here. Who won what was sounding like a war to end all wars between the Controllers and those whom they would control. Or kill. What Kas didn't know was why.

"If you have that ring and you're so sure the empress will speak to whoever returns it to her, why don't you just take it yourselves?" Kas asked. He noticed Ossi and Mira react to his question and look to Tacito for his answer. "It doesn't seem you need us at all."

Tacito and Sofia shared a look, and it was Sofia who spoke next.

"You are welcome to stay here, in the cave, or in the village," she said, ignoring Kas's question. "We will give you food, drink, and warm beds for the night. I apologise that we will not be joining you. I have things to attend to before we leave in the morning."

"We? Wait, you're the emissary?" Kas couldn't believe that something clearly very important to them would be entrusted to a child, no matter how mature she seemed to be.

"You think I make a poor emissary?" There was a note of humour in Sofia's voice.

"No, well," Kas floundered. "I mean, you're very young…"

He met Sofia's eyes and was hit with an intense feeling of having lived a very long time. Kas blinked and suddenly it was just the little girl smiling at him, the feeling gone completely. He shook his head, trying to shake the discomfort that was now almost overwhelming. Kas had no idea why, but his intuition was screaming at him to leave this place and never return.

"We are honoured that you will join us, Druid Sofia," said Ossi with a bow. This time, Kas was grateful to Ossi for bringing things back on track. For covering his rudeness. Why had he decided to insult the only people who could remove their collars?

Which reminded him. "And, uh, when will you be able to take these off?" Kas tapped his collar, trying to sound polite and respectful.

Tacito's cheeks flushed, and he looked genuinely embarrassed. "Ah, yes. Forgive me, but I think it best if we remove those in the morning, don't you?"

CHAPTER THIRTY-ONE

KAS

Kas barely slept that night. He'd thought he would drift off the moment his head hit the pillow, what with walking half the length of the continent and this being the first night in a real bed in over eight years. The cot in the rebel headquarters didn't really count. Not compared to the mattress that seemed to mould to his body and the feather pillow.

But sleep eluded him, his hand constantly reaching for his collar, his mind racing.

Tomorrow.

He would get his collar off tomorrow. What would it be like? The object Sofia had produced that would free Kas and his friends hadn't looked complicated. Maybe she'd simply touch it to the metal around his neck and the collar would just drop off. Or perhaps there would be some ritual, long and involved.

One question plagued him, though. One fear. Kas had opened his mouth to ask several times, but closed it, too afraid of the answer. He'd been wondering about it ever since the collar was clamped around his neck, though it had always been an academic exercise. Like wondering about their families. It didn't matter, because he was never going to get the collar off. But now he was. Tomorrow he'd be free, and all he could think was: would his magic be the same?

Kas didn't know of anyone who'd had their collar removed before. Wasn't sure the City Druids had even thought about it, tested it. His mind drifted to the cave. All the Druids of the Veil were sitting there, enchanting, their collars by their sides. It gave him hope, but not much.

The Druids were just... different. They were the only tribe who never produced non-magicals. Though there were some pretty dark rumours about how that had come to be the case. But something had struck Kas in the cave that he was almost certain hadn't been noted by his friends. The Druids were testing their enchantments. Which meant Druids were both magicals *and* object wielders.

Who knew if the collars even worked the same on them? Besides, with their ability to remove them at will, perhaps the effects—whatever they might be—were lessened. They were still able to regularly connect with their magic.

Kas had been cut off from his magic for eight years. What if it simply no longer worked? Like a flame starved of air. Or maybe it would be like an atrophied limb. Could he restore it to what it had been, or would his magic always be crippled?

Sweat broke out across Kas's forehead and he kicked the covers back, as if the sweat were from the temperature in the room and not his anxiety. He'd always thought the magic didn't matter that much to him. That it was simply another aspect of who he was, but only as important as how fast he could run, or how strong he was. That it wasn't important to who he was as a person.

That was what he'd always told Salomon. What he thought he believed. And while he'd missed it immediately and longed to have what felt like a part of him back, not having magic hadn't bothered him at the camps. Not in terms of his confidence. But there, none of the prisoners had magic.

And magic's absence had been a great equaliser. They'd all gotten to know each other as people, not based on what they could do. Of course, the shared struggle of the camps had bonded them, too. But it had been different. And now, with the prospect of his collar being removed so close, with the idea that he might not have his magic, or that it might not be as powerful as it once had been, Kas felt terrified.

Who was he without it? He felt embarrassed in anticipation, imagining seeing people who'd known him back then. Seeing their faces when they realised he couldn't do what he once could. Their sympathy and pity.

Kas sat up, giving up on sleep entirely. He padded over to the window, keeping his steps as silent as he could. Ossi grunted and turned, but his breathing remained steady. He couldn't hear Mira, but he didn't sense a change and assumed she was still sleeping.

It was dark outside, but despite the trees surrounding the settlement, he could see the sky starting to lighten. Dawn wasn't far away.

Kas turned quickly as he heard the door click softly shut.

"Sorry," Mira whispered. She glanced over to where Ossi continued to snore softly and tiptoed over to Kas, sitting in the chair next to him.

"Where have you been?" Kas asked.

"I couldn't sleep. I wanted to wander around the camp, but then Davide found me and showed me around. I assume someone saw me and let him know," Mira said, seeing Kas's forehead crease. "But he gave me a lovely tour and then let me hang out in the caves."

"He let you stay there by yourself?"

"Well, no, he introduced me to a couple of Druids who were working and they showed me what they were doing. And then Davide returned a little while ago and escorted me back here."

Kas returned his gaze to the blossoming day. The sky was now red near the horizon, but still a deep blue if he craned his head out the window, looking up. So beautiful, and yet, something about this place, about the Druids, had him on edge.

"I mean, it's reasonable, I guess," said Mira thoughtfully. "What if I got lost, or wandered off into the path of the soldiers?"

"True," said Kas, sitting back in his chair. "But it does feel an awful lot like there's something they don't want us to see."

Mira nodded. "Which is odd, right? Because I'd have thought the uncollared folk in the cave would be the big secret."

Kas nodded back at her. "Although, since we're here to get our collars off, the fact that they can remove them isn't so taboo."

The pair lapsed into silence, both lost in their thoughts. Kas struggled to think of what else the Druids might be hiding. Maybe they weren't hiding anything at all. Maybe Mira was right, and they were escorting their guests for their own safety. Maybe they were just weird. And though Kas held that his last thought might still be true, he also felt there was something else going on here. Something the Druids were hiding.

He said as much to Mira, and the small woman agreed.

"But to be honest, I don't think I care to know what it is," she said. "They're going to take our collars off today, and then we're out of here."

"Yeah, but with one of them with us."

"I do not mind little Sofia," said Ossi from behind, making them both jump.

"Gods above, Ossi, when did you get up? And how are you dressed?"

"I may be large," said Ossi, eyes shining with mischief, "but I can move softly."

"You slept in your clothes, didn't you?" Kas guessed.

"A Jatte never reveals his secrets."

"Do the Jatte even have any secrets?" Kas teased.

"It would boggle your mind."

A small cough from the door had them all turning, and before them stood Sofia.

"Does the wood from your trees not creak at all?" Kas asked, glaring at the old cabin they were in as if it had personally offended him.

"Perhaps your ears don't work," offered Ossi with a smile. Kas rolled his eyes at his friend.

"Good morning, Sofia," said Mira pointedly. "Are you ready for us?"

"We are. Please, follow me."

Kas had thought they would return to the cave, but instead, Sofia led them along a different path. They wound through a different part of the forest, this section leading them up a hill. Kas was embarrassed about how out of breath he was until they turned a corner and he saw just how high they had climbed.

The Druid village was laid out below them, closer than when they had spied it on their way in, but they were now higher up. The trees surrounding the village covered the various tracks like the one they had followed this morning, and the one that led to the caves.

To his left was the mysterious clearing where he could see the tip of the white stone.

"What *is* that?" he asked Sofia, pointing.

Sofia glanced around and saw what had caught his attention. "That is one of our sacred sites," she said simply. "A peaceful place for us to commune with the Ancients."

She started off again, leading them along a path that wound up into the mountains.

"Are the Ancients your gods?" asked Kas, hurrying to catch up and walk beside her.

"The Ancients are important to us, but no, they are not to us as your gods are to you."

"Do you believe in any gods?" Kas asked.

"No," said Sofia. "We don't believe that there are higher beings that created or control the world. Instead, we believe that all the worlds are energy, and what matters are the interactions between the different energies."

Kas blinked. She'd said it simply enough, but it was such a strange concept, and unlike anything he'd ever heard before. "So, like how we're interacting now?"

"Yes." Sofia inclined her head. "But also how we interact with the plants and the animals, and even this mountain. When the energies are in harmony, everything functions at a higher level. But when the energies are in conflict, there is damage and despair."

"So, how do the Ancients fit in?" Kas asked, trying not to puff despite the incline. Sofia didn't seem at all phased by the mountain's steep incline. Kas supposed her energy must be in harmony with it.

"We believe that the first peoples of the world were completely in tune with everything around them. But as they grew and developed, some fell out of harmony with the world. Eventually, those who were in harmony increased that connection, and left this world."

"Left? Left how?"

"We do not know. Perhaps they assumed another form.

Perhaps their relationship with the energy allowed them to travel great distances. Perhaps they became one with the energy." Sofia almost whispered this last option and Kas glanced at her, registering the reverence on her face before it returned to the pleasant mask all Druids seemed to display.

"What happened to the others?" Kas asked. "The Ancients who fell out of harmony?"

Sofia smiled at him. "They became us."

Kas fell into silence, unsure of what to say to that, but also focussing on breathing as the mountain path seemed to become steeper still. Thankfully, in a matter of minutes, Sofia announced they'd arrived and the group gratefully spread out onto a plateau. It was a large area, big enough to hold dozens of people comfortably, and if the used campfire in the centre was anything to go by, apparently it often did.

Mira stumbled over to one of the logs near the firepit and collapsed onto it, sucking in breaths that didn't seem to provide relief at this altitude. Ossi wandered over and sat beside her, and Kas felt better to hear him also breathing deeply.

Kas moved to the edge of the platform and turned, looking up at the mountain behind him. It was as if he was standing on a smaller peak that was missing its apex. As if a giant had lopped the top off. He scuffed at the ground with his foot. It was smooth. Perhaps from the visitors it had received over the years. Though in that case, it wouldn't be smooth all over.

He looked out over the land, uneasy, as if the giant who had cut the top off the mountain might be out there. He sensed Sofia standing next to him.

His eyes again found that strange white stone, as if drawn there by unseen forces. From this height, Kas could see it was a stone plinth. A great hunk of white stone, long and tall. Whether it was carved or not, he couldn't tell. Perhaps it had been made by the Ancients Sofia had mentioned. That might explain why it was so important. Kas wondered if perhaps the plateau was made by them, too.

A shuffling drew their attention and Tacito appeared, accompanied by Davide, both men wandering onto the plateau as if simply out for a morning walk.

"Ah, we're all here. Excellent." Tacito shuffled over to Sofia, handing her a cloth bag and standing by her side. Davide remained near the path. Whether that was to warn them of anyone approaching, or to prevent anyone from leaving, Kas couldn't tell.

"We've brought you up here because we've not removed a collar that has been intact for so long before. We can't say what will happen, but should any of you experience a sudden burst of your powers, we felt it best for us to be somewhere less visible. And less populated." Sofia reached into the bag, rummaging around before pulling out a rod similar to what she'd held in the caves the day before.

She studied it, eyebrows furrowed, glancing up periodically at each of their necks. Then she handed the bag and the rod to Tacito and walked over to where Mira and Ossi were still seated.

"May I?" she asked Mira, gesturing at her collar. Mira nodded and sat tensely as Sofia ran her small fingers around the metal band.

Sofia's frown deepened, and Kas felt panic rising in his chest. Something was wrong. What if their collars were different and the Druids couldn't help them? Worried as he was about the impact of the collar on his magic, Kas didn't think he could bear the chance at having it removed snatched from him like that.

"They are different," Sofia said eventually.

"Will the rods work?" Tacito asked.

She ran her hands around the band one more time and then shook her head. "No."

Kas's stomach dropped, and his whole body slumped. He saw the devastation in Mira and Ossi's eyes too.

The Druids appeared oblivious to the reaction of their guests. Both Tacito and Davide moved closer to Sofia, and they continued talking among themselves.

"Ah, I see what you mean," Tacito said, running his own fingers along Mira's collar. Mira looked very uncomfortable to be surrounded by Druids, all reaching for her neck. As if sensing this, Davide moved to Ossi and asked to examine his collar, and the larger man hunched down, allowing easier access.

"It's as if it's a continuous band," Davide said, fascination in his voice.

"Forgive us," said Sofia, finally remembering the three, now devastated, guests in their midst. "We have not examined collars like these. Ours are made differently, it seems."

"So you can't help us?" Kas said, trying and failing to keep the dejection from his voice.

"I believe we still can," said Sofia, nodding at Davide, who had switched with Tacito and was examining Mira's collar while Tacito, on his tiptoes, ran his fingers over Ossi's.

"We use the rod for our collars," Sofia explained, monitoring Davide closely. "There is a small hole in the underside, and with the enchanted rod, we can unlock them, in a sense. But your collars have no holes. If I am correct, then the reason for this is that a Druid should be able to remove them using only our magic. They would not wish to use such a collar on us, as they would either need to collar us all, or the collars would be completely pointless."

"It is possible they would use these ones if they decided

we were all a threat," Tacito said to Sofia, who nodded, eyes still fixed on Davide.

"We will need to plan accordingly."

Davide was fully focussed on Mira's collar, his face beginning to show strain, though all Kas could see was the man lightly touching the collar around his friend's neck. Whatever he was trying wasn't working.

"It's not a simple enchantment," he eventually said to his fellow Druids as sweat broke out across his forehead.

"If removal does not work," said Sofia, her head cocked to the side, "perhaps we could alter the original enchantment."

Tacito raised an eyebrow as if this had not occurred to him, and he returned to Ossi, having moved to watch Davide's attempt, and placed his fingers on Ossi's collar.

After a while, Tacito, also showing strain, said, "Ah yes, they've used two, I think. Woven together."

"It might be more," Davide grunted back. "I feel a third."

"One to bind, one to block, but what would the third do?" Sofia asked of no one in particular.

"Who knows what those Collaborators would do or why," said Davide, uncharacteristically bitter. It seemed his efforts required all his energy, and he had none for the mask they usually wore.

But Sofia looked up at his remark, not in anger, but as if he had solved the problem. "We need to think as they would," she said. "Not one to block. But three. Perhaps they couldn't find an enchantment to block all magics and so imbued one for magicals, one for spells, and one for objects."

Both men continued concentrating for a beat, and then Kas saw comprehension dawn in their eyes.

"I think you're right," Davide grunted, Tacito nodding.

Both men continued to strain, but seemed more focussed now, as if they could see the way forward.

"I've got it," said Davide eventually, and with a thunk, Mira's collar dropped to the ground. "They've woven the blocks around the bind," he said to Tacito, drifting over to help the older man.

Sofia and Kas moved to Mira, who was touching the pale strip of skin on her neck, her eyes wide in wonder.

"How do you feel?" Kas asked, sitting beside her and touching her shoulder.

"I feel..." Mira searched for the words. "Whole."

Apparently satisfied that there had been no adverse effects, Sofia snatched up the collar, examining it.

"How about your magic?" Kas asked. "Do you need something to help test it out?"

Mira shook her head, but closed her eyes. "I feel the power," she said. "But it's... distant."

Kas could hear the two Druids murmuring near Ossi, but all else was silent. He stopped himself from peppering Mira with questions, despite his own fears. The Druids fell silent and all Kas could hear were birds crying. Three ravens landed nearby, and Mira opened her eyes.

"Well?" Sofia asked, her eyes shrewd on Mira.

Mira shook her head. "It feels slippery. Like I can grasp it, but then it slips."

"What if we got you some supplies?" said Kas. Spell casters usually needed potions to assist with their spells. Though some powerful ones could cast with words alone. He remembered seeing Adeline trying once, eventually resorting to hiding a potion in her sleeves to make it seem as if she'd succeeded.

Mira nodded tentatively. Kas could feel her hesitation. Her desire to prolong the hope that her magic wasn't damaged.

Sofia, still clutching the collar, headed for the cloth bag she'd left on the other side of the firepit and returned with a small vial. As she handed it to Mira, Tacito said, "I've got it," and Kas heard the clunk of Ossi's collar. He restrained himself from rushing to Ossi, feeling that Mira needed his support.

Taking the vial from Sofia, Mira threw it on the ground, saying, "Enflagrio."

Nothing happened.

Kas put a comforting hand on Mira's back, rubbing it softly. A look passed between Mira and Sofia.

"Why don't you check on Ossi?" Sofia said to Kas. "And then we'll get started on yours."

Kas looked to Mira, who nodded, and he left them talking quietly as he approached Ossi.

"How do you feel?" he asked.

"Strong," said Ossi.

"You always feel strong."

"This is true." Ossi smiled at Kas. Seeing Kas's anxiety, Ossi grew serious and introspective. "I see what Mira was saying," he said eventually. "It feels... patchy."

Ossi walked to the end of an unoccupied log and squatted down, getting his hands as far underneath as he could. Then he pushed up, trying to lift it. He managed to lift it and hold it at his waist before he dropped it.

"With my power," he said. "I could have flipped it with one hand."

Kas looked to the Druids. Tacito and Davide had their heads together, examining Ossi's collar and talking in whispers. Mira and Sofia were also talking softly.

Ossi took a couple of deep breaths and squatted to try again. This time he paused, as if waiting for something. When he did eventually stand, he lifted the log much easier than before.

"It's there, it's just…"

"Patchy?" Kas echoed.

Ossi nodded. "Like a muscle I haven't used."

"Perhaps it will return with time and practice," Sofia said, moving towards them, Mira in tow.

Ossi shrugged. "Perhaps. I am still strong. As are our non-magicals. It will not be an issue if it does not."

"Same," said Mira. "I mean, I've gotten by without it for this long. I think I'll be okay if it doesn't return."

Sofia looked at Kas. She seemed to know that Kas did not feel the same way. If his magic was gone or damaged, he was going to be devastated.

"Have a seat," said Sofia gently. "Let's get started."

CHAPTER THIRTY-TWO

KAS

Kas tried to remain still as Sofia's fingers traced the length of his collar. He breathed deeply to slow his thumping heart and tried not to glance over at Mira and Ossi in case their magic had suddenly returned at full power.

"This will be easier if you remain still," said Sofia so softly only Kas could hear.

"Sorry," he said.

The collar felt heated, as if Sofia was pouring her magic into it. But he may have been imagining it. Maybe it was just because he was so focussed on it.

Sofia was murmuring to herself, but Kas couldn't make out what she was saying. Eventually she said, "Ah," and then he knew it wasn't his imagination. His collar grew hot —uncomfortably so—and just as he was about to say something, he heard a faint click, and it dropped from around his neck.

He looked at Sofia in surprise, but the small girl simply smiled at him before snatching the collar from the ground and examining it closely, as she had Mira's.

"Do you feel it?" she asked him.

Shaking slightly, Kas felt inside himself for his power.

The connection almost made him cry. He'd been cut off from it for so long, and when he felt it flowing once again through him, it was like being whole again.

"Yes," he whispered.

"And?"

Kas closed his eyes and took a couple of deep breaths. He examined the flow, noticing it spurt. Like a bucket being poured with jerky movements, rather than a smooth motion. As if the flow were interrupted somehow.

"I see what Ossi was saying. It feels patchy—like it's not a smooth flow anymore. And slippery, like Mira said. Before, it was a part of me, and now I feel I have to reach for it, and it's hard to grasp." Kas wasn't sure he was explaining it well, but Sofia nodded, turning the collar over in her hands.

Kas continued to reach for his power. Now that he understood what his friends had been describing, he also understood why they did not seem as worried. Ossi's power was an enhancement of what he already had. If he could get used to the ebb and flow, he could use it as such. And for spell casters, they only really needed their magic when creating potions and during the actual casting.

Kas's magic required sustained access to his power. Everything he used to be able to do would be next to useless without it. And he wouldn't be able to free Tia. Nausea gripped his stomach. Tia was trapped, collared, and alone. He'd been so sure that it would be easy to free her once he had his power back.

But now...

Kas fisted his hands. It had to work. He needed to free Tia. To see her again. To make sure she was alright. His heart fluttered at the dream he'd had of sneaking through the Kikachi village and opening the door to wherever they had her trapped. How she'd fling her arms around him in relief. How her lips—

"Are you ready to try it?" Sofia asked gently.

Kas nodded, pushing the daydream from his mind. It *would* work. He would save Tia. He looked at the firepit. In the past, he could have ignited it with barely a glance. But now, staring seemed to do nothing, though he thought he saw the air shimmer, as if the coals were hot.

Frustrated and afraid, Kas thrust his hand out, willing his magic to work. He felt something snap into place inside of him and a small flame burst from the firepit.

Everyone cheered, even the Druids, but Kas felt sick. He knew he should be grateful it worked at all, especially with Mira's and Ossi's experiences. But he'd *felt* his power. It felt like it used to, but the flame… it was barely enough for the firepit. He used to feed all four kilns at the potters. Was this all he could do now?

"How about the other?" said Sofia softly from his side.

Kas looked sharply at her. How could she know? The little Druid simply held his gaze, her eyebrow raised.

Kas took another deep breath and reached for the light.

Gasps told him it had worked. Relief flooded him. If this still worked, he would be okay with his elemental magic being damaged. Kas walked around the fire, but as he reached halfway, he heard the reactions of his friends seeing him.

"How did you do that?" Mira asked.

Kas looked at his hands, blinking back tears of frustration. He hadn't intentionally let go of the light. And worse, he hadn't felt it slip. What good was invisibility of you never knew when it would reveal you? How was he going to help Tia now? His daydream turned to a nightmare image of Tia grasping the bars of her cage and crying as he was hauled away by soldiers.

Ossi crossed to him, placing a comforting hand on his shoulder.

"It will get better," he said.

Kas heard the conviction in Ossi's voice and wished he shared it. He nodded at him, and they walked back to the group.

The Druids had been in hushed discussion but broke apart as the two men approached.

"Do you mind if we keep these?" Sofia asked, holding up Kas's collar.

The three friends nodded. Kas would be happy to never see that thing again in his life. Sofia nodded back and handed the collar to Tacito, who put it with the others in the cloth bag.

"We will need to examine them further," said Sofia. "They were ostensibly made simply to block the magic of the wearer. But that should not affect your magic as it has. I suspect there was a hidden enchantment woven into your collars, and we shall seek to understand its purpose."

"If you can," Kas said, his voice sounding smaller than he would have liked. "Will it fix whatever is wrong with our magic?"

Sofia looked sympathetically at Kas. "It is possible," she said in a tone that suggested it was unlikely. "Tacito will lead the investigation into the collars from here. And since I will accompany you south, I can monitor your magic and see if it begins recovering on its own, with time and use."

"And take Tia's collar off too," said Mira.

"And remove Tia's collar," Sofia agreed.

Kas didn't share the relief he saw on Mira's face. He was still stuck on how they were going to free Tia without getting caught themselves.

"What about the other Kikachi?" asked Ossi.

The other Druids cast a look at Sofia, but she held Ossi's gaze. "It is not the right time for that."

"But if the Controllers are about to invade, surely we'll need them to be able to fight," said Kas. "And if there's something in the collars that has weakened our magic, they'll need time to recover."

Sofia levelled her gaze at Kas and again he felt the weight of the ages bearing down upon him, before she was simply a little girl again. A little girl who seemed to be in charge.

"If we remove the collars now, what do you believe would happen?" she asked.

"Well, they'd be free for a start," said Kas.

"And what would they do with that freedom?" Sofia pressed.

"They'd fight the Empire," said Ossi. "First to free their village, and then to recover their people from the camps."

Sofia gave Ossi a pleased nod. "Precisely. Removal of the collars from the Kikachi, or Jatte, prior to the Empire agreeing to the cessation of annexation would result in a civil war. And when the Controllers arrive, they will quickly decimate the entire southern lands, with you all weakened from your infighting."

It did not escape Kas that the Druids assumed they would be bothered neither by the Empire's civil war, nor by the Controllers.

"This is why speed is of the essence. We must meet with the empress and convince her to end the annexation and settle the terms, inclusive of the removal of collars, with enough time for us to restore everyone's magic—however that will be achieved—before the Controllers arrive."

Kas felt an intense pressure fill him. He wanted to head off now. They had already wasted too much time. Why hadn't the Druids removed their collars last night? They could have already been travelling.

"We have time enough," Sofia said, as if sensing Kas's anxiety. "But we must not squander it."

"Well, let's go then," said Kas. "We'll need time to assess Tia's situation before we figure out how to break her out."

"You can turn invisible," said Mira, awe still in her voice. "That's why you wanted your collar off before we broke her out, right? So you could just wander in and grab her."

"I can't turn her invisible," said Kas. "And my magic is patchy like yours. I might get right in the centre of the Kikachi village and suddenly reappear."

Mira opened and closed her mouth, as if about to argue, then realising she couldn't debate Kas's magic into full strength.

"Perhaps it will be stronger by the time we reach the forest," said Sofia.

They all heard the finality of her tone, and Tacito picked up the cloth bag with the collars inside. Sofia turned to her fellow Druids, and they clasped hands, saying their farewells, before Tacito and Davide waved and wished the group luck, then began to descend the mountain.

"Well, are you ready?" Sofia asked them.

"Don't you need to get your things?" Mira asked.

"What things might I need?" Sofia asked.

"I, uh..." Mira looked helplessly at Kas and Ossi, who both shrugged at her. "Nothing, I guess."

"Excellent, then we should be off."

The small girl hurried to the mountain path, the three friends walking quickly to catch up. Kas thought they might awkwardly catch Tacito and Davide with how fast Sofia was walking, but when he looked ahead, the two Druids were nowhere to be seen.

CHAPTER THIRTY-THREE

TIA

Tia paced like the caged animal she was. She focussed on her breathing and kept a steady mantra in her head, trying to convince herself everything would be fine.

It was hard. If half of what the witch doctor had been telling her was true, everything would definitely not be fine.

Aurora and Fabian had managed to sneak in a few quick visits after discovering she was there, but it had now been days since she'd seen either her sister or her brother, and she was trying not to feel abandoned. She didn't want them to take the risk to come see her, but now she felt like a kid again, sitting around while the grown-ups were too busy for her.

The witch doctor's guard outside paced past her door, causing Tia to jump. She jumped every time someone came near her door, worried it was the witch doctor. His visits were truly awful. He'd given up torturing her for information on her long-dead siblings, clearly having decided whatever had happened to them, they weren't something he needed to worry about.

Instead, he leered at her while talking about how holding her captive was going to convince her siblings to swear loyalty to him, and then the rebellion would be over. One last use for her until he handed her over to the Empire soldiers.

She was jumpier today. It was the deadline for her siblings to give up. Valto had told Fabian and Aurora that if they didn't publicly declare their support for him and give up the names of those who had been part of the rebellion, he'd hand Tia over to the soldiers for them to do with as they wished.

Today, either Valto would be accepted as the leader of the Kikachi and the destruction of their culture would be complete, or she would be handed over to the soldiers and returned to the camps. Or worse. Tia didn't know which she feared more.

Suddenly, a ruckus sounded back towards the village centre, and the guard yelled, his footsteps fading. Tia pressed herself against the door, trying to peer through and see what was going on. Had something happened to her siblings? Or were they attacking? Was the real rebellion beginning?

"Tia," Aurora hissed, making her jump.

"I'm here. What's going on?"

"It's just a distraction to get rid of the guard. I needed to speak to you."

Tia's stomach dropped. She closed her eyes. Of course her siblings would give her a chance to voice her opinion on her fate. A small, selfish part of her had hoped her brother and sister would make the decision for her. That she wouldn't need to be involved in the impossible choice.

"Stay true to the cause," Tia said without waiting for her sister to ask. What else could she say? Sacrifice everything, everyone, and all that we are so that she could be free? Or as free as she could be with a collar around her neck and the witch doctor all but guaranteeing that she would need to flee her tribe.

Her sister hesitated. "Are you certain?"

"I've heard what the witch doctor has been doing. He tells me himself. He's so proud. Pitting families against each other. Telling them that sacrifices are required to heal their children. And from the sounds of it, the people are beginning to believe it's necessary. That it's what the Goddess wants."

Aurora's silence confirmed it, and Tia closed her eyes, hating the witch doctor more than she thought possible. He'd told her how he'd convinced the people that their Goddess was vengeful. That she believed in an eye for an eye. That by now, almost every family had a reason not to trust any other, or was too fearful to do so. This was how he was maintaining power. No one dared join together. Except for the rebels, and even they were few.

That Valto was comfortable telling Tia what he'd been doing, and why, made her feel worse. Either he had no intention of letting her go, or he knew that with her collar, it didn't matter what he said. She was powerless to help her people.

"There's no other choice," Tia whispered to her sister, her heart breaking. "You need to stop him."

"Tia, I—"

"Just answer me one thing," Tia interrupted. Her resolve was barely hanging on, and if Aurora suggested there was a way to defeat the witch doctor without Tia being handed to the guards, she wasn't sure she could argue against it. And she knew there was no way to achieve both outcomes.

"What is it?" Aurora asked.

"Valto keeps implying that my mother wasn't my mother.

It's clearly a poor attempt to unbalance me, but... I just need to hear it from you." Tia felt silly even asking, but Valto's efforts had paid off. His subtle pauses, his tones, that smile. Never coming right out with it. But it tapped into something that Tia could barely remember, and Valto's suggestions had taken root. Tia had been waiting to ask one of her siblings, and now seemed like it might be her only chance.

Aurora paused, and Tia's heart sank even as it began to pound. "Aurora?"

"Tia..." Aurora seemed to search for the words, but her tone struck like a bell, smashing Tia's world. "This is not the time. Let's deal with Valto and then—"

"It's fine," said Tia. She felt numb. Having been so desperate to clarify Valto's taunts, suddenly she didn't want to know. She didn't want to hear the truth. "You need to go. Tell Valto the deal's off."

"I don't know if I can lose you again," her sister whispered back, voice cracking. Tia clamped a hand over her mouth to stop the sobs from escaping while the tears streamed down her cheeks. She forced her mind to become blank, clinical. She could cry later. Now, her people needed her.

"I'll be fine," she lied. "I got out of the camps once. I can do it again."

Tia felt Aurora hesitate, and then she whispered, "Alright, sister."

And just like that, Tia's future was gone.

She returned her sister's farewell, not really hearing or understanding whatever Aurora said. And then she was alone again.

Tia moved away from the door, no longer worried about what happened outside, or who might come in. Her time was limited. Despite what she'd told her sister, as soon as she'd made the decision, she'd known. There was no way the soldiers would send her back to the camps. They would execute her for sure. Returning an escapee told the other prisoners that escape was possible. They would never allow it.

How many days did she have left to live? How many hours?

Some time later, the door opened. Tia saw Valto enter, but she was barely paying attention. She didn't care that he was there. He couldn't hurt her now. And she didn't want to waste what she had left of her life listening to him rant.

"... devious liars, the pair of them. I'm sure you were as convinced as I that they cared about you. Apparently, we were both wrong."

Tia stared past the witch doctor and through the open door. She missed the woods. She'd spent far more of her life in the camps than in Ravenswood Forest, but it was home. Regardless of whatever her mother's secret was, it was in her blood. She longed to run through the trees, to splash in the river, to see the stars winking through the canopy. She inhaled deeply, savouring the crisp, fresh scent of the trees and the bushes and the dirt.

"Enjoy it while you can," sneered Valto, annoyed Tia was daydreaming instead of listening to him.

Tia looked directly at Valto and was satisfied seeing him recoil slightly at the look in her eyes. She was already dead. There was nothing he could do to hurt her.

Tia opened her mouth, taking a step towards him, but before she could say anything, a loud voice boomed outside.

"Hail, Shifters of the forest!"

Valto whipped around, staring out the door, but in no rush to confront whoever was out there. It was a soldier's voice that responded.

"What business have you here, Troll?"

A tiny spark of hope lit in Tia's chest.

Ossi?

"I wish to trade!" Ossi was speaking much louder than necessary, clearly trying to create a distraction. That he was being so obvious was making the soldier nervous, and much as he tried to keep his voice steady, it wavered as he answered.

"The Shifter market is not open to outsiders. If you wish to trade, I recommend you head for the city of Lorendell."

"Shifters of the forest!" Ossie ignored the soldier and raised his voice again. "Come trade with me! See my wares —trinkets from all across Valoris!"

Tia could hear movement and murmuring as her people moved towards the commotion to see what the Troll was yelling about.

"Why are they not moving him on?" muttered Valto, annoyed.

"You're the leader of the tribe," Tia shot at him. Though she would not call him Matriarch. "Why don't you go and move him on yourself?"

The witch doctor turned, glaring at Tia. If he left now, he was essentially following her direction. If he stayed, he looked weak and scared. He moved towards her.

"The soldiers can deal with the Troll," he sneered in her face. "Though I don't doubt they have numbers enough to deal with you, too. I think I'll find some to remove you from my storeroom. I have better uses for it than housing you."

He turned and strode out of the room, slamming the door behind him.

"What a jackass."

Tia jumped and squealed as a voice came from nowhere, flinching again as Kas materialised in the store-room's corner by the door.

"Kas! What the... how did you... but..."

Kas smiled and crossed to Tia, engulfing her in a hug.

"It's okay. We're here to get you out."

"But—Kas! Your collar." Tia touched Kas's bare neck where his collar used to be. The skin there was paler and softer than the skin around it.

"Yeah, it feels weird." Kas frowned. "My magic is still there, but it's harder to access. Like a muscle that's wasted from lack of use."

"But you can clearly still use it," Tia said, hope in her tone. She cared about Kas, of course, but most of her worry was for herself. If the collars had robbed her of the magic she'd never had a chance to use...

"Oh yeah," said Kas quickly. "It's there, and Sofia seems confident we'll reach our old levels."

"Sofia?"

"She's a Druid. They're the ones who got the collars off," said Kas, smiling warmly at Tia. "It's tricky, but they figured it out. Sofia will take yours off once we're out of here."

"Really?" Tia's eyes grew wide as she gazed into his, barely daring to hope it was real.

Kas nodded, and Tia flung her arms around his neck, giving a little squeal of excitement. Kas hugged her back, his strong arms around her. She could feel his heart pounding, his breath on her neck. She tentatively pulled away, but then their faces were so close to each other and his lips were on hers.

"Kas, no," Tia pulled back quickly, shock and surprise on her face.

"Sorry, I thought... sorry." Kas's eyes widened in alarm, and then he looked away and wouldn't meet her eyes, his face a deep red.

"It's just—"

"You don't have to explain. I shouldn't have—come on, we need to get you out of here."

Tia wanted to grab his hand and explain, but he was right. There wasn't time now. She would talk to him later.

"How are we going to get out?" she asked, trying to break the tension and put the focus squarely on the mission. "He shut the door, and it locks automatically."

Kas had moved to the door and glanced at Tia, clearly still embarrassed, but with a flourish pushed the door gently and Tia watched as it easily opened a crack and closed again.

"I blocked the catch while that guy was talking." Kas's nose scrunched in distaste as he spoke of the witch doctor. "I'm going to use my invisibility. Let me go first and I'll make sure no one's looking. Then I'll open the door for you. You're going to walk quickly, heading straight, and then a slight right. Go directly for the trees. Don't run. The movement will attract too much attention."

Tia nodded and then gaped as Kas disappeared right in front of her. She was going to have to ask him about that. Right after she cleared the air between them. Why did he have to kiss her? She moved to the door, resisting the urge to push it open and run. Had she given him some signal? She didn't think so, but who knew with Empire men?

The door opened, breaking into her thoughts, and Kas's disembodied voice urged her again to move swiftly, but calmly. The fresh air hit her like a cool embrace and her heart swelled as she looked up at the trees and smelled the forest again.

Keeping her legs moving, Tia forced herself to stare at the edge of the clearing they were moving towards. She desperately wanted to look around. To see her people. Really look at her village. Not to mention she wanted to see what was going on with Ossi, who was now loudly trying to sell goods to the soldiers who were attempting, without success, to physically remove him.

As she neared the edge of the clearing, Tia let out a sigh and relaxed. She'd made it. She was free.

And then Kas materialised directly in front of her.

"Kas! You're visible," she hissed urgently.

But she wasn't the only one who had seen.

"Hey!"

The soldier's voice rang out, followed quickly by Valto's.

"She's an escaped prisoner! Get her!"

Tia ran.

CHAPTER THIRTY-FOUR

TIA

CRASHING THROUGH THE WOODS, Tia followed Kas as he blinked in and out of visibility. He led her around the outskirts of the village before turning abruptly away.

Tia glanced back and saw chaos. Ossi was still arguing with a bunch of soldiers, but more had started after the fleeing pair. Before she turned back, several villagers jumped in front of the soldiers, halting their pursuit.

"Aurora! Fabian!" Tia stopped completely, horror descending over her as her siblings led the group blocking the soldiers. They would be sent to the camps for sure.

"We have to go," said Kas, appearing at her side and grabbing her arm.

"We have to go back for them!" She tried to pull her arm from his grip.

"Whatever the soldiers will do to them is going to happen now, no matter what we do," said Kas, gently but still firm. "Don't let their sacrifice be for nothing."

Tia let him pull her away. She felt awful. A coward. Who ran away and let their siblings suffer so they could be free? She should stay and fight. And yet, she continued to follow Kas.

The sounds of fighting faded as they moved deeper into the woods.

"Right up here at that log," Kas said, keeping her moving.

Tia felt ill, but resolve filled her. Kas had said someone was there to take her collar off. Once they had, she would go back for her siblings. Fight alongside them. Free them too.

Assuming they're still alive.

"She's here!" a voice called from behind them. Some of the soldiers had made it past the rebels and were close on their heels.

"Faster," Kas urged unnecessarily as they both surged forward, Tia aware of roughly where Kas was from the breaking branches and bushes moving violently.

They cut left and then left again, and soon the yelling of the guards was farther back and sounded less urgent. Kas told her to slow her pace and conserve energy.

"We left Sofia at the edge of the forest," he explained. "So we have a ways to go."

Sofia. The Druid. The person who would remove her collar. Still, the farther they moved away from her siblings, the more intense her desire to get back to them.

Kas flashed back into view in front of her. What if there was something wrong with her magic, too? Maybe she would flicker between her human and animal form. Nerves grabbed her. She'd been collared so young, she'd never even been exposed to the Testing. What if she didn't have magic at all?

Her heart strained in her chest. If she couldn't shift, how was she going to get back and help her siblings? Nerves turned her legs wobbly, and she almost stumbled.

She *would* have magic. Her parents were both powerful shifters. Her father's other children had been older than her, and they had all been shifters. And it was laughable to think her mother's magic wouldn't have passed to her.

And yet... Tia shook the fears away. The most she needed to worry about was what form she would assume. In her dreams, she was always something large and powerful. A lion, or a panther, or a bear. But what if she could only become a rodent?

I could have slipped under the door and escaped.

She would make it work. Whatever she shifted into, she would use it to save her family.

"We're almost there."

Tia blinked. She'd been so lost in her thoughts she'd lost track of where they were and was surprised they had reached the edge of the forest so quickly. But looking around, she saw they still were a little ways off.

"Tia!" Mira rushed out of some bushes and gave Tia a quick hug. "I'm so sorry. I just ran. I should have stayed. I wanted to get you out sooner, but I thought I should get help—"

"It's fine." Tia smiled. "You were right to run. Thank you for getting me out at all."

"Okay," said Kas, materialising beside her. "Mira's going to take you to Sofia. I'm going to head back in case Ossi needs help shaking the soldiers."

The women had time to nod and Kas was invisible again, Tia watching the forest give away his position as he hurried back to find Ossi.

"So," she said, turning to Mira. "Kas can turn invisible."

Mira's eyes widened. "Right? He kept that quiet. When I found him, he told me without his collar he'd be able to rescue you more easily. But he wouldn't tell me how."

Kas flickered back into view before they lost sight of him in the trees.

"All of our magic is a little patchy," Mira said, touching

Tia on the shoulder and leading her towards the edge of the forest. "Sofia thinks there's something hidden in the collars that affected it. The Druids are looking into it. But it's getting better. All of us were practicing with it on the way here, and it's less patchy now."

Tia frowned. Kas had appeared several times during their flight. That was better? Her anxiety at the removal of her own collar increased.

"How does it feel having your magic back?" Tia asked, trying to distract herself.

"It's amazing," Mira gushed. "I mean, it's tricky to use. I have to time it right."

Tia recalled she was a spell caster.

"But I can feel the power again." Mira's eyes were lit with an energy Tia hadn't seen in the shorter girl before.

"I can't wait." Tia smiled.

"Are you nervous?"

Tia nodded.

"I'm sure you'll be fine. Do you know what kind of animal you might be?"

Tia shook her head. "It can be random. Sometimes you'll have a family that are all predators, and then one kid will be a rabbit."

"That would still be cool," Mira said, her eyes wistful.

Tia nodded. There was nothing wrong with being a rabbit. But she needed to become something that would help her save her siblings.

They walked in silence for a bit, Tia straining to see if she could hear the conflict back in her village. She couldn't, of course. It was too far away for them to hear. And if she could, they would have been in trouble. Now that the adrenaline had worn off a bit, Tia felt the full weight of guilt for escaping. That her escape had jeopardised her family, her people. She was almost certain there was something she could have done to help instead of running.

"Tell me about this—Sofia, was it?" Tia asked. She was curious, but was also desperate for a distraction.

Mira nodded. "Sofia's a Druid. She's... well, maybe I'd better start at the beginning."

The walk was pleasant as Mira filled Tia in on everything that had happened from when she found Kas until they had broken her out.

"So, let me see if I've got this straight. Sofia's about ten, but she's the Druid they've sent to talk to the empress about the looming Controller invasion."

"Yep." Mira nodded.

"And depending on how that conversation goes between little Sofia and the empress, the Druids may or may not want to help us stop the Controllers from destroying all the other tribes in Valoris."

"That's about the gist of it." Mira nodded again.

They shared a look.

"Druids are *weird*," said Tia.

"I guess it depends on your perspective," said a small voice from behind a tree the women had just passed. Both of them flinched.

Tia looked down at the small girl. She did look ten years old. And an ordinary young girl at that. Nothing immediately stood out that would explain her being the one selected to meet with the empress to decide the fate of the world. Though now that she thought about it, Tia wasn't sure what she might have expected to see that would explain it.

"You must be Tia," said the little girl, holding out her hand in greeting. "May the power of the universe embrace you."

"Goddess's blessings," Tia responded. "I'm pleased to meet you, Sofia. Especially as I understand you might be able to rid me of this." She tapped her collar.

"Indeed I can," said Sofia. "Please kneel."

"Is this like getting knighted?" asked Tia nervously as she complied. Was this going to be some weird Druid ritual? The little girl summoning some ancient magic and channelling it into the collar? Was Tia going to have to swear an oath to the Druid gods? Did they even have gods? Tia had the feeling they didn't. She remembered hearing that they worshipped the world, but they called it a universe for some reason. Wasn't it something about energy?

"No," Sofia said, reaching over and lightly touching the collar. It felt warm all of a sudden. "I'm just short."

Tia tried to stem her impatience and was proud of herself for only asking twice how much longer it would take. Suddenly the heat of the collar was gone, a thunk telling her it had fallen to the ground in front of her.

Power enveloped her body, rushing to fill every inch. It was a sensation she'd never felt before, so wondrous and heavy. She felt like she could thrust her arms out and magic would flow, Empire-style.

Sofia quickly picked up the collar and Mira appeared in front of Tia, next to Sofia. They were both smiling at the look of awe on Tia's face.

Suddenly, that wondrous flow spluttered within.

"That seems usual, based on the experience of your friends," said Sofia, seeing Tia's face fall.

"But it's getting better," said Mira.

Tia took a deep breath. No time like the present. And she had to get back and help her siblings.

"No," said Sofia, taking a step towards Tia. Her voice was quiet, but somehow felt like it rang out like a gong.

"What do you mean 'no'?" Tia demanded.

"It's not safe to test your magic yet."

"How did you—"

"Tia!" Ossi lumbered towards her and caught her up in a giant hug.

"I missed you too." She squeezed him back. "You got away alright?"

"Yes. Kas started a fire."

"Kas!" Tia's exclamation was stifled slightly by Ossi's embrace.

"It was just a little one," Kas's voice sounded from behind Ossi. He sounded embarrassed. Tia was grateful he hadn't been capable of starting a big fire in the forest.

"Don't worry," said Ossi, placing Tia back on the ground. "I will not try to kiss you."

"Ossi!" Kas appeared beside the Troll. His face looked like it would never not be red again. "I told you that in confidence."

"Wait, who kissed who?" asked Mira, looking around the group.

"No one," said Kas.

"Kas kissed Tia," said Ossi.

"Ossi!" Kas looked like he wanted the ground to swallow him up.

"You kissed her?" Mira asked Kas before looking at Tia in confusion. "But Tia likes girls."

"Mira!" Now Tia looked horrified.

"What? You do."

"You like girls?" Kas asked, his voice sounding strained. "I thought Shifters were more... fluid."

"Kikachi," Mira corrected him.

"And we are accepting of people's preferences," said Tia, trying to stem her annoyance. "Men, women, both, multiple partners—"

"Multiple?" Kas's eyes bugged out of his head.

"Why not?" Tia challenged.

"Do you... I mean, not that it matters..." Kas looked like his face might start another fire and Tia felt a spark of pity for him.

"I prefer women, and one partner at a time," she said. "I wanted to tell you when we were alone and not being chased."

"I'm sorry," Kas said, staring at the ground. "I mean, I should have known—"

"How would you have known?" Tia asked, her voice hardening dangerously.

"I mean, it's pretty obvious," said Mira quietly. Tia shot her a look, and Mira shrugged.

"I meant I shouldn't have kissed you," said Kas, flustered.

"Because you should have known I like girls?" Tia asked, anger rising.

"I like everybody," said Ossi loudly, smiling at everyone.

"Perhaps we should be going?" suggested Sofia.

"I've never had a boyfriend or a girlfriend," said Mira, almost to herself.

"What is your preference, Sister Sofia?" asked Ossi.

"According to all of you, I'm ten. I don't like anyone," said Sofia.

Mira scoffed, muttering something that sounded like, "Ten my ass," and Sofia cast her a curious look.

"I need to help my siblings," Tia announced, moving back towards the village. "I don't expect you to join me—"

"The soldiers have them," said Ossi, sobering up. "Once you were far enough away, all those interfering with the soldiers surrendered and the soldiers took them to a prison wagon."

"Then I need to hurry. Maybe I can break them out on the road like the rebels did with us."

"You will help them more by coming with us."

Everyone stopped, Sofia's voice ringing out with that power that seemed to reverberate to the core. Tia glared at her.

"How's that?"

"We are going to meet with the empress. Convince her to abolish the annexation. As a part of that, and in preparation for the upcoming war, I will urge her to close down the prison camps."

Tia looked at the small girl, not allowing the kernel of hope to bloom. End the annexation? Close the camps? Was it possible? She hardened herself again. Of course it wasn't going to happen. If all it took for the empress to do what was right was for someone to ask her, she would have ended annexation as soon as she took the throne.

"I believe the empress will do it," said Sofia confidently.

Tia snorted. "Oh yeah? And why's that?"

"Because the Controllers are coming. And if the Empire tries to stand alone, especially in the state they're in, they will be decimated. I believe the empress will end annexation. If not because it is the right thing to do, then out of self interest."

Tia's mouth pursed. That sounded more believable. But could she risk it? Gamble the fate of her siblings on it?

"If we attack the wagon," Ossi said, his deep voice soft behind her, "then even if we save your siblings, the soldiers may punish the rest of your people."

That was true, and Tia hadn't even considered it. But her siblings were all she had. The last of her family...

"The soldiers were not mistreating them. Once they surrendered, the soldiers let them walk to the wagon and get in by themselves."

Tia closed her eyes. Damn her siblings or damn her people. Either way, she was a coward and an asshole. She wished she was with them. Suffering too, instead of free and collarless. Then she felt incredibly selfish for wishing that.

A soft hand wrapped around hers.

"Come on," Mira said gently. "Let's go make the empress release them."

Tia nodded, sniffling and blinking, refusing to cry, and they all started walking.

Kas fell in beside Tia and she slowed her pace, allowing a small gap to form between them and the group.

"I'm really sorry," said Kas. "I shouldn't have kissed you. That was very presumptuous of me. I just thought... I don't know what I thought. But I shouldn't have assumed."

"Thank you," said Tia. "You shouldn't have. But I forgive you."

"Is it okay if we never mention it again?"

Tia laughed. "I won't," she said. "But I can't make promises for Ossi."

Kas groaned and Tia smiled as the light increased, the trees thinning as they reached the border of the forest.

"Wait," Tia said, stopping again and looking at Sofia. "My people—can you take their collars off?"

"No," said Sofia, softly but firmly.

Tia glared at the little girl in frustration. "Why not? I'm not asking for us to attack the soldiers. Just to free my people. You have the power right there in your hands."

Sofia cocked her head to the side, considering Tia. "The time is not right."

"There's no better time! Look at all of us. You said it will take time for our magic to get back to full strength. And you said the Controllers are coming. Free them from their collars now and let them heal."

"If we remove their collars now, they will fight the soldiers, will they not?"

Tia hesitated. "If the soldiers give them reason to."

Sofia levelled a look at Tia that told her the girl did not believe for a second that the Kikachi would seek, if not revenge, then to rid their village of Empire soldiers.

"And if, for whatever reason, your people did attack the soldiers, that would bring about a civil war between the Empire proper and the Kikachi, would it not?"

"Sure." Tia nodded, frustrated. She knew the Druids didn't have to worry about such things, but surely even she realised if conflict kicked off with her people and the Empire, it wouldn't be small. Not with how the Empire had treated them. What did she expect? What was the girl's problem?

"Such a war at this time does not move the world towards Unification. And if the Kikachi and the Empire are weakened by a war with each other, both will be obliterated by the Controllers when they come. Your people's collars will be removed at the appropriate time, but that time is not now."

Rage grew within Tia. Who was this little girl to determine the time to free her people from oppression? She didn't know how they had suffered. How they were still suffering. Her siblings would never have been caught had they been collarless. She never would have been caged.

"Careful now," Sofia warned. "Heightened emotions can spark unintentional shifting, especially in those with little control over their powers. And your power is... temperamental, as is the case with your fellows who've had their collars removed. Shifting now would be very ill-advised. And let me counsel you, it is best you discover your animal form when you have a firm grip on your power, and in private."

"This isn't private enough for you?" Tia gestured to the empty forest around them.

Sofia made a show of looking around and then thinking. "The time is not right."

Tia thought she might hate that little girl.

CHAPTER THIRTY-FIVE

KAS

"It just... turned up?"

The empress was turning the ring over between her fingers, her eyes locked on it, but her tone made it clear exactly how unimpressed she was with Sofia's explanation for how she came to be in possession of the most prized piece of jewellery in the Empire.

"Yes, as I said," said Sofia. Kas's eyes flew to the little girl in disbelief at her exasperation. She was impatient with the empress's fixation on how they found her ring. Hadn't he warned her that she might be suspicious about that? At any rate, he wasn't sure getting annoyed at the empress was the best way to bring her on side.

"As in it fell off a wagon? Or perhaps it simply rolled into town on a stiff breeze?"

Kas shifted in his seat, uncomfortable and wanting to fix the tension. But he was also unclear on how the Druids had come by the ring he himself had tossed off the bridge all those years ago. And he didn't think mentioning the last time he'd seen it would help the current state of things.

"What matters, Your Majesty, is that it is here now,

returned to you. However, we have more important things to discuss and little time for idle chatter."

It was like the air was sucked out of the room. Kas and his friends tensed, all freezing in place like rabbits hoping the wolf might find a target other than them. He couldn't help but dart a look at Sofia. The girl looked completely relaxed, but for her desire to move the conversation along.

His eyes tracked to the empress, and then he quickly pulled them away before she saw him looking. The empress was fuming. But there was something else in her eyes, too. Something fleeting that he hadn't fully grasped. Perhaps whatever it was explained why they'd not been kicked out yet.

The silence stretched, and he chanced another glance at the empress. She had sat back in her chair, arms crossed. The empress cast a look at the soldier sitting to her left. She'd introduced him as Master Sandison, but he was wearing the uniform of a simple infantry soldier. Kas had almost fainted at seeing him, convinced they were about to be arrested and returned to the camps.

But Master Sandison had greeted them all with a friendly smile, despite his intimidating stature. And he hadn't so much as flinched at Ossi, who was over a head taller than the soldier, and far bulkier. Kas had thought the lord was going to interrupt Sofia a couple of times, but then he'd seemed to think better of it and had closed his mouth.

Now he offered the empress a reassuring smile and a shrug. The empress's hard expression remained, though it softened slightly at the man's smile, and she sighed loudly.

"Okay then, Lady Druid, what are these *important things* we must discuss?"

"The Controllers will invade, and soon. They will be here before the solstice. And if you are not ready, the continent will fall by spring."

The entire room gaped at Sofia. Why hadn't she said anything earlier? They'd asked why she needed to speak with the empress. And they'd travelled all the way from the Druids' village to Ravenswood Forest to the city, and not once had she mentioned the impending invasion. Not so much as suggesting they hurry up when their pace slowed, or offering an opinion when they'd thought to set up camp early.

A faint ringing began in Kas's ears. So soon. War would be here so soon. He'd been daydreaming as they travelled from the forest to the city about finishing his task and starting the life he'd dreamed of for so long.

His talk with Ossi had helped, and Kas had begun thinking about what *he* would do with the rest of his life, whether or not his brother was a part of it. Kas could still imagine carving a life for himself in the City of Stone. It was what he knew, and the part of him that would always love his brother also longed for things to change with time.

But Kas had also imagined travelling. Spending time with Ossi and his people. Or living in the forest with Tia and learning about her people.

Now he felt sick as all his dreams were dashed. He wouldn't be settling into a peaceful life in the city, whether or not he reconciled with Salomon. Or fishing each day with Ossi. Or laughing with Tia about his pathetic attempts to woo her Kikachi friends.

His hopes of a normal life leaked through his fingers. A life where he didn't have to worry about invasions and slavery and the end of the world. If Sofia had mentioned this before, he'd have dropped her and the ring at the gate and wished her good luck. Which, now that he thought about it, was probably why she'd said nothing.

"I am here on behalf of the Druids of the Veil because we wish to understand the steps you propose to take to repel the Controller invasion," said Sofia, apparently unaware or unaffected by the current mood of the room.

Ice seemed to emanate from the empress. In fact, Kas noticed the water glasses on the table begin to frost. It seemed the empress was a powerful water mage. And if she lost her temper, they might all be frozen solid and then shattered by a simple tap.

"The steps *I* propose." The empress's voice was dangerously low and controlled. The way people spoke before their rage erupted. Anger burned in her eyes. "Let's see. The rebels have betrayed me. Instead of taking my coin to bolster the city guard, they took it *and* that of one of the nobles—I don't know which one, though I have my suspicions—and are now creating far more havoc and violence than ever before. I have no idea if this is the rebels' own plan, or if they are now acting on the noble's behalf."

Kas's stomach dropped. Salomon's deal. His brother had double-crossed the empress. Had that been Salomon's plan all along, or had he simply found a better deal with this noble? Either way, the empress was fuming, and whoever she decided was to blame would swing. Kas just needed to make sure that it wasn't his little brother. Even with Salomon's betrayal, Kas couldn't stand by and see his little brother executed.

The empress stood, pacing as her voice rose. "The people are ready to revolt. They say I have no control over my own city, much less the Empire. They're staging protests, no doubt organised by the traitorous nobles on my council. So between the people and the rebels themselves, unrest in the entire city is at an all-time high."

The empress whirled back to the table from the window she'd drifted to. "The Shifter colony is on the brink of war and my general tells me the Trolls have started challenging their guards to duels, stating that if the soldiers can't win a fistfight, they shouldn't be guarding the settlement. It won't be long until they break out entirely."

The empress took a breath, returned to her seat, and leaned towards Sofia. "So no, I have no steps to propose for your Controller invasion. I likely will not be alive to see it. So I suggest you find someone else to burden with the defence of the continent. Assuming, of course, the Controllers come at all," she muttered.

Kas felt his anxiety spike. If it was he who the empress's ire was focussed on, he'd have been overwhelmed by shame. And yet, though Sofia lowered her head and studied her hands, she did not seem as upset as he would be now, let alone when he was as young as Sofia appeared.

Something gnawed at the back of his mind. She didn't act like a kid. But then, the Druids were all pretty weird. Either way, it didn't sit right with Kas for anyone to speak to a kid like that. Even if that kid was proclaiming the end of the world. And even if you were the empress.

"Sorry, Your Majesty, but—" The empress's eyes whipped to Kas's, and he wanted to melt into the floor, but he forced himself to continue. "I mean," he said, gesturing at Sofia, "she's, what? Ten? I know it's a lot, and she was a bit presumptuous, but she's just a kid."

The empress blinked at him. Master Sandison looked at Kas, a mixture of admiration and pity on his face. Mira shuffled uncomfortably in her seat. Kas assumed he was about to be executed for impertinence.

The empress looked from Kas to Sofia and back. "You think..." She looked to Sofia again and back to Kas. "You think she's ten?"

Kas felt so wrong-footed he just stared blankly at her and said, "What?"

"You think the Druid is ten years of age?"

Master Sandison rubbed his face with his hand, not

entirely covering his smirk. Kas prayed for the power to turn back time and keep his mouth shut.

"Uh..." Kas looked at Sofia in confusion. The girl ignored him, examining her fingernails. "Yes?"

The tension broke, the empress and the lord's son sharing a look—hers surprised exasperation and his amused pity. Mira caught his eye and gave him a sympathetic smile.

"Druids age differently, boy," said the empress. Kas felt himself bristle at the empress calling him 'boy'. She was, what? Three years older than him? But that was not the point, and this was not the time. "How old are you, Lady Druid?"

Sofia shuffled. "It's often hard to keep track. We don't care for the measurements of time in the same way you do. Let's say, one hundred? Give or take."

Kas now gaped at Sofia and missed the empress casting him a look as if he were intellectually slow. Kas wanted nothing more than to melt into the floor.

"Your Majesty, your refreshments," said a maid, placing a tray on the table and setting out some small pastries, as well as a pot of tea and some cups. Her arrival provided a convenient interruption, and Kas prayed to all the gods that the discussion moved on as soon as she was done. "Do you need anything else, ma'am?"

"No, thank you Adeline."

Adeline?

Kas whipped his eyes to the maid. "Addy?"

"Kas?"

"You two know each other?" the empress asked.

"We grew up together," said Adeline. Her voice held a pointed tone.

The empress shot Adeline a look, one eyebrow raised. "Is this *him*?"

Adeline nodded, looking embarrassed, but the empress

returned her gaze to Kas. He had the distinct feeling he was being appraised. The longer the empress's eyes roamed over him, the more uncomfortable he felt.

"I mean, I can see the appeal," the empress said, as if considering the purchase of a horse for her stables. "You have good taste."

"Thank you, Your Majesty," said Adeline. She seemed pleased by Kas's discomfort, which only increased it. He felt he had missed the topic and now couldn't follow the conversation.

"If we might perhaps return to the discussion of the impending invasion?" Sofia said politely.

"Ah yes. The problem that, as I pointed out, appears to be almost exclusively yours." The empress sipped her tea. "In fact, now that I think on it, it does strike me as odd. In over three hundred years of successive invasions, not only have the Druids not once been the targets, but you have barely registered the slightest factor of care for those affected."

The empress took another sip, her face pleasantly blank, as if they were friends discussing the weather. The rest of the room stared at Sofia.

Kas wondered again why the Controllers had left the Druids alone. Surely having some slaves who could create powerful magical objects would be appealing? Or some who might be able to defeat the wards?

Sofia smoothed the folds of her cloak. "We are the Keepers. We do not engage in the politics of men."

"A," said the empress quickly, "sexist. And B, the invasions have never been political. The Controllers want nothing but slaves. There is no bargaining with them."

Master Sandison gave a little cough. "We might be straying slightly off topic..."

"Yes, okay," the empress agreed. "Back to my point,

which is that some might say it's a bit rich, or at least odd, that you are only now coming to me and demanding action."

Sofia lifted her cup to her lips, but replaced it before drinking. "Before, the Controllers were not set on complete annihilation. As the Keepers, we are charged with protecting the various sacred sites of the world, and waiting for the signs that the Unification has begun."

"So what? Are you worried about your sites? Are the Controllers going to knock over your stones?"

The empress had barely finished speaking when she flinched, and even Kas sat back as a wave of anger seemed to wash over the room, like a warning shot of what could be brought upon them.

"We now believe the change in strategy of the Controllers may be heralding the commencement of the Unification."

Kas still had no idea what this 'Unification' the Druids kept talking about was, but it felt ominous, and the look the empress gave the soldier seemed to confirm his instincts.

"It is imperative," Sofia continued, seemingly oblivious to the effect of her words, "that the annexation is ended before the invasion commences. To build the army you need to repel the Controllers, you will need to free the tribes, remove the collars, and release the political prisoners from the labour camps."

Sofia's demands were met with a stunned silence. Kas was supportive of all those things, but to demand them of the empress? He braced himself for her anger, wondering if she would yell, freeze them, or both.

But the empress merely massaged her temples, sighing. "I understand your position, Lady Druid. But unfortunately it does not change mine. I am in no position to help you, regardless of whether or not I want to. The cessation of the annexation is something that must be done correctly if we are to avoid a civil war. And I have neither the support, nor the resources to do it safely. And I can't see that changing anytime soon. Not until I have at least the capital under control and have dealt with this rebel issue."

The empress glanced at Master Sandison, but the soldier was staring at the table, his expression blank. She looked from Ossi to Kas, and then considered each of the people at her table.

"Adeline?"

"Yes, Your Majesty?"

"I'm not sure I trust this man's judgment." She stared right at Kas. "It seems to me he might be prone to missing cues and often fails to see fantastic opportunities that are right in front of him."

Adeline lowered her head, a broad smile on her face. Kas's own face burned. Apparently, he was currently missing one of those cues the empress was referring to.

"You know him. Do you think him capable of helping us take care of Lord Flighty? Or persuading the rebels to join our side?"

Adeline looked up at Kas. Her eyes were intense, a complicated array of feelings warring within her. She glared at Kas, a flash of hurt and anger in her eyes, but then it subsided and he saw the warm look that was his friend. Catching his eyes, Adeline mouthed, "Trust me".

"If you require the acquisition of evidence to convict Lord Flighty, there are few others who would be better suited, Your Majesty. Certainly no one I can think of who could do what you require quite so discreetly. As for the rebels, most of the people we grew up with are now among their ranks, and they all have a great deal of respect for Kas," Adeline said. "And they would certainly follow him over his brother."

Kas's insides froze. What was Adeline doing? If the empress knew his brother was deputy leader of the rebels, she'd probably have Master Sandison run him through right here.

"His brother?" The empress glanced over at Adeline.

"Salomon," said Adeline, giving the empress a look Kas couldn't decipher. "Kas's younger brother is Salomon Ironstone."

The atmosphere charged immediately, and Kas felt his blood literally run cold. Of course. The empress didn't need Master Sandison's sword. She could kill him with her magic quicker than the soldier could draw it.

"His brother is the leader of the rebels?"

"Deputy leader," Kas corrected, as if that mattered.

There was a silence and then Master Sandison said, "When the rebels double-crossed us, they attacked a convoy leaving from the north barracks, headed to supply weapons to the outposts. From the reports, Jori arrived on the scene, telling his men to stand down. It's unclear from the witnesses what happened exactly, but after the fighting concluded, Jori was among the dead."

Kas met Master Sandison's eyes and saw what the man had not said aloud. They thought Salomon had killed Jori. But Salomon wouldn't have done that. His little brother was ambitious, but surely—

Kas's mind returned to the south tower. Salomon had betrayed him. Had turned Kas over to the guards simply to get his older brother out of his way. An escapee of the camps, it was a strong possibility he would have been killed. Kas had to believe Salomon didn't know that. That he had assumed Kas would be returned to the camps. And Salomon didn't know how bad they were, not really.

His anger flared. *Stop making excuses for him.* Salomon wasn't ten anymore. He was a grown man. And he had betrayed Kas, even knowing the consequences were dire. Just to get him out of the way. But Salomon was still his little brother. And even with his treachery, Kas couldn't leave him to die.

"Salomon will listen to me, Your Majesty," said Kas with a confidence he did not feel. "But if I can't convince him to order his men to stand down, I can convince the men to leave him. Especially once we cut the purse strings."

The empress considered Kas. She glanced at Master Sandison again, but he was now eating a sandwich and missed her look. She frowned at the soldier and looked again at her ring.

"You are loyal to your brother," she said.

"I love my brother," Kas said slowly. "And the man that I know would not be behaving as you describe without a good reason." Kas tried to focus on the little boy he'd known, not the man he'd met weeks ago. But he couldn't get the look in Salomon's eyes out of his head as his little brother had given him up to the guard. "But if I am wrong, Your Majesty, then I understand what must be done."

The empress looked at him then, her penetrating gaze piercing to his soul. She worried her bottom lip, thinking.

"I suspect it is Lord Flighty behind all of this," she said eventually. Kas felt a weight leave his chest. "He stands to gain the most, and the rebels did seem amenable to working with me before his interference."

"What do you need from me?" Kas asked.

"Us," Tia corrected. Mira and Ossi nodded.

The empress took a deep breath. "If Lord Flighty has been paying the rebels to cause chaos, there will be a paper trail. A man so used to business dealings as he is will likely keep things he shouldn't because he is used to documenting in order to see what has been profitable. But he is not stupid. He would not keep such evidence somewhere easy to find."

The empress turned her ring over again in her fingers. "Ideally, I would need someone skilled in shadow work to retrieve the evidence for me." She looked from her ring to Kas, eyeing the conspicuous light band of skin around Kas's neck. "The person who stole this ring would be perfect." Kas's heart froze. "I wasn't in the palace at the time, but I heard no one caught sight of them at all. Even when the alarm triggered."

There was a charged silence. Kas's mind raced, trying to think of something to say. Something that wouldn't sound guilty. He willed the blush not to redden his face.

"What I need," the empress said, sitting back in her chair, the tension diffusing immediately, "is for you to somehow acquire evidence proving that Lord Flighty is funding the rebels and directing their current activities. I have a meeting with them tomorrow afternoon. Bring me the evidence by that meeting, and I will allow you to take my terms to the rebels."

Kas sat up, eager to get going. But the empress wasn't finished. Her eyes, though still cold, were tinged with sympathy.

"If you cannot find what I need, I will need to move against the rebels themselves. While they are causing trouble, I cannot bring the nobles to heel, and without their coin and armies, we will not have a hope against the Controllers."

Kas swallowed, his throat suddenly dry and constricted. He nodded. He knew she had to act. At least he had this chance to save his brother and his friends.

"Adeline?" The empress turned her head slightly, eyes not leaving Kas's. "Go with them, will you? I'll need someone involved that I can trust."

CHAPTER THIRTY-SIX

CASSANDRA

"Can we trust them?"

Cassandra had been asking herself the same question. But the frightening truth was, she had no choice. She exhaled heavily as Lukas followed her through the corridors, matching her frantic stride easily.

"Adeline trusts Kas," she said. "And I trust Adeline."

"You barely know her," Lukas said reasonably.

"True, but being in such a dearth, as I am, of trustworthy allies, I'll take a new friend over an old enemy."

Lukas's silence spoke volumes. This was the exact opposite of her father's favourite saying.

"You're better off trusting an old enemy," he'd tell them. "They'll never surprise you. If your new friend betrays you, you'll never see it coming."

But Cassandra had had enough of following her father's advice. He was the one who had left her this mess to deal with. Whether by his creation or continuance, he'd bequeathed her an Empire on the brink of implosion with an invader at their door. It was time to try things her way.

"What I'm really worried about is what happens next," Cassandra said, rounding a corridor and almost colliding with two servants. The servants hastily hugged the wall, lowering their eyes and bowing. Normally she'd apologise, but today she was so preoccupied she barely noticed.

"You mean the Controllers?" Lukas asked.

"Well, yes, they're certainly a problem. But I mean, after the mission to get the evidence." She rounded another corner, this time keeping far to the right, but the corridor was empty. "Either it doesn't work out and we're back to square one. Or worse, they're caught and there's nothing I can do about it. Or the mission is a success and I have to deal with that."

"You're worried about confronting Flighty?" Lukas asked. He didn't sound at all out of breath, whereas Cassandra was huffing slightly. Of course, his legs were longer, and to her knowledge, he wasn't wearing a corset.

"No, *that* I'm looking forward to. But what will the others do? We're hoping with him gone they'll follow the power and fall in line. But what if they don't? What if they leave?"

"Good riddance."

"We need their armies. Their resources." She slowed, turning to face her childhood friend. He looked at her seriously, really listening. She felt seen by him. He reached out and held her arms. His touch was gentle, but he was so strong, and held such confidence. It made Cassandra feel like everything was going to be alright. Even though she knew it wouldn't be.

"Whatever happens, we'll face it together. And if the nobles are going to run, better it happen now so we can adjust our strategy. But if the evidence is found and we can prove Flighty's a traitor, you need to act accordingly. Execute him immediately. Show your strength."

It was what Cassandra had been intending to do, but

the harsh tone was unlike Lukas. She searched his eyes, but they were suddenly unfocussed, as if he were far away.

"You were always so against execution. What's changed?"

Lukas blinked, dropping his arms and frowning, his eyes cast downward. "Yeah, I guess I was. I suppose border duty has changed me. I have seen the direct impact of treachery. It's not something that can be let go. Especially at this level."

Cassandra reached out, touching his arms as he had hers. His upper arm was warm and rock hard under her hand, and she rubbed him sympathetically. It was distracting how he'd filled out. She removed her hand. It was a ridiculous dream. Lukas was clearly not interested in her, and even if he was, everything he'd said about the life he wished for himself was the anthesis of marrying the empress. And whatever else she might be, she would never not be the ruler of the Empire.

Sadness stabbed her heart. The idea of being with Lukas was freeing to her. They would rule together, a true team. She would be able to trust him to take over when they had children. Cassandra shook the thought from her head. It was not to be. It would not do to dwell on such dreams.

Besides, it was entirely likely the Empire would collapse in civil war, and if that didn't finish them off, the Controllers would. She could worry about her love life if she was still alive next winter.

"Would you mind coming to the meeting?" Cassandra asked Lukas. "I know your family needs you, but—"

Lukas gave an exaggerated bow. "It is my honour to serve you, my liege. I remain your most humble servant."

She slapped him on his shoulder and he gave her a wink, his broad smile lighting up his face. "I was already planning on being there. And if we need to stall for time, I'll provide a briefing on the border. I've been around senior officers enough to know how to draw out a briefing for hours."

Cassandra smiled after Lukas until he'd rounded the corner, and then, smile dropping, she backtracked until she reached the stairs leading down. The servants were the only ones who used them, but luckily she met no one as she quickly descended two floors. Hurrying through the back corridors, Cassandra reached the reinforced door and, checking that no one was watching, pulled a key from her dress, unlocked it, and hurried through.

"Your son is here. He's grown into an impressive young man."

The prisoner visibly relaxed, deflating as he sat on the straw pallet and rubbed his face with his hands. She could see him shaking, but pushed her emotions away, willing herself to be cold.

"But he's worried about you," Cassandra continued. "A letter would put his mind at ease. And you know what they say. A distracted soldier..."

Is a dead soldier.

The words hung between them. Lord Sandison, her father's oldest friend, glared up at her.

"As I told you last time, I will write no more letters. Lukas is right to be worried." Lord Sandison gestured around the cell. "Kill me, or let me go. But I'm done playing your games."

Cassandra stared blankly at him. Could they fake his death, perhaps? An accident while he travelled?

When did you become such a monster?

Cassandra pushed the thoughts away. Curse her father

for leaving her this mess. Why had she not released Lukas's father the minute she took the throne and was informed of who lived in their cells? How was she ever going to resolve this in a way that didn't see Lukas hating her forever? Her stomach turned. He probably should hate her forever.

Lord Sandison slowly got to his feet. His bones creaked, and as he shuffled to the bars where she stood, Cassandra noticed his hair was disgustingly thin. She would fix this today. If she had to keep Lord Sandison detained, it didn't have to be in squalor in a dungeon.

"But you won't let me out," he said to her quietly, the way he used to speak to her when she was little. "Not now."

There was a slight glint in his eye. He could tell she felt awful. That's why he was playing the kindly old father of her best friend. Cassandra's eyes hardened.

"Do you really want to push me to end this?" she asked. "Because if you're done with our charade—the charade we agreed on together—then I will choose to resolve this matter with honesty. Are you really so ready for your family to discover you're a regicide? They'll lose everything. The estate, the islands. Lukas will have to return to the front in order to support his mother and siblings."

Lord Sandison's eyes flared dangerously. "You'd really send him back there? You of all people know what it's really like. I thought he was your friend."

Cassandra's retort died on her lips. She did not want Lukas to return to the border. She also didn't want him to discover that his father had murdered her own, poisoning him slowly, until he died painfully.

Her guilt about keeping the man in a cage abated. This was not how she would have chosen to deal with him. It was what her father had decided when he'd discovered his friend's treachery. There was no stopping his own death, but despite everything, he'd not been able to return the favour and execute Lord Sandison.

But despite the cruel nature of the punishment, Lord Sandison was not blameless here. He'd killed her father. Somehow, in her guilt, that fact often somehow slipped her mind. All she saw was her best friend's father languishing in a cell.

"I'm in this position because of old men and their lies," she hissed. "You killed my father. I don't know why he decided to hide you away instead of executing you as you deserved, but here we are. I'm doing my best to spare your family as much as possible from the pain caused by your actions."

Lord Sandison took a step back from the bars, his face crumpling like old paper. "As am I," he said quietly. "But after all this time, I realise that keeping up this charade only continues the pain for them. I'm drawing it out. I think it's time we ended things. Let them feel the pain of my loss, address it, and move on. It's the least that I owe them. That we owe them. Don't you think?"

Cassandra's mind reeled, running a million miles an hour through options, quickly discarded, trying to find a way forward that didn't lose her Lukas forever. Nothing fit. Nothing would work.

"Please," Lord Sandison whispered. "Please let me die."

She turned from the cage. From the skeletal form of the man who'd been like a second father to her growing up. She walked as fast as she could to the stairs, and when the man was out of view, she bunched her skirts and held them to her mouth as she screamed.

CHAPTER THIRTY-SEVEN

EMILIA

EMILIA STOOD IN THE ALLEYWAY, glancing around and tapping her fingers impatiently against the daggers strapped to her thighs. He was late, and this meeting was unnecessary. What she needed was to be back in the castle, shadowing Lukas and waiting for the meeting the empress had called with the nobles.

So much had happened, and this meeting would be key, she knew it. Though part of her wished someone else could be tasked to monitor it instead of her. As important as the meeting was, she'd much prefer to follow the odd group of heathens who'd arrived without warning and set all this in motion. Something about them—especially the one in charge, Kas—had snagged her attention and refused to let go. But alas, none but her could cross the wards and enter the palace.

It had surprised Emilia that the empress had bothered to meet with them personally. The Divine Prophet would never have done such a thing. Someone would need to have made it through layer upon layer of lesser priests, all of whom would have had to be willing to stake their lives on the person having something of extraordinarily high value to get a similar meeting with the ruler of the Divvinium.

But this leader of a legion of sinners had made time for them herself. Emilia was trying desperately not to allow an iota of respect for the woman to grow. But the more time she spent spying on her, especially with how open she was with the soldier, the more Emilia couldn't help but appreciate that she really did have the interests of her people at heart.

Voices sounded from the end of the alley, and Emilia jumped, hands flying to her weapons. But the voices faded. Just some Empire folk walking through the Merchants' Quarter. She took a deep breath to calm herself and straightened from the fighting stance she'd dropped into. Emilia wasn't usually this jumpy, but she also wasn't usually this visible. She'd grown comfortable living as a wraith in the palace and hadn't unbent the light in weeks. But she couldn't very well meet him while invisible. It wouldn't do for her handler to learn of her secret talent.

Casting her gaze to the end of the alley, she watched another group of heathens walk by. So much laughter here. You didn't hear laughter in the streets back home. Such frivolity was frowned upon. The One True God wanted respect and sacrifice, not laughter and games. Still, the genuine happiness she saw in some of the Empire's citizens seemed... beautiful. Not the indecent debauchery she'd been told was rampant here.

The briefings they received about the people who lived in the City of the Damned made them seem like devils. A people who valued gluttony and who laughed at those without while gorging themselves sick on decadent indulgences.

But as with most things, the truth seemed to fall somewhere in the middle. When she'd first arrived, all she'd seen was the brutal individualism of a people willing to step over anyone in their way. But the longer Emilia had spent in the city, the more she'd started to see some good.

Just the other day an old man with a rickety cart had spared some of his wares for a beggar, even though it was clear the old man was no rich merchant. Emilia had followed him to the market instead of returning directly to the palace, and watched as he adjusted his prices for those without much to pay.

Why was it always those who had so little who were so generous? Emilia thought of the sprawling mansions in Hightown where the soldier's family lived. Not once had she seen anyone from that district lift a finger to help another. Perhaps the One True God should simply obliterate the rich heathens? It seemed to her the poor could be saved.

Casting her eyes to the sky, Emilia frowned and began fiddling with a small ring on her little finger. Her handler was late. She hated tardiness and strove to never let another wait on her. It bothered her when she wasn't afforded the same respect.

Maybe something had gone wrong? Had her handler been discovered? Unlikely. Unless he'd literally been found on his way to the meeting, she'd have heard about it before she left the palace. A mind controller within the city walls? The palace would be in a panic. More likely, Sigmund didn't give a shit about making her wait because she was a woman.

Her mind turned back to the empress's meeting. And to Kas. Something about him intrigued her. Not to mention, he seemed to have enormous respect for all the women around him. They were his equal, or even his better, and he had no issue with it. They all seemed to work together. The Troll had been the same, but something about Kas had locked him in her mind, and she couldn't shake him out. It didn't hurt that he was nice to look at.

A scuff sounded from the other end of the alley, and she spotted a cloaked figure shuffling towards her. Emilia swore silently at herself. She should have sensed him before he even turned into the alley. But she had been too busy daydreaming about a boy. She angrily evicted all thoughts of the Empire folk from her mind and got her head in the game.

As he approached, Emilia ducked into a side alley where they could meet without worrying about being seen from either of the main thoroughfares. He followed her, pushing back his hood so she could see his face, but leaving it over his head so it could be pulled down quickly if needed. She followed suit, noticing his heavy breathing. Her handler had become comfortable here. He was out of condition. Emilia filed that information away in case it became useful. It was an affront to the One True God to fail to maintain the vessel He had provided for his people to serve him.

"Light and blessings, Emilia," the older man puffed.

"May His control grant you peace," Emilia replied by rote. For the first time in her life, the traditional greetings sounded odd to her ear. 'Light and blessings'. It felt light in the City of the Damned. Everything here was colourful, and the sun reflected off dazzling displays in the markets and shone through coloured glass in their temples. While the Divvinium preached this was sinful opulence, if the One True God wished them light, wouldn't he wish for them to celebrate His colours too? It was so dreary in the north. So monotone. Perhaps that was why they prayed for light.

"Thank you for meeting with me, and I apologise for my tardiness."

She was required to meet with him and he didn't sound at all sorry, so Emilia said nothing.

"You are tracking the unfolding events?"

"Yes, Erus Dunat. In fact, I really should be back in the palace. The empress may be meeting with others in the lead up to the council meeting tomorrow."

It pained her to call Sigmund Dunat by any kind of honorific, especially 'erus', which was usually reserved for the high priests. But he insisted, and though she knew he would never dream of trying such a thing were they in the north, it was easier just to use it here than cause trouble.

"The empress is of little concern for now." Sigmund dismissed her with a wave of his hand. "Lord Flighty is preparing. It's why I was late. I wanted to watch his meeting with Baron Shamble."

"You were with Vikram?"

That made no sense. There were a dozen Imperius in the city, all spying on and, where required, influencing key figures in the Empire. It worked because they remained separate. And no one else could bend the light as she could. Her comrades all had to infiltrate their proxies' homes and remain close by without being spotted. Doing that with one person was hard enough. Unless their proxies were together, the spies only ever met directly with Sigmund, who exchanged information as required. And Sigmund had been clear that such meetings were to take place away from the proxies.

"I meet with all of my subordinates," said Sigmund with pained patience. He'd not once come anywhere near the palace. Nor to any external locations she had advised him that her proxy was visiting. "I met with Reiko, then Vikram, and now you."

Emilia's blood froze in her veins even as her heart began pounding.

"Reiko is here?"

Sigmund smiled at her ignorance and clear distress. "Of course." As if he didn't purposefully keep the Imperius's isolated from each other. "He arrived in the city before you did."

Emilia's head swum. Though she'd managed to be removed from Reiko's patrol under the guise of shadowing the soldier who might leave for the palace at any minute, it'd been another week before he'd actually set out, Emilia his unexpected guest.

Apparently, she needn't have bothered. Reiko must have been sent to the Empire's capital that same day they'd met with Patron Smolka. Emilia forced her mind back to what Sigmund was saying. Apparently happy with his blindside, he'd returned to discussing the council meeting.

"This is a key point in our strategy," he explained, as if Emilia was particularly dim. "She is going to call for aid in preparation for our invasion. It is essential that this meeting goes the way we want it to."

"Of course, Erus." Emilia tried to keep her face pleasant. "Which is why I should really get back—"

"You are not to interfere with the meeting," Sigmund interrupted.

"What?" Emilia's brow arched. "But, respectfully, I haven't had a chance to brief you on the true purpose of the meeting. It seems premature to dictate the strategy."

"Lord Flighty suspects the empress is going to seek their support for an increased presence on the border." Sigmund wore a smug grin, confident as he was that with all of his information feeds, he saw the bigger picture. He also, like most of his fellows, had an issue with women, and had informed her at their first meeting that the empress was weak and would be dethroned within the month, and that Lord Flighty was the true power in the Empire.

She was going to enjoy this.

"That's not the purpose of the meeting at all." Emilia tried to keep her face neutral as the grin slid from Sigmund's face.

"Oh?"

"The empress has discovered that Lord Flighty is funding the rebellion. She has a team tasked with locating evidence of his treason. She intends to confront him with the evidence at the meeting."

Sigmund turned his gaze to the ground, his eyes flicking over the dirt and trash, processing this new information.

"If her thieves do not succeed, she will look foolish, further diminishing her position."

"And if they do succeed?" Emilia felt they would. She felt another pang of desire to accompany Kas and his team and watch them infiltrate Lord Flighty's properties. She was curious to see them in action. Yes, that's what it was. A professional curiosity.

It occurred to Emilia that she hadn't yet told Sigmund about the empress's ring. It seemed she'd been unprotected for years. That at any point during that time, they could have seized control of the empress and therefore the entire Empire. Emilia looked into Sigmund's eyes and saw the raw hatred burning there. He would likely suggest that upon her arrival in the palace, Emilia should have at least tried to gain control of the empress, and therefore, the blame for the missed opportunity of the past eight years belonged solely to her. Emilia decided not to rectify the oversight.

"Unlikely," Sigmund said dismissively. "Lord Flighty's assets are well guarded."

Other than the two Imperius who managed to get in to his house, one of whom has been living there for the past six months...

"But if they do," Emilia pressed, "and the empress

disposes of Flighty, the others will fall under her command and unite."

"If the empress disposes of Flighty, the others will resent her and revolt," said Sigmund confidently. "Your orders remain the same. Do nothing to influence the meeting." He paused, thinking. "But you are to ensure your proxy does not intervene on behalf of the empress. We wish to weaken their bond. Make her feel she is completely alone. That she has no one."

Emilia's stomach sank, but she bowed as Sigmund dismissed her. It felt wrong to isolate the empress. But she was projecting, she knew it. They taught students at the elite academy for espionage about projection. About feeling empathy for those you observed. Emilia had been alone her whole life. Her aversion to isolating the empress was misplaced sympathy for herself. And she wasn't really alone. The One True God was always with her.

But the words felt empty all of a sudden, and as Emilia reached the end of the alley, she checked that no one was watching and wrapped the light around her like a comforting blanket. Her thoughts whirled through her head, confused and unsure.

All the stories painted the empress as a cold, godless woman, intent on leading her sinners in a life of debauchery and blasphemy. But it was clear the empress really did care about her people. In fact, the Empire didn't seem to be the threat the Divvinium claimed they were at all.

They weren't preparing a crusade against the Divvinium, intent on wiping their religion from the continent. In fact, left to its own devices, the Empire would probably destroy itself. The gap between those who had everything and those who had nothing was so stark it turned Emilia's stomach. The Divvinium had its issues, but at least it believed in equality.

Emilia paused, her thoughts tripping her up. The Divvinium preached equality, and sure, it seemed to care for its citizens more than the Empire did, but were things equal? She could apply for any role in the Divvinium, but she'd never get something a man wanted. No women were ever permitted a leadership position, despite preaching that they were permitted to apply.

And wasn't that another form of imposed class disparity? She looked around. But it wasn't this extreme. She might not be able to advance, but she wasn't starving on the streets. Which brought Emilia back to her original thought: How could the Empire be a threat to the Divvinium when they were too busy starving their own people in the streets?

From the sounds of things, it wasn't the Empire seeking to destroy the Divvinium, it was the Divvinium who wanted to annihilate the other religions.

Emilia looked around at all the people going about their lives in the city. They were laughing and joking, hurrying and peddling. Was this truly blasphemy?

She understood that their false gods offended the One True God. But what place was it of theirs to come and force them to see the light? If they all wanted to worship their false gods and be damned for all eternity, shouldn't they be allowed to make that choice?

Emilia shivered, glancing up at the sky as if the One True God might be watching. She tried to shake the thoughts from her mind. Doubting her orders was an offence to the One True God. And whatever these southerners wanted to do, Emilia certainly didn't want to be damned for all eternity.

Sighing, Emilia slipped through the people and carts slowly winding their way across the main street towards the palace. She needed to shake off these doubts. She was the best spy in the whole Divvinium. She had never failed a mission. Hades, if she'd been born a man, she'd probably be the grand cleric of espionage by now.

Emilia quickened her pace, trying to convince herself she was not angry at the treatment she received due to her gender. Not mad that Patron Smolka had acted as if she was being bestowed a great honour in being selected to come here. Despite clearly having just told Reiko he was headed to the city, too. No wonder Reiko had been happy to storm off and leave her be.

Emilia told herself she was professional. No matter what the rest of them did, the games they insisted on playing, she would follow her orders. She would serve the Divvinium. She would do what was required of her in service to her God.

But were those orders really in the name of the One True God, or were they for the benefit of the Divine Prophet himself?

She paused at the drawbridge. What could she really do to advance their mission by hanging around the palace, waiting for a meeting that she'd essentially been ordered to do nothing in anyway?

And she'd not been specifically ordered not to follow Kas and his team. Not been told to return to the palace *immediately*. Feeling lighter than she had in a while, Emilia turned, setting off to find her new targets. Huge though the city was, if there was one thing she'd learned about the people of the Empire, where there were problems to be solved, ale was involved. There were three taverns close to the palace. Emilia headed for the dingiest one.

CHAPTER THIRTY-EIGHT

KAS

The team exited the palace, automatically aiming for one of the seedier taverns nearby. The Drunkin' Pumpkin was close to Hightown, but in the Servants' Quarter, and the gentrification hadn't yet turned it into one of the trendy pubs that dotted the city.

As they walked, they attracted stares and conspicuously stolen glances from the citizens of Lorendell. Some people went out of their way to give the group a wide berth, and at least one skinny man let out a little cry of surprise and hurried back into the shop he had exited.

Kas nervously rubbed his neck. Ossi and Tia's tan lines from their collars weren't as obvious as Kas and Mira's, but they were still relatively obvious. Maybe they all should have stayed in the palace grounds to plan. Or asked the empress for some scarves.

"It's not our necks that give them pause," said Ossi, falling in beside Kas.

"How do you know?" Kas asked. He rubbed his neck again, now seemingly unable to keep from drawing attention to his thin band of pale skin.

"When was the last time you saw a Troll, a Shifter, and a Druid walking the streets of your city?"

Kas blinked. Trolls were occasionally seen in Lorendell, and people behaved very much like they were now—keeping their distance. But a Shifter? Kas couldn't remember ever seeing one, though they were spoken about enough that Tia was easily identifiable. Certainly no Empire-born looked like she did. And while there were the City Druids, they seemed to never leave the palace, though Sofia's grey cloak marked her for who and what she was.

"Why is it the tribes don't mix more?" Kas now asked Ossi. Though Lorendell was Kas's city, he had no idea why the other tribes didn't visit, but the Jatte were the travellers. They were the only tribe who regularly visited the others.

Ossi shrugged. "My grandfather said it is because of the Controllers. That it was their warmongering that kept the tribes suspicious of others."

"Do you think that's what it is?" Kas asked.

"Maybe. My grandmother told me that at one time, the tribes were fluid. Visitors were common, and people even relocated, choosing to live in other tribes. But despite that, the leaders of the tribes could never get on the same page about helping each other. I can see how that might be difficult. If I lived elsewhere and my people were attacked, I would return to fight. And I would resent my adopted home if they did not offer support."

Kas tried to imagine the streets of Lorendell teeming with people from all the tribes. Shops run by Jatte or Kikachi, or even the Druids. A thought struck him.

"What about relationships?" he asked. "You know, intertribal ones?"

"They happen from time to time," Ossi said. "They are rare, but not unheard of."

"But, where do they live?"

"My mother was an Empire woman. She came to live with us for a time, but our ways are so different. She found it confronting and she missed the familiar comfort of her city. My father offered to move with her, but she knew his heart was with his people, and that he would not be accepted here."

Kas fought to keep his mouth closed, his jaw wanting to drop. He knew Ossi was small for a Jatte, but he'd never wondered if there was a reason for that. "So she left you?" he asked gently.

"No, my father thought it important for me to be with her, and so I lived here for a time." Ossi smiled, looking around. "I don't remember much other than it felt like a great adventure. But eventually it became clear that I have more Jatte blood than Empire, and my mother didn't want me treated poorly because I was different. So she returned me to my people, but visited often, and my father brought me here whenever he could."

The pair lapsed into silence as Kas tried to imagine a young Ossi running around the same streets he had grown up on. He thought to ask if Ossi wanted to visit his mother while they were in Lorendell, but before he could, Tia had called to him, and Ossi sped up to walk with her and Mira.

The group wove its way through the streets, and Kas found himself walking with Adeline. Kas felt happy that Adeline was with them. Of all people, she knew what Salomon meant to him, and when he'd first turned to thievery to support himself and his brother after their parents died, she'd come with him. They'd actually been a pretty good team.

But then they'd grown older. Kas realised he could turn invisible and Adeline had had to get a job, and she hadn't the time to go with him anymore. And now she had a plum job in the palace. Perhaps that explained the look on her face. Like being here was the last thing she wanted. Still, it hurt. Perhaps she'd finally outgrown him.

"I know this is outside your usual duties," Kas said to her, giving her the grin that usually softened her eyes, no matter how mad she was. "But I'm glad you're here. I'm glad we're together."

Adeline did not smile, and the look she cast him was devoid of those soft eyes.

"Have I upset you?" Kas asked. His heart constricted at the idea of hurting Adeline. She was his best friend, and everything felt like it would be alright when she was around.

Her eyes finally softened upon hearing the alarm in his voice. "No, it's just... it's nothing. I'm glad we're together, too." She smiled, but her last words sounded strained. Like she was convincing herself as well.

"You'll like everyone," said Kas, eager to capitalise on the melting of her mood. "Well, I mean Sofia's a bit odd," he said, lowering his voice, "but Mira's lovely, and Ossi's a great guy. And I bet you and Tia will hit it off. You're a lot alike."

Adeline's eyes narrowed again, the frosty exterior descending. "I'm sure she's *amazing*."

Kas blinked, confused by the sudden change in his friend. Her sudden hostility towards Tia.

"Adeline?" a haughty voice called from across the street, and Kas turned to see a tall, thin man walking towards them. He couldn't be much older than Kas, but dressed as if he were middle-aged and in the style that Kas associated with social climbers.

"Shit," Adeline muttered.

"I thought that was you." The man cast a look over their group, his nose scrunched in displeasure as he immediately decided they were not worth his time.

"I really must have my watch back," the man said in a

gratingly arrogant tone. "I gave your... *belongings*, such as they were, to your sister and told her to have you return it to me. Honestly, I didn't think you'd be so petty."

Kas gaped as Tia and Mira shared a look before they ushered Ossi and Sofia away, the four of them huddling at the side of the road, trying to look as if they weren't listening.

"I don't have your watch, Micah," Adeline said in the strained tones of someone tired of explaining things that were never heard. "I told you that. My sister told you that. I still don't have it."

"It's just that I need it for the ball this weekend—" Micah continued, not hearing Adeline at all.

This was the man Adeline had been engaged to marry? No wonder she'd been so upset that night in the rebels' tavern. At least it sounded like she'd dumped him. But there was no way Kas was about to let anyone talk to his friend like that.

"Mate," Kas interrupted. "She said she doesn't have your watch. I suggest you leave it."

Micah's eyebrows touched his powered wig, and he looked stunned that someone such as Kas would dare to address him directly. Kas saw something dawn behind Micah's eyes, and the thin man looked from Kas to Adeline and back, his incredulity growing.

"Is this *him?*" Micah asked, appalled.

The empress's voice echoed in Kas's head, asking the same question, and he was hit again with an intense feeling of missing something that was right in front of him.

"It doesn't matter," said Adeline quietly, turning her gaze to the cobblestone road.

"It is, isn't it?" Micah's disbelief turned to glee as Kas's anger at missing the joke grew.

"Look, we've got to go," Kas said, gently taking Adeline's

elbow to lead her away. "She doesn't have your watch. Leave her alone."

Micah scoffed, sidestepping to block them. "I do hope the two of you are happy together," Micah said snidely. "I'm certain he will provide you with everything you deserve."

"What is your problem?" Kas asked, trying to guide Adeline around the man, but finding Micah once again in their path.

"No problem, good man," Micah said, buoyant now. "When my ex-fiancée told me she'd found another, I had no idea that he would be so..." Micah made a show of looking Kas up and down. "*Poor*. But you do seem a far better match for such a harlot." All the glee had gone from Micah's voice in an instant and he spat the last word at Adeline, spittle hitting her face.

A large hand dropped on Micah's shoulder, turning him. Kas had never seen Ossi so angry. If he'd been in Micah's place, he'd probably wet his pants.

"Please do not speak to the lady like that," said Ossi, glaring down at Micah, who seemed to be trying to collect himself and close his mouth.

"I'll speak to her however I like," said Micah, some of the arrogance returning to his tone, though his wavering voice betrayed his fear. "I suggest if *you* wish to speak to her, you simply hop in line. Or will he need to pay for the pleasure?" Micah sneered at Adeline. "Do you charge by the hour now?"

Ossi took a step forward, forcing Micah to back up several steps.

"I'll ask you one more time not to speak to the lady like that," Ossi said dangerously.

"How dare you presume—"

"And then," Ossi interrupted, taking another step and forcing Micah back farther, "I won't *ask* again."

Micah's face went instantly pale and his mouth bobbed, as if still talking, but his brain had the sense to withhold the words. Micah backed up from Ossi, who continued to stare menacingly at him, and cast his eyes instead back to Kas and Adeline. Finding a safer target, he began walking away and, from a safe distance, called snidely, "Have a wonderful life together. I'm sure your hovel will be lovely."

Kas looked at Adeline. She was bright red and looked deeply unhappy, though she brightened as her eyes found Ossi.

"Thank you," she said to him.

"No one should ever speak to you like that," Ossi said with a small bow.

The women rejoined them and they set off again, Ossi moving the women along quickly to create a gap for Kas and Adeline to speak.

Kas wracked his brain, trying to think of the best way to restart the conversation. Micah had made it sound like Adeline had left him for Kas. Maybe she'd just needed an excuse to end things?

"Look," started Adeline, saving Kas the trouble. "I'm sorry about that. It's just... I just... I guess I heard what I wanted to and got the wrong end of the stick. It was my mistake. And I didn't tell you because I really didn't think you'd ever meet Micah, so..." she trailed off.

Mistake? What had she—

Oh.

Kas's mind searched back through the conversations they'd had since he escaped the camps. How he'd mentioned missing her so much that he'd dreamed about living with Adeline in a little house here in the city.

Shit.

And now that he thought about it, she'd been so happy. So quick to assume he felt that way about her. Because...

Kas felt ill. Because *she* felt that way about him. He'd always seen her as a friend. His best friend. He'd never even considered Adeline like that. To be fair, he'd really only started thinking about girls at all just before he'd been caught and collared. But Adeline?

He glanced at her now. Willing himself to see her as she was, not how he thought of her—a thirteen-year-old girl. Kas blinked.

She was beautiful. Thin for an Empire woman, but strong from her years of housework. Her lips were full and her eyes such a deep green. How had he missed it?

"Look, Addy—"

"It's fine, Kas. It was my mistake. I was probably just looking for anyone to give me an excuse to leave Micah's miserable ass."

Kas heard the lie in her voice, but before he could say anything, Ossi fell back level with them.

"He was not worthy of you," Ossi said simply. "No man should ever treat you like that. A woman like you should be worshipped."

Adeline giggled, slapping at Ossi's shoulder and telling him he was laying it on a bit thick. But her eyes were bright. Like they had been when she'd looked at Kas earlier.

"He's right," Kas said, panicking. How had he not seen her before? Really *seen* her? And now he was going to lose her just as he realised what had been standing right in front of him? Adeline and Ossi turned to look at Kas, giving him the distinct impression that he was intruding on their conversation. "I mean, that guy was a knob. You deserve so much better."

"Thanks Kas," said Adeline, smiling. "And you deserve happiness too. Tia seems lovely. I'm happy for you."

"They are not together," said Ossi, offering Adeline his arm. She took it, looking up at him curiously. "Kas kissed her, but she prefers women, and so she did not wish to kiss him back."

Adeline tried to stifle a giggle, but he saw her shoulders shake as Ossi led her towards the group, their heads together as they spoke words he could no longer hear.

Perhaps it was good that he couldn't hear. Kas looked at the ground, wishing again that he possessed earth magic that would allow him to open a nice, deep chasm and jump.

"Kas?" Tia called back, her brow furrowed, wondering why he'd stopped.

"Coming," Kas called and hurried to catch up.

He remained at the back of the group for the rest of the walk, trying to make sense of his feelings. Adeline was his friend. And so was Ossi. So it was good that they seemed to like each other. And Ossi would definitely treat her better than her ex-fiancé.

And Kas wasn't interested in Adeline like that. Right? He was just reacting to realising his friend liked him. But the feeling that had hit him when he'd looked at her and *really* seen her... he'd never felt anything like that before. He told himself it was love for a friend. His oldest friend. That feeling hadn't changed when he realised she was beautiful.

Kas struggled with his thoughts for the rest of the walk to the tavern, and as he walked through the doorway behind Ossi and Adeline, still arm in arm, he couldn't help feeling like he may have missed his opportunity for happiness.

CHAPTER THIRTY-NINE

KAS

SAT around a dark table in the back corner of the tavern, the group was now furnished with drinks, and a plate of snacks had been largely decimated. Kas had made an effort to block out the thoughts and feelings that stabbed him with every giggle or casual touch between Ossi and Adeline. He'd given up trying to convince himself to be happy for them, instead telling himself he didn't have time to think about it at all. He had a mission to complete, and not much time to do it.

Adeline had given them all a rundown of what she knew about Lord Flighty, which was quite a lot. She'd never actually worked for the man, but apparently the maids gossiped.

"So we're looking at his house, and three business headquarter buildings here in the city," Kas summarised, thinking. "But who knows how many other properties he might own outside the city, or even on the islands."

"That's right," said Adeline. She smiled at him like she used to. When they were friends.

"But it's unlikely what we need is outside the city," said Tia, grabbing another hunk of bread. "If he doesn't travel regularly, I can't imagine he'd trust a courier to transport incriminating documents."

"That's true," said Mira. "But how are we going to break into and search four buildings before this time tomorrow?"

"Four that we know of," added Ossi.

"His house should be easy," said Adeline. "Most noble houses use one of the housekeeping companies to cover staff absences. They maintain a roster of temporary staff available at short notice," she explained, seeing some blank looks. "So if a maid is too sick to work, this company will send someone for the day to cover her duties."

"But how will we know if someone is sick?" Kas mused. "And then we'd need to intercept the messenger..."

"We'll know they're sick if we make them sick," said Adeline.

The group looked at her.

"What? Not seriously ill, just sick enough to not go to work."

"Do you have a poison that will work?" Kas asked.

"Not on me, but I can pick up supplies and make one pretty quickly." She looked down the table at Mira. "But you might have a better one."

Mira looked slightly alarmed. "No, no. I'm sure whatever you have in mind will be great."

"Perhaps now is the time to tell them, dear," said Sofia, sipping on the ale that Kas had needed to purchase for her, the barkeeper glaring at her very presence in his tavern.

"Tell us what?" Tia asked as Mira shot Sofia a look and blushed.

Sofia simply inclined her head at Mira and reached for some cheese.

Mira sighed, closing her eyes. "I'm not a spell caster," she admitted. "I'm a full magical."

"That's great," Kas said, wondering why she'd kept it a secret. "Which element do you wield?"

"I'm not... I'm not from the Empire."

Silence met that pronouncement, and everyone waited for her to continue. But Mira seemed unwilling to say more. Sofia, however, had no such hesitation.

"Mira is a Communicator magical."

"You're from the Comunicator tribe?" Adeline asked, eyes wide. "Didn't the Controllers..."

"I am Nadair, and yes, the Controllers wiped my people out. My parents smuggled us across the border before it was too late. But refugees weren't welcome in the south." Bitterness entered Mira's tone. "We knew we'd be collared if they realised who we were. But Nadair look similar enough to pass ourselves off as Empire-born, and when I was separated from my family, I thought it safer to continue the lie."

Kas felt a pang of empathy for Mira. He'd lost family too. But he hadn't lost his home, not really. Sure, he lost his parents, then their house, and had needed to move to the slums. But he'd had Salomon. He'd still had the city. He'd had Frank and Adeline and all the familiar faces he'd grown up with. He could visit the alleys he'd played in as a child. Mira had none of that.

Looking at her now, knowing who she really was, he could see the subtle differences in her ears, her eyes, even her hair colour that should have marked her as a Communicator from the start. Now that he knew, he was floored he'd ever believed she was Empire-born.

"That's why the soldiers tried to arrest your family, isn't it?" asked Tia gently.

Mira nodded, sniffling. "They killed them," she said. "When my father said to run, I went one way, and they all went another. There was a crack, and I smelled fire. I heard the screams..." she whispered.

Tia pulled Mira into a hug and the rest of the group fell into a sombre silence. They had all lost people they loved over the years, but at least their tribes remained. Mira had lost her family, and had no home to return to.

The mission suddenly weighed heavier on Kas. Not only was he fighting to save his brother—the only family he had left—but if they weren't successful, the Empire would never unite and soon, they would all be in Mira's shoes.

Mira wiped at her face, extracting herself from Tia. "I can communicate with birds. Any type. But mainly ravens."

Kas blinked at her. The Communicators could communicate with animals, hence the Empire dubbing their tribe the Communicators. What had Mira called them? The Nadair. He'd need to remember that. Kas suddenly recalled the three birds that had come to the mountaintop when their collars were removed.

"You can communicate even with what the collars have done?" Kas asked.

"Yes," Mira said. "I can't communicate with as many of them at a time as I could. And sometimes I call for one and another comes. But unless we specifically need a flock of eagles for an attack, we should be fine."

"That will prove excellent for surveillance," said Ossi, laying a comforting hand on Mira's shoulder. She smiled up at him. "Birds can go many places we cannot. And no one pays them any mind."

"And we can work out a code, perhaps with the number of pecks, and send each other messages if we're separated," Mira said.

"Like three taps for trouble," said Tia.

"What if you miss a tap?" asked Adeline. "Then you think it's just two taps and so everything's fine."

"The birds can repeat the code," said Mira.

"How would we send a code?" asked Ossi. "The birds can't understand the rest of us."

"You'll use them like a flare. If something's wrong, or you've found the evidence, you'll signal the bird and it'll come and find me and let me know what's going on. I'll take care of the rest."

"But how do we signal them?" asked Tia, frowning as if puzzling over a complex math problem.

Mira sighed. "You can give them a treat. Then—"

"What treat do we give birds?" Kas asked.

"They like cashews," Mira said shortly. "Then—"

"Where are we supposed to get a bunch of cashews in the middle of a food shortage?" Adeline asked.

"Bill's grocer?" Kas suggested.

Adeline shook her head. "He closed two years ago."

"How do we make sure we give the right bird the treat?" Ossi mused. "Presumably birds who aren't in on the plan also like cashews."

A small wooden bowl of slightly stale peanuts slammed onto the table, making everyone jump. Kas hadn't even seen Mira get up.

"They're not cashews," said Adeline quietly.

"They will do." Mira sat heavily, working to keep her frustration in check. "We will use ravens. I will tell all the ravens I can communicate with that a human offering a nut is the signal. The ravens will carry the message to me, whether or not it is their preferred treat."

"If that's the case, the nut seems a little unnecessary," said Ossi quietly.

"Perfect," said Kas loudly before Mira could respond. "That's settled. If we need help or find the evidence, we'll use the signal, and Mira will do the rest. If a bird lands near you and taps three times, repeatedly, head back here and we can regroup and address whatever the issue is."

No one seemed overly satisfied with that—Mira was still clearly frustrated and everyone else was struggling with the logic of what had seemed like a simple idea. Kas brought them back to the task at hand.

"It's good we'll have a way to communicate, because I think we're going to have to divide up into teams. We'll send two to the house. Do you think you can take two of the maids out?" Kas asked Adeline.

She considered it before nodding slowly. "I think so. Then someone could be in the kitchens while I look around the house."

Kas shook his head. "I don't think you should be a replacement. You're too recognisable. You've worked in noble houses, and now most of their staff would know you work for the empress. And even if they don't, we can't risk you being seen in his house and then someone recognising you in the palace."

Adeline didn't look happy, but she nodded. "Fair enough. Where do you need me then?"

Kas looked around the group. "Well, I think we send Tia and Mira to the house."

The two women nodded, though Adeline looked thoughtful.

"I can see that Mira isn't Empire-born now that I know it, though I didn't question it before," Adeline mused. "But Tia is obviously a Shifter. She'll stand out. The poison is complex, but I should have time to make a glamour potion. I can brew enough for you too, Mira, just to be safe."

"I didn't know you could do that," Kas said, impressed. Glamour potions were tricky spells. If Adeline could make one that would allow Tia to pass as Empire-born, she must be more powerful than he'd thought.

"I'm proud to be Kikachi," said Tia. "I don't care if these city folk stare at me."

"Yes, but since you're infiltrating Flighty's estate, it's probably best if you're forgettable," said Adeline.

Tia's mouth pursed to the side. "Yeah, fair point."

"Thanks Addy," said Kas, keen to move things along. "Okay, so that leaves me, Ossi, Adeline and—"

"I shall not be joining you," said Sofia. "I will return to the palace."

Kas opened his mouth, about to argue. He couldn't see what she would achieve at the palace. The empress had made it quite clear that she wouldn't entertain discussions about preparing for the invasion until they had helped her. But then, he wasn't sure what he would task Sofia with anyway. What did one do with a centenarian who looked ten years old?

"Great." He nodded at her, and she raised her mug to him before drinking some more. "Then Tia and Mira to the house and the rest of us to his businesses. Do you think we need to tail Flighty himself?"

There was a brief silence as everyone thought.

"I think that would be wise," said Ossi. "He may say something, or lead us to another property that we don't know about."

"Then I'll take that job," said Kas. "Hopefully my invisibility holds out. And it'll be a good opportunity to work on it."

"We'll take the three businesses between us," said Adeline, looking at Ossi.

"Good. If you split up, you should be able to cover them easily."

"Sure," said Ossi, smiling at Adeline in a way that ignited a fire in Kas's belly. Adeline returned his smile, and Kas had no doubt the two would conduct their surveillance together.

"Okay." Kas forced his eyes from them and back to the

group at large. "So we've got our jobs, and we're clear on Mira's signal," Kas hurried on before the discussion on the signal could start up again, "so it might be best if we split up from here. Tia and Mira aren't needed until tomorrow." He turned to them. "Maybe see if we can get a couple of rooms here and then anyone who's got some down time can use them to rest." He looked back around the group, not making eye contact with Adeline. "Adeline will make her poison and the glamour, and I'm sure Ossi will help if needed."

"I'm sure he will," Tia teased.

"And I guess I'll try to find Flighty," Kas finished, ignoring Tia.

Mira looked over at Adeline and Ossi. "Tia and I can start surveillance on the businesses while you make the poison."

"Thanks," Adeline said with a smile before turning to Kas. "Head to the forge at the edge of the Merchants' Quarter and the Servants' Quarter," said Adeline. "Ask for Finneous. He works in their store. He'll have an idea of Flighty's schedule since he used to drive his carriage."

Kas nodded his thanks. "Alright, all going well, we'll meet back here tomorrow by midmorning. Obviously if you find what we need earlier, send a message. Once we know the location, we can plan how we're going to get the evidence. And if we don't know where it is by midmorning... well, we'll deal with that if it happens."

The team split up, wishing each other luck as Ossi and Adeline slipped out of the tavern and Tia and Mira headed to the bar to ask about a couple of rooms. Kas wandered to the door, wanting to ensure space between him and his friends.

He should be happy for them. For both of them. But instead, Kas just felt more alone than he ever had in his life.

CHAPTER FORTY

EMILIA

Emilia pulled her hood down, making sure it was hiding her face as she wove around the citizens of Lorendell. Her discomfort at remaining visible was outweighed by her fear of losing Kas if she ducked into an alley to disappear.

The tavern had been so crowded she'd been forced to enter without the security of invisibility, and after observing the meeting, she'd followed Kas from the tavern without thinking about it and was now tailing him as he made his way to the forge the girl—Adeline—had mentioned.

She'd seen the looks Kas had shot Adeline and the Troll she'd been flirting with, giggling and pressing her shoulder into his. Kas had been upset by it. Had he and Adeline dated previously?

The idea of it made her frown. Emilia decided pretty, giggly Adeline must be stupid if she let someone like Kas go. Though she couldn't fault the girl's taste. The Troll was pretty handsome. If you liked huge guys with muscles for days and deep blue eyes.

She hurried as Kas disappeared around a corner, slowing again once she had him in sight. No, Adeline could keep her Troll. Emilia was far more taken with the tall, strong, but agile and thoughtful man who apparently had the same secret power that she did.

Emilia shook her head. She was curious about Kas—that was it. At first it had just been because she'd never met a man who was such an egoless leader. Someone who surrounded himself with such a diverse group and seemed to truly value their opinions. And now it was purely about learning if the invisibility he'd referenced was the same as hers.

Nothing to do with how handsome he was or how his eyes sparkled when he laughed. Emilia took a sharp inhale, berating herself and pulling her focus back to the mission. What was wrong with her? The fate of the entire Divvinium was at stake, and she was daydreaming about an Empire heathen.

Kas hurried into the forge's shopfront, and Emilia made her way to the entrance of an alley across from it. She pressed into the shadows and wondered if she should pull the light around her and follow Kas inside. But by the time someone else opened the door, allowing her to slip inside, it was probably going to be Kas on his way out.

Still, she pulled the light anyway and felt immediate relief at being invisible once more. She could see Kas through the shop's window. He was making small talk from the easy interaction, but she could see the urgency in his eyes.

All of them were conscious of the limited timeframe, but Kas above the others was anxious. It was his brother on the line. Emilia had heard much of what the infamous rebel leader had been up to. The man—little more than a boy, really—was causing chaos for chaos's sake. Violence was the aim of almost all the missions the rebellion now undertook, and it didn't seem to matter who the casualties were.

A far cry from the gentle man currently charming a shop worker so that he could save his brother and the Empire. If she hadn't known they were brothers, she never would have guessed it.

The door opened, and Kas set off, Emilia now in invisible pursuit. She wondered at his urgency. She herself had no siblings, but she felt if she had one like this Salomon, she probably wouldn't be busting her ass to save his.

But then, she wasn't as good a person as Kas.

Emilia frowned as she once again wondered how the One True God could be so angry at these people that he wanted them obliterated. Sure, some of them were assholes. She'd seen a rich man bump a middle-class woman the other day. The woman had landed in a mud puddle and the man had kept walking, not even glancing back to see if she was alright.

But then she'd seen a poor man taking his meagre supplies home with him after work. The man had stopped to give some of his food to a kid who was begging in the streets. In the Divvinium, no child would be forced to beg for food on the streets. The idea of letting anyone, let alone a child, suffer like that was abhorrent—though apparently not to the Empire. Though that one man had cared. Even not having much himself. It troubled her. What issue could the One True God have with him?

Kas stopped suddenly, and Emilia dodged people and carts and found a safe spot along the outer wall of a shop where she could watch him. He moved, also finding a spot, keeping his eyes on the upper level of a building across the road from them both.

Nothing happened, and Emilia decided he must be waiting to see if Lord Flighty turned up or exited the building. Her mind began to wander again and her feeling of guilt grew.

She shouldn't be here. She should be back in the palace, keeping an eye on things there. She should be watching the empress. Listening in on her conversations with the soldier. Nudging the soldier's responses to guide them along the path that would open the door for the Divvinium's invasion.

Her orders were to ensure the soldier didn't support her in the meeting. Sigmund didn't understand the intricacies of such a position. Didn't get that you couldn't leave them be and then suddenly manipulate him to not support her, and then leave him to answer her questions about why he hadn't.

That kind of tweak to a relationship needed to be choreographed. Perhaps you build them up beforehand, driving them closer together, and then afterwards blame the lack of support on something she said, either in the meeting or before it, and then you needed to make him leave for a bit, so she could worry and obsess on it.

That's what drove a wedge. That's how you made someone feel alone. That was how you distracted the leader of an empire so much that she'd focus on her boyfriend rather than the impending crisis.

But Sigmund didn't get it, and Emilia suddenly didn't feel like making him look good. She would normally do it anyway, because she took pride in her work. But now... she didn't *want* to drive a wedge between the empress and her soldier. She didn't *want* to put in the hours required on such a manipulation that Sigmund would neither recognise nor credit. She didn't *want* to weaken the Empire so the Divvinium could simply crush it in one blow.

The thought came so suddenly it took Emilia by surprise. She didn't want the Empire to fall. All of these people to die. But if she didn't prepare the way, then the fighting would be intense. Maybe the destruction would simply be far worse. But surely they deserved the right to fight? To have some autonomy in what happened to them?

Emilia banished the heavy thoughts from her mind. Her focus was the empress, but part of that was at least understanding this mission, if not influencing it. Whether or not the soldier supported her in the meeting would be of little consequence if Kas showed up with evidence of Lord Flighty's treason and the man was arrested and executed.

And while she knew it served the Divvinium for Kas's mission to fail, a part of Emilia wished him and his friends success. Lord Flighty was a knob. Emilia would be happy for him to be brought down a few pegs, rather than killed, but then, she wasn't going to shed any tears for the man if he died. She'd spoken to Vikram outside the palace after one of the council meetings. He'd said he didn't need to influence Flighty much at all. And obviously Vikram had no control of him in the meetings. No, that was all Flighty himself.

Kas pushed off the wall and began casually walking, looking at the buildings, before settling across the road from Emilia, next to the building he was watching. Emilia could see the tension in him. The worry if he was wasting his time waiting. If he should be off looking for Flighty elsewhere.

Emilia wondered if she should be following the others. If she was honest with herself, what she should have done was follow the small Druid back to the palace. See what she was up to. There was nothing more for the Druid to say to the empress, so why was she going there?

Maybe she should have followed Adeline to see what poison she was brewing. Some Imperius's loved having spell casters as proxies. If she learned what poisons Adeline could make, she could feed that back to the Divvinium. Perhaps such poisons could be brewed and unleashed in the populations' water supplies in the lead up to battles.

Emilia was confident that she hadn't needed to follow

the Shifter and the Communicator. Vikram had been inside the house. Anything worth learning, he should have found. And the only mystery the two women held in Emilia's mind was how they'd formed so strong a bond so quickly. But maybe that was just the animal connection.

Emilia knew she should report the presence of the Communicator to Sigmund. If one got away, maybe there were more. Hades, maybe she should follow the Communicator purely to listen in and find out if she knew of other survivors. But Emilia didn't want to do either of those things. The longer she spent in the City of the Damned, the more she wondered if it was truly necessary to wipe out the other peoples of Valoris. And a small part of Emilia felt that if the small Communicator had managed to escape the purge, then good luck to her.

No, Kas was the right target to follow, Emilia convinced herself. If anyone was likely to locate the evidence, it was him, which meant if she were to influence the mission, he was the key. Also, it was his power she wanted to study. Needed to study.

A carriage pulled up and the grating accent of the unnecessarily rich reached her ears even from over the road. She saw Lord Flighty alight and hurry into the building, as if trying to minimise the time he might be in the proximity of the common folk.

Emilia darted across the road and followed Kas, who had slipped down a side road that paralleled the building. She peered around a corner as he checked to see if he was being watched. A gasp slipped from her lips as Kas suddenly grew pale, as if he were somehow faded. Like an illustration rather than real life. He was duller than he'd been moments ago.

Two men exited from a back door and Kas darted in,

slipping through just before the door closed. The men didn't so much as blink at him.

He's invisible. But I can see him. Maybe because we share the power?

Emilia frowned, a memory tugging at her. Walking through the ruins up north with the soldier. She'd thought that boy had seen her as he hid with his friends. But maybe... could that boy also have the power? Could that boy have been Kas?

The men finished their break and headed for the door, throwing it open and lurching inside. Without thinking, Emilia rushed for it, but she halted before she entered, allowing it to close in front of her.

Kas would be able to see her. That changed things. She couldn't very well barge inside as she usually would. She would have to be careful now. She would have to find another way.

CHAPTER FORTY-ONE

TIA

"I'm just saying I think we could have found another way."

"And I'm just saying that if we could have, we would have, but you still haven't been able to come up with another option, and we've really only got a few hours to make this work," said Tia, She glanced at Mira, whose lips were pressed into a straight line.

Tia understood how she felt. She wasn't feeling like a superstar for poisoning two innocent women so they could infiltrate Lord Flighty's estate to look for evidence that would likely see the man executed. She tried not to think about the possibility that the women would be implicated if this went wrong.

"Look," she said, her tone softer. "I get it. I feel like an asshole too."

"I know." Mira waved her off. "I know you're in the same position. And to be fair, I didn't really think about it much until now. It's probably more nerves than guilt."

Tia knew Mira was lying. She did feel guilty. Tia knew that, because she felt guilty herself. And she knew Mira.

Mira was a better person than she was. Softer and kinder. This had to be eating at her.

"So, when we get there, presumably they'll allocate us our roles," said Mira, clearly trying to get into the right head space.

"That's what Adeline said would happen." Tia nodded. "She said the women she poisoned usually worked house-keeping, but that sometimes they shuffle the staff when temps come in. So they might put us anywhere."

Mira nodded, dodging around a pack of men so sooty they could be nothing but chimney sweeps. "And then what's our plan? Should we try to find a way back to each other? Or try to look around separately?"

"A lot will depend on where they put us," said Tia. She'd been thinking about this most of the night, unable to sleep. If at least one of them got assigned to cleaning, they should be fine. But if they were given roles without much access to the house... "It'll be fine," Tia said, as much to herself as to Mira.

"Of course it will," Mira said, trying to hide her nerves. "We'll play it by ear then. And I suppose if we need to get out of there, either because we've found the evidence or, for another reason, we could rendezvous somewhere?"

"I think head for the tavern," said Tia. "If there's a chance to find the other person, or signal with your ravens, great, but if not, just head for the tavern."

Mira nodded and Tia didn't add that the tavern was best because if something went wrong and one of them was caught, the other person could reunite with the group to help figure out what to do.

They walked the rest of the way in silence, each lost in their own thoughts. Finally, they reached the estate and Tia hesitated, her hand on the wrought-iron gates.

"How do I look?" Tia asked, turning to face Mira.

Mira's brows knitted as she looked Tia over. "Same as when you took it. It'll work, but…"

Tia nodded, pulling the ridiculous bonnet to try and cover as much of herself as she could, before similarly adjusting Mira's for her. Mira would be fine, but the potion hadn't been as effective on Tia as everyone had wanted. They were never going to be able to do anything about her height, but she'd hoped the potion would make her paler than it had. At least she could try and keep her ears hidden.

Oh well, now or never.

"Are you ready?" Tia asked. *Are you okay?*

Mira nodded. "We'll be fine," she said, more confidence in her voice this time. "Worst thing that could happen is we find nothing."

Tia shot Mira a smile. She knew how nervous Mira was, and that she was able to pull herself together like this and focus on the mission was impressive.

"True. Either way, let's try to be out of here at least thirty minutes before we have to meet back with everyone."

Mira nodded, and they pushed through the gates and walked to the house. Tia arched her neck back, looking up at what was more a mansion than a house.

"I'm glad we don't really have to clean this place," she muttered.

"No kidding. Maybe we did those ladies a favour."

With a final grin at Mira, Tia pushed open the door and led the way inside.

"About time you pair showed up," a rough voice called the minute Tia's foot hit the floor. "Come on then, no time to dawdle."

Tia and Mira shared a look as they followed the woman, who could only be the head of housekeeping, across the entrance hall. The woman was imposing, taller than both of them, and twice as wide. But she wasn't plump. Tia wouldn't have been surprised if the woman said she spent her time away from work engaging in some of the illegal pit fighting some of the less reputable taverns ran.

"Okay, let's see what they sent me this time," the woman said to herself, turning on Tia and Mira and running an appraising eye over both of them. If her expression was anything to go by, she was not impressed.

"What am I supposed to do..." she trailed off, shaking her head. "Either of you ever worked in a place like this before?"

Tia and Mira glanced at each other, a silent agreement to try honesty passing between them before they shook their heads.

"Always sending me the new ones. Have to have a word I will, but nothing to be done about it now." The woman's eyes snapped back to Tia, narrowing suspiciously. "You've something of a Shifter about you, you do. All tall and skinny." The woman looked like she might spit in disgust, but not having been asked anything, Tia opted for silence.

"You one of these half-breeds I've been hearing about? Taking all the food from the good people of the Empire? Well I won't have you in the house."

Tia saw red. She completely forgot about the mission and opened her mouth to respond, but luckily Mira kept her head and got in first. "She's not a half-breed. Rumour is she's some noble's bastard."

The head of housekeeping reevaluated Tia, her eyes narrowing and raking over her again. "Could be the Earl Windcoat," she said eventually. "He's skinny as a beanpole and randy as a rabbit."

Tia felt her rage subside as the large woman huffed, satisfied she'd solved the mystery of Tia's heritage. The woman looked about to dismiss them before her eyes landed properly on Mira and narrowed again.

"You look weird too," she said suspiciously.

"I'm an orphan from the slums," Mira said immediately. The story worked just as Kas had told them it would. The woman's expression changed as if smelling a pile of trash and she was suddenly keen to be rid of them.

"Fine, you"—she pointed at Mira—"down to the kitchens. Raelene will tell you what's what. And you"—she pointed at Tia—"out to the stables. Boys need a hand cleaning it up. Lord Flighty saw it last night and pitched a fit. It's the boys' job, but they won't do it right. You make sure they do."

And with no further explanation, the large lady stormed off. Tia and Mira looked at each other. This was going to be harder than Tia had suspected.

"I don't know that they'll let me out," Mira worried. "I can't imagine I'll be allowed to do anything but peel and maybe chop vegetables."

"That's okay," said Tia, her mind running too. "Kitchens are full of gossip. You might learn where the evidence is without having to go anywhere. I might have more freedom. If I can get things going, I might be able to excuse myself to try to find Brunhilda," she said, nodding after the large lady, "and have a poke around upstairs."

Mira giggled at Tia's nickname for the head of housekeeping, and nodded. "Don't try anything rash, though."

"You either. I'll come find you when it's time to go. I suspect I'll be able to get away, but you might need some help."

Mira nodded and with a whispered, "Good luck," to each other, they separated and went about trying to find where the kitchen and stables were respectively.

Tia felt she had the advantage. All she had to do was to head back outside and circle the building until she found the stables. But instead of heading back through the front door, she moved forward, deciding to have a look around while she could.

The house had more rooms than seemed necessary, even for a rich person. And while Tia could identify the dining room from the long table and the sitting room from the cigar smoke, she had no idea what the purpose of half the others was. But none of them seemed to be an office, and she didn't have the time to move the large oil paintings to check for hidden safes.

Opening a door, Tia found herself looking at a smaller version of the sitting room. Perhaps this was for more intimate gatherings? Or a place to take the more exclusive members of your dinner party?

Glancing behind her, she pushed through the door and wandered around. There were a couple of tables with drawers. Not desks, but still. If Flighty spent time in here with select visitors, it was possible he'd left something in here.

"What are you doing?"

Tia jumped halfway to the nearest table and whirled around, finding a severe-looking man in the doorway. He looked to be slightly older than Tia and the entitled air, coupled with the similarity to the subject of most of the paintings, had her certain this must be Lord Flighty's son.

"Forgive me, my lord," Tia said with a bow. "I'm new. I was looking for the stables."

"Well, you won't find them in here." There was curiosity in his tone, but it softened and a smile flickered at the corner of his mouth as he looked at Tia more closely.

"No, my lord. I thought maybe one of the doors led outside, and when this one didn't, I thought to look out the window to get my bearings. I've not been in a house this big before." Tia had fallen into a cringeworthy parody of the accent she'd heard some of the Empire folk from the mines using. She'd done it without thinking and now held her breath, hoping that he didn't pick up on it, or ask more questions that forced her to keep using it.

But the man simply smiled and jerked his head. "The house is a little over the top. Come on, I'll show you the way."

Tia bowed again, forcing her features into a grateful expression, but inside she was cursing. She was supposed to be forgettable. Now, if something went wrong, Flighty's son would definitely remember her.

"I'm Bryon, by the way." He smiled at her.

"I'm honoured to meet you, my lord," said Tia.

"And what's your name?" he asked, his voice amused.

"Ah." Tia's eyes flew around the hallway, looking for inspiration. They landed on the red curtains. "Scarlett, my lord."

"I'm pleased to meet you, Scarlett. And I hope we run into each other again."

Tia simply smiled at him as he opened a door and pointed to the stable. She didn't correct his assumption that she was a new permanent member of staff. Nor did she appreciate the way he held the door, forcing her to squeeze past him, their bodies touching.

She hurried away, only relaxing slightly when she heard the door shut. The stables were larger than most of the houses she'd seen in other areas of the city. It was a double storey building, and she vaguely wondered why. Not like the horses wanted a view. She entered through an open walkway and followed the voices she could hear until she found two young men sitting in one of the stalls.

Both looked at her in alarm at being found taking a break, but then relaxed, perhaps seeing she wasn't the head of housekeeping.

"I've been sent to help you clean," Tia said, looking pointedly around at the lack of cleaning taking place.

"Ah, not to worry," said one of the men, who looked at least five years younger than Tia. The other didn't look old enough to be working at all. "We've got a system. You're welcome to stay here, or you can head back and tell her we've got it under control."

Tia glanced back at the house. She could leave now and have a look around, but it seemed busy inside the house. And if Bryon Flighty was still wandering around, no doubt Brunhilda was patrolling too, lest the young master see cracks in the ship. Maybe she should wait here for a bit before heading back in.

"I might stay here for a bit," she said, the men giving her knowing smiles. "But I'm happy to work. Is there anything I can do?"

"You see," the older one explained, "our system relies on the fact that Lord Flighty only ever comes out here about four times a year. He yells and then forgets about it. We cleaned it once, but by the time he came back, it was dirty again. So now he yells, and then we keep our heads down so everyone assumes we're cleaning, and then everything goes back to normal."

Tia smiled at him. She could get behind a system like that. "How about I sweep out the entry? That way, if anyone pokes their head inside, it looks like you've done something, and if the lady in charge looks this way to see if I'm doing my job, she'll see the dust billowing."

The men looked at her with appreciation. "That'll work," the older one said, smiling. "Shame you're a temp. We could use more people like you around here. I'm Clay, that's Ewan."

Ewan waved at her, and Tia waved back, grabbing a broom before hesitating. "How do you know I'm a temp?"

Clay jerked his head towards the house. "She never sends the household staff out here unless they're temps and she doesn't think she has time to teach them. She doesn't trust the other maids not to gossip about her, and she doesn't care what we have to say."

"Fair enough," Tia smiled at him and she headed away and began sweeping.

Tia settled into the rhythm of her work. Focussing on the mission had allowed Tia to distract her mind from straying back to Valto and his claims about her mother. But now, the monotony of sweeping had her turning everything over in her mind. Analysing Valto's body language, his tone, Aurora's tone when Tia had asked her about the truth of Valto's implications.

She was busily reading in to the length of the pause Aurora had taken before responding to Tia's question when laughter broke out from the stall where Clay and Ewan were hiding, and with an effort, she brought her mind back to the task at hand.

Clay and Ewan seemed friendly enough, but she could tell they were savvy, and if she was going to get anything out of them, she had to time it right.

This way, Tia could hopefully fade into the background enough for the men to continue their conversation. And if not, then at least she'd look like she'd been cleaning when she headed back to search the house.

Her clothes pulled at her as she swept. Adeline had managed to get maid outfits for her and Mira, but they didn't fit well, and so had been pinned to help them look less suspicious. But the sleeves were longer than she was used to, and the stupid cloth hat thing kept flopping over. As she swept, one of the pins began scraping her softly. She knew they were on a timeframe anyway, but she couldn't finish this mission fast enough.

Finally, the men's voices returned to a steady stream of general chatter and complaints about work. She eased herself closer, inch by inch, aiming for a spot where she could hear them. She wasn't in a rush, confident they wouldn't be talking about anything useful for a while.

As expected, when she could finally make out the comments, there was nothing interesting to hear. They didn't like the head of housekeeping, there was a new contender in the pit fighting, they didn't like the head of housekeeping, the recent rain would mean they'd have to clean the carriage tonight, they really didn't like the head of housekeeping.

They droned on so much that Tia had almost tuned them out when finally she heard something that snapped her senses in check.

"Did you hear about the convoy that got hit?" Clay asked. Tia assumed Ewan shook his head, because Clay kept going, "Food and mail for the soldiers at the labour camps. Can you imagine? How angry would you be, stuck at one of those places, and then not only does your letter from home get pinched, but you're stuck with crappy food?"

"What would they want letters for?" Ewan asked.

"They don't want them," Clay said dismissively. "It's not about *what* they're hitting."

"What do you mean?" Ewan asked.

Clay lowered his voice, and Tia struggled to hear. "I heard the boss talking. He's apparently got hold of their strings now. He's telling the rebels to cause as much chaos as possible. Show everyone the empress has lost control of the city."

Clay sounded impressed, but Tia could hear the slight tinge of disapproval in Ewan's voice. "Sounds like he's just wasting the food. My mom could hardly afford bread last week. Baker said he had to put the prices up because he couldn't make it fast enough for the demand. All the rebels are doing is making it harder for the rest of us."

"Ah, you're not seeing the bigger picture," Clay said. "The rebels have been trying to oust the empress for years with no luck. But the boss, he sees the bigger picture. I'll bet he has her out before the year's end."

"No way," said Ewan.

"Mark my words," said Clay. "He's got a plan. And he's putting it into action."

"Like you'd know," Ewan said. Tia could tell he'd had enough of listening to Clay about this.

"Of course I would. Who takes him to his office? The one no one else knows about. I wait out front and he goes in with his papers and comes out with empty hands. Trust me, he's got a plan, and he's running it from there."

"It's probably just his business records," said Ewan.

"He has plenty of places to keep those records—"

The boys' discussion moved onto internal estate staff politics and Tia tuned them out. A secret office? Clearly not so secret if his driver knew. And was telling everyone. But still, a place that wasn't well known where he stored all sorts of paperwork sounded just like what they were looking for. Shame Clay hadn't mentioned where it was.

Tia was trying to decide if it was worth joining in the conversation when a raven landed before her and pecked the ground three times.

The signal!

Mira needed her.

CHAPTER FORTY-TWO

MIRA

"No, not like that!" The cook sighed heavily and said in a loud parody of muttering under her breath, "Stupid girl."

Mira bit back the response she wanted to give. She'd been biting back responses most of the day. The cook and her offsider were clearly annoyed to be lumped with an untrained temp. Mira was sure she'd been able to follow their directions on some of her tasks. But when she'd displayed the onions she'd diced exactly as shown—she'd even kept the example batch to check her work against—the cook's assistant had said they weren't diced enough and when she gave them to the cook, having pretended to return to her bench to remedy them, they were apparently *too* diced.

After that, Mira had given up caring about the quality of her work, and instead focussed on staying out of their way in the hopes they would stop yelling at her, or ideally start talking about where the lord of the manor kept his incriminating documents.

She did manage a blissful hour of peace, but then, as if

remembering she was there and deciding to make up for lost time, the cook and her assistant had descended on Mira, deciding that the best training would be for Mira to do all the preparation for dinner while they observed and corrected.

Mira had managed to plead for a trip to the bathroom, during which she had promptly sent a nearby raven to signal Tia for help.

"Don't hold the knife like that!" the assistant cried, pulling it from Mira's fingers.

That was it. Mira wheeled on the assistant, but the door banged open, startling all three women in the kitchen.

"Sorry," Tia said as Mira slumped in relief.

"It's 'pardon'," the chef corrected Tia.

"Pardon for using the wrong word," said Tia. Mira stifled a snort, and the cook opened her mouth to correct Tia again, but Tia kept going before the cook could speak. "Only the head housekeeping lady—"

"Helga," said the cook.

Tia performed a double take. "Is that really her name?" Mira coughed and Tia refocussed. "Right, yes, so Helga—"

"That's Mrs Flack to you."

Tia was almost distracted again, but with a valiant effort, kept herself on track.

"Pardon, Mrs Flack wants to see me and... uh, her." Tia's eyes went wide and Mira silently cursed herself for not thinking of fake names before they entered. But hopefully it wasn't unusual for temps to not know each other.

Luckily, whether or not they should have known each other, the cook seemed to decide that Tia was rude and ill-mannered and she didn't really want to keep the incompetent temp. She simply waved them both away, turning with her assistant, both women loudly complaining about now having to start from scratch to prepare dinner.

"Thank you," Mira breathed as they shut the door behind them and hurried quietly towards the front of the house.

"No worries," said Tia. "Looks like you got the short end of the stick."

"True. Between shovelling manure and dealing with them..."

"I'd pick the manure," Tia finished, nodding. "But I didn't even have to do that."

"What? How'd you get out of it?"

"Where are you two going?" Helga Flack's voice boomed down from the first-floor landing.

Mira looked up to see the large lady glaring down at them.

"Cook's sent me to fetch some provisions for dinner," said Mira. Flack's eyes moved to Tia. "I ruined most of the produce," said Mira, allowing her face to turn crimson. "And we can't send the carriage..."

Flack's eyes grew wide at the magnitude of Mira's alleged kitchen error. "Don't think it won't come out of your pay, girl," she said, turning away. As she strode away, she called, "And don't be long!"

Mira grabbed Tia's hand, and they jogged for the door and kept running down the driveway, not stopping until they shut the gate behind them.

"I'm really mad about my pay," said Mira, and Tia started laughing.

"I really think those girls we poisoned got the better end of the deal," said Tia.

"No kidding! I'll put money on them calling in sick tomorrow as well. Make the most of it."

"I would," said Tia. "Did you find anything out? The stable hands mentioned a secret office that Flighty has, but not where it was."

"Oh, I might know." Mira's face lit up. "The cook was bemoaning that one of the other girls wasn't here that she wanted to step in instead of me. I think the girl had worked in the kitchens before."

"When the poor woman who always works there was pulling another sickie so she didn't have to hate her life?"

"Probably. Anyway, the assistant said the maid was 'at Bletchley' and then they started talking about 'the scanner' and how the maids hate cleaning at Bletchley because Flighty yells at them whenever they have to dust the scanner. Any idea what it means?" Mira asked. "'Cause I don't."

Tia frowned, thinking. "I think we passed a Bletchley Road on the way into the city, but we can ask Kas or Adeline. They'll know. No idea what a scanner is. Something that scans?"

"Thanks, Professor," Mira said, bumping Tia playfully. Now that she was out of that kitchen, the sun seemed brighter, the colours more intense, and the weight of the pressure she'd felt was gone. It shouldn't be, she realised. They still had only a couple of hours to find the evidence the empress needed, and only a couple more to retrieve it.

She looked over at Tia and found her smiling too. "I'm not sure we're cut out for actual jobs," Mira mused. "Look at us after a couple of hours. I don't know that we were this happy even after we got out of the camps."

Tia laughed. "I know, right? Maybe we're just not cut out to work for assholes."

"Tell you what," said Mira. "I already thought Adeline was nice, but I have a whole new level of respect for her."

"No kidding," said Tia, thinking about it too. "She's been doing that for, what, ten years? More?"

"Probably more. They seem to start work young here."

"*Some* people start work young here," Tia corrected.

Mira nodded. They'd both had a long and passionate

discussion about the class system in Lorendell. Both of their tribes had a hierarchical leadership structure, but neither had the distinct divides between the haves and have nots that existed here.

"Either way," said Mira, not wanting to deviate back into a discussion that she knew would engulf them for hours they didn't have, "huge respect for Adeline."

"Completely agree. After you," Tia held the door to the Drunkin' Pumpkin for Mira with a mock bow.

"Why thank you." Mira inclined her head as she entered.

The two women headed for the table in the corner at the back, where the group had gathered the day before. They'd barely sat and were considering ordering something to eat and drink when the door opened again and Adeline and Ossi started towards them.

"Bet they did surveillance together," Tia whispered.

Mira looked up at the pair. They walked closely together, firmly in each other's personal space. As they walked, their fingers brushed against each other's, and both hands twitched as if wanting to reach for the other.

"Are we even sure they surveilled anything?"

Tia snorted. "Maybe a bedroom somewhere."

"How would that even work?" Mira wondered. "He's enormous."

Tia ducked her head, snorting with laughter. Mira slapped at her to control herself as the couple approached the table.

"Hello," Adeline greeted the women happily, Ossi pulling a chair out for her.

"Hello you two." Tia grinned. "Been having a good time 'surveilling', have we?" asked Tia, sketching air quotes.

Neither looked the least bit embarrassed as they smiled at each other. Mira was so happy for them she felt a little sick. She tried not to wonder if anyone would look at her like that.

"Ossi wanted to stay with me," Adeline said.

"For safety," Ossi added, nodding seriously at Tia and Mira, his eyes sparkling.

"Uh huh," said Tia.

"Did you learn anything?" Mira asked as the door opened again, but strangers entered, not Kas.

Both shook their heads. "Nothing," said Adeline, her brow creasing. "I don't think he's using any of them for his... shadier dealings. But it's just a feeling. I guess we won't know for sure unless Kas managed to follow Flighty inside any of them." Adeline's eyes swung to the door as she mentioned Kas, and they all automatically copied her.

"We didn't see him," said Ossi, returning his gaze to the table. "Kas, I mean. Or Lord Flighty. I don't suppose he turned up at the house?"

Mira shook her head. "Flighty was gone before we arrived, so if Kas was following him, he would have left too."

"He didn't stay in our room," said Adeline, with only the slightest blush at admitting she and Ossi had slept in the same room.

"Nor ours," said Tia.

"Did you discover anything at the estate?" Ossi asked, turning their thoughts from concern about where Kas was.

"Yeah, that it's a terrible place to work," said Tia. "I hope your workplaces weren't like that," she added to Adeline.

"I had some special ones," Adeline admitted. "But from what I hear, Flighty's is the worst. They have trouble keeping people."

"I don't doubt it," Tia said. "But I did find out that Flighty has a secret office. They said it's on Bletchley. That's a road, isn't it?"

Adeline nodded. "Bletchley is at the back of the Merchants' Quarter. Though I thought it was mostly storage."

"Good for privacy then," said Ossi.

"And the cooks mentioned there was a scanner there," said Mira. "Do either of you know—"

"A scanner?" Adeline interrupted, already on her feet, eyes wide. "We need to go."

They hurried after her, all piling out of the tavern and following Adeline as she led the way to Bletchley Road.

"What is it?" asked Mira, moving up beside Adeline.

"A scanner is an enchanted object kind of like the Testing Orb," she replied. "They're very rare and *very* expensive. You put it above a doorway and it will glow as someone enters, telling you about their magic and its strength."

"But it might not register Kas's invisibility, right?" asked Tia, understanding Adeline's panic.

"No, but it would at least alert for his elemental magic," said Adeline. "Which would tell Flighty someone was there. And if he couldn't see anyone..."

"I'll send some ravens," Mira said, gesturing to the skies and surrounding building roofs. "They should be able to see if Flighty's carriage is there. I'll send some others," she said, gesturing again and a number of birds flew off in all directions, "to scout for Flighty's carriage through the city. See if we can find him."

Mira kicked herself for not sending some earlier to keep an eye on Kas and Flighty.

"Thank you," said Adeline. "Hopefully they're on the other side of the city, and so Kas is safe and we can try to break into his office."

The group hurried on, all looking expectantly at Mira

any time a bird made a sound. She kept shaking her head, wondering if she should ask the birds to be quiet for a bit.

But then a mournful cry came, and Mira looked up as the others looked to her.

"They've found Flighty. His carriage just pulled up at the office on Bletchley. We're not going to make it in time."

CHAPTER FORTY-THREE

KAS

KAS TROTTED along behind the carriage. He could easily have turned invisible and hopped up on the back since there was only the driver, no footmen, but his magic was still unreliable and the last thing he needed was to be seen riding on the back of Lord Flighty's carriage.

Besides, the physical activity kept him awake. Despite what was riding on their mission, Kas was deeply bored.

He'd followed Lord Flighty all yesterday evening, and this morning, and it had been hour upon hour of people kissing his ass. No wonder the man was so bloody arrogant. Kas didn't miss the narrowing of eyes and looks of disgust—possibly with themselves—that appeared on faces after the man left, but Kas had discovered that Flighty was the kind of man who would enjoy that just as much as people loving him.

He was all about power and control. So far, Kas had found nothing redeeming about the man. He'd also found nothing to indicate where he might be storing anything incriminating about himself. Flighty had met with a man Kas had seen in the rebel warehouse, but all Flighty did was hand him a sealed note, and then the carriage drove away.

Kas considered going after the note, but it was more important to remain with Flighty for now.

In fact, the only interesting thing Kas had learned so far was that he was not the only one following Lord Flighty. Everywhere they had gone, both the night before and this morning, a strange cloaked man with his hood down had been as well. His presence was odd, and Kas could tell neither Lord Flighty nor his staff realised the man was following them. But so far, the man had done nothing, and so Kas had left him alone.

As they pulled deeper into the Merchants' Quarter, Kas perked up a little. There was nothing down here that related to the businesses within the city that they knew Lord Flighty owned or was affiliated with. Maybe Kas would finally discover something useful.

He'd better find something useful. Kas glanced at the sky. He probably had an hour or less before he needed to head back to the tavern. The carriage slowed and so did Kas, moving over into an alley that led between two buildings and seemed to be currently used for storage. He hid behind some wooden crates and watched as Flighty got out of the carriage.

"Be back here before lunch," Lord Flighty snapped at the driver. He turned and strode towards the door on a building that looked unoccupied. The driver didn't need to be told twice, and he jerked the reins, heading off no doubt to wait nearby.

Kas hurried over as the door closed behind Lord Flighty. If he didn't want his carriage parked outside, this might very well be the location they'd been looking for. A secretive building that he didn't want associated with him. What would Kas find inside?

Kas did a quick circuit around the building, checking for other entrances and, having decided that the only real potential, other than the front door, was an upstairs window, accessible via a rickety-looking set of ladders and walkways, he headed back towards the front.

Slipping into an alley and pulling the light, Kas then poked his head out, checking if the coast was clear before he headed to the front door. In this part of town, no one was particularly looking at anyone else. They were all too busy or too tired and simply focussed on their own work with the aim of getting it done and getting paid. Even the cloaked man seemed bored. He made no move to go inside and was instead wandering down the street, looking in at the warehouses and lumber yards.

Confident no one was looking his way, Kas pulled open the door and walked inside. It was a mess. There was dust everywhere, and cobwebs coated the ceiling. The floorboards and walls looked rotten, as if they might break at the slightest touch. There were rooms to his left and right, but they were similarly run-down and contained musty wooden boxes and furniture covered in sheets. There was a rustling, and Kas didn't want to think about what might be living in there.

Mouldy carpet ran up the stairs in front of Kas. From what he could see of the pattern, it had been hideous and time hadn't made it any better. He squinted. It was hard to tell because of the pattern, but the dust didn't seem as thick in the middle.

Kas had been starting to doubt his eyes. Surely someone as rich and powerful as Lord Flighty wouldn't stand to be in such a dump. He'd have thought that if Flighty had bought the run-down building, he'd have had people working on it night and day before he dared to step foot inside. And yet, he saw the man walk inside with his own eyes.

Kas tentatively tested the first step. Unlike the rest of the building, it felt solid. He continued to the top of the stairs and found a hallway stretching the length of the building, heading off left and right. The runner from the stairs also carpeted the hallway, and though the doors were closed, they looked and smelled like downstairs had. All but one.

The door at the end of the hall to Kas's right was well made and new. He crept towards it, not wanting Lord Flighty to suspect anyone else was here. The last thing Kas needed was Lord Flighty looking up at the door as he tried to squeeze through. Opening it would be enough of a gamble.

Pressing his ear to the thick wood, Kas held his breath, listening for any sign of what Lord Flighty might be doing in there. He could hear papers rustling and the scratching of a pen, but without knowing the layout of the room, there was no way to know if he was facing the door or not.

The shadows were shortening, and Kas took a deep breath. There was no time to do this properly. No time to wait for Flighty to leave or to go and get his friends. Kas was so focussed on his task he'd completely forgotten about Mira's ravens and didn't even think about sending one for help.

He pushed the door open a crack. There was no squeal of hinges, or intake of breath from a startled lord, and so Kas pushed it a little more.

The room was huge. It had clearly been expanded into the room next door and was outfitted with bookshelves, paintings, a lounge setting, and row upon row of cabinets made for document storage. And right in front of the door Kas had pushed open was a huge desk made of oak or walnut, or some other expensive wood that Kas had probably never touched in his life.

And sat behind the desk, looking right above Kas's head, was Lord Flighty.

The man was frowning, his eyes now scanning the doorway, moving through and over Kas, unable to see him, but somehow searching as if he knew Kas was there. Kas froze, and eventually Lord Flighty returned his gaze to his papers.

Breathing a little easier, Kas slipped through the door and crept into the room. He started for the desk. Risky, but he also felt anything to do with the rebels would be a recent matter. It'd either be on his desk or in easy reach, rather than filed away in one of the cabinets. Plus, Kas felt his time slipping away. Perhaps it was wishful thinking that he might spy a document titled 'How I'm Helping the Rebels and Why' and be able to grab it and run.

A board creaked and Lord Flighty's head whipped up, his eyes bearing straight through Kas.

"I know you're here," Lord Flighty said loudly. "Better for you if you reveal yourself now."

Kas panicked. How could he know? An unlatched door and a creaky floor couldn't have the man so confident of an intruder. Especially one he couldn't see.

Lord Flighty rose and walked around his desk, passing within inches of Kas as he strode to the door, closing it and whirling on the room, his eyes scanning again.

Kas moved as silently as he could over towards the window. His steps were painfully slow, his heart beating so loudly he was sure Lord Flighty would hear it. Sweat beaded on his brow and a slice of panic took him, thinking were it to fall, it would give him away.

Doubt started to creep across Lord Flighty's face, but the man took a couple of steps back towards his desk, stopping where Kas had been when the floorboard gave him away. Lord Flighty's arms reached into the air, grabbing for Kas, who was thankfully out of arm's reach.

"Reveal yourself," Lord Flighty commanded. "Do so

now, and I may be amenable to working out a way for you to make up for breaking into my office."

Kas could imagine the uses Lord Flighty might put an invisible servant to. He had no intention of doing any of it. He was so close to the window now, all he wanted to do was dive through. Thankfully it was open, Lord Flighty perhaps seeking to air out the stench of the building. As if seeing it at the same time, Lord Flighty's steps sounded, crossing to the window, right along the path Kas had taken.

Clicking sounded on the other side of the room. It sounded to Kas like a pebble bouncing on the floorboards. Thankfully, Lord Flighty thought it worth investigating and hurried over, again moving around with his arms out, like a blindfolded child trying to find his friends in a game.

Kas allowed himself a breath and took another step towards the window.

"Ah, there you are," Lord Flighty's voice sounded.

Kas looked down at his body and then at Lord Flighty, who was now staring right at him.

CHAPTER FORTY-FOUR

EMILIA

Emilia hid among the shelves, willing Kas to make it to the window. But then he turned visible.

Why did he do that?

From the look on Kas's face, it hadn't been intentional. Emilia carefully and slowly slipped between another set of shelves, positioning herself between Lord Flighty and Kas. She told herself it was to ensure she was out of the way and to better observe the interaction. Certainly not to get involved. Imperiuses did not get involved unless it furthered the cause.

She saw Lord Flighty's eyes narrow as he took Kas in. The excitement she'd seen when he'd realised someone was in his office, but invisible, faded. He no longer saw an opportunity. Just street scum. Someone beneath him.

Emilia hadn't thought she could like the man less, but she detested him for his judgment of Kas. His failure to see his value now that he presumed his background. So like her own betters, who dismissed her abilities for her gender.

"Why are you here, boy?" Lord Flighty sneered. "Who sent you?"

She saw the panic in Kas's eyes mix with anger at being

called boy. And for the assumption that he couldn't possibly be acting on his own.

"I'm here to see what you're doing with my brother," Kas said firmly. Emilia nodded to herself, impressed with his cover story, and that he was so quick with it. The best cover stories had a ring of truth, and she knew much of Kas's motivation to help the empress was to help his brother. To save him from the fate he was barrelling towards.

She'd heard much about the young leader of the rebels. If she'd not heard it from multiple sources, she'd have trouble believing that the two were related. Kas seemed so kind, so ready to help others. And this Salomon seemed mean and self-serving.

She had no siblings herself, but she wondered what her life might have been like if she'd had an older sibling like Kas. Someone to keep an eye out for her. To care about her. She imagined she might not have such a hard edge. So much cynicism. Yet Salomon seemed to have almost gone the other way.

And still, Kas risked everything for him.

"And just how did you find this office, boy?" Lord Flighty sneered. Emilia felt the man relax, apparently deciding now that Kas was no threat. She wondered if he had a trinket similar to the scanner above the door to tell if someone was lying, or if his own assumptions meant he was convinced that a street rat couldn't possibly pull the wool over his eyes.

"I followed you," said Kas simply.

Lord Flighty's eyes brightened again, and he looked Kas up and down. "Ah yes, your special talent that let you get in here. Tell me about it."

"I've always been stealthy—"

"You were invisible, not stealthy." Lord Flighty took a menacing step towards Kas. "I wish to know how."

Kas's lips pulled thin, his eyes darting as he tried to think of a way not to tell Lord Flighty about his invisibility. But Emilia already knew there was no way out of that. Any explanation that might work in its stead would be equally valuable to someone like the lord, and it took all her self-control not to whisper to Kas to just tell the man.

"I've always been able to," Kas shrugged. "If I think I don't want to be seen, then I can't be."

Emilia found herself looking at Kas with a similar expression to Lord Flighty, though where hers was a desire to know more, his was a desire to obtain and control.

"Fascinating." Lord Flighty took another step towards Kas, now stroking his greying goatee as his mind whirled. "Well, your knowledge of this location puts me in somewhat of a bind, young man. Only a select few know about it, and they all work for me, allowing me to ensure their silence."

Kas's feet twitched, and Emilia could feel his need to step back as Lord Flighty continued to approach. But to his credit, he held his ground.

"So it seems you have a choice." Lord Flighty came to a stop a couple of steps from Kas, looking down his nose haughtily at the younger man. "Work for me, or I will have to see that you are... disposed of."

Kas's eyes narrowed. "And what would you have me do? If I worked for you."

One corner of Lord Flighty's lips twitched up. He thought he'd won. "Oh, a bit of this and a bit of that. I'm sure I could find a use for someone with your talents."

"Such as?" Kas pushed, not buying for a second that Lord Flighty didn't have something specific in mind.

"Well, let's see. At present I find myself troubled by some of what the empress seems set upon doing. Now, if I had someone who could sneak into the palace, into her private office, her private rooms, I might better learn what she hopes to achieve with these... misguided obsessions. Then I could more easily dissuade her from making emotional decisions that are really not in the best interests of the Empire."

"Not in your best interests, you mean," said Kas as Emilia thought the exact same thing. She was fuming at the empress being called emotional. She took a couple of deep breaths. It was just that she herself had endured men claiming that of her, Emilia told herself. She was not angry on behalf of the leader of the Divvinium's enemy.

Lord Flighty leered at Kas. "My interests do align with those of the Empire," he allowed.

"I will never work for you," Kas said, low and firm.

Lord Flighty frowned in disapproval. "Pity," he said, pulling a dangerously long blade from within his cloak. "Such a waste of an extraordinary gift."

Emilia willed Kas to move, to leap out the window. There was no way Lord Flighty would be able to chase him, and Emilia would put money on the fact that he wouldn't want to call for help out his window. Not when the secrecy of his office was so important to him.

But Kas didn't move. Not his legs, anyway. His hips jerked, trying to walk, then his arms flailed, trying to keep balance when his legs remained rooted to the floor.

"Air magic," Lord Flighty said, taking another lazy step towards Kas. "People assume it's all about blowing things over. But those of us with talent know how to make the air thick, heavy, impenetrable."

Panic took over Kas, and Emilia watched as he swiped at Lord Flighty before his arms were pinned to his sides.

"Now." Lord Flighty took another predatory step towards Kas. "I'm not going to lie. This is going to hurt. A lot."

CHAPTER FORTY-FIVE

KAS

Kas's heart banged in his chest, as if trying to escape the body that had been rendered useless. He reached for his fire, but his ability to conjure flame had abandoned him with the light. Why hadn't he dove out the window the minute he realised Flighty had seen him? Why had he waited, stupidly, allowing the older man to gain control of the situation?

There was a glint in Lord Flighty's eyes. Something that told Kas he was enjoying this. Would enjoy using his knife a little too much.

Kas wanted to close his eyes, but even that was beyond him. So stupid. And now, not only was he about to die, but he'd ruined everything. The empress would never get her evidence. She'd go after Salomon. His brother would likely follow him to the afterlife pretty soon.

Lord Flighty raised the knife, preparing to strike. Not at Kas's throat. Not a killing blow. But across his face. A slash that would hurt and disfigure, but leave him alive. Kas didn't know if this was Flighty's way of encouraging Kas to change his mind and work for him, or whether he just enjoyed causing pain. Maybe both.

He tensed, waiting for the cut. A cloaked figure appeared out of nowhere, lunging for Flighty and knocking him to the ground. Kas's first thought was that it was the strange man who'd also been following Flighty, but this figure looked too small.

The wind that had been pinning Kas evaporated instantly and Kas stumbled, barely keeping from collapsing to the floor beside the incapacitated noble. Lord Flighty was not moving, his eyes closed.

The figure grabbed Flighty's knife, stowing it somewhere in the folds of their own cloak.

"He's out," the figure said, and Kas's eyes widened. The figure was female. "Quickly, grab what you came for and get out of here."

Kas blinked and looked around. The door was still shut. The window was open, but surely he'd have seen someone climbing in. How had she gotten in? And where had she been hiding?

"How did you—"

"Hurry!"

Kas forced himself into action. She was right, this mysterious girl who had saved him. There was no time to chat. Who knew how long Flighty would be out for? He needed to make the most of this gift. And while she was here to help, Kas didn't need to immediately flee. He might still find the evidence.

He lunged for the desk, rifling through the documents, cursing again his rudimentary reading skills. Most of the papers he couldn't understand—tables and charts with numbers and symbols. He snatched up bundles, discarding anything that wasn't writing. Those he stared at, trying to identify simple words. Kas was fairly sure he'd recognise 'rebel'. Hopefully, they hadn't tried to be discreet or use a code.

"Here," the woman grabbed a bundle of papers from Kas and began looking too, positioning herself so she could also see Flighty, who was still on the floor and hadn't moved. "What are you looking for?"

Kas hesitated for a second before he decided the secrecy of the mission was trumped by needing to locate the evidence swiftly. Besides, the girl had been hiding here somewhere. She probably heard everything he'd said.

"I need something linking Flighty to the rebels," he said. "Proving that he's working with them, or directing them."

The cloak bobbed as she nodded and they fell into silence as they flicked through the pages. She was much faster and Kas felt his cheeks heat, hoping she didn't notice. She finished her pile and grabbed the one he'd discarded. Kas pretended not to notice, but was grateful she was double-checking. He finished the rest of his and moved to a nearby cabinet and began flicking through files.

"Here's something," the woman called eventually. "It's a letter to a Salomon, and it's asking him to prioritise attacks on the palace's convoys, as well as cause as much chaos in the city as possible."

"It really says that?" Kas asked, his embarrassment at not recognising the document subsumed by his surprise at finding something so obviously incriminating.

"Yep." She handed it to him with a bundle of papers. "Now, get out of here, and I'll take care of him."

"Take care how?" asked Kas, worried now. If she killed him, this would all be for nothing.

"Don't worry, he'll be fine. I'm just going to make sure he's okay and then I'm going to stage things in here, so when he wakes up, he'll think he knocked his head or something."

"He won't remember me?" Kas asked. His brows furrowed. That seemed unlikely.

"I don't think so," said the girl. "With a head injury like

this, often there's an element of memory loss. If I make it look like he hit his head, he's more likely to accept that explanation and think seeing an invisible man was a dream."

Kas hesitated. She knew then. Yet she seemed neither surprised nor interested in it, when everyone else was fascinated by such an unusual magic. Perhaps she'd had time to be amazed when she'd been hiding wherever she'd hid, and was now too focussed on the task at hand. Which was fair, considering she was letting him go and risking Flighty waking up while she was still there. He glanced around, wondering again how he'd missed her, but that wasn't the question he asked.

"What's your name?"

"What does it matter?"

"I'd like to thank the person who saved my life."

The woman hesitated, but when she answered, there was a smile in her tone. "It's Em—Emily."

"Well, thank you, Emily. Thank you so very much for saving my life. If there's anything at all I can do to repay you—"

"You can hop out the window and do whatever it is that you're going to do with that document," she said. "Otherwise all this will have been a waste."

"Yeah, you're right," said Kas, clearing his head with a shake and crossing quickly to the window. "If I can repay you, though—"

"Go!"

Kas pulled the light around him and hopped out the window. He was down the ladders and heading up the street in no time, clutching the evidence firmly. As he glanced around, he could see the other cloaked figure, still milling around aimlessly in the street. Did he not know his partner was up in the office? Or maybe they weren't working together after all, and the similarity in their attire was mere coincidence.

Kas hurried around a corner and let the light go as he began to jog. He'd lost so much time. He needed to find his friends and get back to the palace. Or maybe he should go straight there.

His mind turned back to Lord Flighty, and he suppressed a shiver. The glint in his eye when he'd advanced on Kas with the knife was pure evil. He would have enjoyed hurting and killing Kas. And now he knew about Kas's gift.

Emily had said he needn't worry about that. That Flighty might not remember. But that seemed unlikely. A farfetched thing to hope for. Better to assume Flighty would remember and prepare for that. Prepare for someone to come after him who apparently enjoyed causing pain and who knew Kas could become invisible. Because Flighty would come after him. There was no way he'd be willing to leave Kas alive now.

Kas tried to stuff the documents in the pocket inside his jacket, but they were too bulky. He glanced at them, frustrated again that he couldn't read them easily. Emily had been looking at the top one, so he took the top few pages and tucked them in his pocket, and clutched the remaining pages tightly.

These documents would solve everything. Now he could save his brother and his own life. Because once the empress had them, Lord Flighty would be executed for treason. Just so long as he didn't come to and find Kas before he made it to the palace.

"Hello, brother."

Kas jerked to a stop as Salomon dropped off the wall and landed in front of him.

CHAPTER FORTY-SIX

EMILIA

EMILIA WATCHED AS KAS LEFT, making sure he was far enough away before she even started cleaning things up in Lord Flighty's secret office. There was no need to rush, other than the possibility of Lord Flighty's people coming to look for him. Lord Flighty himself wasn't going to cause her any issues.

She'd grabbed his mind the minute he raised the knife. Dropping her invisibility, she'd gained his attention, and that one look had been enough for her to gain control. As she tackled him to the ground, it had simply been a matter of ordering him to lie there and keep his eyes closed.

Satisfied Kas was safe, she turned back to the room. She'd tidied the documents they'd been going through out of habit, but now she went and grabbed a pile, throwing it in the air so the documents fell as if blown by a gust of wind. She frowned as she thought of what she'd seen in those documents. Of the wealth and power this man had taken by screwing over the poorer people in his Empire.

She frowned again, thinking of how Kas had been peering at the papers. Struggling to make out what was there. All children of the Divvinium were taught to read.

They were taught many other things too, but it seemed here in the Empire, you only got the basics of an education if you could afford it. Maybe she'd been too quick to question the Divvinium's plans to invade. Maybe the Empire wasn't such a good place after all.

"Get up," Emilia ordered Flighty.

His brow furrowed and she could feel the hatred emanating from him, but he complied immediately, even with his eyes still closed.

"Open your eyes."

He did so, and the full force of that hatred hit her. Emilia smiled. Lord Flighty's breathing became more strained as he fought against her control.

Interesting.

Emilia wasn't expecting such a strong will from the man. Had assumed he was little more than a spoilt rich fool who had received everything anyone could ask for, but still wanted more. Felt he deserved more. And she could sense his frustration at the situation, but the ability to fight an Imperius, especially one as strong as she was, was rare.

A shame. Were he not so self-serving, he might have done well for them in the war.

Emilia increased her smile and strengthened her grip on his mind and, with a word, Lord Flighty stilled. His eyes still showed defiance, but his body was calm and relaxed once more. Normally, Emilia infiltrated with more finesse than she had with Lord Flighty. Even when she took full control, they barely registered her. But then, she hadn't had much time, and to be honest, she hadn't cared to be gentle with the man.

On rare occasions, an Imperius could damage a mind when taking control. They were all taught to avoid this, as it usually rendered the proxy incapable of performing what-ever action was desired. Emilia couldn't remember the last time she'd simply reached out with her power and grabbed someone as she had with Lord Flighty. However, it didn't seem to have hurt the man at all. Aside from his pride, since he was aware of her incursion. Though that would not be an issue for long.

"On my order, you will do the following," she said clearly, looking Lord Flighty dead in the eye, not flinching at the seething rage there. "You will not notice that anything is missing from your office. As far as you shall remain aware, the document is here, safely on your desk. You will not remember anyone else being in this office with you. As far as you shall remain aware, you were alone the entire time you were inside. You will not remember that there was a young man who had the power of invisibility. As far as you shall remain aware, there are only the known magics and invisibility is not one of them. You will not remember me. As far as you shall remain aware, you have never seen a Controller," Emilia made sure to use the southern term for her people. "None are in the city."

Emilia thought, looking for loopholes. She didn't need to be perfect, but she did need to influence enough that the lord would go straight from here to the palace for his meeting and not to the guards.

Just for fun, she added, "If anyone ever suggests to you that Controllers are within the city walls, you will become irate and tell them they are both wrong and stupid for thinking so." She didn't know if that would work, but it was worth a shot. Though from the sound of things, he may not be alive long enough for it to matter.

"All you shall remember from today is that you were working at your desk, and then the wind blew some of your documents onto the floor. Once you have picked them up, you will notice the time. You will think you have worked so hard that time got away from you, and you will call for your driver to take you to the palace for your meeting. Move to your desk and sit there."

Lord Flighty obeyed immediately, and Emilia moved to the window, crawling out and perching on the small landing outside as she looked back, making sure she had eye contact. She would need to put her order in effect and then disappear. Frowning, she called back in, "Once I give you the order, you will fall asleep for one minute. When you wake, you will assume it's because of the gust of wind. Forget."

Her order sounded in the air like a bell and Lord Flighty fell immediately to sleep. Pulling the light, Emilia hurried down the ladders and onto the street. The rush of managing to save Kas and get away was immediately dampened as she saw Vikram wandering casually back towards the office. The man wasn't even trying to hide. At least he had his hood up, but they were supposed to keep to the shadows, and it wasn't like this part of town was lacking in places to hide.

Anger bubbled up as she thought of the risks she took every single day being in the palace. She realised how close she'd come to being caught when Kas had turned up. It was only her abundance of caution—overcautiousness, as she was often criticised—that ensured she maintained her cover despite her invisibility. She hadn't become lax, as Vikram clearly had.

Vikram wasn't even listening in. Hadn't thought to go to the window as she had. In fairness, perhaps this was a regular occurrence, and Vikram had spent hour upon hour squatting up there for no reason. Still, that laxness meant he had missed a pretty key piece of information today. Thank the One True God.

Her heart began to pound again as she thought of what might have happened to Kas if Vikram *had* done his job properly.

As she hurried away up the street and back towards the palace, Emilia told herself she had acted because this meeting needed to play out as intended. That a fractured court was a necessary step in preparation for the invasion.

Not because she cared about Kas.

She took a deep breath, shocked at the risks she'd taken. All for a man she didn't know. An *Empire* man. And she had revealed herself to him. Almost given him her name. May as well have, as close as the name she'd given him was. Thank the One True God he hadn't seen her eyes. Of that, she was sure. No Empire-born would see her red eyes and not react.

Emilia dodged carts and carriages as she scuttled along the main road. Now that the adrenaline was wearing off, the full extent of what she'd done—what she'd risked—started to set in. She'd not even thought about whether or not to help Kas. She'd just done it. Reacted on instinct. Why was her instinct to help him? Because she had a crush?

No. She shook her invisible head. She didn't have a crush on an Empire man. She was curious about him because they shared a gift, that was all. But in her heart, she felt the lie. Felt the flutter when he'd looked at her. At the gratitude in his voice. At what she could ask for in return for that gratitude.

Emilia stopped dead in the street and was almost run into by a group of maids hurrying for the market. She wished for a cold trough of water in which she could dunk her head. Now was not the time for a stupid, girlish crush. And Kas was certainly not the object for it. She was a professional. The best in her field. She needed to pull her head back into the game.

Emilia walked with resolve. She had her mission. She would carry out her mission. No more deviations. No more helping the other side.

She almost lost her footing at that. Was that what she had done? Helped the other side? No, she told herself, hurrying off again, ducking down a side alley that she knew would get her to the palace quicker. No, she wasn't helping the other side. Like she said before, she was aiding her own mission in ensuring the meeting took place as planned.

And whether Kas lived or died had no effect whatsoever on the impending war. So there was no harm in her keeping the handsome man alive a little longer.

As she looked up at the looming palace, she thought grimly that the impending war was likely to be bloodier than either side realised. There was a good chance both she and Kas would be dead before the year was out.

She stepped onto the drawbridge, no longer worried about the drop. She was used to it by now. And as she made her way to the council chamber, she decided that since her time was likely limited, she could save whomever she wanted. After all, if she would be dead soon, she may as well have something nice to look at in the meantime.

CHAPTER FORTY-SEVEN

KAS

"Kas, did you get it—" Adeline's voice cut out as she saw Salomon. Salomon simply waved at her, smiling at the group.

"Hello everyone," Salomon drawled. "Kas and I were just having a chat."

"Yeah, but we need to go," said Kas, trying to step around Salomon. His younger brother stepped back into his path.

"Why the rush, big brother?" said Salomon. "It's been a while since we caught up."

Kas glared at Salomon and bit back the comment he wanted to make about the last time they saw each other. Something was off. Even the Salomon who'd turned him over to the city guard hadn't been this... obnoxious. Perhaps being leader of the rebels had gone to his head?

"Look, Salomon, we need to get going."

"Got somewhere to be, do you?" Salomon leered.

"Yeah." Anger piqued and Kas couldn't stop himself. "We're cleaning up your mess and helping the empress bring down Lord Flighty."

"Kas!" Tia and Adeline said together. He didn't listen.

"Double-crossing her like that—what were you think-ing? That'll just earn you and the rest of the rebels a rope each in the square. But we've got a chance to fix it. The empress gets Flighty and then she's going to forgive the rebels. All of you. She's even going to give you a legitimate role."

"Brother," said Salomon, fixing the lapels of Kas's coat. "I *have* a legitimate role. Sure, it'll be more difficult without Flighty's resources, but that guy was annoying as all the hells. Besides, he's already given us a lot. I can't imagine he was going to keep that up."

"Salomon," said Kas, shocked. He felt stupid for being shocked, but the part of him that couldn't stop loving his little brother was still hoping Salomon had just gotten a little lost.

Kas wanted to say something profound. Something so jarring or meaningful that it got through to his brother and brought the boy Kas had known back. But he couldn't think of the words.

This man in front of him had no intention of changing. He didn't want Kas's help. He didn't think he needed help at all. He *liked* the chaos and violence of the rebels' current direction. A pit formed in Kas's stomach. He didn't know this man at all.

"Kas," Salomon said, mimicking Kas's plea. "Now that both Jori and Flighty are out of the way, I can finally move the rebels in the direction I really want."

Salomon's evil smile made Kas feel sick.

"And what direction is that, Salomon?"

"Ah, big brother, I can't say. But if I were you, I'd leave town. I can't guarantee your safety if you stay. Oh, and—" Salomon snatched the bundle of documents from Kas's hand. "Thanks for these. Might be able to get a parting gift from Flighty for them."

Salomon scaled the wall like it was nothing, and was gone. Kas's friends were yelling, Adeline telling Kas to stop him with his elemental magic, Tia telling Mira to send her birds to peck Salomon until he dropped them, Ossi suggesting Tia try shifting.

"It's fine," said Kas, repeating himself loudly when no one listened.

"It's not fine!" said Adeline. "He just took our evidence."

"Here." Kas pulled the papers from his coat. "Check them," he asked Adeline quietly. "I think this is what we need. The rest were ancillary."

Adeline scanned a few lines, her eyebrows reaching for her hairline. "Oh yeah, this is good."

She handed the documents back to Kas, and he put them in his pocket.

"We need to get going," said Mira. "The meeting should be starting. We'll have to hurry to make it before it ends."

"We were worried about you," Tia said to Kas as they hurried up the street. "Mira's spies saw Lord Flighty headed to his secret office, and we'd heard there was a scanner there."

"What's a scanner?" Kas asked.

After they told him, he said, "Well, that explains it," and he told them how he'd been busted.

"Wait, so Lord Flighty saw you and knows you can become invisible, and so did this random mystery girl?" said Adeline, worried.

"Yeah, but she said he probably wouldn't remember," said Kas, the words sounding weak, even to him.

"Oh, well, that's fine then," said Ossi in a rare show of sarcasm.

Ossi's worry, more than the others, put Kas on edge. "Well, it happened, and I can't do anything about it now.

Hopefully, Flighty is headed for the meeting and he'll be executed before he can mention my magic."

A silence fell on the group, the only sound their breathing as they hurried through the Merchants' Quarter.

"Well, it seems the worst that can happen is that he tells the empress and her council," said Ossi. "And then what would they do?"

"Nothing," said Tia, shooting Kas a reassuring smile. "I know you've needed to keep it secret, but she said once the city is sorted, she'll be shutting down the camps, so it's not like they're going to lock you up."

Kas nodded, but his stomach felt like ice. He'd not even considered that. And even without the camps, what if the empress or her nobles felt his power was too dangerous to allow to roam free? They could very well collar him again and lock him in the dungeon.

"I'm sure the empress will value your talent in the upcoming conflict," said Ossi, as if reading his mind.

"Sure, if it worked properly. If it had held for a few seconds more, none of this would be an issue."

"If it had held for a few seconds more, you wouldn't have been able to get the evidence," said Mira gently.

Kas gave her a halfhearted nod. That was true, though he told himself he could have waited outside the window and gone back in when Flighty left. But then they might not have made it to the meeting in time. Especially if Salomon had been waiting for him.

"You did good," said Adeline, giving him an awkward hug as they continued to hurry to the palace.

"Thanks Addy." He smiled at her.

"What's all this about?" Ossi said, frowning.

The group slowed, though they were short on time. Citizens were exiting houses and businesses and wandering slowly towards Hightown. There was no rush, but plenty of curious chatter.

"I don't know," said Kas, "but they're going to make it harder to get to the palace. And we're already late."

"That man is dressed like your brother," said Ossi, pointing.

Kas saw them then. Rebels. Spread out in the crowd, urging people forward, knocking on doors and entering the shops and taverns.

"What in the Goddess's Green Garden are they doing?" said Tia. Adeline shot her a curious look at the unfamiliar saying.

"I don't know, but it can't be good," said Kas.

Salomon had been cocky, but also unworried. He'd barely flinched when Kas told him his benefactor was likely to be executed. Ice filled Kas's veins. Whatever Salomon had planned, Kas just knew it had to be bad. And much as he'd had it with this stranger in his little brother's skin, he couldn't live with himself if innocent people got hurt.

"Adeline, take these and go. Hurry to the palace. You'll get in faster than we will, anyway." He thrust the evidence into her hands. "The rest of us are going to go figure out what Salomon's got planned. Once we know, we'll send word." Kas nodded at Mira.

Adeline nodded and hurried off.

Kas took a deep breath. "Right, let's go find out what's so interesting."

CHAPTER FORTY-EIGHT

CASSANDRA

THE EMPRESS TAPPED the arm of her chair, the only outlet she was allowing for her agitation. The meeting was *not* going well. Lord Flighty had arrived in a foul mood, and then, as if he knew she wanted to keep them all there, had negated every subject she'd tried to raise for discussion, either explaining why it needed to wait for the next meeting, or agreeing to matters he'd previously had a staunch objection to.

She glanced out the window again. The shadows were lengthening. Adeline and her friends should have been back by now.

"If there's nothing else, Your Majesty?" Lord Flighty said, raising slightly out of his chair as if making to stand. Viscount Cuddy followed suit.

Sycophant.

In some ways, Cuddy disgusted her more than Flighty. At least Flighty had his own schemes. His own endgame. Cuddy seemed only to desire to kiss Flighty's boots.

"Actually, I think Master Sandison had something he wished to raise." Cassandra looked pointedly at Lukas.

Her friend had been no help at all. In fact, he'd made

417

things a hundred times worse. If she'd had even one member of the council back her up on any of the topics she'd raised, they could have sparked a discussion. But all Lukas had done was open his mouth and close it again, without saying a thing.

Lord Flighty made a show of resuming his seat and looked expectantly at Lukas. Lukas smiled at Cassandra. Hope flared in her chest. He hadn't somehow forgotten that the entire point was to draw out the meeting for as long as it took Adeline and her friends to find the evidence and bring it to the palace.

Lukas turned to the rest of the council and opened his mouth. And then he closed it. His brow furrowed, as if he'd forgotten what he was going to say. Lord Flighty raised an eyebrow, leaning in towards Lukas before sitting back in faux exasperation and smiling his sickening smile at Cassandra.

"It looks like our young Master Sandison doesn't have anything to raise after all."

"No," Lukas said, speaking his first word of the meeting. "I did... I wanted to..." His mouth bobbed open and closed again, the furrow above his brow increasing.

"It's okay, lad," said Lord Flighty, getting to his feet. "We all forget what we were going to say from time to time. But I really must be going. Come to my estate sometime. I miss your father and am curious to hear what news you have of him."

"Wait," said Cassandra, getting to her feet too, her hands splayed on the table. The room looked at her in surprise. "We need to... uh..."

"Controllers," Lukas spluttered, as if the word had cost him significant effort to get out.

There was a pause as everyone waited for Lukas to continue, but he did not.

"Anything specific about the Controllers?" Lord Flighty asked. "Or are we just worried about them in general?"

There were snickers around the table.

"I think we need to consider expanding the wards," said Cassandra, inventing wildly. A vague memory popped into her head. Her father and Lukas's complaining after a council meeting where they'd wanted to ward the city gates. The nobles hadn't wanted to, for some reason. Though she was clutching at anything, she now wondered why in the world they weren't already warded.

"Whatever for?" said Lord Flighty dismissively. "The wards at the border are sufficient. While they are in effect, any wards for the city will just be telling us what we already know."

"The Controllers are coming," said Cassandra. "And our border wards are largely untested. I think we should ward the city walls so that we would be alerted should any enemy spies attempt infiltration."

"There is no evidence the Controllers are coming." Lord Flighty actually waved Cassandra's concerns away.

"They are coming," said Cassandra, her temper rising. "In fact, we have no real way of knowing if they aren't already here."

"That is preposterous," said Lord Flighty, becoming suddenly angry and slamming his hands onto the table, causing everyone to jump. "And you are both wrong and stupid for thinking so."

A charged silence fell, though Cassandra thought she heard a small giggle. Perhaps someone's way of dealing with secondhand embarrassment. Everyone sat wide-eyed and waiting for Cassandra to respond.

Cassandra herself was shocked. Never had Lord Flighty been so blunt. He'd never lost the grip he held on his temper. Even Lord Flighty looked somewhat stunned at what had left his mouth. She could see his mind working as his eyes flitted about the room, trying to figure out how to play his outburst.

Cassandra stood. She was going to have to address his insult. Perhaps she could wax lyrical about how insulting it was and buy time for Adeline to bring the evidence.

"Never in my life—" she began in a low and dangerous tone.

The door burst open and Cassandra inwardly sighed, feeling like she was the one who'd been let off the hook.

"Apologies, Your Majesty." Adeline appeared at her side, dropping into a deep curtsey that didn't entirely hide how ragged she looked. "These just came for you."

Cassandra gave Adeline a grateful smile, with just enough curiosity to let the girl know she'd be asking what happened later.

Adeline gave a little nod and hurried out of the room, closing the doors behind her.

Cassandra made a show of looking at the papers. She felt the men in the room straining to discover what she held. She looked up at Lord Flighty, just as curious as the rest. He seemed happy that the interruption had derailed Cassandra's dressing down and had no idea he was now in a far worse position.

"I do not believe what I am seeing," Cassandra said, her voice dripping with disapproval. "I hope this isn't true." She turned her eyes back to the papers. "But I don't see a way it can be anything but."

Lord Flighty sighed, his confidence back in full force as he had the gall to look annoyed with her theatrics, clearly thinking it was merely another ploy to extend the meeting. "And what, pray tell, do your papers tell you?"

Cassandra threw the papers on the table dramatically.

"That it is *you* who has been funding the rebels."

There was a satisfying collective intake of air and the other nobles looked at Flighty, shock in their eyes.

"You've been paying them and directing their activities. And by the looks of this," she said, snatching up and rustling the papers at him before tossing them down again, "your main aim has been to undermine the Crown."

"That's preposterous," Lord Flighty said, not even deigning to look at the papers.

"Is it?" Cassandra said, drawing herself up. "For years the rebels have been engaging in smaller operations, largely focussed on securing food and supplies for the poorer populations. But lately, their singular focus appears to be undermining me. A focus, it would seem from your antics in this very room, that you share."

Baron Page moved to the head of the table, where Cassandra had thrown the papers. He picked them up, his bushy eyebrows drawn close as he concentrated. It wasn't long until they reached for his hairline, his face paling.

"Emery..." He turned to Lord Flighty. "Is this true?"

"Of course it isn't, Zachariah. It's some made-up nonsense this *girl* has manufactured because she is abundantly aware of what we can all see, plain as day. She is not cut out to rule."

Even Viscount Cuddy moved away from Lord Flighty when he referred to the empress as a mere girl. All the nobles seemed eager to use physical distance to avoid being associated with him. That was good. Cassandra smiled.

"Let me see that." Baron Shamble wobbled over to Baron Page, taking the documents. Soon, he too was staring at Lord Flighty with confused alarm.

"Emery, whatever were you thinking? This... this is treason."

Cassandra's heart swelled with joy. They had said it, not her. This was going perfectly.

"Don't be daft." Lord Flighty scowled. "Come, Pol, we're leaving."

Lord Flighty was halfway to the door before he realised Viscount Cuddy was not behind him. "Pol?"

Viscount Cuddy took a few steps, but instead of following Lord Flighty, he stopped next to Baron Shamble, holding his hand out for the papers. He stared at them, his eyes barely moving. Cassandra wondered if he was even bothering to read them, or if this was for show.

The viscount raised his head and looked at Lord Flighty. "How could you?"

"This is a lie!" Lord Flighty strode back towards his fellow councilmen. "Don't you see? I'm being set up!"

"It doesn't look that way, Emery," said Baron Page.

"Are you all this stupid?" Lord Flighty was now in a panicked rage. "They're forgeries. She's scared because I am the power in this empire. Because I have the ability to lead. Because I should be the emperor!"

The room fell into a tense silence. Lord Flighty's eyes were wide, alarm in them now as he realised he'd gone too far.

Lukas stood, finally, and moved to stand between Flighty and Cassandra.

"Guards!" Cassandra called, her voice loud but controlled, in stark contrast to Flighty's. Metal clinked as four armoured guards entered the room, their feet striking the floor as one as they stood to attention before their empress. Cassandra kept her eyes on Flighty. Her face was stern, but her eyes flickered with satisfaction. "Arrest Lord Flighty for treason against the Empire."

CHAPTER FORTY-NINE

CASSANDRA

Lord Flighty dove around Lukas, his hands claws, reaching for Cassandra, his eyes sparkling with madness. Lukas moved to tackle the lord, but paused as if suddenly unsure what to do. The guards moved, but were too far away. Cassandra hesitated, so surprised by Lord Flighty's actions that she froze.

"Solidify!" called a female voice.

Lord Flighty's legs froze, causing him to topple mid-stride, falling to the floor a mere step away from Cassandra.

The room erupted.

"Move!" the guards called, two pushing through to guard the empress, the other two moving to secure Lord Flighty. The barons hurried to get out of the way of the guards, knocking over the chairs and a valuable vase trying to clear the area.

"Out of order!" screeched Viscount Cuddy, pointing at the door.

Cassandra looked over, as if in a daze. Adeline was standing there, looking shocked.

"I've never cast without a potion before," Adeline said blandly to no one in particular.

Cassandra's frazzled mind absently thought Adeline must be quite powerful. It was exceedingly difficult to cast a spell with only words. Especially with such precision.

"It is forbidden to attack a noble in the palace with magic!" Viscount Cuddy seemed abnormally angry about Adeline's actions, and Cassandra realised he was worried about being arrested alongside the friend he'd so readily supported. "Arrest her!"

"It is forbidden to attack *anyone*," Cassandra corrected Viscount Cuddy, shaking off her daze. "Or to use magic in the palace at all. Unless authorised by me."

Viscount Cuddy's rouged face paled as Cassandra's cool anger fixed on him. "And seeing how *your* friend, Lord Flighty, was trying to attack *me*, I authorise Adeline's use of a spell to prevent him from doing so."

Cuddy seemed to shrink back, and Cassandra became aware of the nobles' eyes on her. Waiting for her decision. She raised her chin, casting her eyes purposefully around the room, meeting each of the noblemen's in turn.

"We will reconvene here tomorrow to discuss what has happened and the changes we will make moving forward. For now, you are all dismissed."

She turned to Lord Flighty.

"Lord Flighty, you have been arrested for high treason. I hereby sentence you to death."

It was the only sentence available for the crime of high treason, yet there was still the sharp intake of air from the witnesses, indicating their shock at the outcome. Perhaps they had expected leniency. Or that Cassandra would hold Lord Flighty in the cells and conduct a more thorough investigation.

But Cassandra had all the evidence she needed, and Lord Flighty was a cancer that would doom the Empire to extinction when the Controllers came for them. She no longer had time to consider luxuries such as involved investigations or leniency.

The guards dragged Lord Flighty from the room.

"Hold him in the cells, but prepare the gallows," she told one of the remaining guards. "He swings before the sun sets."

The guard drew to attention with a snap and bowed before hurrying from the room.

"We should leave," said Lukas, appearing at Cassandra's side, eyeing the nobles. Viscount Cuddy was whispering with Baron Page. If she stayed in the room, it was likely they'd try to talk her down. At least delay the execution until tomorrow, when they could rally support and have her change her mind.

And it might work. Cassandra wasn't happy that she was about to kill a man. Even if that man was Emery Flighty. And given the situation with Lukas's father... If they gave her an out, she may well take it. And then she'd be worse off than she had been before. This would all be for nothing if she didn't come out of it with the respect of the nobles. Or at least their fear.

"To my rooms," Cassandra said, nodding at Adeline, letting her know she was to follow. "I must prepare."

They left the nobles to their hushed chatter and hurried along the hallway. Cassandra glanced at Lukas, eyeing him suspiciously. What had that been about? Not once had he backed her up in the meeting, and then, when she was attacked, he'd gone to save her, but stopped. If she didn't know better—

"I'll get your mourning gown," said Adeline, interrupting Cassandra's thoughts and bringing her back to the task at hand.

"No, bring me my black doublet and pants. The tall boots too. I want to look more warrior than princess."

Adeline nodded and headed to the wardrobe.

Cassandra cast another glance at Lukas. He seemed oblivious to any issue. He wasn't even tense as he headed to the window.

"Crowd's already gathering," he commented, looking down into the square below.

Cassandra opened her mouth but was silenced by a tapping at the window next to the one Lukas was peering out of.

"That's Mira," said Adeline, hurrying out of the closet, her arms full of black clothing. "Three quick taps. That's the code for trouble."

"It's a bit late for a warning," Cassandra muttered, grabbing the clothes from Adeline and laying them on the bed to decide which to wear.

"It's not about us. Something's wrong. Something in the city."

CHAPTER FIFTY

EMILIA

EMILIA WOUND her way carefully down the palace stairs. She should stay with the empress. Monitor what she intended. Assess for any opportunities. But instead, she dodged the palace staff, all in a frenzy, and aimed for the exit.

The meeting had gone as expected and Emilia had played her part. The soldier had been an unhelpful ally to the empress, and she could feel the empress's frustration at her childhood friend.

And when Lord Flighty moved to attack her... Emilia frowned. She'd reacted on instinct, intent on doing what was needed to ensure the soldier was useless. So focused on her task, Emilia hadn't initially realised he'd been moving to protect the empress from a physical attack.

And when she realised she'd left the empress vulnerable, Emilia had felt bad.

Moving down the stairs, Emilia ducked into a side corridor to avoid a bustling group of maids.

What am I doing?

Protecting Kas was one thing. If she hadn't, the meeting wouldn't have happened, and Lord Flighty wouldn't be about to be executed. All of this chaos served the Divvinium and therefore the One True God.

But wanting to protect the empress?

Emilia continued down the corridor, heading for a back staircase that would be less busy. The idea of the empress coming to harm should have made Emilia happy. What better conditions for the invasion than the head of the Empire injured or dead? But the idea made her feel ill.

She had been here too long, she told herself. She'd grown attached to her targets, projecting more than she'd thought possible. She felt invested in them. Worried about them. But they were the enemy. Weren't they?

She needed fresh air, and Emilia knew she'd be expected to observe the execution. So she'd left the soldier and the empress and was heading outside. Though now, as Emilia looked around, she realised she'd taken a wrong turn somewhere. This was not a part of the palace she'd been in before.

Emilia looked around, wondering if there was another way besides backtracking, but voices made her freeze.

"I told you not to seek me out. It is too risky."

At the deep, male voice, Emilia ducked into a small alcove that didn't entirely fit her body. Hopefully the owner of the voice wasn't a burly city guard who might brush against her and wonder at the unseen object.

"How could I not? I examined the collars. There's only one reason for what you hid in the weave. You need to stop —this is madness."

Emilia held her breath as the tiny Druid who'd been part of Kas's group walked past, imploring a taller, thin man, wearing the browner cloak of the City Druids.

"It's not madness, it's the will of the Ancients," said the man.

"They would never want this. Francisco said—"

"Francisco," the man spat in derision. "He fears change. He is too attached to the role of Keeper. The Unification demands change. Requires action. We are doing the work of the Ancients. Work those of you who remain in the north are too fearful to do."

"But what you plan is not the answer!" the little Druid said emphatically. "It will likely destroy us all..."

Their voices faded as they moved further away, and Emilia knew she should follow them. Whatever they were talking about sounded pretty important. But if she missed the execution, she'd be punished. And she hated being around the Druids. Something about them was just creepy.

Telling herself she'd follow up on the Druids later, Emilia pushed out into the sunshine, the day completely at odds with the event she was about to witness.

Across the drawbridge, Emilia was surprised to see the throngs of people heading to the square. She could understand the spectacle of execution—especially that of a noble—but word couldn't have spread this quickly.

Across the way, she saw Vikram looking a little lost as he made his way against the crowd. Honestly, how the man had been accepted as a spy, Emilia had no idea. His father wasn't even that important.

She moved quickly, touching his arm and leading him into the back alleys she'd come to know. The two moved away from the crowds and Vikram took the lead, taking them to a roof where he had apparently arranged to meet Erus Dunat.

"I didn't know they were going to kill him," Vikram admitted to Emilia as the two stood at the edge of their roof, watching the citizens of the City of the Damned flock to the market square.

Emilia remained silent. Of course Sigmund hadn't passed her information along. She wondered what they would do with Vikram now. He might get another proxy. Or they might send him home. He seemed more suited to the front lines than working behind enemy ones, but the idea made Emilia sad. They were far from friends, but Vikram didn't go out of his way to make her life difficult, and that was close to friends in her book.

"My fellow Imperius," Sigmund said, appearing on the roof behind them.

Emilia and Vikram muttered their greetings in unison, bowing at their master.

Sigmund strode to the edge of the roof and nodded at the crowd as if everything was going according to his plan.

But what is *his plan?*

"Vikram, it seems your proxy might no longer be tenable for our cause. You are now in support of Reiko. The mission is to support and inflame the riot. Maximum chaos."

"Yes, Erus." Vikram bowed.

"Reiko has the lead. Position yourself up there." He pointed to some taller roofs at the opposite end of the square to the gallows. "And when I signal, decommission your proxy."

Without hesitation, Vikram bowed and left.

Ice spread in Emilia's stomach. She saw the plan now. A proxy on the ground to whip up the crowd, all packed into the square. An assassin ensuring the right outcome, causing panic. Even those unmoved by words would fear for their lives with arrows flying.

It was perfect for the Divvinium's invasion.

But Kas was down there. She'd seen him easily, accompanied as he was by his Troll friend. And again, she felt that uncomfortable feeling gnawing at her conscience. Were *these* the people they should be targeting?

She cared not whether Lord Flighty died by the

empress's hand or by Vikram's, but she did not see the fashions of the rich down in that square.

"Busy day in the palace, Emilia," drawled Sigmund.

"Yes, Erus," Emilia said, bowing her head.

"Busy day for the Divvinium." She could feel his smile as he imagined the boons these deaths would earn him. "Watch the festivities if you wish, but hurry back to the palace to observe the fallout. And we will meet soon. If the boys do their jobs properly, we may need to think about retasking you."

He left, clearly heading to a better vantage point. Emilia's heart sunk. Sigmund was planning something, and it was definitely not going to be good for her. Her eyes found Kas again, relieved to find him at the edges with a clear exit. Her eyes flitted to the tall roof and she spotted Vikram there in the shadows.

If only the Empire soldiers were as observant. Her mind raced, trying to think of something, anything she could do to, if not avert the tragedy brewing before her eyes, to shift it. To focus the Divvinium's power on those who deserved it.

But there was nothing. Nothing she could do without branding herself a betrayer.

She toyed with the idea of warning Kas. Maybe she could let him know. Or somehow lead him away before things got bad. But Sigmund was watching. And Reiko was around, somewhere. What if they saw?

Emilia dropped off the roof, landing softly on the ground, and began to make her way back to the palace. She didn't want to watch anymore. She'd hear what happened in the opulent halls of the enemy's leader.

Out of habit, she offered a prayer for their victory. But she was no longer sure whose victory she was really asking for.

CHAPTER FIFTY-ONE

KAS

Kas sat next to Ossi, up high on the wall that surrounded the town square. Most days, the square was alive with temporary stalls, and the crier was atop the platform, calling out announcements and messages.

Today, the gallows had been erected, and the gathering clouds were dark. The empress must have had more faith in Kas and his friends than Kas had thought. There were citizens milling around. More than usual. It wasn't every day one of the upper class swung. It was usually the poor. The mood was almost festive with it. It turned Kas's stomach.

But what had alarmed him and had him signal Mira to send word to the palace was that most of the gathering citizens were rebels. They were massing in the square and he wasn't the only one who'd noticed. The guard detail had doubled, and they were working to create a larger buffer between the crowd and the gallows.

The team had decided to split up: Kas and Ossi, Tia and Mira. Kas had seen Salomon, his red hair flashing through the crowd, but whenever he'd drawn close, his little brother had disappeared. It happened enough that Kas realised he was being messed with, and so he and Ossi had climbed a wall, and now they were waiting for Salomon to come to them.

"Hello again, big brother. Fancy seeing you here."

Kas flinched as Salomon dropped down next to him. Kas had been expecting him, but his little brother had still got the jump on him.

"Hello, Salomon. I see you're here to join all your friends. I presume you're too busy to try to have me arrested again."

Salomon laughed, humour absent from the sound. "I have better things to worry about than you, brother." His tone was light, but he couldn't completely hide the bite in his words.

"Why'd you do it?" Kas knew it wasn't the time. The Empire was about to tear itself apart; he shouldn't be thinking about how his little brother betrayed him. But he'd been unable to shake it from his mind, and he might not get another chance to ask. "I told you I'd get it off." Kas indicated his naked neck. "We could have had a life together. We could have had the dream."

"*Your* dream," Salomon hissed, raw anger in his voice. "Why would I ever want that life? Forever in your shadow? You dream of a world that revolves around you. Where you have your trusty sidekick there when you want him. But I'm my own person, Kas. I want a life where I'm in the light."

Kas stared at his little brother, his jaw hanging as he tried to understand his brother's anger. Not once had he tried to overshadow Salomon. In fact, at every opportunity, he'd put his brother first. He'd tried to reflect any light he found on himself back onto his brother. How had things gone so wrong that Salomon hated him? And so fiercely.

"Salomon," Kas stammered. "I want that for you, too. I want us both to have a good life. A great life. I just wanted those lives to be together."

Salomon scoffed, and Kas felt his own anger stir.

"Look, we can talk about this later, but right now we need to work together. There's a bigger threat than the Empire. We need to band together to fight it. You need to stand your people down."

Salomon smiled at Kas. It was a dark, twisted leer that held no light.

"Haven't you realised, brother? You don't tell me what to do anymore. It kills you, doesn't it? That I've risen so high. That people like me. Respect me. Follow me. Not you. You'd love it if I stood them down. What, so they can be rebranded and put under your control? Please." Salomon exhaled mockingly. "I'm not that stupid."

Kas went to try again, but Salomon stood.

"Enjoy the show." He smiled cruelly. "You and your Troll friend."

Salomon glared at Ossi, and without another look at Kas, he leapt onto a roof and out of sight.

"Your brother is not what I expected from your stories," said Ossi.

"He's not what I remember," Kas said sadly, gazing after Salomon.

Ossi straightened next to him. "The empress has arrived."

Kas looked to the platform and saw the empress and the prisoner appear, flanked by several guards. "Let's hope they got Mira's message."

"Citizens of the Empire," the empress called to the crowd. Almost immediately, the rebels began heckling and jeering, drowning out whatever else the empress was trying to say. She made several attempts to regain control of the crowd, but none were successful.

Lord Flighty raised his head and the crowd fell silent.

"It would appear, Your Majesty, that the people do not wish to see me killed."

Some of the regular citizens laughed, starting to call out that they did, in fact, wish to see a noble hang. But they were quickly drowned out by the rebels booming support for Lord Flighty's words.

The empress began to speak and was immediately drowned out again by raucous voices. She closed her mouth, frustration evident on her face, and Lord Flighty opened his, the rebels falling quiet again.

"It seems you are not in control, Your Majesty. Perhaps you should step down? Hand the crown to someone who can rule an Empire."

The crowd erupted, and the guards stepped a little closer to their empress.

"We don't belong to any empress!" a voice called from the back, and resounding cheers thundered in the square. Kas knew before he looked that the new speaker was his little brother. Salomon continued when the crowd settled, "We don't belong to any lord, either."

The cheering of the rebels had a harsher tone now, and Kas realised that, on the platform behind the empress and the condemned man, were the other powerful nobles of the city.

"For too long, the rich have been squashing our heads into the mud with their expensive boots."

The cheering was now lower, more of a growl.

Sick realisation hit Kas. He knew what Salomon had planned.

"It'll be the food riot all over again," he muttered.

"What's a food riot?" asked Ossi, tension on his face as he watched the crowd turn.

"Salomon's going to have his men storm the platform to

kill the empress and all the nobles. He wants to take them out all in one go."

"He'll never succeed." Ossi frowned. "The guards will clear the platform before the rebels get anywhere near it. There's at least one hundred of them between the crowd and the gallows."

"Exactly," said Kas. "All that will happen is the poor will be killed and maimed."

The crowd started moving, Salomon's voice riling them up, building into a frenzy. The front rows began to press into the guards, and Kas saw many of them were regular citizens. They looked terrified. He imagined his parents looked the same right before they were killed.

"People of Lorendell!" Kas didn't remember getting to his feet, and he was surprised to see some heads turn his way. "Think about what you are doing. We are here because justice is to be witnessed. We are here because a citizen of the Empire tried to use you as pawns in his own scheme. He tried to use you to increase his wealth while keeping you down in the dirt."

He saw Salomon shift, worried, as the crowd listened to Kas and began to calm from their frenzy.

"Don't listen to him!" Salomon called.

Kas raised his voice even louder. He was at the advantage. Where Salomon was behind the crowd, Kas was in the middle. They could all hear him better, and most could see him from where he stood on the wall.

"The empress is about to dispense justice to this man. She doesn't care that he is rich. She doesn't care that he is a noble. She treats each of her citizens the same. Now is not the time for violence. Now is the time for justice."

There was murmuring in the crowd, and Kas could see doubt cross some faces. The frenzy Salomon had whipped up was dying out, and Kas could even see some people taking the chance to leave the square.

He looked to the platform and saw the empress looking at him. She gave him a grateful nod, a smile on her face. He nodded back and indicated to the crowd. She could address them now.

An arrow flew from a roof behind where Salomon stood. A scream sounded from the crowd as the arrow lodged in Lord Flighty's throat.

The guards reacted immediately to the attack against those on the platform. The empress was shielded by four guards and the platform was evacuated in seconds, Lord Flighty's body abandoned as his blood pooled around him.

Kas scanned the roof for the assassin. There was a hooded figure standing in the shadows, lowering a longbow. Before Kas could get a good look, the figure ducked away, and his attention was stolen by the mayhem below. The fighting wasn't as crazed as it might have been. Many of the citizens and some of the rebels had left before the arrow had been fired, and others still were pushing for the exits rather than heading into the fray. There would be no repeat of the food riot that had killed his parents, but innocent people were still trapped in the square.

Kas searched for his brother, but he was no longer standing on a cart behind his people. There was a flash of red hair in the crowd, and Kas felt his heart contract. What if Salomon was hurt? Killed? And their last words were full of hate and hurt.

His brother had changed. He'd changed so dramatically that Kas didn't like the man he'd become. But Salomon was his flesh and blood. And no matter how he felt about his little brother, he did not want him to die.

Without thinking, Kas dropped down into the crowd and began pushing to get to his brother. There was a thud as

Ossi dropped down behind him, and Kas felt a swell of gratitude for a friend who would follow him without hesitation into this melee. Then he heard Ossi's gleeful roar and remembered he was Jatte. He loved fighting.

"Watch out!"

Kas turned to see a sword swinging at his head and ducked. Ossi slammed the man wielding it in the chest and he went flying. Ossi roared at the sky and went about clearing a path.

Kas spun around to see who had shouted the warning and was grateful to see Tia and Mira there. Despite his gratitude, his heart sank. He'd hoped they were somewhere safe.

Tia snatched up the sword, dropped by the man Ossi had sent flying, and Mira was clutching an iron bar. The smaller girl looked terrified, but there was determination in her eyes.

With Tia and Mira to watch his back and Ossi tearing a hole through the brawling crowd, Kas went in search of his little brother.

CHAPTER FIFTY-TWO

TIA

THE SWORD WAS TOO big for her, but Tia was used to the pickaxes from the quarries and swung the sword as if she were digging for salt in the north. Her arms jolted painfully as she blocked a guard, his eyes in full-blown panic as he swung his long sword blindly, not caring who he hit. She pushed him away with her sword and watched to make sure he didn't attack again. He didn't, swinging instead at the group of rebels pinning down two other guards near the north wall of the square.

The fighting was bloody and chaotic, and the heat of several fires that had caught from the blasts of fire mages was not helped by the gusts of wind. Rather than put the fires out, the wind simply blew hot, and Tia felt she was fighting in an oven. As they moved, Tia was careful to not look carefully at what she trod on. Or who.

If they were smart, they would have fought their way to the exit and headed for safety. But Kas wanted to save his brother. It was understandable. If the situation was reversed and she saw her brother in danger, nothing would stop her from getting to him. But Kas's brother seemed like an asshole. And this whole riot was pretty much all his fault anyway.

But this wasn't about Salomon. It was about Kas. Tia's stomach dropped with piercing guilt as she rammed her sword into a large bearded man who'd been about to cleave Mira's head in two. She understood Kas because her own brother *was* in danger. When push came to shove, she *had* left him in danger and ran away to keep herself safe. She had no idea if Fabian or Aurora were okay. If they were alive or caged, as she had been.

Tia ripped her mind away from her family and focussed on keeping herself and her friends alive. She would return and help her family. But she couldn't do that if she was dead.

A man rushed up from behind and Tia was about to thrust her sword through his chest, but suddenly he collapsed and Mira stood back up. She'd smashed his legs with her iron bar. They smiled at each other, Tia giving Mira a little nod of thanks. She'd already killed too many people today.

Mira looked up, and Tia followed her gaze. A flock of birds whizzed out of the sky, diving and pecking and distracting people from killing each other. Tia's eyes found the hooded figure that had fired the arrow that started the riot. Something about the figure bothered her. The rest of the rebels weren't hooded. And the hooded figure had just seemed... different.

One of the rebels lunged at Kas, his arms outstretched. Kas hit him with three fireballs in a row, and then sent a line of fire into the path of three rebels headed their way. But the fire flickered and died and the largest of the men advanced on Kas, his hands outstretched menacingly, lightning crackling between his fingers.

Mira moved between the two men, but another man

stepped forward and suddenly Mira was caught in a small but powerful whirlwind. Her little body was thrown around in the air before being slammed into the ground with a sickening thud.

Magic flew around the square in full force, guards fighting rebels and ordinary citizens fighting for their lives. The air turned humid as fire and water were cast against each other. Ice shards flew past Tia's face and the ground beneath her rumbled. She hurried to Mira's body, crumpled on the ground. Her friend did not move.

"Mira?" she shook her, but Mira was oblivious to Tia's efforts to rouse her.

"Mira needs help!" she called to Kas and Ossi. Both men turned, eyes flaring with concern as they saw Mira.

Ossi began pushing back towards them, and Kas raised his head, bellowing his brother's name into the crowd.

"Salomon!" He looked around frantically.

"Mira can't wait," Tia called to Kas as Ossi reached them and stood protectively over the two women. "We don't have time to find your brother."

He scanned the crowd around them once more, and then Kas hurried over, crouching over Mira with Tia, gently checking her neck for a pulse.

"I will carry her," said Ossi, using his height to look for the best way out.

"The palace will be locked down," Kas said, his hands now gently pulling Mira's eyelids up as he looked into her eyes. "There are no other healers in this part of the city. And she needs help fast."

"How far to the nearest one?" Tia asked him, looking at her friend's limp body, barely aware that the frenzied fighting was dying down.

Kas looked around. "Too far. The fighting's moving to the streets. They'll be clogged with people fighting or fleeing. And the guards will probably set up checkpoints at the gates between districts. It'll take too long to get through."

"I will make room," said Ossi, his voice dangerously low.

Kas shook his head as his hand palpated Mira's skull. "You'll just attract the guards. They'll hold you up and it'll take longer. Besides." Kas glanced around the square, bodies littering the ground, some still alive and moaning. "They'll be swamped. They may not prioritise... someone who isn't from the city."

"Can you not help her?" Tia asked, watching Kas. "You seem to know what you're doing."

Kas shook his head. "My father was a spell caster, and he knew a lot about healing, but his speciality was potions. I don't have anything with me to make something for her."

Tia stood and looked around frantically, as if the solution would simply appear in front of her. She'd grown close to Mira. There was something calm about the smaller girl. She'd been through so much, but she always had a smile on her face and was quick to ask about others if they seemed down. She couldn't die.

Her eyes caught Ossi's, the huge man looking at her curiously. "Perhaps it is time for you to shift?" he said gently. "Maybe your animal form is something that might help us."

Tia felt the blood drain from her face. What if she couldn't do it? No one had ever told her how. She'd been too young. What if she was able to shift, but her animal form was something that wouldn't help?

"I don't know," she said, anxiously looking at Mira. "What if..." Her voice died. Mira would do it for her.

Kas rose and put a reassuring hand on Tia's arm. "We've got nothing to lose, Tia. Just give it a try." His eyes were gentle, and Tia nodded. She could try. For Mira, she could try.

Tia closed her eyes, feeling stupid and suddenly very aware that she had no idea what to do. She thought about magic. About animals. She conjured her memories of the shifters in her tribe morphing into various animals. They'd always made it look so easy. Why had no one ever mentioned how to do it?

"For me," Kas said quietly in her ear, "I need to focus on my centre. When I do, there's like a ball of energy there. It's hard to describe."

Tia nodded. She'd try anything at this point. She took a deep breath and closed her eyes again, focussing her attention on her heart. Nothing happened.

All of a sudden, she felt it. Kas was right. There was something inside her. A ball of energy. It felt powerful and cool, like liquid metal. Tia reached for the energy with her mind, taking control of it and pushing it out until it engulfed her. She felt the energy shimmer over her.

A sense of power coursed through her. She felt strong and more alive than ever before. But she felt the same. Nothing had happened. She didn't feel larger or smaller or any different. It was going to take too long to learn how to use the magic to achieve the shift. She'd failed Mira.

The screams from the crowd intensified. The fighting must be almost done, the victors picking off the last of the losing side. Then she heard a gasp from below and Ossi's low chuckle.

Tia opened her eyes and stretched her wings.

Wings?

Kas and Ossi were staring up at her. Tia frowned, slowly becoming more aware of her body.

"Tia," said Kas, awe in his voice. "You're a freaking dragon!"

CHAPTER FIFTY-THREE

KAS

Kas walked slowly through the square. A day had passed since the execution of Lord Flighty. Or was it murder? Could you murder a man condemned to die? Kas shook the thoughts away. It didn't matter. Lord Flighty was dead. And so were over a hundred citizens, rebels, and guards.

Blood stained the courtyard stones, but most of the bodies had now been removed. Word was that a pyre would be erected on the river. Until then, the dead were being housed in one of Lord Flighty's warehouses, already claimed by the empress.

Kas had been there this morning. And now he was back in the square by the gallows.

There was no sign of Salomon.

Some of the people he'd spoken to said they saw Salomon leave the fight early on. One man claimed Salomon had fled the moment the arrow hit Lord Flighty's neck. Either way, Kas hadn't found him among the dead. He had to believe his brother was still alive.

For now.

The guards were going door to door through the city,

their numbers bolstered by the private armies of the nobles. For once, the empress and her lords had united. They would have the rebels rounded up by nightfall. He prayed Salomon would go with them quietly.

"This was not a good fight."

Kas looked up at Ossi, who was surveying the blood-stains sadly.

"Is there really such a thing as a good fight?" Kas asked.

"There is." Ossi nodded. "But this was without honour. And innocents should never be collateral damage."

"How is it going up there?" Kas nodded at the palace.

"They are still arguing. But the empress is asserting her authority and the others seem to be accepting it. For now."

"They seem to be working well together to find the rebels," Kas commented.

Ossi nodded. "And once that is complete, they intend to approach the minor tribes and invite them to a summit here in the city. They will discuss how to dissolve the annexation in a way that is acceptable to all, but ensures everyone stands together against the Controllers."

Kas nodded, but that seemed like a pipe dream. He couldn't imagine the Kikachi forgiving the Empire fast enough to stand with them against the Controllers. It seemed the Kikachi would be more likely to join with anyone seeking to destroy the Empire.

"I'll be interested to see how they manage to get representatives to agree to come to the city, let alone agree to join forces."

"It has been suggested that I might act as an envoy to the Jatte," Ossi said. "And that Tia might be able to approach the Kikachi, but... well." Ossi looked to the sky. "In unrelated news, some of the nobles think the greater threat is a dragon that was reportedly seen flying north. They wish to get a hunting party together."

Kas smiled, imagining the looks on the faces of anyone who had seen Tia fly over the capital and north towards the Druids. His smile faded a little. It was too soon to hope to hear anything. Hopefully, the Druids were able to help Mira. And hopefully, no one was seriously hunting Tia.

"Kas, there you are. Hi Ossi."

Kas turned in time to see Adeline give Ossi a different smile from the one she often gave him. Then she winked.

"Hi Addy," said Kas, trying not to be jealous. He loved both of them, and if they were happy together, then he should be happy too. If he'd realised his feelings for Adeline at long last, he had no one to blame but himself for being too late.

"The empress is asking for you both." She tore her eyes away from Ossi and looked at Kas. "I think she wants some more supporters on her side when the talks resume. I don't know why the nobles are reluctant to even approach the minor tribes. If we can't work with them, we're all doomed."

"They don't want to give up their wealth," said Kas, kicking the ground in frustration. "Even if giving a little means they won't die or be enslaved."

"On the bright side." Ossi grinned. "If the Controllers come and we're still divided, we can just get Tia to shift into a dragon and fly us all to safety."

"Wait, what?" Adeline looked at Ossi in confused alarm.

"I'll tell you later," Ossi said.

"Alright." Kas didn't want to think of them together *later*. "Let's go help save the world."

EPILOGUE

Francisco watched from the shadows as Kas left the courtyard with the Jatte and the empress's maid. The boy had come much further than he'd hoped, and yet had so much further to go.

As the old Druid walked to the city gate, no one bothered him. He walked like a wraith through the streets, watching the chaos as the Empire went through the difficult and painful process of uniting. It would be for the best, but there would always be casualties in such things.

The Druids had been the Keepers for hundreds of years now. They well knew the pain that would come. The world was shifting, and the time of the Druids' stewardship was over. The Unification was beginning.

Finally outside the City of Stone, Francisco took a deep breath and turned his eyes north. So much still to do. And so little time. After what felt like an age of waiting, the time was suddenly here, and he felt impossibly unprepared.

Glancing back at the palace, Francisco was filled with a desire to get as far away from that place as possible. He didn't want to deal with the arguing and the politicking. And something in there just felt *wrong*.

But they needed his help, and it was his destiny to guide them in the right direction.

He still had a part to play in what was to come. His destiny was to shape the future for the good of everyone, or fail and doom the world entirely. He needed to prepare.

But not today.

Today he would walk and enjoy the beauty of the world.

Before it all burned to the ground.

BOOKS BY K.T. HOLDER

<u>The Highacren Prophecy</u>

Regent (free prequel novella)

Royal

Return

Reign

Rogue (free bonus chapter)

<u>The City Chronicles</u>

Rise of the Divvinium (free prequel novella)

City of Stone

City of Shadows

Echoes of the Divvinium (free bonus novella)

City of Sorrow

ACKNOWLEDGMENTS

Thank you for reading City of Stone! I had such a great time writing this book, and I'm really enjoying the series. This world is so much fun to play in, and I hope you're enjoying diving into it too.

Again, a huge thank you to my wife! She is my biggest supporter and I'm so lucky to have her by my side.

I also need to thank my furry little writing companions. Ducky, Biggie and Butters, thanks for keeping me company and making sure I take breaks.

A big thank you to Courtney at Elevation Editorial. Thanks again for all your help with this story! I think everything we added (and took out) make it such a better story.

Thank you to Damonza for the awesome cover!! The team was fantastic to deal with and every design they created was amazing. If you're looking for a book cover, go to Damonza - you won't be disappointed!

The beautiful map is thanks to Rachael at Cartography-bird Maps (www.cartographybird.com) and it is stunning!! If you need a map I can't recommend her enough, she's obviously talented and was a pleasure to work with.

I can't thank my advanced reader team enough! I really appreciate all your feedback and support, and I love hearing your perspectives. A special shout out to Alex and Kathleen for your ideas and suggestions.

A special thank you to Terzah for reading all my books (even though they're not her usual genre) and giving heaps of advice and support. I owe you a glass of Kendall Jackson and a big glass of ice!

And the biggest thank you is for you! I can't tell you how amazing it is to me that other people are reading my books. I really appreciate you sharing my stories and I hope you enjoyed this one!

If you did enjoy the story, please consider leaving a review on Amazon or Goodreads, or really anywhere you like! They really can make a difference, especially in helping other people find my books, and it'll go a long way to letting me keep writing stories for you.

Feel free to head over to my website (www.kthold er.com) where you can sign up to hear about book releases and other fun things! If you sign up, you get Regent, an exclusive prequel novella to the Royal series, for free!

You can also get updates by following me on Facebook and Instagram, and I'm also on Goodreads and BookBub!

Thanks again!